CW00823091

Fallout

Fortress Security, Volume 16

Rebecca Deel

Published by Rebecca Deel, 2023.

FALLOUT

First edition. January 10, 2023.

Copyright © 2023 Rebecca Deel.

ISBN: 979-8215793428

Written by Rebecca Deel.

To my amazing husband, the love of my life. Thanks for your constant encouragement and support. I love you.

Chapter One

Willow Knox woke to the overwhelming scent of copper and a sharp pain from a raging headache. Frowning, she opened her eyes to identify the source of the smell and saw an endless darkness. Her breath froze in her lungs at seeing nothing but blackness. Had the hotel experienced a power outage?

Another scan of the area showed nothing. Still pitch black. Her breathing became more labored. Not now, she admonished herself. She could panic later.

How could there be such an absence of light? Where was she? Not in her bed at the hotel. The surface under her back was too hard. The floor? Did she pass out or possibly stumble over something in the darkness and hit her head?

Willow tried to sit up and couldn't. Something heavy pinned her down. Had the nightstand or lamp toppled on top of her?

She shoved at the weight and sucked in a breath. Rather than feeling the heavy, hard wood from a piece of furniture, Willow's hand clamped around an arm. A hairy, muscled, and limp arm.

Her heart surged into an erratic rhythm. Someone else was inside this room with her. A man.

Willow fought tidal waves of panic. This wasn't Mexico, and she wasn't in the hands of a murderous cartel specializing in human trafficking. She was safe. At least, she had been before she woke up sprawled on the floor with no memory of how she'd ended up there.

Jacking up her courage, Willow said, "Who are you? What are you doing in my room?"

Silence.

She thumped the man's shoulder. "Hey, buddy, I'm talking to you. Get off of me."

No response.

She never invited Ballinger Research clients to her hotel room. Interviews were conducted in public places and, if she was comfortable with the client, Willow searched through records at the client's home during the daytime. She never brought strangers to her room. So, who was this man?

Willow's grip on the panic started to slip. She needed to get away from the stranger before she lost it completely. If she panicked, she'd be even more vulnerable.

She sucked in a breath to scream but coughed as a thick, coppery scent stung her nose and throat. What was that smell? Blood. Had she injured herself when she fell?

Willow followed the man's arm to his shoulder. She pushed and shoved until she moved his body enough to slide out from underneath him.

She scrambled to her hands and knees. Moving slow, Willow crawled to the left and into a cold, sticky pool of liquid. Water? A soft drink?

A hard shudder snaked through her body. Coppery scent and liquid meant something more sinister than a soft drink. Oh, man. This was so bad.

She needed light. If she could find her phone, she could use the flashlight app to see. Where was her phone? She didn't feel the familiar lump in her pocket.

Willow shifted to the right and away from the sticky pool and bumped into something hard. A table? She stretched out a hand and connected with a chair.

Thank goodness. A lamp sat on top of the table. Willow gripped the arms of the chair for balance and stood.

After swaying a few seconds, she steadied and slid her hand across the table until she touched the lamp. Light flooded the room, momentarily blinding her.

When her eyes adjusted, she turned to confront the silent man in her room.

Horror exploded inside her. Willow screamed.

Blood pooled around Graham Enright, his lips blue and his skin gray. His body was riddled with knife wounds. A knife lay nearby, blade stained with blood.

Why was Enright on the floor of her hotel room, dead? She searched her memory and came up blank.

So much blood. She shuddered. Was all of it Graham's or had she been injured, too? Willow glanced down at herself and grimaced as she plucked at her clothes. Blood covered her hands and stained her shirt and jeans.

A heavy pounding on her door caused Willow to jerk.

"Open up. Police."

She stared at the door as the pounding came again. Keeping the police waiting wasn't wise. She'd look guilty.

Willow squashed hysterical laughter. She couldn't look much more guilty than she did with a dead body on her floor and blood on her hands and clothes.

She wiped her hands on her jeans since she would toss her entire outfit into the trash if the police gave it back to her. Unlikely.

Walking to the door on shaky legs, Willow twisted the knob. A wave a dizziness crashed into her. She braced her hand against the wall as two uniformed officers stormed into the room.

A third officer with a baby face came toward Willow as her knees buckled. He caught her with an arm around her waist and eased Willow to the floor. "O'Riley, we need an ambulance here."

An older officer pulled his attention from Graham's body to glance at Willow and Baby Cop. "She injured?" O'Riley asked.

"Can't tell, sir. She's covered in blood."

O'Riley grabbed his phone and called the dispatcher. After a short, terse conversation, he slid the phone into his pocket. "Ambulance is on the way. So are the detectives and the coroner."

The world began to spin. Willow moaned.

"Ma'am, are you hurt?" Baby Cop asked.

Her field of vision narrowed until darkness swallowed her whole.

#

Chapter Two

Max Norton checked his phone again, disappointed not to see a text from Willow. He'd messaged her as soon as he was airborne so she'd know he was safe and on his way home. No response. She always responded to his texts. Until today.

Seated next to him in the cabin of the Fortress jet, Brody Weaver nudged Max. "Everything okay?"

"I don't know." He frowned. "I messaged Willow three hours ago, and she hasn't responded."

"That's not like her. Maybe Sage heard from her." Brody grabbed his own phone and shot off a text to his wife. Less than a minute later, his phone lit up with a response that had him scowling. "Sage and Poppy haven't heard from her for the past twelve hours. They made plans for a video chat at noon, and Willow never answered her phone. They're packing bags, getting ready to leave for Tucker's Gap."

"I don't like this. Tell them to wait. We'll land in Nashville in an hour. If I still haven't heard from Willow by then, I'll go to Tucker's Gap."

Brody's lips curved. "I like the plan. The girls won't."

"Tough. I don't want Sage and Poppy walking into a possible hornet's nest without us." He didn't want them in danger. "I'll find out what's happening. If I need help, I'll let you know."

Concern knotted his gut. Even if he had upset Willow with his question before he deployed, why didn't she respond to her best friends? She wouldn't want to worry Sage and Poppy. If she'd immersed herself in research and forgotten the video chat, Willow would have sent the sisters a message to apologize and reschedule the chat.

Max rubbed his jaw. "Something is wrong, Brody."

A slight nod from his friend. "We'll find her."

"No, *I'll* find her. I need to do this alone."

Brody's eyes narrowed. "What did you do?"

Yeah, that was a definite warning. "Nothing."

"Max."

He blew out a breath. If anyone other than a teammate had cornered him, he'd refuse to answer. Not an option with a member of the Texas team, especially his team leader. "I asked her to go out to dinner with me."

Silence, then, "On a date?"

"Yeah."

Brody groaned. "Too soon, my friend."

"It's been six months." Six months in which Willow had slowly healed from the nightmarish ordeal in Mexico that scarred her inside and out. "I didn't push for a commitment, Brody. I asked her to consider a real date. I've been moving our relationship forward at a snail's pace and giving her plenty of space."

"How did she respond?"

He flinched. "She didn't," he muttered. "Willow froze."

"Too soon," Brody repeated.

"I'm crazy about her, and she's comfortable with me." Max glanced at his friend. "She'd dumped me into the friend zone. I had to do something to make her see me as more than a friend."

"You could have waited a few more months in the friend zone. She went through an experience at the hands of a sadist that no woman should have to endure. She's working through enormous PTSD and trust issues, especially with men."

"I know exactly what Willow survived," he said, voice low.

Brody stared at Max. "She told you some of what she went through?"

"Willow told me everything." In excruciating detail after he showed her a few of his scars, souvenirs from his time as a captive of a cult leader when he'd worked undercover as a cop. Max promised her the complete story one day.

His team leader studied Max. "You've walked in her darkness, haven't you? That's how you acquired the scars."

Max shrugged. "Close enough."

"She won't talk to Sage and Willow about what happened in Mexico."

"They weren't raped by an egocentric monster. She doesn't want Sage and Poppy to walk through her nightmares."

"You told her about your experience?"

"She knows the gist." He'd forced himself to share a little so she'd know he understood, that she didn't have to hide what she felt from him. Anger, bitterness, rage, and sorrow were familiar companions. Facing them head on with her in the dark watches of the night didn't scare him. "I wanted her to know nothing she feels will push me away. I've been there and come out the other side." Most of the way.

"I'm glad she's talking to someone besides the counselor. If she needs more help, you'll tell me."

The last statement was an order, not a suggestion. Having grown up with Brody, Sage, and Poppy, Willow was a good friend. They cared about her and viewed her as family. "Yes, sir."

His phone rang. Max glanced at the readout on his screen. He straightened. "It's Willow."

"On speaker."

He swiped his thumb across the screen and tapped the speaker button. "Are you all right?"

A slight pause, then, "This is Officer O'Riley with the Tucker's Gap Police Department. Are you Max Norton?"

Max's heart skipped a beat, then surged into a frenetic pace as adrenaline poured into his bloodstream. Had Willow been in an accident? "Yes. What happened to Willow?"

"We're not sure yet. We found her covered in blood in her hotel room with a body."

The former cop in Max stirred to life in an instant. "Her injuries?" Whose body was found in her room?

"Don't know. The ER doc is examining her now. Ms. Knox passed out less than a minute after we entered the room. She drifted in and out of consciousness in the ambulance. Every time she surfaced, Ms. Knox asked for you. She's disoriented."

"I want to talk to her," he demanded. "Now."

"Hold on. I'll see if the doctor will let me in the room and if she's awake." After a couple of minutes of mumbled conversations and thumps, O'Riley's voice came through the speaker again. "You're in luck, Norton."

Another thump, then, "Max." Willow's voice sounded weak.

"Are you all right?"

"No."

Disoriented. He needed to be more specific. "Are you injured?"

"I don't know." She began to cry. "I can't go through this again, Max."

His blood ran cold as the implications of her statement hit him like a ton of bricks. No. Please, God, no. Not again. "We're still in the air, an hour from Nashville, Willow. As soon as we land, I'm driving to Tucker's Gap. I'll be there in three hours. Hold strong for me, baby."

More fumbling, then O'Riley was back. "The doc just kicked me into the hallway. He'll run tests on Ms. Knox. When will you arrive?"

"Three hours." Sooner if he could make it happen.

"She'll still be in the hospital. I asked the doc to run a tox screen."

Max's hands fisted, and his jaw hardened. "Willow was drugged?"

"What is your relationship to Ms. Knox?"

He thought fast and made a snap decision to ensure he wouldn't be kept from Willow's side. "We're engaged."

Brody's eyebrows soared.

"She's not wearing a ring."

"Didn't have time to buy the ring before I went out of town."

"I see. We're in Tucker's Gap Hospital. If the doc releases Ms. Knox, I'll let you know. Otherwise, I'll leave word at the nurse's station for you to be granted access to her."

"Appreciate it." He'd also be doing some ground work on his end to make sure O'Riley and his buddies didn't stop him. Max had friends in very high places with pull in the military and law enforcement communities. To be by Willow's side, he'd call in every marker if necessary.

He ended the call and immediately placed another one to the Fortress Security CEO, Brent Maddox. His boss answered on the first ring despite the late hour.

"Yeah, Maddox."

"It's Max Norton."

"What do you need?"

"Time off. Willow Knox is in the hospital."

"What happened?"

"Not sure. Tucker's Gap cops found her in her hotel room covered in blood and with a body. She might have been drugged."

"Take backup."

"I want to scope out the situation first. If I need help, I'll ask one of my teammates to drive to Tucker's Gap."

"I don't like it."

"Tough, sir."

When his teammates heard his response to Maddox, all conversation died.

"Got something to tell me, Norton?"

"No, sir."

Maddox gave a bark of laughter. "In other words, mind my own business."

"I didn't say that." But he was thinking it. Willow was his. End of story. He just hadn't convinced her yet.

"I'll let that slide for now. Don't bank on that for long."

"Understood, sir."

"Permission granted for leave. I expect regular updates, Norton. Keep Weaver informed as well. How can we help?"

"Two things. One, I need Zane to find out if anything is circulating online about an incident in Tucker's Gap, Tennessee." Zane Murphy was the Fortress tech geek. If any information was online, he'd find it.

"Done. Second?"

He sighed and manned up. "I need an engagement ring."

#

Chapter Three

Max parked his SUV in an empty slot near the emergency entrance of the Tucker's Gap hospital. The parking lot was brightly lit, a contrast to the darkness of the pre-dawn hour. Two patrol cars were parked a short distance away, the officers nowhere in sight. They were probably stationed inside.

Although he hated to be unarmed, Max didn't want anything to keep him from Willow's side. Besides, plenty of things were available to use as weapons if he needed to protect himself and Willow. Max had no problem using lethal force with or without a weapon. No further harm would come to Willow on his watch.

He unlocked his floorboard gun safe and stored his weapons. With identification in hand, Max walked into the emergency room and headed for the nurse's station. A cop lingering nearby sized him up, eyes hard. Max ignored him, focusing on the woman behind the desk. "I'm here to see Willow Knox."

When the nurse glanced his direction, the officer moved closer, alert. "Who are you?" he demanded.

"Max Norton. I'm Willow's boyfriend."

"Identification."

Max handed over his Fortress identification and waited while the officer examined his credentials.

After a beat, the officer handed back the wallet.

"Where is Willow?"

The other man pointed at a second cop at the far end of the corridor. "Inside that exam room. The doc's with her. So is Officer O'Riley. He'll stay with her. Protection."

Right. Protection if she'd been targeted and a guard if she was guilty of murder. Max didn't need the warning. He knew how the game was played. Until proved innocent, Willow was a suspect in the death of Graham Enright. His friend, Zane, had called with an update as he reached the outskirts of Tucker's Gap.

His jaw hardened. Why had Enright been in Willow's hotel room? Based on the cop's expression, he was going with the obvious conclusion that Willow slept with or planned to sleep with Enright until something had gone horribly wrong and she'd killed him. The cop's assessment was dead wrong but he didn't know Willow or about her experience in Mexico.

What was the Enright heir doing in Willow's hotel room? More important, how did he end up dead?

Max strode down the hall and extended his cred wallet to the officer at the exam room door. "O'Riley is expecting me."

After a cursory examination of Max's identification, the officer handed back the wallet and rapped on the door.

A man with salt-and-pepper hair and cop's eyes, and wearing a uniform opened the door, blocking entrance to the room. His gaze connected with Max's. "Norton?"

Max nodded and showed his identification.

After a moment, the cop stepped back. "I'm O'Riley."

Entering the room, Max's gaze zeroed in on the woman in scrubs lying on the bed with her eyes closed. He crossed the space separating them in seconds. "Willow."

Her eyes flew open. "Max." She sat up and swung her legs over the side of the bed. A second later, she was in his arms.

Stunned, he wrapped his arms around her by reflex, slowly tightening his hold by degrees, giving her plenty of time to break free if she felt trapped. This was the first time Willow had touched him voluntarily. "Are you all right, sweetheart?"

She shook her head, her body beginning to tremble.

Dumb question. Of course she wasn't all right. How could she be when a man was murdered in her hotel room? "Are you injured?"

"I don't think so but I don't know."

Max understood what she couldn't bring herself to verbalize. She didn't know if she'd been sexually assaulted. The question was why didn't she remember?

The only answer that made sense was Willow had been drugged or someone had knocked her out. Based on her response, he was going with the former. If that was the case, only the doctor would be able to tell if she'd been an assault victim for a second time. Man, he hoped not. Willow had been through enough.

He kissed her temple. "No matter what happened, we'll deal with it together," he murmured. "You aren't alone any more."

She wrapped her arms tighter around his waist. "Thank you for coming. I shouldn't have called you," she whispered. "You just returned home after being gone for a month."

"I will always be here for you." He lowered his head until his lips brushed against her ear as he whispered his next words. "I told O'Riley we're engaged."

"Better hope my father and brothers don't receive that memo."

Max chuckled, positive if the men in her family heard the news, they'd come after him with both barrels loaded. He'd be lying if he said that wasn't a concern. Max could handle himself. Defeating three ticked off, protective men determined to safeguard Willow would be a challenge.

He eased back to slide his hand into his cargo pocket. Max pulled out the diamond ring Maddox had given him at the airport. Praying it was a decent fit to support the story he'd spun for the cops, Max slid the ring on the fourth finger of her left hand.

Satisfaction filled him. A perfect fit. Playing to the riveted audience of cops and medical personnel, he raised her hand to his lips and kissed her palm, holding her hand firmly when she subtly tried to pull away. Hopefully, she would get used to his touch fast. Otherwise, Max's claim of being her future husband wouldn't hold water. "I'm sorry your ring wasn't ready before I left town, Willow."

Max turned his head to look at the woman with a stethoscope draped around her neck and wearing a white coat. "What can you tell me about Willow's injuries?"

"Ms. Knox has bruises and scrapes. No internal injuries. We're still waiting on the results of the tox screen."

He steeled himself. Might as well address the elephant in the room because ignoring it wouldn't help Willow or him. The sooner they knew the truth, the better. "Any signs of sexual assault?"

Willow inched closer to Max.

"We need to know, baby," he murmured. "Well, Doc?"

"I didn't see signs of sexual assault but I'm still waiting on the results of the rape kit."

Just hearing those words made him want to hurl. When Willow shuddered, Max scooped her into his arms and placed her gently on the bed. He sat beside her and again took her hand in his. This time, she didn't try to pull away. Progress.

Although he couldn't hurry the tests or the healing process, he would be there for Willow every step of the way. If the tests showed no assault, the possibility of it and enduring the assault exam would resurrect painful memories.

"We need the test results as soon as possible, Dr. Conroy," O'Riley said.

"I'll check with the lab again, Sean, but tests take as long as they take. Can't afford to make mistakes."

"I understand, but nudge the lab rats along, will you?"

Conroy's lips curved. She motioned for the nurse to follow her from the room. At the door, she paused and looked over her shoulder at Willow. "Ms. Knox, press the call button if you need assistance or if you need a break." With a warning glance at O'Riley and Max, she exited the exam room with the nurse on her heels.

Seconds later, someone rapped sharply on the door frame, and two men in conservative suits and ties entered. The detectives had arrived.

The men nodded at O'Riley, and the older one came to Willow's bedside. "Ms. Knox, I'm Detective Cohen. This is my partner, Detective Warner. We need to ask you a few questions about what happened in your hotel room."

Willow's hand trembled in Max's. "Ask. I doubt I'll have answers."

His eyes narrowed. "Why not?"

"I don't know what happened."

Willow's answer wouldn't go over well. As a cop, Max had been suspicious every time a suspect claimed amnesia. More often than not, the suspect lied.

Cohen stared. "You expect me to believe that?"

"Watch it, Detective," Max said softly, a clear warning in his voice.

"Who are you?" Warner demanded.

"Max Norton. Willow and I are engaged." He smiled. Well, more a baring of his teeth. "I used to be on the job in Texas. Willow is cooperating to the best of her ability."

"She's lying."

"She's innocent until proved guilty. Treat her with respect or you'll be speaking with her lawyer instead of obtaining information."

Cohen stared hard at Max for two beats before shifting his attention to Willow. "You say you don't know what happened last night."

"That's right."

"Let's start earlier in the day. What do you remember?"

She took her time answering the question. "I remember leaving the hotel yesterday morning and driving to the Enright estate."

"What is your relationship to Graham Enright?"

"I barely knew him."

"Were you lovers?"

She flinched. "No. What part of 'barely knew him' don't you understand?"

"Are you sure, Ms. Knox? Lying to the police is unwise."

"She answered your question," Max said. "Move on." That earned him a glare from both detectives. Tough. They weren't badgering Willow.

"What time did you arrive at the estate, Ms. Knox?" Cohen asked.

"A few minutes after nine."

Max breathed a little easier. At least she was able to remember part of the past 24 hours.

"You had an appointment with Graham, spent time with him and hit it off?"

Willow shook her head. "I interviewed Oliver Enright, Graham's father."

"You're a reporter?"

"A genealogist. I work for Ballinger Research."

Detective Warner glanced up from his notes. "You're an heir hunter?"

"Hunting heirs is one of the things I do. I also research family trees for historical purposes when a client requests that service. The information is for family use."

"I've heard your name mentioned in the news media."

She stiffened.

"Don't you write books, too?"

Willow nodded. "With permission from clients, I've written and published five books about the black sheep in their family trees."

Cohen snapped his fingers. "You wrote a book about a pirate, right?"

"Smiling Jack."

"Yeah, that's the guy. Good book. Always like stories about pirates. So, you drove to the Enright estate and interviewed Oliver Enright. How long did the interview take?"

"Two hours."

"Did you also speak to Graham?"

"No."

"Did you see him?"

She shook her head. "The housekeeper showed me into the library where Oliver waited. When the interview ended, I returned to the hotel."

"Housekeeper walked you out?"

"No one was around."

"What time did you arrive at your hotel?"

"Noon."

"But you said the interview lasted two hours. The Enright estate isn't that far from your hotel. Sure you didn't stop to meet Graham?"

"What is it with all the questions about Graham? No, I didn't meet Graham. I hit a road construction detour, got turned around, and had to backtrack before I found my way to the hotel."

Cohen frowned. "Say I believe you although I don't see how it's possible to get lost with GPS on your phone. What did you do when you arrived at the hotel?"

"Dropped my computer and research materials in my room, and went to the hotel's restaurant for lunch. Afterward, I returned to my room and worked on the Enright family tree until dinner." She sighed. "That's where things become murky."

"Did you leave the hotel for dinner?"

"No."

"You sure about that? You said things are murky."

"I'm not positive, but it's a reasonable assumption."

"Why?"

"It's dark early at night this time of year. I never go out alone after dark, especially in a strange town."

"Ever?"

Her gaze broke away from Cohen and shifted to Max.

He gave a slight nod. She needed to answer the question because Cohen and Warner would look at security camera footage to check her story.

"No." No elaboration.

Max sighed. Nothing like waving a metaphorical red flag in front of the cops.

The detectives and O'Riley straightened. "Why not?" Warner demanded.

"You can't expect us to believe that." This from Cohen.

Willow scowled. "I don't care what you believe, Detective Cohen. It's the truth."

"Why won't you go out at night?" Warner repeated.

She took a deep breath. "I was…" Willow fell silent, tears trickling down her cheeks. She turned her face away from the detectives and pressed it against Max's shoulder.

"I've got you," he murmured, wrapping his arm around her shoulders. He would always have her back.

"You were what?" Cohen snapped.

"Willow was taken captive six months ago by a Mexican cartel into gunrunning, drugs, and human trafficking," Max said. "I shouldn't have to tell you the trauma Willow suffered. She's still working through some issues. Leaving her home at night is one of those issues."

Cohen stared at Willow a moment as though puzzled at her answer, then his eyes widened. "You're Colonel Knox's daughter. I saw your story in the news."

Warner whistled softly.

Max lightly cupped the back of Willow's head with his palm. "Everyone in the country saw that story. A high-ranking military officer targeted by his own wife and her lover made the rounds on the news cycles for several weeks, especially since Willow's stepmother targeted her as well."

"Bad business," Cohen muttered.

"True story," Willow said, voice choked.

The detective speared Max with a glance. "Must make your personal relationship a challenge."

He shrugged. "We manage."

"She goes out at night if you're with her?"

"What do you think? She feels safe with me. Last night, I wasn't with her."

A snort, then Cohen turned back to Willow. "So, you probably didn't leave the hotel for dinner. You still had to eat. Did you meet someone for a meal in the hotel's restaurant?"

"I don't know. I can't remember. However, I don't know why I would meet anyone, especially Graham. I don't eat meals with clients or their families when I'm working."

"Why not?"

"Ballinger Research pays for my hotel room. They allot me a certain number of days to complete the research on site. I finish the work in the office. Not only that, the client also pays based on the number of hours the project takes to complete from start to finish. I don't have time to waste."

"Makes sense. You said you especially wouldn't share a meal with Graham Enright. Why not?"

"I told you. We were barely acquainted. I said hello once or twice when I was at the estate or his father's office. I never carried on a conversation. Why would I eat dinner with him?"

"Maybe you were two-timing your man. A lonely woman with her boyfriend out of town. Who would blame you for going on a date or two with an attractive companion, maybe indulging in a little personal one-on-one time in your hotel room? Who would know, after all?"

She scowled. "I would. I don't cheat."

"You sure about that? We'll check the hotel's security cameras," he warned.

"Go ahead. I don't have anything to hide."

"That you can remember," Warner said with a sneer.

"Enough," Max said. "Move on or leave and call Willow's attorney."

"This isn't your case."

"Willow is mine, and I will protect her."

"Interfering in our investigation will land you behind bars, Norton. You used your street cred as a former cop to get into this room. You won't get a pass on interference."

"We're on the same side, Cohen. We all want the truth."

"Even if the truth lands your future wife behind bars?"

"Willow didn't kill anyone."

A sneer from Warner. "Yeah? Then why did we find her fingerprints all over the murder weapon?"

#

Chapter Four

Willow stared at the detectives, horrified by the news they delivered with grim expressions and deep suspicion in their eyes. How had her fingerprints ended up on the knife used to kill Graham?

She didn't know Graham. Why would she kill him?

Willow searched her sketchy memory again, looking for answers to what happened in her hotel room, and came up with nothing. Finding her prints on the knife didn't make sense. She hadn't brought a knife or gun to Tucker's Gap.

Despite urging from her brothers and father, she didn't own knives except the ones for kitchen use. Her gun was locked in a safe in her closet at home. "That's impossible."

"It's a fact." Cohen folded his arms across his chest. "How do you explain that?"

"I can't. The knife isn't mine." Was it possible Graham brought the knife to her room? Maybe, but she came up against the same problem. She wouldn't invite Graham to her room for any reason because she didn't know or trust him. The only men she trusted were her brothers and father, Max, and Max's teammates.

"You know that but you can't remember anything about your lover's tryst with Enright." The disdain in his voice accompanied a matching expression on his face.

Her cheeks burned. "There wasn't a tryst," she insisted.

"Sorry, Ms. Knox." His tone said he wasn't sorry at all. "I don't believe you. I think you invited Enright to your room, and something went wrong. Maybe he got rough, and you panicked. Makes it self-defense. Given your experience in Mexico, any jury would understand. Let's not waste each other's time, all right? Tell us how it went down, and we'll put in a good word with the DA for you. You might even get off without any prison time, given your recent history."

"We're done here." Max stood. "You're throwing mud at the wall to see if anything sticks."

"Her prints on the murder weapon don't constitute mud, Norton."

"You know better. What you have isn't enough. She doesn't have cuts on her hands or defensive wounds. No witnesses have come forward to support your tale. I'm not buying the story you're selling, and neither will a judge. She told you everything she knows, and now Willow is invoking her right to consult with an attorney."

Cohen shifted his narrowed gaze to Willow. "Ms. Knox, are you going to allow Norton speak for you or do you have a mind of your own?"

Nice. Her choices were to confess to murder or admit to having as much spine as a wet dishrag. "Contact my attorney." She'd have to get on finding one. Perhaps her boss knew an excellent criminal attorney. The way things were looking, she'd need the best in the business to keep her out of jail.

The detectives scowled. "Don't leave town," Warner said. He flipped the page on his notebook, pen hovering over the surface as he eyed Max.

"We'll be speaking again soon, Ms. Knox. You can count on it." Cohen shifted his attention to Max as well. "What about you, Norton? Where have you been during the past 24 hours?"

He smiled. "Out of town."

"Be more specific."

"Okay. Out of the country."

The detectives stared. "Are you trying to be cute?" Warner demanded. "If that's your goal, you're falling short of the target. You're ticking us off. That's not wise."

"I work for Fortress Security, and our missions are classified. My team has been deployed out of the country for the past month. I was in the company jet returning to the states with my team when

O'Riley called to tell me Willow was in the emergency room. After the jet landed in Nashville, I drove straight here."

"Mission," Cohen said thoughtfully. "What does that mean exactly? You sell security systems overseas or something?"

Max chuckled. "Fortress does sell systems overseas but I'm not on an installation team."

Speculation lit the detective's gaze. "You're a bodyguard or something?"

"Or something."

A soft whistle. "Black ops?"

Max remained silent.

Cohen dragged a hand down his face. "I'll take that as a yes. Great. So you're not just blowing smoke. I've heard of Fortress through the grapevine. Tough outfit."

A shrug. "We get the job done."

Understatement. From what Willow understood, they never failed, no matter the odds stacked against them.

"Since you won't tell us where you were, will anyone confirm you were out of the country until a few hours ago or do we have to take your word that you're telling the truth?" Warner sneered.

"I'm reaching for my wallet," Max said.

"Afraid we're trigger happy?"

"Just a precaution." He removed two cards from his wallet and handed one to each of the detectives. "Call Fortress any time day or night. Someone will confirm when I left the country and when I returned. Don't ask for details. You won't get them."

"Would they lie for you?"

"If my life was at risk, yes. That's not the case."

"But you and Ms. Knox are engaged. Wouldn't they feel obligated to protect her like they would you?"

Willow tensed. She didn't want Max to be in trouble with the Tucker's Gap police because of her.

He squeezed her hand in silent warning without taking his attention from the detectives. "No."

"We'll check on your whereabouts, Norton," Cohen warned. "Ms. Knox might not have the skill or stomach to kill Graham Enright, but you're the top suspect in my book."

"I'd be disappointed if you didn't suspect me, and it wouldn't give me much hope that you'd find the real killer."

"Oh, we'll find him." He paused deliberately. "Or her."

Warner narrowed his eyes. "You love Ms. Knox, Norton."

"We're engaged. What do you think?"

"I think you'd kill any man who hurt your woman."

Max stared at Warner. "Don't think much of me, do you? If someone tried to kill Willow, I'd do anything necessary to protect her and not feel a moment's guilt. I want justice for her, and that includes seeing the perp behind bars. You seem to think I'm an assassin for hire. That's not what we do."

"You telling me that you don't kill people in the course of your job?" Warner scoffed. "I don't believe you."

"Didn't say that. When we confront terrorists, things happen fast. I kill in defense of my teammates and our principals, not because I'm an assassin."

"But you would kill to protect Ms. Knox."

"To spare her life and mine, absolutely. That's not what happened with Enright."

"We're back to Ms. Knox killing him in self-defense."

Max snorted. "We're back to you finding the real killer who isn't Willow."

Cohen handed his card to Max and turned away. "Tell her attorney to get in touch. We need to have another conversation with both of you once Ms. Knox is released from the hospital." He inclined his head toward O'Riley. "Officer O'Riley will wait and escort you to the station."

Before the detectives left, Dr. Conroy returned and motioned for them to stay. "The initial tox screen is back."

"What's the word, Doc?" Sean asked.

"The lab found Rohypnol in Ms. Knox's bloodwork."

The detectives looked as stunned as Willow felt. She stared at the doctor. Good grief. No wonder she couldn't remember anything. One of the side effects of Rohypnol was memory loss.

How had she been drugged? A shudder wracked her body. Even more troubling was not knowing what happened to her during the time her memory had gaps.

Warner slid her a hard look. "You gave yourself the drug. We'll be checking the restaurant's cameras for proof."

Cohen held up his hand to forestall more comments from his partner, Max, or Willow. "Send me the results, would you, Doc?"

"Of course. I'll send the rest of the test results as soon as they're available, too."

After a nod, he left with Warner on his heels.

O'Riley eyed Max. "What's your plan once the detectives speak with you and Ms. Knox again?"

"First priority is to get a room at a different hotel."

The cop gave a slight nod. "Need a recommendation?"

"I have my own resources, but thanks."

He slipped a hand into his pocket and handed Max a card. "In case you need to contact me later. I'm not sure what's going on but the drug in Ms. Knox's system makes me question her guilt in Enright's death."

"Appreciate the contact information."

"Yep. I'll wait in the hall until you're ready to go."

After O'Riley left the room, Dr. Conroy walked to Willow's bedside. "I'd like to keep you here until the test results are back."

"How long will that take?"

"A few more hours." She squeezed Willow's hand. "I hope to release you by noon. I'd release you now except under the circumstances I'm afraid you might need further treatment."

Circumstances she couldn't remember. Stomach churning, Willow gripped Max's hand tighter. "I understand." All too well.

"If it turns out you were assaulted, Ms. Knox, I'll ask a counselor to talk to you."

"No."

"Ms. Knox, I'd strongly advise you to reconsider."

"I already have a counselor." Marcus Lang and his wife, Paige, were wonderful plus they had become good friends in the past six months.

"I see." Another hand squeeze. "I'm glad. Be sure to contact the counselor as soon as possible no matter how the results turn out. What you've experienced will likely stir up bad memories."

Willow gave a nod without committing one way or another. Chances were good, though, that Max would insist. He was the one who introduced her to Marcus and Paige. The couple had helped her through some difficult days but she hoped their counseling services wouldn't be necessary again.

"I'll return when the rest of the tests are ready," Dr. Cohen promised. "Your nurse will arrive soon to hook up an IV to flush the drug from your system. Rest. We'll talk about your next steps before I release you."

"Thanks, Dr. Conroy."

She smiled, patted Willow's arm, and left the room.

Max released her hand. Willow felt bereft, almost as though she'd lost something vital or precious.

"May I hold you?" he murmured. "Please?"

Tears stung her eyes as she nodded.

He wrapped his arm around Willow's shoulders and eased her against his chest. His other arm circled her waist in a loose hold. "I meant what I said, Willow. We'll get through this together."

"What if..." She couldn't even voice the awful thought. The prospect of working through another physical assault was daunting.

"Let's wait for the facts rather than assume the worst."

She sighed. "You're right. We'll know soon."

"Do you mind going through the past 24 hours again with me?"

"Why? I don't remember enough to keep myself out of jail."

"The evidence of Rohypnol will help with that." Max rested his cheek against the top of her head. "Indulge me."

She recounted what she told the detectives. When she reached the point in her recitation when she believed she went to the hotel's restaurant for dinner, something flashed through her mind too fast to catch. Willow stopped talking in mid-sentence, frowning.

"What is it?"

"I'm not sure. It's probably nothing."

"But may be something. Tell me anyway."

"Something flashed through my mind but disappeared before I could grab it."

"Something or someone?"

She scowled. "I can't remember."

"Will you try something for me?"

"Of course. Anything." She paused for a second, then qualified that with, "Anything within reason. I'm not into jumping out of airplanes or cliff diving."

He chuckled. "Close your eyes." When she complied, Max said, "Relax against me, and let your mind drift. What did you work on yesterday afternoon?"

"The Enright family tree."

"What did you do?"

"I traced Oliver's and Martha's history as far back as I could."

"Find anything interesting?"

She wrinkled her nose. "Oliver's idea of fidelity is flexible."

"An affair?"

"More than one."

A grunt. "How often did that happen?"

"A lot."

"Huh. Doesn't say much for his character, does it? How long have he and Martha been married?"

"Fifteen years. She's the latest Mrs. Oliver Enright. There have been three others. Martha is the one who has lasted the longest."

"He had multiple affairs?"

She gave a wry laugh. "Oliver should have a revolving door on his bedroom."

"Any skeletons in the family closet?"

Willow frowned. "Maybe."

"Explain."

"Four murders in the family during the past ten years, all unsolved."

#

Chapter Five

Max's brows knitted. "Four unsolved murders. Do you think the Enrights have a serial killer stalking them?"

"Or living among them in plain sight." Willow wrinkled her nose. "It sounds like something out of a horror movie. Although I might be wrong, I don't think I am."

His gut knotted. A serial killer coming after him? Bring it on. He'd wipe the floor with the killer and go home at the end of the day without a smidgen of regret. Someone evil gunning for Willow was unacceptable.

To catch a serial killer, you had to think like one. Willow couldn't do that. The woman at his side didn't have an evil bone in her body.

Max's lip curled. On the other hand, he could think like a serial killer. His childhood and later capture and torture at the hands of a cult leader helped him tap into the darkness hidden inside evil men.

He studied Willow's troubled expression. Max had believed Willow's job as a genealogist was safe. Researching family trees shouldn't have been dangerous. Now, he would always wonder if she was safe while he was deployed on a mission with his team. "Have you run across something like this before in your research for Ballinger?"

"No, thank goodness. I've discovered an embezzler, a few pirates, a smuggler, a pimp, and a direct descendant of a king of England, but never a serial killer."

"Good. The last thing you want is to attract the attention of a serial killer. They believe they're the smartest person in the room and will go to any lengths to prove it. A nosy genealogist would be perceived as a threat to exposure and automatically become a target."

"Oh, come on. How would I be a threat to anyone? My job is to create a chart and possibly a narrative for family use."

"A killer would fear discovery through your research."

"Sorry to disappoint, but I've found nothing that points to a killer's identity, just an indication that someone is working behind the scenes."

"If you found a pattern pointing to the identity of a killer, wouldn't you feel obligated to report it to the police?"

Willow narrowed her eyes. "I wouldn't let him get away with murder."

"Have you found a pattern in the Enright family background?"

Her gaze skittered away from his.

Max's heart sank. "You have." He wanted to slam his fist through the nearest wall. She should have been safe. Instead, Willow had walked straight into the path of a killer. "What did you find?"

"All the victims were stabbed to death."

He closed his eyes a moment. "The next time my team is deployed, I'm tempted to hide you in my duffel bag and take you with me. At least then, I'd know you were safe."

She smiled. "I'll pack my running shoes so I can keep up with you."

"What's your next step?" He wanted her to go home and hide in a safe room until he tracked down the person who murdered Graham Enright and ensured Willow was safe. Not going to happen, though. Willow was too strong to hide from life no matter how difficult the path she walked.

"Once the sun comes up, I have to call my boss. He won't appreciate it if I wake him from a sound sleep. Rusty Ballinger has a two-month-old daughter who has her days and nights mixed up. If I'm lucky, I'll still have a job at the end of the conversation, and Ballinger might have a client. No guarantees on either. If my company keeps Oliver Enright as a client, Oliver will probably request a different genealogist since I'm a suspect in his son's death."

He squeezed her shoulder, grateful she allowed his touch. "Close your eyes again."

She rested her head against his shoulder and complied.

"You researched the Enright family tree during the afternoon. Did you leave the room for any reason?"

"No."

"Did anyone come to your room?"

"No. Wait. Maybe." Willow growled. "Sorry. I saw another flash of something. This is so frustrating."

"But you are remembering bits."

"Tiny pieces that mean nothing and don't help."

"It will." He needed to contact Zane Murphy and ask him to find hotel security cam video. Anything that cast doubt on the story the Tucker's Gap detectives were spinning would help. Max's goal was first to keep Willow out of jail, then track down the real killer to make sure Willow's name was cleared and she remained safe. "In your mind, go to the door and open it. What do you see?"

She was silent a moment, then sighed. "Nothing. I'm sorry, Max. This isn't working."

"Let's keep going. In your mind, go to the hotel's restaurant. Do you see the host or hostess?"

Willow stilled. "Yes. It's a host. He's harried, answering the phone to take reservations as well as arranging seating for people coming to the restaurant."

"Excellent. Did you have to wait to be seated?"

She shook her head. "I caught him in a lull."

"The waitress took you to a table. Where did you sit?"

"Corner table on the left side of the room."

"What did you eat?"

Silence.

Max glanced down at her. "Do you remember?"

"I'm not positive, but I think it was a salad or possibly just a dessert."

"Good. Did you drink iced tea, water, or something else?"

"Soft drink." Her lips curved. "A diet drink."

He grimaced. What was the point? "Did someone stop at your table or join you for dinner? Someone you didn't expect?"

More silence, then, "I don't know. My memory is totally blank. How can I remember my drink but not if someone sat with me?"

"Rohypnol creates weird holes in memories."

"Will I ever remember everything?"

"Probably not. You remembering as much as you have is amazing. We'll check the security camera footage."

"What if the cameras don't help?"

"We'll talk to people who interacted with you yesterday. Someone knows something. We'll figure things out, Willow."

"We need to do it yesterday. Otherwise, I'll spend time behind bars. I'd rather not become best buddies with hard-core inmates at the local jail."

"You won't."

"You can't know that."

"You didn't kill Enright."

"The Tucker's Gap police aren't convinced."

"The drug in your blood work has created doubt. I'll find out who killed Enright."

"*We'll* find the killer. This is my mess, and I'll help clean it up. I hope you can clear my name." She nudged him. "I'd hate to miss out on our engagement by being a jailbird."

Max chuckled, glad to see a glimpse of her humor. "Sorry if I'm causing you awkward moments. An engagement was the easiest way to obtain access to you."

Her face flushed. "I don't mind. I kind of like it."

"Why?"

"Being engaged, even if it is pretend, makes me feel normal, as though I'm not damaged." She waved her hand. "I'm sorry. That probably doesn't make sense. Ignore me."

"No chance of that happening. Ever." Max cupped the side of her neck, his thumb stroking her jaw. "Willow, you aren't damaged."

Her gaze skated away from his again. "How can you say that after what happened in Mexico?"

"Not damaged," he insisted. "Dented."

She huffed. "Big dents."

A light tap sounded and the nurse stepped inside, pushing a cart. "Ms. Knox, I'm Candace, your nurse. I'm here to hook up an IV to flush the Rohypnol from your system."

"Any word on the rest of the test results?" Willow asked.

"Not yet. Dr. Conroy requested a rush, though. Hopefully, you won't have to wait much longer. In the meantime, let's get this IV started. The sooner we flush the drug from your system, the better you'll feel." Minutes later, Candace pushed her cart from the room.

As the door closed behind the nurse, Willow yawned. "Sorry," she murmured.

"Don't be. Sleep is the best thing for you. Rest. I'll keep you safe."

"You haven't slept, either."

He wouldn't go into a deep sleep until one of his teammates arrived to keep watch while he rested. "I'll be fine until we're in a place where I know you're safe."

"That's not fair to you, Max."

"I wasn't drugged." He started to go sit in a chair when Willow laid her hand on his forearm. He froze. "What is it?"

"Stay. Please."

"Are you sure?"

She nodded. "I feel safer when you're close."

Definite progress. Perhaps they were moving out of snail gear to turtle speed where their relationship was concerned. "Scoot over." When she complied, he raised the head of the bed and reclined against the pillow, stretching his legs out beside hers on the mattress.

Willow sighed and relaxed in Max's embrace. "Thanks."

As if he would turn down any request from Willow. "Any time."

In less than five minutes, Willow was sound asleep. Max relaxed deeper into the pillow and, by minute degrees, settled the woman in his arms more fully against his chest, hoping his body heat and heartbeat would help Willow sink into a deep sleep.

He allowed himself to drift. A combat nap his military coworkers at Fortress called it. Operatives learned to sleep lightly in enemy territory. As far as Max was concerned, Tucker's Gap was behind enemy lines which meant he would remain on guard until someone he trusted had his back.

An hour later, he became alert when footsteps approached and a familiar deep voice spoke to O'Riley in the hallway. What was his teammate doing here? He should have been recharging himself.

Seconds later, Jesse Phelps peered into the room. Seeing Max was awake, he walked to the bedside. "How is she?"

"All right for the moment. When we receive more information, that may change."

"What does the doctor say?"

"Willow was drugged with Rohypnol."

Jesse scowled. "Rape kit results?"

"Pending."

A slight nod. "Won't be easy no matter what the results are."

He inclined his head in silent agreement. "Why are you here?"

"You needed backup. The rest of the team will come if we ask." His lips curved. "Might come even if we don't. Sage and Poppy are lobbying hard to come to Tucker's Gap."

"Figured. They're Willow's best friends. They'll want to be here for her." Max sobered. "It's not safe. Brody and Logan should keep their women away."

"Why?"

"A serial killer might have murdered Graham Enright."

"You serious?"

"Afraid so. In researching the Enright family history, Willow discovered four people in the past ten years have been stabbed to death."

"Suspects?"

"Don't know. I doubt Willow pulled police reports. She stumbled across the murders while researching the family tree."

"I'm glad she didn't look too deep."

"Someone may think she knows too much."

When Jesse's eyebrow raised in a silent question, Max told him about Enright's murder in Willow's hotel room.

"Any chance she invited Enright to her room?"

"None."

"You sure?"

"He's positive," Willow said curtly. She opened her eyes and glared at Jesse. "I barely knew Graham, and inviting any man to my hotel room is out of the question."

A nod from Texas team's medic. "I understand. How are you, Willow?"

"Angry and afraid."

Without thinking, Max kissed the top of her head.

Willow's breath caught and her gaze shot to his.

Oh, man. He could have kicked himself for that slip. Although it was an instinctive move, he might have set their relationship back several steps. "Should I apologize?"

After a pause, she whispered, "No."

He smiled. "Just as well. I wasn't going to apologize anyway."

Jesse snorted, drawing their attention back to him. "If that's your idea of romance, Norton, you need some serious tutoring."

"If you're volunteering your expertise, I'll pass because you haven't dated in more than two years." Neither of them were in the running for best dating candidate.

"Who had time?" the medic demanded. "Between training as an operative and paramedic, all I've done is study and deploy with you clowns. Saving the world is hard work."

True statement. All Fortress operatives worked hard to get into top shape and stay there. The medics, however, heaped medical training on top of everything else.

Another knock sounded on the door. Dr. Conroy walked in. She paused when she saw Jesse. "Who are you?"

"Jesse. I'm a paramedic, and a friend of Willow and Max."

Tension left the doctor's shoulders. "If you had been another police officer, I would have insisted you leave. My patient has had too many visitors over the past few hours."

She shifted her attention to Willow. "Ms. Knox, your test results are in. Do you want the gentlemen to step into the hallway while we discuss the results?"

Max wanted to insist the doctor tell him as well but he didn't have the right. Not yet. He hoped to change that. How fast depended on Willow.

The woman in question looked at him.

He made himself say the words. "Your choice."

Willow shifted her gaze to the doctor as she pressed her body tighter against Max's side, as though bracing for a body blow. "You can speak freely in front of Max and Jesse."

"Are you sure, Ms. Knox?"

"Positive. Please, don't make me wait any longer."

"No indications of sexual assault."

Max breathed easier. Thank God. "You're sure?"

"Positive. I don't understand why someone drugged Ms. Knox with a date-rape drug and didn't assault her, but for her sake I'm glad they had another purpose in mind."

"So are we."

Conroy eyed Max. "Would it have made a difference in how you felt about Ms. Knox if the results had been different?"

"No. Never." No hesitation in his answer. Yeah, he'd care a lot if she had been assaulted again. Max would feel like he'd failed to protect Willow from one of the monsters of the world. The monsters should never touch her. She was special.

His fast response seemed to satisfy the doctor. She shifted her focus to Willow. "I strongly recommend you contact your counselor as soon as possible. You've been through a trauma sure to bring bad memories to the surface."

"I will."

The doctor studied her a moment. "Do I have your word?"

Willow stiffened. "I don't make a habit of lying, Dr. Conroy."

"All right. I'll put in orders for you to be released. Your nurse will remove the IV and bring your discharge papers. If you change your mind about our counseling services, let me know. I'll be glad to arrange an appointment for you. Also, don't hesitate to return if you notice new symptoms." She squeezed Willow's hand, nodded to Max and Jesse, and left.

Jesse's expression was grim. "We need to call Zane."

Chapter Six

Max pulled out his phone and called Fortress Security's tech and communications guru, Zane Murphy. His friend answered on the first ring.

"Yeah, Murphy."

His eyebrows rose at the other man's curt greeting. "It's Max Norton. You sound a little rough around the edges, buddy."

A low laugh came through the phone's speaker. "What you're hearing is the aftermath of a night spent comforting a little boy with an ear infection."

He flinched. "Ouch. Hope he feels better soon."

"Thanks. What do you need?"

"Other than a solid eight hours of sleep, your hacking skills."

"Nothing I like better than circumventing the system. Who am I bedeviling with my computer today?"

"Tucker's Gap cops. I need everything they have on the murder of Graham Enright, and I want you to hack into the security system of the Royal Hotel in Tucker's Gap."

"No problem with the murder file. What am I searching for at the hotel?"

Max summarized what happened to Willow. "If anyone interacted with her or entered her room, I want to know and see their faces. I want identification on each person."

"The identification is more challenging, especially if they don't have a record. In addition, Phantom will be in a hot zone soon. I'm their tech support."

"Don't worry about a deep search. Security cam footage of Willow will be enough to get me started. I don't mind legwork. If I need further help, I'll let you know."

43

"Good enough. Max, don't do legwork on the ground alone, especially since you might have a serial killer stalking Willow. These guys are more dangerous when cornered and desperate."

His hand clenched tighter around the phone and caused the plastic housing to creak in protest. He was very familiar with the danger of dealing with serial killers. "Jesse is here, too. We'll watch over Willow as well as guard each other's backs, Z."

"See that you do. I don't want to lose another friend."

Max stilled, unused to hearing the note of sorrow in Zane's voice. He'd overhead bits of conversation from other operatives who knew Zane well and remembered this was always a difficult time of year for the tech wizard. He'd lost his entire SEAL team to an IED a few years earlier and ended up in a wheelchair from his own injuries. Max's throat thickened. "I hear you, Z. We'll be careful."

"Good. Anything else I should know about your situation?"

"The Tucker's Gap detectives investigating Enright's murder will call soon to confirm that I wasn't near their town when the death occurred. They're wondering if I'm their culprit."

"Figures. I'll make sure they know you were out of pocket during the time of the murder. When the boss arrives, he'll want an update."

"I'll call as soon as I can. I also need a lawyer for Willow."

"She's under arrest?"

"The possibility looks unlikely but I want an attorney with her when she's questioned by the police again."

"Understood. How soon?"

"Imminent. We're waiting on the discharge paperwork now. They left a babysitter to make sure we don't skip town before they grill us again."

"I'll call Maddox and find out who owes him a favor and lives in the area. Stall. Do you need a lawyer, too?"

"Not once you vouch for me. The detectives would love to pin the murder on me as a jealous boyfriend defending his future wife against a man who tried to hurt her."

"Future wife? Anything new you want to share with the class?"

"No." Not yet, at any rate.

"Give me a list of bullet points to cover on this phone call."

"Confirm I wasn't near Tucker's Gap, and Willow and I are engaged. These detectives aren't the trusting sort. They wanted to know if Fortress would lie to protect me."

A snort. "Sounds like there's not much hope they'll solve this murder or the others."

"No kidding. They haven't connected the previous four murders together even though the same family and method of death is involved."

"Not good. All right. I'll cover for you with the cops. Want me to send the security cam footage to Jesse as well?"

"I'd appreciate it. Make sure the footage can't be traced back to you. I'll send a copy of it to the detectives to keep myself out of the local jail. I can't protect Willow if I'm behind bars."

"No problem." Zane paused. "Phantom's calling in." He ended the call.

Max returned the phone to his pocket.

"What's our next move?" Jesse asked.

"Analyze security cam footage and get the cops off our backs."

"After you sleep," Willow insisted.

"We'll rest after the police interview." Willow still looked as though she would fall down any moment in exhaustion. The only way she'd sleep more was for him to rest, too. After being awake for more than 36 hours, Max was reaching the end of his endurance.

Candace returned to the room with a handful of papers. She smiled at Willow. "I hear you're ready to leave us, Ms. Knox."

"I hope you don't take this wrong, but I can't wait to get out of here."

The nurse laughed. "I don't blame you. Let's remove your IV first, then we'll go over the discharge paperwork. After that, all of you should go out for a good breakfast. Nurse Candace's orders."

Jesse smiled. "Music to my ears. I'm starving."

Candace flashed him a grin and blushed before she removed the IV.

Amused, Max's lips curved. Without trying, Jesse attracted female attention wherever he went. Maybe their schedule would slow down now that they were back from deployment. With a month off, perhaps the team's medic would have time to go on a few dates before the team returned to the work rotation.

After Candace finished going over the paperwork with Willow, she left them alone with one last glance at Jesse.

"I think you made another conquest," Willow said, amusement in her voice.

Jesse lifted one shoulder in a half shrug. "If she lived closer, I might try. She's kind and cares about her patients, a good indication of character."

O'Riley tapped on the door and poked his head around the jamb. "Candace said Ms. Knox has been released. Ready to go to the station? The detectives will be anxious to ask more questions."

Yeah, he bet. "Not yet." Max wanted to feed Willow while he waited for her lawyer to arrive. He refused to take her to the station until she had representation. "You hungry, O'Riley?"

Eyebrows rose. "I could eat. Why?"

"We're starving, and Willow needs to eat before the detectives question us again. You know the interrogation won't be short." Nothing he could do about it. The best he could do was feed her and make sure she had a hot drink to take with her into the interrogation room. "Where do you recommend that we eat?"

"Millie's Diner. The place isn't much to look at on the outside but the food tastes like my grandma's cooking. Millie and my grandmother are best friends and known county wide for their cooking."

"Sold," Jesse said. "Sounds perfect."

"We know Cohen and Warner told you to make sure we don't skip town." Max helped Willow sit up. "Come eat with us. Our treat. You can escort us to the station after the meal."

"Well..."

"When are you off duty?"

The cop grimaced. "Two hours ago."

"Then you definitely deserve a meal for working overtime."

"The detectives don't know Willow has been released," Jesse pointed out. "We'll go to the station straight from the diner. A ninety-minute delay won't matter to the investigation."

"I suppose it's all right. No more delays, though. I'm on duty tonight so I need to sleep."

"Fair enough." Max took Willow's hand and escorted her from the emergency room. He told himself he was keeping in line with the story he'd told the detectives about the engagement. In truth, he wanted to hold her hand for himself because if he was touching Willow, he knew she was safe.

How pathetic was that? Nothing would happen to Willow on his watch whether he was touching her or not. He knew now that danger was circling ever closer to her, and he'd remain alert until the killer was dead or behind bars. He didn't have a preference on which option came out on top. As long as Willow was safe, Max was good with it.

Within minutes, Max, Willow, Jesse, and O'Riley were seated at a corner table in Millie's Diner. The place was full, the wait staff moving fast to take orders and deliver food to customers.

When Wanda, the waitress, breezed by to take their orders, she patted O'Riley's cheek and called him Handsome. The burly cop blushed like a teenager but stood and kissed Wanda's cheek. She waited until he returned to his seat before she said, "Now, what can I get for you folks on this fine morning?"

Willow said, "I don't know what will settle on my stomach."

Max squeezed her hand. "Are you feeling sick?"

She nodded.

"That's a common side effect," Jesse murmured. "Try oatmeal or a bagel with some herbal tea."

"Our oatmeal is a best seller," Wanda offered. "Millie makes it from scratch from her grandmother's recipe. We have a variety of toppings to choose from or you can eat it plain. We also have mint tea. My granny swore mint tea was the only thing to fix an upset stomach."

Willow smiled. "Oatmeal and mint tea sound wonderful. Thanks for the suggestion."

"Sure thing, dear." The motherly waitress took the orders from the men and hurried off to inform Millie who manned the kitchen.

"What are the chances of me having access to my clothes and computer today?" Willow asked.

"Not very good," Max said. "The detectives and crime scene team have to process the hotel room. After that, they'll want computer techs to look at your laptop."

She groaned. "The laptop is the property of Ballinger Research, and contains all of the Enright information."

"Do you have an off-site backup for your research?" Jesse asked.

"I do, but my boss still won't be happy to know his laptop is in police hands."

"Does he have something to hide?" O'Riley asked, eyebrow soaring.

"Not that I know but we're privy to confidential information about our clients and their families. Ballinger is considered a premier private investigation agency. We take client confidentiality seriously."

The cop bristled. "We don't gossip to anyone who asks."

"You can take the chip off your shoulder now," Jesse said wryly.

"Her accusation isn't fair," O'Riley snapped.

"Willow wasn't accusing your department of being unprofessional, but Max and I used to be on the job. We know how cop shops work. Gossip is a favorite pastime. Information leaks."

The other man sighed and held up a hand. "Yeah, you're right. Sorry, Ms. Knox. The department's been getting a bad rap lately from the local news agencies. I'm a little sensitive."

Wanda brought a tray loaded with coffee, juice, iced tea, and Willow's herbal tea to the table. "Here you go, folks. I'll be back with your food in a minute." She turned to Willow. "Millie said if the mint tea and oatmeal don't settle to let her know, and she'll send out a toasted bagel."

"Tell her I appreciate her thoughtfulness."

"You bet, hon." The older woman hustled off to the next table to take an order, then went to the kitchen. She returned two minutes later with their meals.

By unspoken consent, the four concentrated on eating instead of talking about anything to do with the Enright case.

While Max ate, he kept an eye on Willow. Although slow, she steadily consumed the oatmeal and sipped her tea.

Wanda stopped by the table again when they were almost finished. "Would you like coffee or tea to go?"

"That would be great," Max said. "Thanks."

"Coming right up." She headed back to the kitchen and returned minutes later with large to-go cups. Wanda handed one cup to Willow. "Millie sent you a mix of honey, chamomile, and vanilla. The guys have coffee strong enough to dissolve metal. No cream, no sugar. Just straight-up lethal."

Max grinned. "Perfect. Thank you, Wanda."

"Don't thank me yet, buddy." She waved a slip of paper around. "Who gets the bad news?"

Jesse held out his hand. "That would be me." He winked. "Does that mean I get a larger piece of apple pie when I come in here for dinner?"

"Well, now, that should earn you some credit. Just tell the girl who waits on you that I said to serve you an extra portion."

"You got it. I'm looking forward to dessert."

She patted his shoulder, then turned to O'Riley. "Don't be a stranger, you hear, Sean?"

"Yes, ma'am. I'll be back soon." As Wanda moved off to assist other customers, O'Riley's cell phone rang. He checked the screen and grimaced. "It's Cohen."

O'Riley swiped his thumb across the screen and pressed the phone to his ear. "O'Riley." A pause, then, "Yes, sir. We're on the way to the station now." His eyes widened as he listened to the detective. "I'll pass the word, sir." He slid the phone into his pocket and turned to Willow. "Your lawyer is waiting for you. Must be someone high powered because Cohen's in a lousy mood."

Wouldn't surprise Max. People from all walks of life owed Maddox favors. "We shouldn't keep the detectives waiting any longer. Might blow back on O'Riley," he said as he stood and helped Willow to her feet.

"I'll appreciate staying out of the dog house," the cop muttered. "Cohen and Warner have a lot of influence in the department. Might hurt my chance at a promotion next month if they lodge a complaint with my sergeant."

Max escorted Willow to the SUV and buckled her seatbelt while they waited for Jesse to pay the bill. He took a step back and studied Willow's face. She was still too pale for his liking. "How do you feel?"

"Better than when we left the hospital. I'm still tired and shaky, though."

"The next few hours will be tough. Cohen and Warner might call the session an interview. This will be an interrogation. They plan to grill us like trout. If they can find a way to pin the murder on us, they'll do it."

"Don't they want to find the real killer?"

"We're strangers in town and a quick, easy solution to the murder. This is a small town, Willow. You can bet Tucker's Gap doesn't have a lot of high-profile cases to solve. The mayor, town council, police chief, and anyone else in power will be clamoring for a fast arrest. Who better to pin the murder on than strangers?"

She sighed. "Great. I'm here to do genealogical research and might end up going to prison because of someone else's handiwork."

"I won't let that happen."

"You're not a miracle worker, Max."

"Trust me. Please."

Her gaze locked on his. "That's a tall order for me."

"I know," he murmured. "But I have a great incentive for keeping you out of the local pokey."

Willow's lips curved. "What's that?"

"You haven't agreed to go to dinner with me yet."

She gave a short laugh. "Not asking for much, are you?"

"It's just dinner, Willow."

"You're asking for a date and a commitment. I'm a bad bet, Max."

"So am I but you're worth every ounce of effort. I'm a patient man. As long as you don't tell me no, I still have hope."

"And if I say no?"

He leaned in closer. "I'll do my best to change your mind." His lips skimmed over hers, then he moved away. The last thing he wanted to do was spook her. Willow was moving the right direction, toward him. "Don't say no."

Max glanced over his shoulder and noticed O'Riley watching them from inside his cruiser, speculation in his gaze. Did he suspect the engagement was fake?

Jesse left the diner and gave Max a chin lift to indicate he was ready to go.

"I'll be back," he said to Willow.

"Something wrong?"

He shook his head. "No need to keep Jesse tied up at the station for the next few hours. I'd rather he find us a place to stay."

"Ask him to look for a big box store where I can buy clothes." Willow tugged at her scrub top. "I can't keep wearing scrubs."

He closed her into the SUV and talked to Jesse on the sidewalk. A minute later, the medic drove away.

Max stopped by O'Riley's vehicle and talked to the other man. "Lead the way, O'Riley. We'll follow you."

"Where's your friend going?"

"To find a new hotel. I don't want to stay in the Royal Hotel with Willow. She's not safe there."

A slight nod. "Make sure you stay on my tail, Norton."

Max climbed into his vehicle and followed the cop from the parking lot. When they arrived at the station, Max helped Willow to the asphalt. He wrapped his hand around hers. "Ready?"

She squared her shoulders. "Yes."

"Let's get this party started."

Chapter Seven

Max approached the desk sergeant. "Max Norton and Willow Knox to see Detectives Cohen and Warner. They're expecting us."

The grizzled cop tilted his head toward the chairs against the wall. "Take a seat. I'll tell them you're here."

Max led Willow to the plastic seats and turned to O'Riley. "Thanks for watching over Willow until I arrived."

O'Riley gave a slight nod. "Hope everything works out." After saying goodbye to Willow, he left.

Max sat beside Willow and threaded his fingers through hers. "Wonder how long the detectives will keep us waiting."

"I'm surprised they haven't arrived already."

He considered what he'd observed at the hospital. "They'll keep us waiting at least fifteen minutes."

"Why?"

"Power play."

"Too long. I say five minutes."

"We'll see who's right." He glanced at Willow. "Care to place a wager on it?"

"What kind of wager?" She sounded suspicious.

Smart woman. He was up to something sneaky. Couldn't lose if he played his cards right. "If I'm right, I win a kiss from you." Max waited for her reaction. If she blanched at the forfeit for guessing wrong, he'd back off. If she didn't, Max would have the kiss he craved from Willow.

She sucked in a breath. Rather than look horrified, Willow seemed excited by the prospect. "What if I win?"

Max's pulse kicked up. Willow hadn't refused his suggestion of a kiss. A sign she trusted him? "Name your forfeit. I'll gladly pay up."

Her cheeks flushed a deep pink. "A moonlight beach walk with you."

He stared. Hartman, Tennessee wasn't near a beach. Did Willow realize she'd asked him to take her out of town? "Deal," he said before Willow retracted the request.

No matter who won, Max couldn't lose. A kiss or a weekend at the beach? No contest. He'd happily pay the forfeit. Might score a kiss in the moonlight on the beach. In fact, he'd claim a kiss on the beach anyway. Win-win for him. Hopefully for Willow, too.

Max kept an eye on his watch. When the time ticked past Willow's five-minute mark, his lips curved. A kiss was in his near future.

After 25 minutes, Detective Warner appeared in the bullpen doorway and motioned for Max and Willow to follow him. No apology for keeping them waiting, just arrogance and swagger as he led them through the maze of desks, perps, and cops and down a long hallway. Yep, definitely a power play.

Warner motioned Willow into a room on the right. "My partner is waiting for you."

Max peered into the room. Cohen, seated at a scarred wooden table, frowned at him. Max walked inside with Willow and pulled out the chair on the opposite side of the table for her.

"You can go now, Norton," the detective said curtly. "Warner has plenty of questions for you while Ms. Knox and I chat."

"O'Riley said Willow's lawyer was here. Willow won't answer questions until her lawyer is in the room." Max sat in the chair beside Willow's. "Warner can do something else while we wait."

"Hey," Warner protested. "I have better things to do than accommodate your need to hold your girlfriend's hand. If she's innocent, Ms. Knox has no reason to worry."

Cohen leaned forward, gaze fixed on Max. "Unless you're afraid she'll rat you out as the real killer."

Willow straightened. "You can't be serious."

Max rolled his eyes. "You're wasting your time, Detective. I didn't kill Enright."

"Guess we'll see," Warner said. "Hope you have proof of your innocence because I think you're our man, and I can't wait to see you behind bars with the rest of the lowlifes. If you're lucky, your woman will wait for you to be released from prison. She'll be an old woman, though."

A uniformed officer appeared in the doorway. "Detective Cohen, Catalina La Roche is demanding to see Ms. Knox now. She finished her phone calls."

A dark expression settled on Cohen's face. "Yeah, yeah," he muttered. "Send her in."

Warner groaned. "Why did it have to be La Roche?"

The detectives turned to Willow. "You have high-powered friends," Cohen said.

Under the table, Max squeezed her hand. No need to inform the detectives she'd never met La Roche.

Willow smiled. "I see you know her."

"We've crossed swords in court. She's very selective in her choice of clients. How did you hook up with her?"

The sound of heels tapping up the hallway forestalled any comments. A woman dressed in a black jacket and pants, and a royal blue blouse, wearing sky-high heels entered the interrogation room with a leather satchel slung over her shoulder. Her blue eyes glittered as she stared with evident distaste at Cohen and Warner. "Detectives Cohen and Warner, we meet again. At least this time we're not in a courtroom."

"Not yet," Warner muttered. "Could happen soon."

Catalina La Roche gave a toothy grin. "Don't bet on it, Warner." She set her satchel on the table. "I need ten minutes with my client. After that, we'll be ready." A glance around the room had her eyes narrowing. "Turn off the recording equipment, gentlemen."

Warner cursed under his breath as he strode from the room with Cohen on his heels. They slammed the door behind them.

Max signaled for silence as he watched the light on the ceiling camera mounted in the corner. When the light went out, he said, "It's safe." He held out his hand to La Roche. "Max Norton. This is Willow Knox. Thanks for coming on short notice."

The lawyer's smile warmed. "I owe Brent Maddox a huge debt. Representing an innocent woman is a small price to pay for him saving my sister's life. I consider this a down payment." She sat in the chair Cohen vacated. "We don't have much time, folks. Tell me what I need to know."

La Roche took copious notes as Max and Willow brought her up to speed. When they finished, she capped her pen, dropped it on the notepad, and sat back. "I see why the detectives want to pin this murder on one or both of you. Quite a feather in their caps to wrap up the case so quickly. This isn't the crime capitol of the world. They've only had two murders a year for the past decade. Enright's death is big news and will generate pressure to make an arrest."

"You live here?" Willow asked.

"An hour away, close enough to know how the town works and the crime rate." She grinned. "Criminal defense is my bread and butter. It's my business to know the crime statistics. So, Ms. Knox, you're my priority now."

"What about Max? I don't want him in trouble because of me."

"Fortress will vouch for Mr. Norton's location at the time of the murder. Their amazing operatives can't be in two places at one time." She patted Willow's hand. "He'll spend time getting to know Detective Warner."

Max groaned. "That was mean, La Roche."

The lawyer laughed. "You're tough, Norton. You can handle a surly detective. Besides, the longer you keep him occupied, the less time he has to double-team your lady."

Couldn't argue with her logic. For Willow, he'd throw himself into the task.

"A few more questions, Ms. Knox. I need you to be honest. If you lie to me, I'll walk away from your case so fast your head will spin. Nothing, including my debt to Maddox, will keep me here."

Willow looked wary. "What are your questions?"

"Did you kill Graham Enright, self-defense or not?"

"No."

La Roche watched Willow for a couple of beats. "Did he rape you?"

Willow flinched. "Not according to the emergency room doctor."

"Do you agree with the assessment?"

"I suppose."

"Rohypnol is a date-rape drug. Why would he give you the drug if he didn't intend to assault you?"

"I don't know if he drugged me."

"Did you drug yourself?"

"No."

"You exhibited a strong reaction when I asked if Enright assaulted you. Was it the idea of rape or personal experience?"

Max held his breath, wondering what Willow would say. When she bowed her head, he murmured, "Tell her. The detectives know which is why they believe I'm responsible for Enright's death."

"Talk to me, Ms. Knox," the lawyer urged. "We're running out of time."

With her gaze glued to the scarred wooden table, Willow summarized her experience in Mexico. "I didn't kill Graham, Ms. La Roche, and I don't know who did. I don't remember anything after going down to dinner."

The other woman sighed. "Let's hope security camera footage and possible cell phone pictures and recordings will give us enough to boot you off the suspect list."

After a sharp rap, the door opened. Cohen stepped in. "Time's up, Counselor. Norton, Detective Warner is waiting for you in the room across the hall."

Max pushed back from the table, stood, and bent to kiss Willow's cheek near her ear. "Answer truthfully but don't volunteer information," he whispered. "Listen to your lawyer. Send her to get me if you need me."

To La Roche, he said, "Willow is still recovering and has only slept two hours. She needs a break in an hour." He'd make sure he took one then so he could check on Willow.

"No worries, Mr. Norton. I'll keep an eye on her, and I'm sure Detective Cohen will be happy to accommodate her needs." She speared the detective with a hard stare. "Won't you, Detective?"

"Yeah, sure. Whatever I can do to make her stay more pleasant." He sneered. "Can we get on with this?"

"By all means. The sooner we finish, the faster I can go into the office." La Roche nodded at Norton. "She'll see you soon."

He brushed his mouth over Willow's in a barely-there kiss and left the room. Max crossed the hall and closed the door behind himself.

Warner pointed at the chair across the table from him. "Sit."

"Want me to bark, too?"

A scowl. "Shut up and sit down."

"My feelings are hurt." Max pulled out the chair and sat. He glanced at the camera in the corner. Yep, recording in progress. "Does this mean we can't be friends, Warner?"

A snort. "We ain't ever going to be friends. Let's get on with this, shall we?" Warner opened the manila folder on the table in front of him. "Did some research into your background."

Max stilled. The detective was bucking for a promotion. "Wasting your time, Warner."

"Mine to waste." He jabbed a finger at the file. "Says here you were a highly decorated cop, commendations all over the place as well as a penchant to land in the hospital."

Because he took the most dangerous assignments. "So?"

"You have a death wish?"

"At one time."

"But not now."

"No."

"What made you change your mind about dying?"

"Willow."

The detective rolled his eyes. "What do you know about Graham Enright?"

An hour into the session, Max's phone vibrated. He held up his hand to Warner. "Hold on a second."

A scowl. "Hey, this isn't social hour. I'm a busy man."

Max glanced at the screen, satisfaction filling him. "This pertains to your case."

Warner stared at him through narrowed eyes. "Yeah? What do you have?"

"Security cam footage from the Royal Hotel."

He straightened. "How did you get that? We're still waiting on a warrant."

"Anonymous friends in high places." And one supremely talented computer hacker. "Want the footage or not?"

"Yeah, I want it."

"Email address?" Max sent the video footage to the detective. "Want to watch the footage while I check on Willow?"

"I'm the one in charge here."

He shrugged and stood. "Suit yourself, but I'm going across the hall. Thought you'd want to make good use of your time since it's valuable."

"Sit down, Norton."

"In ten minutes. You already have confirmation from my employer that I was on an overseas flight at the time of Enright's murder. You're spinning your wheels trying to pin the murder on me. In case you forgot, Willow was drugged a few hours ago, and I'm worried about her. Since I'm not a viable suspect, I'm taking a short break to check on my woman."

Max left the room.

Chapter Eight

"Come on, Ms. Knox," Detective Cohen scoffed. "Nobody with two brain cells to rub together will believe you. I'm not buying your story."

Willow clasped her hands under the table, hoping the camera didn't pick up on her fear. Deep inside, she felt bone-deep terror. The person who constructed this frame job was a skilled craftsman. In Cohen's place, Willow wouldn't believe her story either.

What scared her the most was Max was in the middle of this mess and the Fortress operative would protect her with his life if necessary. She didn't want him or his friends hurt on her account.

Max Norton was a good man Willow wanted as more than a friend but she was broken inside. He deserved better than a woman who hated the dark so much she wouldn't go outside her house alone at night. Didn't matter that she lived in a safe small town with a low crime rate. Her imagination went wild when she stepped outside her front door after sunset.

Willow's heart hadn't received the message that Max might not take a chance on her. It raced every time he touched her. A simple brush of their hands sent her pulse rate into the stratosphere.

Butterflies took flight in her stomach every time he looked at her with those gorgeous chocolate-brown eyes. She loved chocolate and had a fondness for Max. The other men from the Texas team were like her brothers. Strong, protective, and annoying.

Resisting the masculine appeal of Max's teammates was easy. Max was in a category all his own, and Willow had discovered she couldn't resist him. Instead of resisting, perhaps she could grow strong enough to be with a man of Max's caliber, the woman she'd been before Armando broke her down. That woman was still there deep inside, hiding. Time to bring her out of the darkness and into the light.

Cohen slapped the table, making Willow jump. "Ms. Knox, pay attention. I'm not playing around. You're in serious trouble. If you don't answer all questions to my satisfaction, you'll find yourself in a steel cage. Perhaps then you will cooperate."

"That's enough, Cohen," La Roche warned. "I'm losing my patience with you. Your interrogation techniques are abusive and uncalled for, especially under the circumstances. My client is innocent until proved guilty. You don't have proof."

"What do you call the fingerprints on the murder weapon and a dead body in her hotel room? How much more proof do I need, Counselor?"

"She was drugged," the lawyer snapped. "Easy enough to press her fingers to the hilt of the knife."

"Got an explanation for the dead body?"

"That's your problem, not mine. Part of my job is to ensure you don't bully a traumatized victim into confessing to something she didn't do."

A snort. "Your innocent victim is as guilty as sin and should spend the rest of her life in a cage. I'm making it my business to see that's where she ends up."

Willow's blood ran cold. Memories of her captivity in Mexico flooded her mind. Fear, hunger, isolation, despair, pain, and degradation had been constant companions following the "training sessions" with Armando and his merry band of thugs. All those emotions came back in spades in a split second.

Her lips twisted. Even the doctor in Armando's employ had volunteered to train Willow for her life as a sex slave. The man had been given free rein to do as he wished to Armando's captives. Between the physical abuse and drugs, Willow's future had been bleak. After her time in captivity, Willow knew she wouldn't survive long-term behind bars.

The door to the hallway flew open and Max stepped inside. "Break time." His eyes glittered as his gaze locked on Cohen. "Now."

Willow stared. Max was furious. Had Warner made him angry or did something else spark his temper? She'd never seen Max angry except on the Mexico mission. In her presence, Max always exhibited patience and kindness.

"Get out, Norton," the detective snapped. "I have work to do, and you're interfering. Care to guess my next step if you don't leave immediately?"

La Roche pushed back from the table and stood. "Enough, Cohen. Mr. Norton is right. Ms. Knox needs a break. I need to call my office and check in anyway. I'll return in a few minutes." She stared pointedly at Cohen. "Turn off the camera, Detective. I'll wait until the light goes out before I leave the room. You may not turn on the camera again until I return."

Muttering curses, Cohen left the room, shoulder checking Max on the way out.

Once the light on the camera winked out, La Roche patted Willow's shoulder. "I'll be gone for fifteen minutes, more if I can stretch it out. Don't restart the party without me."

"No worries. I'd love to bail on this party, but I have a feeling Detective Cohen would object." She wrinkled her nose. "I'd prefer not to end up behind bars with Big Bertha and her friends."

The lawyer laughed. "I don't blame you. Relax a few minutes. I'll see if I can find more herbal tea for you." She closed the door, leaving Max and Willow alone.

He drew her up and into his arms, holding her against him in a grip Willow could break easily. "How are you holding up?"

"Not great," she admitted. "I'm so tired I'm punchy."

"Not surprising. You need to sleep, and the drug is still in your system." He eased her closer and gently coasted one hand down her back and up again before settling it at the nape of her neck. "I overheard Cohen berating you while I was in the corridor."

She gave a wry laugh. "What you heard was the latest of many rants. Ms. La Roche has been issuing increasingly stern warnings to Cohen to back off. He's only doing his job, but this is grueling."

Max tightened his hold. "I'll talk to him."

"I can handle it, Max." Maybe. The short break would help Willow reestablish her equilibrium. The trick would be to maintain her balance when the detective sat across the table from her. Max didn't need to know how vulnerable she felt.

He should be concerned about himself, not her. The former cop would be a prime target behind bars. She couldn't let that happen.

"You shouldn't have to handle it. There are ways to obtain information without being abusive."

"Would you say that if you were in his shoes?"

"Why do you have to be so logical?"

"We're friends. You can't be objective."

Max eased back enough to look Willow in the eye. "I will never be objective where you're concerned because we're much more than friends. I want to be your hero, Willow."

Her cheeks burned. Didn't Max know he was her hero? He'd stepped into that role the moment he walked into her cell in Mexico to free her. "Only the two of us are in this room. You don't have to pretend."

He trailed a finger down her cheek. "Who said I was pretending?"

Holy smoke. Did he mean that? If he did, was she ready to step into the dating arena again? Willow didn't know what to say so she said nothing.

"Too much?" he murmured when Willow remained silent.

Time to act like Strong Willow instead of Weak Willow. "Wrong place and time."

"Fair enough. Next question. Wrong man?"

"No." No hesitation. Definitely the right man. Once out of this interrogation room, perhaps the right place and time, too.

Satisfaction filled Max's eyes. "I can work with that. Have you remembered anything new in the last hour?"

"Flashes that don't mean anything."

He tilted his head a fraction, gaze intent. "What flashes?"

"Feeling hot, seeing a collage of faces, looking at the restaurant menu. All of those things could be flashes from the past week."

"Flashes of Enright?"

She started to say no but something zipped through her mind.

"Willow?"

"A memory is trying to surface but I can't see it yet."

"Pushing yourself will work against you. The information will come on its own or it won't. You may never remember everything from those missing hours."

"Someone needs to inform Detective Cohen because he missed the memo on drug-induced amnesia. He thinks I'm lying."

An edgy smile curved his mouth. "I'll be glad to pass the message along."

Yeah, he probably would. "No throwing punches to make your point."

"Man, talk about dousing a dream."

Amused, Willow rolled her eyes. "You'll recover from the disappointment."

The door opened, and Willow's lawyer walked in holding a to-go cup. She glanced around, eyebrows soaring. "Where's our intrepid detective? I expected him to be pacing the length of the room, impatient to restart the grilling session."

"Haven't seen him since you left." Max released Willow.

"This is herbal mint tea, Willow. If you need something carbonated to drink, let me know." She handed Willow the cup along with a packet of sweetener, then returned to her seat at the table. "Cohen will return sooner or later. How do you feel?"

"In need of a long nap."

"Same. Brent Maddox doesn't believe in keeping regular office hours so apparently no one else should either. This is brutal."

Max chuckled. "Welcome to the world of Fortress Security. We're on duty 24 hours a day, and so are our lawyers."

"Plural?"

"Definitely plural. Maddox employs hundreds of bodyguards and operatives, any one of whom might run afoul of the law and need a top-notch lawyer to keep them out of the local jail."

La Roche looked pleased. "Top notch, huh? Good to know Maddox respects my skills."

Max inclined his head. "The boss recognizes quality when he sees it, and he only hires the best. Don't be surprised if he offers you a full-time job."

"I'd consider it."

Detectives Cohen and Warner opened the door and stalked inside the room. Willow's stomach knotted, dread growing. Were they ready to continue the interrogation now? If the questioning went on much longer, she might have to ask La Roche to intervene. Although she wanted to help the detectives find the real killer, Willow was almost too tired to continue. The last thing she needed was to misspeak and end up in deeper trouble.

Max might be right about the drug still being in her system. Willow didn't feel like herself. Her emotions went from one extreme to the other in the space of seconds, and if Detective Cohen pushed her too far, Willow might lose her temper. Not a good plan for staying out of jail.

Cohen surprised her. "Both of you are free to go."

Willow stared. That was it? They could leave without more grilling? As hostile and as sure of her guilt as the detectives had been, the sudden change in tactic didn't make sense. Were they hoping she'd let down her guard and reveal her guilt by mistake?

As though he knew how off balance she felt by this turn of events, Max wrapped his arm around Willow's waist and tucked her against his side. "You don't look happy, Cohen. What gives?"

"You forwarded security camera footage to my partner." He glared at Max. "I don't want to know how you got it, by the way. Did you watch the footage?"

"When would I have had time? I received the footage while Warner and I were cementing our friendship in the interrogation room."

The second detective glowered at Max. "Zip it, Norton."

Max gave a mocking sigh and shook his head. "There you go, hurting my feelings again."

"What did you see?" Willow asked. If the detectives were letting them leave, did that mean the recording showed something to prove she was innocent?

"Enough to create doubt as to your guilt." Cohen's tone was grudging.

La Roche bent to retrieve her satchel. "Quite the ringing endorsement of Ms. Knox's innocence, Detective Cohen. Is this your idea of an effusive apology for badgering my client?"

He glared. "Don't push your luck, Counselor."

"Wouldn't dream of it." She gave him a bright smile. "If you wish to interview my client again, contact me, not her. Am I making myself clear?"

"Wouldn't dream of questioning Ms. Knox without an appointment no matter how critical and time sensitive the questions."

Willow scowled. Really? He was going with a guilt approach? "That's not fair, Detective. I cooperated with you, and I want

Graham's killer caught. If I can help, I will." But not until she'd taken a nap.

Whether her memory would return was anyone's guess. If it didn't, Willow wouldn't be much help to the detectives. Neither detective responded to her statement nor apologized for the horrible way they treated her.

Max urged Willow toward the door.

La Roche trailed them through the police station and out the front doors to the sidewalk. She handed each of them her business card. "If you need my services again, call me. Mr. Norton, send me a copy of the security footage. I want to review it in case we're called back into the interrogation room. In the meantime, be careful and keep an eye on Ms. Knox. I don't like how this is shaping up."

"Neither do I. Don't worry. Willow is my top priority." He shook La Roche's hand. "Thanks for your help. We owe you."

A quick smile. "I'm glad I was available. Take care, both of you." After a wave, she walked to her car and drove from the parking lot.

Max lifted Willow into the passenger seat of his SUV. He rounded the hood, slid behind the wheel, and drove from the police station, turning in the opposite direction from the Royal Hotel.

He activated his Bluetooth and called Jesse. His teammate answered on the first ring.

"Yeah?"

"Where?"

"Sparrow's Nest Inn." He rattled off the address. "We're in room 300."

"Suite?"

"Yep. You finished entertaining the detectives?"

"They turned us loose. Zane sent me the hotel security cam footage. I passed it on to the detectives. They saw something to make them question their belief in Willow's guilt. We'll examine the footage ourselves after we've slept."

"Good plan. Since Willow isn't in imminent danger of going to jail, we can take a break before we start tracking a killer."

"We just left the police station."

"You'll arrive at the hotel in an hour. I figured you'd want Willow out of town."

"Thanks, Jesse. See you soon." He ended the call and, at the next red light, input the inn's address into his SUV's navigation system.

Willow finished her herbal tea as Max turned into the parking lot of the Sparrow's Nest Inn. She smiled. "It's charming and quaint. Are you sure we'll be safe here?" Willow glanced around uneasily. She hated to sound like a woman afraid of her shadow but she'd been drugged in a supposedly secure environment.

"We're safe for the moment. If that changes, we'll find a new place. Jesse would have checked the inn before he booked a suite. Security is our business, Willow. We wouldn't stay in a place unsafe for you."

Max opened Willow's door and held out his hand. "I'd go to the store to buy clothes for you, but I thought you'd want to go with me."

"You don't feel comfortable buying women's underclothes, Max?" she teased.

His cheeks flushed. "It's not my favorite thing to do but I've shopped for my mother and sisters when they were in a time crunch. Buying foundation garments was a painful part of the trip." Max's lips curved at the edges. "I'm almost sure my sisters sent me shopping for bras and panties as a punishment for reading their diaries."

Willow laughed. "You didn't."

"I did, and I'm not sorry, either." He helped her to the asphalt and took her hand in his as they walked toward the inn. "My sisters tortured me."

"How?"

"They interrogated my girlfriends and embarrassed me by spilling all my secrets." When she grinned, Max said, "Hey, this is serious. Don't I get any sympathy from you over their betrayal?"

"How old were you?"

"Fifteen. My twin sisters were eighteen."

"Why did you read their diaries?"

"A few of their friends thought I was cute. I wanted to know which ones and possibly score a date or two."

"You couldn't tell which ones were interested?"

"Afraid not."

"So, you wanted an older woman, huh? Didn't you have a girlfriend at the time?"

He sighed. "I should have known you'd take their side. In my defense, I was only a dumb teenager and couldn't think of another way to find out in a hurry what I wanted to know."

Willow was still laughing when Max opened the door and ushered her into the lobby and to the bank of elevators.

After a short ride, they knocked on the door to room 300. Jesse opened the door and motioned them inside. He handed Max a key card for the suite.

Willow glanced around the interior. "This is beautiful." The decor was sweet and homey.

"Max and I will share a room. You have the other one." Jesse indicated the room on the left. "That one has the best view of the gardens."

Sweet. "Thanks, Jesse."

"I'd offer to take your luggage into the room but you don't have anything with you."

"I'll check with Cohen later this afternoon," Max said. "I'm afraid they won't release the scene for another day at least."

"Probably not. Want me to take the first watch?"

Max shook his head. "I've got it. I have to report to Maddox and Brody, anyway. Go sleep."

The medic clapped him on the shoulder. "Come get me if anything happens or you need to leave. Otherwise, I'll be awake in three hours."

Three hours? Willow flinched. How could he function on so little sleep?

Jesse squeezed her shoulder gently, went in the second bedroom, and closed the door.

Max took Willow's hand in his. "Come on. Time for you to take a nap."

"What about you?"

"I'll sleep when Jesse's awake." He grabbed his Go bag and carried it to Willow's bedroom. Max pulled out a black t-shirt and handed it to her. "We'll go to the store when you wake."

She clutched the shirt. "Thank you, Max."

"Rest, Willow. I'll keep you safe." After another brief, barely-there kiss across her mouth, Max retreated to the living room, leaving her door slightly ajar.

His words echoed in her mind as she drifted to sleep.

Chapter Nine

Max waited until Willow slept before he made the first phone call. Although tired, delaying the calls would bring nothing but grief from his boss and his team leader. Maddox would chew him up and spit him out while Brody would tear strips from his hide for causing his wife, Sage, more worry about her best friend. Poppy would just lay into him.

He didn't need grief from any of them. Max had more important things to do, in particular slowly romancing a certain genealogist with a beautiful smile and a heart of gold.

"Yeah, Maddox."

"It's Max Norton."

"How's Willow?"

"Shaken up but finally sleeping." He updated his boss, including the news about Willow being drugged with Rohypnol and the resulting memory loss. "The emergency room doctor saw no signs that Willow had been assaulted while unconscious."

"A miracle considering she was helpless. How long was she unconscious?"

His gut twisted at the thought of what Willow might have suffered if the killer had taken advantage of her. "From what I've been able to piece together, about twelve hours."

"Her memory?"

"Still sketchy although small bits are surfacing."

"Has she talked to her father about the incident yet?"

"No, sir."

"He shouldn't hear the news from an outside source. The news media will report on Enright's death and Willow's presence at the crime scene. The story will reach her family before long."

"Yes, sir. I'll talk to her when she wakes."

"Don't delay the conversation to spare her feelings, Max. Her family was hurt by what happened in Mexico, too. Don't add to their trauma."

Max gripped the phone tighter, wishing he could reach through the phone and shake some sense into his boss. Of course, if he followed through on the inclination, Brent Maddox would wipe the floor with him. The Fortress CEO was a decorated Navy SEAL. Time for Max to dial down his anger before he landed himself on his boss's black list. "Copy that, sir."

A chuckle. "How much did that hurt to say?"

"More than is wise to admit to my boss."

Maddox's chuckle turned into outright laughter. "I hear you. What can we do to help, Max?"

"You're already doing it. Zane used his mad hacking skills to obtain footage that kept Willow out of jail. Whatever the detectives saw convinced them to question her guilt."

"What's your next step?"

"Find the person who set up Willow to take the fall for murder and take him down hard."

"You're positive she's not responsible for Enright's death? Willow's experience in Mexico traumatized her."

Anger flared again inside Max. He understood where Maddox was coming from. Still didn't like the implication. "She's innocent."

"You're emotionally involved. How objective can you be?"

True statement. "Enough." Maybe.

"If Enright forced his way into the room or Willow invited him inside and panicked, she could have overreacted, attacked him, and blocked the actions from her memory. She wouldn't be the first victim whose mind protected her from trauma by blocking it."

He snorted. "Doesn't explain the Rohypnol. Willow doesn't have a killer instinct." Max, on the other hand, wouldn't have a problem killing to protect Willow.

"I hope you're right. If you need your team, call them in. Texas team is off mission rotation."

"I will." Max hoped he didn't have to infringe on their downtime. He suspected, though, that his teammates would make an appearance soon. Sage and Poppy would insist on supporting Willow, and that meant Brody and Logan would come with them. His other teammate, Sawyer, would join the party since he wouldn't want to be left out of the action. He liked Willow, too.

"I want an update tonight."

"Yes, sir."

"Watch your back, Max. I don't want to replace an excellent operative." Maddox ended the call.

Max stared at the phone in his hand, stunned by the unexpected compliment. Maddox didn't pass out praise frequently. That Max received a compliment now was gratifying.

He blew out a breath. Time to focus on the next task while he began his watch shift.

Max moved to the sliding glass door leading to the balcony, stood to the side of the frame, and studied the surrounding area. Sunshine illuminated the lush landscape and gardens at the back of the inn.

He would have preferred to be on a higher floor, but the inn topped out at three floors. Jesse had chosen the room's location well, though. The countryside around the inn was flat, especially at the back. A sniper wouldn't get a bead on Willow from high ground or tall buildings near the inn. The inn was located near the end of a long, picturesque lane of low-rolling hills.

Max completed another visual sweep of the area, analyzing trees dotting the landscape, and grimaced. A few trees were tall enough to provide height and cover to make a shot. Couldn't do anything about the trees, though.

He reached up and closed the curtains, making a mental note to remind Willow to keep her curtain closed. Jesse had closed the curtains in both bedrooms before Max and Willow arrived. They couldn't afford to be slack about their safety.

When he was satisfied there were no threats to Willow for the moment, Max called Brody.

"About time," his team leader said. "What can you tell me?"

"I have Willow in a new hotel in a town outside of Tucker's Gap. Staying in town was too great a risk."

"She okay?"

How did he answer that? "She's not in jail."

"How likely is it she'll stay that way?"

"Fifty-fifty shot. Zane hacked into the Royal Hotel's security system and found camera footage of Willow."

"He sent me a copy. Have you seen it?"

Something else he needed to do. "Not yet. Whatever is on the footage created doubt as to her guilt in the minds of the detectives investigating Enright's murder. I'll take that until we come up with something better."

"It's not proof," Brody said, voice grim.

"Nope. The only way to keep her out of jail is identify the killer and point Cohen and Warner in his or her direction. Otherwise, Willow might need the services of her lawyer for more than keeping the detectives from getting too rough in the interrogation room."

"We'll find proof."

Max's lips curved at the corners. Yep, that's what he'd thought. "How soon are you arriving?"

"Tomorrow. You're lucky I talked Sage into waiting until then to make the drive to Tucker's Gap. If she didn't have to finish recording an audiobook, we would have already left Hartman by now."

"Since you're coming anyway, would you stop by Willow's place? She needs clothes, and I don't know how soon the detectives will allow us to leave town."

"That's not the real problem."

He grunted. "I know. Willow won't leave Tucker's Gap until the killer is caught."

"You wouldn't either if you were in her shoes."

"The best thing I can do to protect Willow is find the killer before he finds her."

"You think he'll come after her."

"Wouldn't you if you tried to pin Enright's murder on Willow? He has to be worried the drug didn't block her memory or the effect might fade over time and she'll remember enough to be dangerous."

"Yeah." His friend sounded resigned. "Poppy is coming to lend her research expertise to the hunt."

"So we'll have the whole gang on site by tomorrow night."

"Where are you staying?"

"Sparrow's Nest Inn in Friedman. Sage and Poppy will enjoy the inn. Willow says it's homey and quaint. We're on the third floor."

"I'll reserve rooms for the rest of us. Call me tonight, Max. In the meantime, be careful."

"Copy that, sir." Max ended the call and resumed the watch. Hopefully, things would stay quiet so Willow and Jesse could rest.

Three hours later, Jesse opened the bedroom door. "Anything?"

Max shook his head. "Everything has been quiet."

"Go sleep. I've got the watch. I'll keep your woman safe."

His cheeks burned. "She's not my woman."

"Yet."

"Maybe never."

"From what I've seen since I arrived, you're selling yourself short."

Max's heart skipped a beat before surging ahead. "Willow indicated some interest but it's not a done deal. She might decide I'm not worth the risk. She wouldn't be wrong."

He had no illusions about his suitability for her. Willow Knox deserved better than a rough-and-tumble operative. She needed a gentle man. No one would characterize Max Norton as gentle.

If she needed someone to protect her or kill to keep her safe, Max was her man. The hearts and flowers type he was not.

"Open your eyes, Max. She's already halfway there."

"I hope so but I'm not holding my breath. Wake me if Willow needs me."

"Copy that. Go." Jesse waved him toward the bedroom.

Max took a quick shower, dressed in clean clothes, stretched out on top of the bed, and dropped into sleep.

Three hours later, he woke, fully alert. After slipping his feet into tactical boots and tying the laces, Max rose and walked to the living room.

Jesse turned from his post beside the glass door. "No problems while you slept."

"Willow?"

"Haven't seen her but she'll make an appearance soon. She's been moving around her room the past few minutes. Any news from Fortress or our team?"

"Nothing new from Fortress. Brody is reserving rooms for the team. They'll be here by tomorrow night. Would have been here already except Sage needed to finish recording an audiobook."

A nod. "Have a plan?"

"Working on it. First priority is to figure out if Enright was the target and, if so, who benefited from his death. Willow might have been drugged to prevent the necessity of killing her."

"Second?"

"Determine if Willow was the original target, and Enright died trying to protect her."

Jesse looked thoughtful. "Maybe. The killer might have been spooked after he killed Enright."

He inclined his head though skeptical. Jesse's proposed scenario was possible but Max didn't think it likely. If Willow had been the target and the killer panicked because of Enright's interference, what was to prevent him from killing Willow once Enright was dead? He considered that a beat longer. "What if the killer murdered Enright but was interrupted before he killed Willow?"

A soft gasp had both men spinning toward Willow's room. She stood in the doorway, face as white as snow.

#

Chapter Ten

Horror filled Willow. Was it possible she had been the target, not Graham? "Why would anyone want to kill me?" she asked.

"Good question." Max covered the space separating them in a few strides and took her hand in his. He led her to the sofa and drew her down to sit beside him. "Have an answer for me?"

"Are you kidding? I'm a genealogist. My job description says it all. I research family trees. My career is so far down on the danger spectrum that I can't even see the top. No one would have reasons to kill me. I'm as threatening as a six-week-old puppy."

"Did anything happen to make you feel uneasy while I was deployed?"

Willow shook her head. She hadn't been exaggerating. Her job was just this side of dead boring to other people. While she enjoyed researching family histories, most people didn't understand her enthusiasm.

She'd lost count of the number of people she'd bored to tears talking about her job. The pattern was predictable. They asked about her job with a smile that faded as their eyes glazed during her discourse on the nuances of her work. "I traveled to Kentucky on a research trip. I was gone for two days. The family kept very organized records so I finished my on-site research quickly and returned home to look through copies of documents and complete the family tree. The rest of the time, I prepared for the trip here."

And missed Max like crazy even though she hadn't told Sage and Poppy. They would have teased her endlessly about her interest in the operative.

Besides, she hadn't been ready to talk to her friends about Max. Willow locked her gaze with his. Now, though, she needed advice or maybe a good pep talk to go after what she wanted. Sage, Poppy, and Max had been friends for years.

"You would have told me if something or someone scared you before I left the country?"

One eyebrow rose. "You can ask me that after the number of times I called in the middle of the night because I couldn't sleep? Trust me, if I was afraid, you would have heard about it." She kept secrets from her father and brothers, though.

Willow grimaced. She needed to call her family before the media leaked the news about Graham's death and her proximity to the crime. They had been devastated six months ago. Now, here she was in the middle of another crime. When would life settle down and be normal?

Max squeezed her hand. "What's wrong?"

Nothing like being transparent. "I need to call my family and tell them what happened."

"Want me to do it?"

She stared. "You'd do that for me?" The conversation wouldn't be an easy one. Then again, Max must have made some difficult and painful notifications during his law enforcement career.

"If it would make things easier for you, absolutely. I can explain what happened and the next steps in the investigation. Your father and brothers will ask." His lips curved. "Might be a good idea for me to inform your father about our pretend engagement in case Cohen and Warner contact him."

She frowned. "Why would they call him? He wasn't in Tucker's Gap when Graham died."

"Investigations consist of tracking down tedious details which lead to other tedious details. All of a sudden, one of the details connects to another and to still more after that. In those details, you find the answers to your puzzle. Our relationship, confirming our engagement, and asking your father's assessment of my character are three of those details. If the detectives discover I'm lying about one thing, they'll suspect I'm lying about something else, including my claim of innocence in Enright's murder."

Willow longed to take advantage of his kind offer to run interference with her family. She couldn't, though. Wimping out and allowing Max to inform her family about Graham's murder wouldn't be fair. "Thanks for the offer, Max, but I need to call myself. Dad and my brothers will want to hear my voice to assess for themselves if I'm all right. I don't want to worry them more."

"Hey," Max murmured. "What happened six months ago isn't your fault."

"I know." She knew the truth in her head. Her heart still insisted on feeling guilty.

"Do you?" He cupped her chin and turned her face toward him. "Give yourself a break. How long will you punish yourself for someone else's disloyalty and infidelity? People have the freedom to choose. Every choice has ripple effects." His thumb brushed over her bottom lip, leaving a trail of fire in its wake. "Don't blame yourself."

"Max, hold off on the rest of your discussion," Jesse said. "Willow needs food and caffeine first."

She flashed the medic a smile. Although Willow wasn't very hungry, she would give just about anything for a cup of hot tea. The more she thought about it, Jesse's suggestion of caffeine appealed. Perhaps the inn had green tea.

Max retrieved the room-service menu and handed it to Willow. "Choose whatever sounds good to you. We'll call your family while we're waiting for the food."

Willow scanned the menu, relieved to discover the inn kept a wide selection of teas on hand. She made her selection and wrote her choice on the notepad Max handed her.

Once the men chose their meals, Max called the front desk and placed their orders. He hung up and turned toward her. "The food will be here in 45 minutes. Ready to make the first phone call?"

She nodded. No point in putting off the task. The longer she delayed, the greater risk someone would spot the news coverage and tell her family.

Jesse stood. "Sounds like my cue to make myself scarce." He walked toward the balcony. "I'll be outside if you need me." He closed the door and sat on one of the balcony chairs.

Max rejoined Willow. "Do you mind placing the call on speaker? I'd like to hear what your father says."

"No problem." Max knew everything anyway. Another pang of guilt assailed her. Time to trust her family with the truth. They loved her. She would worry them more if she kept things from them. Willow slid her phone from her pocket. At least Cohen had given her phone back.

Max covered her hand, phone and all, with his. "Let's not use your phone."

"Why not?"

"Someone who is tech savvy enough or has the right connections will be able to trace your location. I'll request one of the Fortress satellite phones for you so we won't have to worry about someone other than Fortress pinpointing your location."

"You're serious."

Max took her phone and set it on the coffee table after making sure the device was turned off. "I am."

"I can use a prepaid phone until Graham's killer is caught. I don't need a satellite phone." How expensive was a satellite phone? She couldn't let Max go to so much trouble and expense for a temporary need. Willow knew without asking that Max would pay for the phone out of his own pocket unless Fortress picked up the expense, and why would they? The engagement was fake.

Max turned and cupped her cheek. "You told me at the hospital the time and place were wrong, but I was the right man. Do you still feel the same?"

Did she dare make the leap? Willow squared her shoulders. No more letting fear rule her life. Time to draw out and nurture the woman she was before Armando put his hands on her. She wanted more than friendship with Max. If she didn't step up now, she might never have the opportunity again.

Willow wasn't blind. Women noticed Max. He didn't notice them in return except for threat assessment. One day, however, that would change. Max might look back at one of the women. If she didn't take a risk now, Willow would have to watch while Max dated another woman. The possibility made her feel ill. "Yes, I still feel the same."

A slow nod, satisfaction gleaming in the depths of his eyes. "So do I. I'm not in a hurry, Willow. We'll take things as slow or as fast as you want. I don't care how slow we move forward as long as we move forward together."

"That's not fair to you, Max."

"You're worth the wait. Communication will be a key factor in our relationship. For us to stay in touch when I'm deployed, you need the sat phone. Our calls and texts can't be intercepted, and our locations won't be compromised. Otherwise, we'll have to confine our communication to the weeks I'm in the country. I don't want to do that."

Willow froze. "You want to communicate with me while you're deployed?"

Max lifted her hand to his mouth and kissed her palm. "I miss talking to you when I'm away from you, Willow. Can't you tell?"

She smiled. "Well, now that you mention it, you're pretty chatty the first few days after you return."

He chuckled. "There you go. Friends don't let friends talk too much." He handed Willow his phone. "Call your family. We'll continue our discussion when you finish."

Was Max still interested in seeing if they had something together? Man, she hoped so. Max Norton was one in a million.

She called her father. As she expected, Colonel Gray Knox answered immediately. Her father always dropped everything to answer her calls which was why she usually called at night so she didn't interrupt his work. "Hi, Dad."

"How's my girl?"

Tears stung her eyes. "I'm fine but I'm involved in something you need to know about before the media leaks the information."

"That doesn't sound good. I'm not going to like this, am I?"

"No, sir, you won't."

"Are you sure you're all right?"

"I promise. This isn't like Mexico."

"Tell me what's going on. Maybe I can help. I have plenty of connections in high places."

She told him everything. Well, as much as she could remember along with what she and Max had pieced together.

"Someone drugged you?" Fury rang in her father's voice.

"Dad...."

"Do these cops have any idea what they're doing?"

How did she answer that question? She didn't know anything about their investigative skills. They seemed competent and determined but Willow couldn't assess their skills. She glanced at Max.

He squeezed her hand. "Colonel Knox, it's Max. I've talked to the detectives. They appear to be competent, sir."

A wry laugh. "That's not a ringing endorsement, son."

"No, sir."

"What are you going to do about it?"

"Dad!" What was he thinking? Max wasn't to blame for the detectives being competent or not.

"It's all right, Willow," Max said. "I would want to know the same thing if my son or daughter was involved in a police investigation. Colonel, I've already started looking into Enright's death. My teammates will arrive tomorrow to help. We're all experienced investigators, sir. We'll find out who killed Enright and keep Willow safe while we get to the bottom of things."

"Is she in danger?"

"Unconfirmed but she might be."

"Because the drug might not cloud her memory sufficiently to protect the identity of the killer."

"Yes, sir. Whoever drugged her brought the Rohypnol with him. Whether Enright or Willow was the original target is the question. With the available information, I can't rule out either scenario."

"I expect frequent updates. I don't want to be blindsided. Once the newsies connect Willow to Enright's death and the debacle with Armando, the story will go nationwide."

"I understand, sir." Max drew in a deep breath. "One more thing you need to know in case the cops or media ask for confirmation. I told the detectives Willow and I are engaged."

"Why?"

"It was the quickest way to access her hospital room. People won't question why I'm staying by her side. I'll be able to protect her without raising suspicions."

"I see." Something in her father's voice said he caught more than Max expressed. "Is that the only reason, Norton?"

Willow's face heated. This was embarrassing. She was an adult and had been living on her own for more than a decade. Yes, her father loved her. That didn't mean Willow wanted him to vet her boyfriends. She could choose her own dates, thank you very much.

"No, sir."

Willow stared at the operative's profile. Oh, boy. Should she run interference? Before she could decide, Max answered her father's question in more detail.

"I want permission to date your daughter, sir."

Silence followed Max's pronouncement, then, "She's a grown woman with a mind of her own."

"You're Willow's father. She loves you and respects your opinion. Giving your permission for a dating relationship will help Willow be more comfortable and open to it."

"What's in it for you?"

His gaze shifted to Willow. "The chance to win the heart of a fascinating woman of noble character and incredible strength."

Sincerity burned in his eyes. He meant what he said. Max wasn't trying to convince her father to accept the ruse to fool the media and police. The engagement might be fake, but he wanted their relationship to be real.

What was she going to do about it?

Chapter Eleven

As Max watched, the realization dawned on Willow that he was telling her father the truth. Would she back away from him, from them, or grab Max's hand and hold on for the potential adventure of a lifetime? He knew which option he wanted her to choose. Pressuring her to accept him as more than a friend would backfire. A short-term relationship wasn't the goal. He wanted forever.

"Willow, is this what you want?" Colonel Knox asked. "Do you want a relationship with Max?"

"I want to try."

"You're either all in or you're not, honey. No waffling. It's not fair to either of you."

Amusement lit her eyes. "Since you put it that way, I'm in."

"You're sure?"

"He's the man I want in my life."

The confidence in her voice brought a slow smile to Max's mouth. Fireworks exploded inside at her declaration. Excellent. Willow was willing to give this dating thing a shot. Maybe, just maybe, he had a chance to win her heart before she learned the truth about him.

He should let her go. He couldn't, not any more. Despite his baggage, Max wanted her in his life. The way sparks flew between them and heat rose every time they were in the same vicinity or when they spoke on the phone, the friend zone was no longer an option. He wanted, needed, more with and from Willow. Max wanted everything. The big question was did she want the same with him? He wouldn't accept less from her.

"All right," Knox said. "If you're sure, Willow, I'll give my approval. Norton, you have permission to date my daughter. Fair warning, though. If you hurt Willow, I will hunt you down and rid the world of your presence. Am I clear?"

"Yes, sir. Crystal clear." He wondered idly if Knox remembered Max worked for Fortress. If anything happened to him, his team would look hard at Willow's family first.

"Dad!"

"You wanted my approval. You have it with reservations. Max is a good friend, but I don't know if he's good enough for you."

"I'm not," Max admitted. The colonel had connections in the intelligence community. Knox would look at the first opportunity to learn about Max's past. Max would look if one of his sisters dated a stranger. In fact, he'd done background checks on every man his sisters had dated from the time he became a cop. Lucky for him, they were married now and he didn't have to vet their dates any more. "Willow is a jewel. I'm a lump of coal." With a penchant for trouble. Max would do his best to keep it from spilling onto Willow.

While he wanted the blessing of the Knox men, Willow's opinion was the only one that mattered. When she knew his past, would she understand why Max had made choices that ended up costing men and women their lives?

Knox uttered a bark of laughter at Max's admission. "At least you're honest."

"I don't lie unless it's in the course of my work and only when necessary. Sticking close to the truth is safer and easier. Spinning too many lies leads to risk of discovery. Too easy to trip yourself up."

"Something tells me you've experienced the consequences up close and personal. You were taken captive in the past?"

More than once. "Yes, sir."

"Tell me about your experience, what tripped you up, and how you handled the aftermath."

"No." His answer was curt and to the point. No way would he discuss the torture he'd endured with Gray Knox or the reason for it. The betrayal still ripped him up inside.

"Confidential?"

"That's correct."

"Is that the only reason?"

"No, sir. I wouldn't tell you if I was free to share the information."

"Willow needs the truth, Norton. Relationships with secrets don't last."

"I'm aware." His gaze locked with hers again. "I'll tell her what I can. If I can't discuss specifics because of national security, I'll let her know. How many secrets have you kept from your family over the years, Colonel?"

"Too many to count, and I paid for it." Bitterness filled his voice. "I understand the reason behind your silence. Be warned, though. I will look into your background, and I'll dig deep, son."

"I'd be disappointed if you didn't, sir."

A snort from Willow's father. "You may regret saying that. I guarantee this won't be the last time we talk. You should also expect more grilling from Will and Trey."

Count him as not surprised by that news. "Yes, sir." Between Willow's brothers and father, Max was more concerned with Will and Trey's opinions of the new turn in his and Willow's relationship.

The Knox men were fiercely protective of Willow, and he'd be stupid to discount that. Max was a lot of things. Stupid wasn't one of them. While Colonel Knox was no slouch, Willow's Special Forces brothers were far more dangerous than their father. They knew how to take care of problems permanently, bury the bodies where no one would ever find them, and skillfully handle interrogation by the police.

A man's muffled voice could be heard in the background over the phone. The colonel murmured a reply, then said, "I need to go, Willow. Call me if anything happens or if I can assist. Call your brothers before they hear this from someone else. If they don't answer their phones, leave a short message. They're due to deploy so they might not be able to take your call."

"I will. I love you, Dad."

"Love you, too, honey. Be careful. Keep Willow safe, Norton, or you'll answer to me." And then he was gone.

Willow made the next call. Her brother picked up on the first ring. "Hi, Trey."

"What's up, Pipsqueak?"

She rolled her eyes. "Is it my fault you're a foot taller than me?"

"You should have eaten more when you were a kid."

"If you and Will had left me more than a mouse portion between you, I would have."

"Yeah, yeah. Same song and dance I've heard since we were kids. Still doesn't change the fact that you're short. You never call during the day so I know something is wrong. What's going on, Willow?"

She summarized what had happened. "I'm fine, Trey, and I'm safe. I promise."

"Try again," he said, voice barely above a growl. "You were inches away from a murder. That has to have an impact on your mental state, and you're anything but safe. Is Max on deployment?"

"I'm here," Max said. "How are you, Trey?"

"I was great until I found out someone is after my sister. Threat assessment?"

"Unknown. We're looking into it."

"We?"

"One of my teammates is here. The rest arrive tomorrow. Fortress is providing tech support."

"Be straight with me. Willow downplays things so we don't worry."

"Hey." Willow scowled at the phone. "Are you calling me a liar?"

"Zip it, Pipsqueak. Does she have injuries, Max?"

"A few bruises and scratches, and residual fatigue from the drug. Her sense of security also took a hit."

"What are you doing about it?"

"Trey." Willow frowned. "You're as bad as Dad. This wasn't Max's fault. He wasn't even in the country when Graham was murdered."

"Answer the question, Max."

Another scowl from Willow. "Don't ignore me, bro."

"If you want to lay into me, take your turn later. First, I want an answer to my question. You're supposed to be a hotshot mercenary for hire, Max. My sister is in trouble. How do you plan to get her out of it?"

"Find Enright's killer and take him down. Once the killer is behind bars, Willow's problem is solved, and we move on to other priorities."

"Do you have anything to go on or are you blowing smoke to get me off your back?"

"We have security footage, and before you ask, I haven't seen it yet. I was a little busy getting acquainted with the detectives assigned to the case. They seem convinced I was the one who killed Enright."

"All right. I want regular updates by text. We may be deployed any minute or I'd ask for leave to help with Willow's security."

"You'll know what I know."

"Are you in the country for a while or do I need to ask friends to act as Willow's bodyguards?"

"I'm on training rotation for the next month."

"I know how shorthanded Maddox is. If your status changes, I want to know about it immediately. Before you leave the country, Max. I don't want Willow left without protection. Hear me?"

"The warning isn't necessary. I won't leave Willow until she's safe. Doesn't matter how long it takes."

A few seconds of silence followed Max's declaration and told him Trey was beginning to understand he had a stake in keeping Willow safe. A very personal stake.

"I thought you two were friends." A wry laugh sounded over the speaker. "Should have known things would change. You're dating my sister, aren't you?"

"Yes." An accurate statement if Willow agreed to an exclusive relationship. Would she take the leap of faith with him?

"Willow, you're okay with this?"

"I'm not a teenager anymore. I don't need my older brothers to protect me."

"Tough. You're getting our protection anyway. After your encounter with Armando, do you blame me for being cautious?"

"I can't let Armando dictate the rest of my life. He's already stolen six months and small pieces of my soul. He doesn't get anymore."

"If you're looking for an apology from me, you're doomed to disappointment. I love you, and I'll always have your best interests at heart whether you want me to or not."

She groaned. "How am I supposed to argue with that? You're annoying, bro."

"But you love me anyway," Trey said. "Max?"

"Still here." He already knew what was coming.

"If you hurt my sister in any way, you'll wish you had never been born. Do we understand each other?"

"You'll have to get in line. Your father and my teammates are in front of you."

"You have no chance to escape retribution." The aggravating Spec Ops soldier sounded smug.

"Probably not. You should ready your weapons."

A gusty sigh. "What did you do?"

"Told the Tucker's Gap police Willow and I are engaged."

"Are you serious?"

"Very."

"Why? Wait. Is there any truth to that claim?"

"No." Not yet. "Telling the police we're engaged was the easiest and fastest way to get to Willow's side."

A groan. "I can't fault you, but that will spark all sorts of questions and throw you into the spotlight. With our family drama in the past six months, the media will run with this."

"I know."

"Yeah, but do you really understand what that means? Your job is conducted in the dark in secret. Anonymity is your friend. The spotlight could sideline your career. Are you willing to take that risk?"

Willow gasped. "Oh, Max. You can't."

He squeezed her hand. "Willow is worth it."

A soft whistle from Trey. "You've got it bad, my friend. Well, best of luck to you. You're going to need it if your name and face are spread across the Net. You'll have a target on your back in neon colors. Willow, be independent and as much of a spitfire as you used to be, but when it comes to matters of your safety, do everything Max tells you to do. Understood?"

"I'm not one of your men. I don't have to take orders from you."

Max grinned at Willow's snippy attitude. That's what he'd caught glimpses of over the past few months. He'd love to see that spirit from her all the time.

"You want to stay safe?" Trey snapped. "Follow Max's lead. I love you, Willow. Watch your back. Max, do your job or I'll take you down before you see me coming."

"Copy that." He ended the call and glanced at Willow. "Two down. One more to go."

"You're enjoying this."

He lifted one shoulder in a shrug. "The conversations are accomplishing two goals."

"Which are?"

"Making your father and brothers aware of what happened and that you have bodyguards."

"What's the second goal?"

Max's gaze locked on hers. "To make my intentions clear. I don't want resistance from the men in your family because I wasn't upfront with them."

Willow studied him. An interesting mix of anticipation and anxiety glittered in the depths of her eyes. "What are your intentions, Max?"

"To win your heart one hug and kiss at a time for however long it takes until you surrender." Max couldn't make himself more clear than that. He wanted Willow to be his and for her to claim his heart for herself.

He hoped she was on board with the program. Otherwise, Max was in for a tough time. His best friend was married to Sage, Willow's long-time friend. Sage's sister, Poppy, was also involved with one of his teammates. If Willow rejected him, Max would still be in close proximity to her. Distancing himself wouldn't be an option. Doing so would fracture his team. That wasn't going to happen if he could prevent it.

Willow's eyes widened. "You're talking about more than dating."

"Are you still in?"

She took her time before answering. Finally, Willow said, "I'm in but I don't know how fast I can move forward from here. This is hard, Max. I think I have things settled in my mind and something happens to set me back, to make the memories return in spades. As soon as they do, the nightmares start again, and I'm afraid to go outside my house in the daytime. I always feel as though at the start, working my way out of the hole one more time."

"It's normal. No matter how much time passes, the memories are still there. You'll beat them back every time they resurface, and you'll come back faster and stronger."

"You may grow tired of waiting for me."

He shook his head. "Never." Max inclined his head toward his phone. "Make the last call."

After a lingering look, Willow punched in Will's number.

When he picked up, Will said, "Talk fast. We're wheels up in ten minutes."

She gave her brother an abbreviated version of events. "I'm fine. Max and one of his teammates are with me. The rest of the team arrives tomorrow."

"You better be or Max and his buddies will answer to me. Keep me in the loop."

"One more thing. The police think Max and I are engaged. If they manage to track you down, back up our story. I don't want to visit Max in jail."

"Copy that. I want a detailed explanation later." Will ended the call.

Willow sighed. "That went better than I expected."

Max's lips curved. "Don't bet on it. Your brother didn't have time to dig into this. He'll find time later." Or worse, Will would send some of his Special Forces friends to do it for him since he'd be out of touch for an undetermined period of time. Will wouldn't leave things to chance. Willow was too important to allow anything to slide.

A knock sounded at the door.

Max rose and tugged Willow to her feet. "It's probably room service, but go to the bedroom while I check it out. If there's trouble, stay hidden. Jesse and I will handle trouble easier if you're safe."

He waited until Willow was out of sight before he checked the peephole and opened the door for the inn worker to deliver their meals and drinks on a large serving cart.

"Do you need anything else?" the teenage boy asked.

"A recommendation for a good restaurant."

The kid brightened. "That's easy. Luigi's, the Italian place over on West Third Street. You can't miss it."

"A town favorite, huh?"

"You bet. Everybody loves the food. It's as good as my mom's."

Max smiled. "That's quite an endorsement. I'll keep Luigi's in mind." He handed Jay a tip. "Appreciate it, man."

After thanking him, Jay hustled down the stairs.

Max closed and locked the door. He pushed the cart toward the living room. "It's clear, Willow."

She returned and breathed deep. "Smells fantastic." Willow helped Max unload the serving cart and set the food on the large coffee table, then sat on the couch.

A moment later, Jesse walked in and reached for the coffee pot. "Learn anything from the Knox men?"

"The detectives haven't been in touch yet, and I'll disappear and never be heard from again if I hurt Willow."

The medic smiled. "Can't blame them. If you mess up, you'll have four more men on your trail, too."

Max rolled his eyes. "I'm not going to mess up." He hoped. His friend grunted. Great. Not a ringing endorsement.

After eating, Max retrieved his laptop. "Let's look at the security footage."

Willow sipped her tea while Max logged into his Fortress email account. "I dread watching this."

Although he understood Willow's reluctance, Max didn't believe they'd see much. He hoped the footage showed enough to get him started.

Jesse sat on the other end of the couch, coffee cup in hand. "I hope we get something useful but I can't see the killer showing his face. He had to know the hotel had security cameras all over the place."

"I didn't look for them," Willow said.

"You aren't a killer," he countered. "The killer paid attention to everything."

She looked disappointed. "I suppose we won't learn much."

"Anything is better than what we have now which is zip."

Max studied the email. "Looks like Z followed Willow through the hotel. The video clips are in order."

"This will be as exciting as watching paint dry," Jesse muttered. "Might as well start at the beginning. I'll take our dishes downstairs and ask the kitchen staff to refill our coffee carafe. Do you need more tea, Willow?"

"Yes, please. Thanks, Jesse."

He rose. "I'll return soon. Go ahead and get started, Max. If you see something, show me when I get back." Jesse pushed the cart from the room.

Max tapped on the screen and settled back to watch the clip. Based on the date stamp, the footage was recorded four days earlier, the day Willow arrived in Tucker's Gap. He made himself watch in order although he longed to skip ahead to the night Willow was drugged. If he skipped the rest, he might miss something important.

After the first five clips, Willow sighed. "This is hopeless."

"We haven't reached the night you were drugged."

"If Jesse's right, we won't see anything." She slid him a glance. "He was right, you know."

Max raised an eyebrow as he tapped on the next footage. "Common occurrence. What was he right about this time?"

"Watching this is boring. I'm not doing anything except walking in and out of the hotel."

"Look out, babe. We're going to shake things up by watching you eat a meal in the restaurant." When she groaned, he laughed.

By the time they had progressed through all the clips except the final four, Willow had eaten in the restaurant four times and interacted with the same people.

Jesse returned to the room with coffee and tea. "Did I miss anything interesting?" he asked as he returned to his seat on the couch and distributed drinks.

"Are you kidding?" Willow glared at the computer screen where the footage showed her going into her hotel room. "There's been nothing."

"So far." Max sipped his coffee and started the next clip. Willow appeared on screen, heading down the empty hall to the elevator. So far, Max hadn't seen anyone following Willow or paying attention to her.

He started the next clip, the one recorded the night she was drugged. In this one, Willow exited the elevator and walked to the restaurant. Max analyzed her body's movement. No sign of impairment. When was Willow drugged?

They continued to watch Willow as she talked to the restaurant's host and followed him to a table at the back of the room.

"You look steady, Willow," Jesse said.

"I agree." She motioned to the screen. "The host's name is Phillip. He works nights and attends college classes in the daytime."

"Did you strike up conversations with him every time you went into the restaurant?"

Willow nodded. "The second night in the hotel, I needed a break to clear my head and went to the restaurant for dessert and tea. I overheard another patron giving Phillip a hard time because the restaurant was full, and he and his family of nine were having to wait to be seated. When the family gave up and stormed off in a huff, I talked to Phillip a while as I waited for a table to open up. I saw a law textbook open on the desk and asked him about it. He was fascinated with my work at Ballinger Research and talked to me every evening."

"He would remember if your behavior was off the night of the murder." Max made a mental note to find out when Phillip's next shift was and talk to him. Maybe he saw something that stood out the night Enright died.

"Probably," Willow conceded. "He's observant. Most of the hotel employees didn't interact with me. They were too busy. Phillip always took time for me."

On screen, the waitress stopped by Willow's table, took her order, and moved on to the next table. Willow took out a notebook and began writing.

Max paused the video. "Do you remember what you were writing?"

She sighed. "Sorry, no. I don't know what happened to the notebook. It's not in my purse."

"What do you normally write in the notebook?"

"Notes about the current case and questions to ask the client."

Jesse grunted. "You might have made a note about something of interest to the killer."

"I doubt the hotel room has been released as a crime scene yet," Max said. "We can ask Cohen or Warner to check. If they didn't find the notebook, we'll at least have an idea of what might have interested the killer."

"That's not comforting," Willow said.

"You might have been the target or Enright. Possibly both of you. Let's finish watching the security cam footage first. After that, we'll call the detectives and ask for an inventory of your belongings."

"What if they refuse to give us information? They haven't shared anything since this mess started."

A slow smile curved his mouth. "If they won't give us the information, I have a friend or two who can get the job done." If Zane didn't have time, Caleb Montgomery would help him out. Like Z, Caleb enjoyed skirting the law. Ironic since his friend was a deputy sheriff in Morgan County.

Jesse leaned closer to the screen as the waitress brought a drink that she set in front of Willow with a broad smile on her face. "Did you order a soft drink or iced tea, Willow?"

She frowned. "I doubt it. I always have hot tea with dessert."

"The waitress acts as though she's delivering a gift from someone," Max said. "Like a man would buy a woman a drink in a bar to set up a date." He glanced at Willow. "Any spark of memory from seeing that?"

"A fleeting impression of confusion."

"Here comes the waitress again," Jesse said.

On screen, the woman brought a tray loaded down with drinks and stopped by Willow's table to deliver a tea pot before moving on to her other tables.

"What kind of herbal tea do you typically order?" Jesse asked.

"Most restaurants have green tea so that's my go-to preference."

The medic grimaced. "I know that stuff is supposed to be good for you, but it tastes like boiled grass. Just saying."

Willow laughed. "Hate to break it to you, Jesse, but coffee tastes like burned rubber to me."

He shook his head. "Sorry your taste buds are messed up. Otherwise, you'd be perfect, and I wouldn't mind challenging Max for you. Now, though, my dreams are dashed. My search for the perfect woman continues."

Max elbowed his friend. "Look."

On screen, Graham Enright strode into the restaurant and headed straight for Willow's table. From the action playing out on screen, the other man didn't hesitate to pull out a chair and sit down beside Willow. Huh. Didn't look as though Enright expected to be rejected. In fact, from this angle, he acted as though he was expected. Had Willow contacted him?

Max hated to consider it. Made him feel disloyal to her. He knew Willow wasn't responsible for Enright's death. However, she could have contacted the man for a business meeting.

He continued to watch the action play out on screen and soon concluded that Willow hadn't set up the meeting. Although Enright's back was to the camera, Willow's face was in clear view and she was uneasy at Enright's sudden appearance at her table.

The waitress cycled back and took Enright's order. She brought coffee for him, and two desserts. "Apple pie with ice cream?" Max asked.

Willow's cheeks turned a pretty shade of pink. "It's my weakness."

"Always a good option."

"Too bad Enright isn't facing the camera," Jesse said. "We could have someone at Fortress evaluate the footage and tell us what he's saying."

"Maybe he could read my lips on the footage," Willow offered.

"I think I can make out what you're saying."

"You read lips?"

"We've all been taking training. It's a useful tool, especially when we're deployed."

She turned to Max. "You can read lips, too?"

"I'm not as good as the others on my team but, yeah, I can."

"What am I saying to Graham?"

Max backed up the recording by two minutes and watched Willow's mouth carefully when Enright walked up to her table and sat beside her. "You said, 'What are you doing here?'"

"This wasn't a planned meeting," Jesse said.

"I told you I didn't ask Graham to stop by the hotel," Willow said tartly.

"I believed you, sugar, but your memory has holes in it."

"Look at Enright's body language," Max interrupted. "He looks taken aback." He paused, then said, "Willow, you're saying that you didn't send him a message to set up a date."

He paused the footage. "Did Enright show personal interest in you before the restaurant?"

Willow shook her head. "He barely noticed me, Max. I saw him long enough to say hello. We never carried on a conversation. Like I told Detective Cohen, I didn't have Graham's cell number. How would I contact him?"

"Someone pretending to be you did send him a message. Might have been a written message rather than an electronic one. If you were determined to get the cell number, you could have asked for it from someone else in the Enright house."

Jesse set his coffee cup on the table. "Any chance someone had access to your cell phone?"

"My phone is never far from my hand." She bit her bottom lip. "I don't want to miss a call or text from Max or the rest of you."

The medic snorted. "I doubt you're waiting for a call from the rest of us, Willow."

Max's heart turned over in his chest at Willow's words. Oh, yeah. He was keeping Willow Knox for his own. Permanently. First, he had to win her heart. Then, he'd build a life with her.

Chapter Twelve

Willow stared at the computer screen, sick to her stomach at the thought that she might have unknowingly encouraged Graham's interest. She wouldn't have asked any man to have dinner or dessert with her unless it was Max. He was the only man she'd been interested in since the debacle in Mexico.

Max's hand wrapped around hers. "What is it, Willow?"

She squared her shoulders. "I didn't set up a date with Graham. Although my memory has gaps, I wouldn't do that." She'd never played the field and wouldn't start with Max.

"I believe you. Let's prove your innocence. Ready to continue?"

Willow nodded.

Max tapped the screen and the footage restarted. Graham must have waxed eloquent because on-screen Willow said nothing for several minutes. She ate her pie and ice cream, and sipped her tea.

She frowned. From her body language, Graham wasn't happy and was making that clear.

Graham gestured with his fork to make his point and dug into his dessert. Looked like a slice of cheesecake.

Whatever he'd said must have upset her because on screen, Willow grabbed the cold drink, swallowed part of it, and made a face at the taste before she set the glass on the table and replied to Graham's comments. "Based on my expression, that's a soft drink. What am I saying now, Max?"

He was silent a moment. "You're telling him you didn't ask him on a date, that you're not interested in a relationship with him because you're interested in someone else." Max glanced at her and winked. "I hope you meant me."

"Who else?"

"Not a ringing endorsement, Max," Jesse teased.

"Thanks a lot. At least I have someone interested in me, buddy. You have no one pining for your ugly mug."

"Ouch, man. That hurts."

The three of them fell silent as Graham said many more things between bites of his dessert. Willow's on-screen self looked more and more uncomfortable as the minutes ticked by. She also glanced surreptitiously as her watch a time or two.

Although she wouldn't have wanted to be rude, Willow would have been mentally scrambling to come up with a reason to excuse herself and go back to her room.

Willow noticed several people sitting near them in the dining room glance their way as Graham continued to speak and gesture with his fork. His voice must have been raised.

Maybe one of her fellow diners would shed light on the conversation. She and Max needed to talk to them before they returned home.

She sighed. Most of the guests at the Royal Hotel had moved on by now. That would make tracking them down tricky. Willow hoped Fortress Security's tech team was as good as Max claimed. They'd have to be to identify and locate potential witnesses, especially if the hotel's management wouldn't cooperate.

Jesse leaned closer to the laptop. "Back up the footage by 30 seconds."

Max complied. "What did you see?"

"Willow's eyes look like they're not focusing. Look at her fumbling with the fork and glass, and she didn't switch back to her herbal tea when she doesn't like soft drinks. There's no way for me to confirm my suspicions with forensic evidence, but my guess is someone slipped Rohypnol into her soft drink before the waitress brought the drink to the table. From what we've seen on the footage, Willow never turned away from the table so Graham wouldn't have been able to spike her drink. That leaves the bartender or waitress, and I can't see either one of them doctoring Willow's beverage unless they were offered a nice bribe."

"Someone probably added the drug when the bartender was distracted," Max said. "Wait until the bartender's back was turned, do a little sleight of hand to distract the audience close by, add the drug, then sit back and watch the show. When Enright helped Willow to her room, it was a simple matter to follow them up and complete the kill. Although I'm grateful, I don't understand why the killer didn't finish off Willow while he was at it. She was helpless. Would have been easy enough to follow through and walk away."

Willow groaned. "I shouldn't have taken a sip from a drink I didn't order much less finish the whole thing. My only excuse is the drug acted fast, I was upset with Graham, or both. I wouldn't think about a potential threat in a restaurant since I wasn't trolling for a date and had no intention of taking a man up to my room."

Max tapped the screen to pause the footage, and his head whipped toward her. "Enright tried to persuade you to take him upstairs?"

She started to say no but something flashed through her mind. Man, this was getting old. Would her memory ever return to normal? "Maybe. I don't know if he assumed I planned to ask him up or if taking him upstairs was his idea. Either way, he would have been disappointed. That was never going to happen."

His jaw flexed. "If your memory clears enough to remember the incident, I want you to tell me what happened."

Willow blinked. "What good will that do? He's dead."

"I still want to know." He cupped her nape. "Please. I don't want to make a mistake with you. You're too important to me."

She trusted Max. Time to prove it. Now, if only her memory would get with the program and provide the answers they needed, she'd be golden. "All right. If I remember more details, I'll tell you."

"Thanks," he murmured, and dropped a kiss as light as a feather on her mouth.

Jesse cleared his throat. "Should I go back to the balcony? I feel like a third wheel."

Max waved that aside and restarted the security footage. Soon, it became obvious Graham suspected something was wrong. Willow groped for her glass, missed and knocked into it, making the glass rock. Graham caught the glass and moved it farther away from her hand. He leaned closer and must have asked a question because Willow shook her head slowly and slumped in her chair, listing to the right.

Based on Graham's body language, Willow's dining companion asked another question and received no response this time. Willow looked out of it. Graham took out his wallet, threw money on the table, and rose. He grasped Willow's arms and helped her stand. When she swayed as though drunk or dizzy, he caught her arm and tugged her against his side. He ignored her clumsy attempts to move away from him and propelled her from the restaurant. More than once, Willow stumbled and would have hit the floor without Graham's assistance.

"Would Rohypnol take effect that quickly, Jesse?" Willow asked.

"Only takes fifteen minutes. According to the time stamp on the footage, Enright helped you from the restaurant 30 minutes after you took the first sip. The effects of Rohypnol last about 12 hours, sometimes longer."

She wrinkled her nose. No wonder she felt awful at the police station. Willow was lucky she hadn't said too much to Detective Cohen. Good thing Max had insisted one of the Fortress lawyers sit in on the interrogation. "Seems as though I'm a lightweight."

"You're a beautiful lightweight," Max said.

Willow's eyes widened. Beautiful? Was he flirting with her? It wasn't necessary. No man interested her except Max.

"Anyone who had been given the drug would have reacted as you did." Max tapped on the next clip that followed Willow and Graham's progress to the elevator. One of the cameras caught Phillip in the background with a concerned expression on his face as he watched their progress. He said something to Graham who replied but didn't stop moving toward the elevator with Willow clamped to his side. "Phillip asked Enright if you were sick, and if he should call the hotel doctor. Enright said you were tired and to mind his own business."

"We need to talk to Phillip, Max. He might have seen something that will help."

"Who do we have here," Jesse murmured.

Willow shifted her attention back to the screen in time to see a person dressed in jeans, running shoes, and a black hoodie with a ball cap tugged low on his head who trailed after them. She studied his movements along with the body profile and decided the person was male. The shoes looked familiar. Coincidence?

The man paused at the edge of the screen, face averted from the camera, while Graham waited with Willow for the elevator to arrive. When the silver doors slid open, Graham practically carried her inside the car. At the last second, Hoodie darted into the elevator, and the doors shut, enclosing Hoodie in with her and Graham.

"We need the Fortress techs to examine this footage and the remaining clips frame by frame," Max said. "Maybe they'll see the man's face reflected on a surface."

Jesse grabbed his phone. "I'll text Zane."

"This guy might not have anything to do with what happened to me or Graham," Willow pointed out.

"A simple conversation will clear it up, but he tried too hard to keep his face away from every camera. He knew exactly where they were located and angled his head away or used the bill of his ball cap to put his face in shadow. If we're lucky, the techs will identify someone who might have taken a photo or video with a phone that allows us to see this guy's face."

"Ask Z to go back through the footage and track Hoodie's progress through the hotel," Max said. "I want to know who this guy is and why he targeted Willow or Enright or both."

After a nod, Jesse sent a text to their friend at Fortress.

Cold chills surged across Willow's skin. "The place to start tracking this man down is the Royal Hotel. We should talk to Phillip, and he'll be on duty tonight."

"You know his schedule?" Amusement filled Jesse's voice. He slid his phone away.

She shrugged. "He told me that he was off on Monday and Wednesday nights because of his class schedule. Otherwise, he works every night to pay for school."

Max watched her a moment, then said, "Do you feel up to talking to him? We can wait until tomorrow if you don't."

She would love to delay the inevitable. However, she wanted answers. No, that wasn't a strong enough word. She needed to find out what happened during her lost hours. Phillip might have the answers Willow sought. "We should go. With luck, the same bartender and waitress will be on duty, enabling us to get the information we need faster."

He shifted his gaze to Jesse, eyebrow raised. "Your medical opinion?"

"As long as Willow doesn't push herself, it's fine."

"All right." Max squeezed Willow's hand. "I'm trusting you to tell me when you've had enough."

"I promise."

A nod. "Let's finish the rest of the footage, then we'll go to the hotel." Max started the next clip. On screen, the elevator doors slid open and Graham carried Willow from the car to her door. He set her down and pushed her back against the wall beside the door, keeping her in place with one hand. Graham tugged her crossbody purse to the front, opened it, and rifled through the inside until he came up with a key card. Seconds later, he opened the door and carted Willow inside.

The door slowly closed. Hoodie appeared at the opposite end of the hallway and raced to the door with a knife in his hand. He caught the door just before it shut and slipped inside.

"Hoodie got off the elevator on a lower floor, then made his way up the stairs to wait for you and Enright," Max said.

Her stomach flipped. "This wasn't a random attack."

"No."

The video continued to run, showing twenty minutes of empty corridor. A newlywed couple Willow recognized from her stay wandered into camera range and out again at the fifteen-minute mark. At twenty minutes, Hoodie exited Willow's room and turned toward the stairs. Soon, he was out of camera range.

Willow groaned. "He kept his head down for the entire trek along the hallway. We still haven't seen his face. No reflective surfaces in sight."

"Not that we noticed on the first pass. We'll find out who he is and track him down," Jesse said. "We're just getting started, Willow."

"Investigations take time," Max said as he shut down his laptop and closed the lid. "We'll drive to the hotel as soon as you're ready."

Ten minutes later, the three of them climbed into Max's vehicle and headed toward Tucker's Gap. Max used his hands-free device to call Detective Cohen.

"Yeah, Cohen."

"Max Norton here. Got a minute?"

"Barely. Make it snappy, Norton."

"Have you released Willow's hotel room?"

A bark of laughter followed on the heels of Max's question. "You should know better than that."

"Any idea when they'll finish collecting evidence?"

"Noon tomorrow is the latest estimate. Why are you in such a hurry? Is Ms. Knox pushing you to get into the room?" Suspicion filled his voice.

Max ignored his questions. "I need a list of Willow's belongings."

"Why?"

"We finally had time to watch the security cam footage. I understand why you released Willow."

The detective grunted. "If I find a loophole in your story, I'll have you back inside an interrogation room faster than you can blink. You're the most likely candidate for the crime."

"Don't waste your time, Cohen. My alibi will hold because it's true. Will you send me the list or should I call Willow's lawyer and have her request it through formal channels?"

"I'd prefer to avoid the legal barracuda."

Now it was Max's turn to laugh. "Don't blame you. Send the list to my email. The address is on my business card."

"What did you see in the footage?"

"I want to know if the killer took something from Willow's room or purse. I didn't see that he had anything in his hand when he left the hotel room. He could have slipped something small into his pocket or under his shirt."

"Like what? Come on, Norton. Be specific. We're supposed to be on the same side here."

Willow rolled her eyes. If that was true, why had Cohen and Warner tried to railroad her into a jail cell?

"I want to know if the killer took Willow's notebook. She keeps track of work-related items in it. The killer taking it might indicate Enright's death was connected to her investigation."

"Or it might indicate her boyfriend had a reason to kill the competition."

"I trust Willow. If our relationship wasn't working for her, she would have told me."

"Unless she's having an affair behind your back. She'd have you and a boy toy on the side. Some people would say it's the perfect setup."

"Not Willow, especially with her background. I'll expect the list soon." Max ended the call.

Jesse whistled. "He's determined to pin Enright's murder on you."

"Cohen and his partner are lazy. They want the easiest solution."

"We'll have to find the real killer for them."

Max's phone rang. He tapped the dashboard screen. "You're on speaker with Willow and Jesse. What do you have for me, Zane?"

"Trouble with a capital T."

"What is it?"

"There's been another murder."

Chapter Thirteen

Max tightened his grip on the steering wheel. "Who's dead?"

"Chip Melton, a bartender at the Royal Hotel."

He groaned, connecting the dots without Zane having to spell them out. "You're kidding."

"Nope. Sorry, buddy."

"Let me guess. He was on duty the night Graham died," Willow said.

"Yeah, he was. Melton worked until 3:00 that morning. He was supposed to report for his next shift yesterday afternoon but he was a no-show. Since that was out of character for Melton, the hotel manager tried to contact him this morning to find out why he missed work. When he couldn't reach the bartender, the manager called Melton's girlfriend. She went to his home and discovered his body."

Max frowned. Man, that must have been rough. Although he felt sympathy for her, they needed to talk to the woman. Perhaps Melton mentioned something to her about Willow. "What's the girlfriend's name?"

"Callie Westover. I sent information on her to your email."

"How did Melton die?" Max asked.

"Same as Enright. He was stabbed. One difference, though. Melton was struck on the back of the head with a blunt object before the killer shoved a blade through his heart."

Cohen and Warner were probably the detectives assigned to the case since the victim had been connected in a peripheral way to Enright's death. "We're on the way to the hotel now to talk to Phillip, the restaurant host on duty the night Enright died. Hopefully, we'll be able to talk to Willow's waitress, too."

"Copy that. The tech team has started tracking the man in the baseball cap through the hotel. They'll do their best to get a picture of his face but no guarantees, Max. Enright's death wasn't an accident. The killer planned it down to the minutest detail. From what I've seen so far, this guy was careful."

"I understand but I need a photo of him yesterday, Z. This guy is escalating and will make another try for Willow before this is over." Possibly more than one attempt. The killer couldn't be sure what Willow remembered. Since Hoodie seemed to be cleaning up after himself, he would come back around to Willow. She was a dangerous loose end. If she remembered his face, Willow could put him on death row.

"Your video footage is a top priority. I'll be in touch when the tech team finishes no matter the outcome. Later." He ended the call.

At the Royal Hotel, Max opened Willow's door and together, they made their way to the hotel's restaurant with Jesse. Willow's friend, Phillip, sat on a stool behind the reservation desk and spoke into a headset, his attention fixed on the laptop open in front of him.

"Yes, sir. We'll have your table ready at 8:00." A moment later, Phillip ended the call and looked up. An expression of surprise was quickly followed by relief when he saw Willow. "Willow, I'm glad to see you. How do you feel?"

"Better. Phillip, this is Max and Jesse. They're looking into what happened the other night. Do you have a minute to talk?"

"We're in the slow part of my shift. As long as I don't leave my post, the manager shouldn't mind. What happened to you the other night? Were you sick? I heard the police were called, and you went to the hospital."

Huh. The hotel management had done a good job keeping a lid on the story. "Willow was drugged with Rohypnol, and the man who helped her from the restaurant was murdered in her hotel room."

Phillip paled. He shifted his attention to Willow. "Are you sure you're all right?"

"The doctor said I'd be fine. Would you mind answering a few questions for Max?"

"How can I help?" he asked Max.

"Did you notice a man in a black hoodie and ball cap who came into the restaurant that night?"

The college student looked puzzled. "Sure. Why?"

"What can you tell us about him?"

"Is he the one who drugged Willow?"

"We need to ask him a few questions. He rode in the elevator with Enright and Willow. He might have seen something to help us identify the killer."

"Wait." Phillip answered a phone call and made reservations for another customer. When he ended the call, he said, "Sorry."

"Do you know if the man in the hoodie is staying at the hotel?"

"I don't think so. I haven't seen him since that night."

"That was the first time he'd been in the restaurant?"

"Yes, sir."

"Why do you remember him?" Jesse asked.

"His baseball cap had Orioles on it. Don't see many of those around here, and my grandfather was a big Orioles fan." A shrug. "I asked him about it but he only said he liked the team. He didn't seem like he wanted to talk."

"Did he wait for a table?" Max asked.

Phillip shook his head. "He opted to go to the bar. I lost track of him after that until he left the restaurant." He scowled. "I should have known something was up."

"Why?"

"Although he left the restaurant right after Willow, he hung back until she and the other guy were in the elevator, then darted inside before the doors closed. It was odd, you know?"

"Did he say anything when he left?"

Another head shake. "I was more concerned about Willow than some man acting weird."

Max pulled out his phone and brought up a photo of Enright. "Recognize him?"

The expression of recognition on his face indicated he did. He opened his mouth to reply, then remained silent.

Guess that answered his question. The kid had been cooperative until this point. Why had he shut off the flow of information?

"Phillip, what's wrong?" Willow asked.

He flicked a glance at Max. "I don't want to cause you a problem, Willow."

Max appreciated the kid's need to protect Willow. He felt the same driving need himself. It was one of the reasons Max didn't understand why anyone wanted to kill her. "Talk to me, Phillip. We know Enright thought he was meeting Willow for a date. Someone duped him into meeting her here."

"I didn't ask Graham to come," Willow added. She turned to Max. "Although I can't prove it, I know I didn't cheat on you. I wouldn't, Max."

"I know. I believe you." He looked at Phillip who had visibly relaxed. "What did Enright say to you when he arrived?"

"That he had a date with Willow."

"How did he seem?" Jesse asked. "Excited, worried, nervous?"

"Excited and a little nervous. He said the date was unexpected but he seemed jazzed about it."

"Excited I can understand if he thought he was meeting a beautiful woman." Max shifted a step closer. "What made you conclude he was nervous?"

"Hard to miss. He glanced around like he was on the lookout for someone watching him. I kept thinking he didn't want anyone to know he was here, that he shouldn't have been here. Maybe like he was feeling guilty or something." Phillip frowned. "He had on a wedding ring so I thought maybe he was having an affair." His cheeks turned pink. "Sorry, Willow."

"It's a logical conclusion," Willow said. "If he was having an affair, it wasn't with me. I would never have been involved with Graham."

"Willow and I are engaged, Phillip." Had to go with the story they'd fed the Tucker's Gap police. Sooner or later the detectives would interview the college kid. "I don't know who arranged the dessert date, but it wasn't Willow. She wouldn't betray what we have together for a short-term fling." That was one thing Max knew would never be a concern when he deployed. Willow didn't cheat. Period.

A nod from the law student. "I didn't think so but I didn't want to cause trouble if I was wrong. Now that I know you're getting married, Willow, I'm especially glad Enright had the wrong idea."

Willow patted his forearm. "Thanks for trying to protect me anyway."

"I didn't do a good job of it. I'm sorry. I thought something was off when your companion practically had to carry you from the restaurant but I didn't question him when he told me to mind my own business. I just thought you were sick. I never suspected you had been drugged. I should have stopped him and questioned him further."

"Not your fault, my friend. It's the fault of whoever put the drug in my drink."

He clearly didn't believe her. "Is there any way I can make it up to you?"

Willow smiled. "You can tell me if my waitress from the other night is working."

He tapped a few keys on his computer. "Do you remember her name?"

"Not off hand. She's a brunette, long hair pulled back in a ponytail, and pretty. She's in her early twenties and a bundle of energy."

His cheeks turned pink. "Uh, that's Marlee Willis." Phillip checked the screen. "You're in luck. She's working tonight. Would you like a table in her section? We're slow at the moment, so she should be able to talk between waiting on her other tables."

"That's perfect," Max said. "Thanks, Phillip."

He grabbed three menus from the stack behind him. "Follow me." Phillip led them into the dining room to the back table in the corner where he had seated Willow on the night Enright had joined her. "Hope you're successful." He returned to his station.

Less than a minute later, Marlee arrived at their table. She recognized Willow and smiled. "Welcome back. I'm glad you're feeling better. What would you and your friends like to drink?"

They each gave Marlee their order. When she returned, Max said, "We'd like to talk to you for a few minutes. Can you take a short break with us?"

She frowned. "Is something wrong?"

"We have a few questions about what happened to Willow the other night," Jesse said. "We're talking to anyone who had contact with her. We'd appreciate any help."

Marlee glanced at the man making the rounds to various tables. "I'm due for a break. Let me tell Mr. Overton, then I'll be back."

"I doubt she saw anything," Willow said. "Is this necessary?"

"We have to ask," Max said. "You might be surprised. Wait staff are observant."

Soon, Marlee approached and sat in the empty chair beside Willow. "I have a ten-minute break. If the restaurant gets busy, I'll have to return to work. You looked pretty sick when your friend helped you from the restaurant the other night, Willow." She leaned closer and lowered her voice. "Did you have food poisoning?"

"Someone put Rohypnol in my drink."

The waitress gasped. "Are you serious?" She held up a hand. "Wait. Do you think I drugged you?"

"No, of course not. We wanted to ask if you saw anything to help us narrow down who did."

Marlee sat back in her chair, arms crossed over her chest. "The first person I'd talk to is your companion that night."

"Why do you say that?" Max asked.

"He was pretty aggressive. I thought I'd have to ask the manager to tell him to calm down or he'd have to leave. He was upsetting Willow and disturbing the other customers around their table."

"Yeah, we saw that on the security footage."

Marlee's eyes widened. "You did? How?"

"We have friends with excellent tech skills."

She grinned. "In other words, you know a hacker."

"Not just a hacker." Jesse winked at her. "A hacker in a class of his own."

"Ha. It pays to have friends in low places."

Time to get the conversation back on track. "The night Willow was drugged, did you notice anyone who stood out?" Max asked.

"What do you mean?"

"Someone who didn't fit in or seemed interested in Willow and Enright, perhaps watching them from a distance."

Marlee was silent a moment, then gave a slow nod. "Now that you mention it, I remember one man whose behavior was off that night."

"Tell us about him," Max prompted. "Where did you see him and when?"

"At the bar two hours into my shift. Chip, the bartender, signaled me to pick up a round of drinks for my tables. This guy was sitting at the bar with his back to the dining room. He didn't look at me even though I bumped into him to avoid colliding with another customer. When I apologized, he just grunted. Anyway, Chip said the guy bought a soft drink for Willow but wanted to remain anonymous."

Excellent. Now they were getting somewhere. "He mentioned her by name, not just the beautiful woman at the corner table?"

"By name," Marlee confirmed. "I thought he knew her."

"Did you see his face?"

"Not really. I glanced at his profile when I apologized for bumping into him but could only see his nose and chin. The bar area isn't well lit that time of evening, and he had a baseball hat pulled down low on his forehead. His face was partially hidden with his beer mug."

"Was he drinking?"

She nodded. "If it matters, I don't know which brand was in his mug. You'll have to ask Chip. He has a memory like a steel trap. Never forgets anything. He'd be able to give you a description of the man, too. Never forgets a face or name. That's what makes him so good at his job."

That amazing ability was also why Chip was dead. "I'm afraid asking him for more information won't be possible."

"Why not?"

Yeah, this was the part of the job Max had always hated. He didn't miss death notifications. "You haven't heard."

Marlee straightened. "Heard what? What's going on?"

No help for it. He'd have to be the one to break the bad news to her. "I'm sorry to tell you that Chip Melton is dead."

She stared. "That's not possible."

"His girlfriend, Callie, found his body a few hours ago."

Tears glimmered in her eyes. "Oh, no. Poor Callie. I'll have to call her on my next break and see if I can help her."

"You're friends?"

"Yeah. She and I grew up in the same neighborhood."

"What do you know about Chip?"

"He was a good, kind man who adored Callie." She swallowed hard. "Chip has a large family, several brothers and sisters. I think he's one of ten kids. He moved to the area when he was hired to work here at the Royal as a bartender. This is so hard to believe. How could this happen?"

"Where was he from originally?" Jesse asked.

"Akron." A tear streaked down her cheek. Marlee brushed it away with a quick swipe of her hand. "Chip was always talking about how much he missed his family and wanted to move closer to home one day. He and Callie planned to marry after she finished college and move to Ohio. They wanted to build a life there."

"Do you know if anyone was giving him trouble here at work or in his personal life?"

"Everybody loved Chip. He never met a stranger, you know?"

"Did the man at the bar speak to Chip in your hearing?"

She shook her head.

"Marlee." Phillip walked up. He'd escorted a family of five to a nearby table and detoured to their table on his way to his station. "You okay?" he murmured.

"Chip is dead," she whispered. "I can't believe it."

"Yeah, I heard about it when I started my shift." He laid his hand on her shoulder. "I'm sorry. I should have told you but I thought you already knew. If you want to talk, I'm a good listener."

"Thanks, Phillip." She pressed her hand over his. "I might do that."

"Um, I get off pretty late but if you don't mind waiting around, we can talk when my shift is over. Maybe get some coffee or something."

Max hid his amusement at the awkward invitation. Too bad he didn't live in the area. He'd like to see if this relationship worked out.

Color flared in Marlee's cheeks. "I'd like that. Thanks for the invitation, Phillip."

He smiled, then returned to the host station.

The cute waitress watched Phillip until he'd settled at his station again. She turned back, saw Max and the others watching her, and blushed. "Sorry. I must seem like a giddy pre-teen after that display." Willow smiled. "Phillip seems like a great guy."

"He is. Phillip is the smartest person I know, and he's funny, too. I love listening to him talk."

"Are you interested in dating him?"

"What woman wouldn't be?" She sighed. "He probably isn't interested in me that way, though."

"He looked interested to me," Jesse said. "How many other men do you know who work late, then volunteer to stay after work even when he's exhausted so he can spend time with you? I bet Phillip is waiting for a signal from you that you're interested in pursuing a relationship."

"You think so?" Hope glowed in her eyes.

"I'll tell you a little secret," Willow said. "When I asked Phillip if you were working tonight, he blushed. He already asked you on a date in our hearing, Marlee. While you're working your shift tonight, think of a fun date for the two of you to enjoy. When you have coffee with him, ask him to go out with you. I'll bet he says yes."

"But he's so busy studying and working. I've never seen anyone study as hard as Phillip. When would he have time to spend with me?"

"Everyone needs downtime," Max said. "Spending time with Willow is the fastest way for me to unwind, even if it's only a phone call or a movie. Ask Phillip to go on a date. You might be surprised how fast he takes you up on the offer."

A beautiful smile formed on her mouth. "I think I will. Thanks for the confidence boost, you guys." She glanced at her watch. "I have a couple minutes before I have to go back to work. Do you have other questions for me?"

"When you circled back to the bar after the guy in the baseball hat followed Willow and Graham out of the restaurant, did Chip say anything about the drink for Willow or the guy who bought the drink?"

"Chip thought it was odd for the man to buy a soft drink instead of alcohol."

Max stilled. Excellent observation. Baseball cap had to have talked to an acquaintance of Willow's to know that she preferred teas, water, and the occasional soft drink. Someone knew her well enough to gamble that she would drink to be polite.

"A smart move on his part," Willow said. "I don't drink alcohol."

"How did he know?" Jesse asked.

"An excellent question." Max turned back to Marlee. "Did Chip mention the other man asking questions about Willow?"

"Not to me. Callie might know. Chip always called her when he got off work, and talked to her on his drive home. She helped keep him awake. I can call her on my next break to ask."

Max shook his head. "We need to talk to her ourselves." He smiled. "Besides, you have a date to plan. Focus on that. Do you mind giving me Callie's phone number? We need to talk to her as soon as possible."

She rattled off the number, then said, "Any suggestions on the date? I'm not very good at this kind of thing. I've never asked a guy to go out with me before, and I don't want to do it wrong. That would spell doom on this relationship in a hurry, and I really want him to like the date and me."

"Never a bad thing to think about dinner or a movie. If he likes sports, tickets to a game would be fun. If money is tight, go to a local high school game or a game at your college."

"Picnics are excellent," Willow offered. "You could even combine a meal with study time if the weather is pleasant. If his schedule is tight, bring dessert and coffee to his place. You can bring your books and study, too."

"I like those suggestions." She looked thoughtful. "I know he likes history. Maybe he'd like to go to a museum with me."

"That's perfect. If he has time, follow it up with dessert and coffee."

"Marlee." Jesse waited until she shifted her attention to him. "Leave the investigating to us, all right? Don't ask anyone questions about what happened to Chip or Willow, and especially don't talk about the man in the baseball cap. It's important, okay?"

She stared. "You think he's the one who murdered Chip, don't you?"

"We don't know. Since we don't, it's better not to risk yourself. If he is responsible for Chip's death, you don't want to draw attention to yourself."

"Marlee, you said Chip had an excellent memory." Max rested his forearms on the table. "Did he mention seeing baseball guy before?"

"Nope, and he would have."

"What about you? Did you see him around here or perhaps in town?"

"Not that I know. Again, I didn't see his face. Most of it was in shadow. The rest was covered by either the hat or his beer mug."

"Phillip said the guy's hat stood out. Do you remember seeing a guy with that hat on around town?"

She thought a minute, frowning. "Maybe."

"Where?"

Marlee remained silent a minute, then sighed. "Sorry. I just can't remember. Is it important?"

"It would help." Max slid his business card to the girl. "Think about it. If you remember where you saw him or anything else you think might help, call me. Day or night."

"You're scaring me," she whispered.

"I don't want to scare you but I want you safe. The faster we catch this guy, the better for you and everyone else involved in this." Especially Willow. Max couldn't get away from the feeling that time was running out to identify this guy before he struck again.

Marlee pushed back from the table. "I need to go."

"One more question. Did Chip mention or joke about his excellent memory when baseball guy was at the bar?"

Blood drained from Marlee's face. "Yeah, he did. He rattled off the drinks on my tray without even looking at the ticket, and teased me about getting better grades in college if I had a memory like his. I'm in danger, aren't I?"

"You're going to go about your business like normal. You aren't going to ask or talk about baseball guy or about Willow. Also, it's best not to go anywhere alone. Wherever you are, carry your cell phone with you, even in your house, apartment, or dorm. Make sure it's fully charged."

"A phone doesn't seem like a good defense against a killer."

"He doesn't know you paid any attention to him. If you don't talk about him or Willow, chances are good he'll assume he didn't make any impression at all. That's what we want."

"We also don't know if he's our guy," Jesse murmured. "He might be someone who thought Willow was hot and wanted to buy her a drink."

Marlee wrinkled her nose. "A soft drink? Come on."

"If you're uneasy or afraid, if something is off and you feel unsafe, call the cops and one of us immediately." Jesse slid her his business card as well. "Our cell numbers are on the back of our cards."

"What if I'm being paranoid and nothing is wrong?"

"Better to be safe. Listen to your instincts. No second-guessing yourself. If you feel unsafe, assume you are and call."

The waitress stood. "Okay. I really have to go before Mr. Overton gets upset."

When she had returned to work, Willow said, "Do you believe she's in danger?"

"Oh, yeah." Max squeezed her hand. "If the killer is baseball guy, Marlee is on his radar. That's not a good place to be." He needed to catch this man before he murdered another innocent person.

Chapter Fourteen

Max tossed twenty dollars on the table to cover the cost of their drinks, and held out his hand to Willow. "We'll stop at the host station and tell Phillip not to ask questions about Enright or you."

"Good idea. I don't want anything to happen to Phillip or Marlee. I'd like something good to come from this situation."

"A blooming romance counts?"

"Oh, yes. A little joy after a heartbreaking loss for two families."

After explaining to Phillip the necessity of keeping a low profile, they returned to the SUV. Max looked at his watch. "We should talk to Callie tonight but it's late."

"The sooner we talk to her the better," Jesse said. "Her life could be in danger."

He was right. Max hoped the initial shock had worn off so Chip's girlfriend could answer a few questions.

"Call first," Willow said. "We'll scare her if three strangers come to her door this time of night. No offense, but you two are intimidating."

"I'll take that as a compliment." Max slid his phone from his pocket and called Callie. Several rings later, a woman answered. "Callie Westover?"

"If you're a reporter, save your breath. I don't have anything to say."

"I'm not a reporter. My name is Max Norton. Marlee gave me your number. I hate to ask, but I need to talk to you for a few minutes."

"Can't it wait? I'm not at my best right now."

"I'm a private investigator, and Chip's death might be connected to an attack on my girlfriend."

"Well..."

"We can talk outside if you feel uncomfortable." Not his first choice. Max didn't want to cause speculation that might trickle back to the killer and place Callie in the crosshairs. "My girlfriend is with me and a friend. Will you permit us to come to your home?"

She was silent a moment, then gave Max her address. "I'm texting my brother. I want him to be here, too."

"That's fine. If he isn't there by the time we arrive, we'll wait in our SUV until he comes."

"All right." Callie ended the call.

Fifteen minutes later, Max parked in front of Callie's home and called her. "Ms. Westover, my friends and I are parked in front of your house. Has your brother arrived?"

"He's here."

"May we come inside the house to speak with you?"

"It's fine since Jason is here."

"We won't take much of your time." He ended the call. "Let's go before she changes her mind." Max opened Willow's door. "Stay behind me and Jesse until we're sure it's safe."

When he rang the bell, the door swung open to reveal a muscular man over six feet tall. He eyed Max with suspicion. "Yeah?"

"I'm Max. Ms. Westover is expecting us."

"She's too nice, allowing you to come when she's upset. I'm not nice. You have fifteen minutes." With one last glower, Jason stepped back to allow them to enter the house.

Max walked in first, followed by Jesse. A young woman near the same age as Marlee sat in an armchair. Jason stood by her side, his hard gaze locked on Max and Jesse.

When he was sure Willow would be safe, Max glanced at Jesse. The medic signaled Willow. She walked to Max's side.

He wrapped his hand around Willow's and said, "I'm Max. This is Willow, and our friend Jesse. Thank you for speaking with us, Ms. Westover."

"Please, sit down." Callie's voice was raspy, her eyes tear-reddened and swollen. "Call me Callie. This is Jason, my brother. Please, sit down and tell us what this is about."

Max sat on the sofa with Willow. Jesse remained near the door. "I understand from Marlee that Chip usually called you on his way home from work."

"That's right. Why?"

"Did he call you the night he was killed?"

She nodded, eyes sheening with tears.

"Did he mention Willow or a man named Graham Enright in his conversation?"

Callie frowned. "I've heard Graham Enright's name."

Jason's eyes narrowed. "That's the guy who was stabbed to death at the Royal." He pointed at Willow. "You're the lady who was with him, aren't you? Max said you're his girlfriend."

"I am. I was drugged in the restaurant that night. When Graham helped me to my room, someone followed him and killed him."

Chip's girlfriend gasped. "That's terrible."

"Callie, did Chip mention Willow or Enright?" Max asked again.

"He mentioned Willow."

"By name?"

She nodded. "He said a guy bought her a soft drink at the bar and sent it to her table. Most people who buy drinks for someone else purchase alcohol. This guy insisted on a soft drink which Chip thought was interesting."

"Did Chip say anything else about him?"

"Not really. The guy just nursed one beer, barely drinking a quarter of it before he left the bar. Oh, Chip said he wore an Orioles baseball cap."

"Why did the hat stand out?"

"It's Phillip's favorite baseball team, and Marlee is crazy about him. She gathers up every scrap of information and socks it away." She smiled. "They'd be good together. Phillip is shy, though. They've worked together for months, and he's never asked her out."

"He did tonight," Willow said.

Callie's eyes widened. "Really? Oh, that's great. I'll have to call her." A tear trickled down Callie's cheek. "Someone should be happy."

"Anything else?" Jason asked.

"Was Chip upset about anything?" Max asked.

Callie shrugged. "The usual stuff."

"What kind of things?"

"Money was tight. With us planning a wedding in the spring, Chip was working extra shifts to save money and pay off bills."

"Anything else?"

"He missed his family. They're tight knit, always in each other's business." Blood drained from her face. "Oh, no. Someone has to tell Chip's family."

"Detectives Cohen and Warner will take care of the notification. It's part of the job, Callie."

"You sound like you know something about that."

"Jesse and I used to be in law enforcement. Was Chip worried about anyone?"

"What do you mean?"

"Did someone give him a hard time at the hotel or threaten him?"

"Everyone loved Chip. He was the best man I know." Her voice broke.

"Did Chip know the guy in the Oriole's cap?"

"He recognized the man's face. Chip saw him on the sidewalk in front of the hotel a couple of times this week. He didn't know the guy's name, though."

Excellent. Perhaps a security camera in front of the hotel had captured Oriole's image. The timing was interesting, too.

"That's it," Jason snapped. "She's had enough. If you have more questions, you can talk to her later."

Max helped Willow to her feet. The odds of him learning more from Callie was slim, but he'd follow through anyway. Over the next few days, Callie might remember more.

He handed the brother and sister his business card. "If you think of anything that might help me figure out who drugged Willow or hurt Chip, call me."

"Wait." Callie stood. "You don't think Chip drugged your girlfriend, do you? He would never do that. He was a protector, not a predator."

"No one thinks Chip is to blame," Willow said. "Since the restaurant and bar were busy, someone might have taken advantage of a distraction and put the drug in my soft drink while Chip's back was turned."

"The Orioles man. You asked several questions about him. Is he the one you want?"

"Maybe," Max said. "Don't mention him or ask about him."

"Shouldn't you tell the police about him?"

"All we know is a guy in a baseball cap sent Willow a drink. He might have hoped to take a beautiful woman on a date, then believed Enright was on a date with her and gave up his pursuit." Not likely but possible.

She stared. "But you don't think so. You think this guy is the one who killed Mr. Enright and drugged your girlfriend. He might have killed Chip."

"We don't have proof. It's best if you don't talk about him, Willow, or Enright. Let the police do their jobs, Callie. They want to find the person who killed Chip. Don't call attention to yourself. Leave the investigation to the professionals."

"Like you?"

He inclined his head. "I want whoever drugged Willow behind bars before he hurts someone else."

"Behind bars or dead?" Jason challenged.

"The preference is always to abide by the law." As long as the murderer cooperated. Max didn't have a preference as long as the man was no longer a threat to Willow. "Thanks for your time, Callie. We're sorry for your loss."

As Jesse opened the door, the large picture window in the living room shattered.

Chapter Fifteen

Reacting on instinct, Max wrapped his arms around Willow and took her to the ground, turning at the last second to take the brunt of the impact with the floor himself. He rolled to flip their positions and covered her body with his, his arms around Willow's head. A flash of light lit up the living room. An explosion rocked the world.

Max grunted as shrapnel pelted him. Warm liquid slid down his body. His legs, back, and shoulders stung. He glanced over his shoulder at the fire spreading across the floor in their direction. They needed to get out of the house.

Jason cursed viciously, and Callie screamed.

"Run," Max yelled.

"Out the back door," Jesse ordered as he leaped to his feet. "Now."

"The front door is right there," the other man argued.

"Do it. Explanations later," the medic snapped. He scooped Callie into his arms and ran for the back of the house as fire spread through the living room.

Jason hurried after them, still cursing and demanding an explanation.

Max surged to his feet, cradled Willow in his arms, and rushed after his teammate. The scent of gasoline filled the air. Thick smoke rolled through the living room and kitchen as alarms blared.

He raced across the kitchen and into the backyard, ignoring the pain in various parts of his body. Max dragged clean air into his lungs and hurried to the far corner of the yard where Jesse waited with Callie and Jason. The medic held his weapon by his side, alert and scanning the area.

Max set Willow on her feet. His gaze swept over her, searching for injuries. He'd hit her hard to take her to the floor in case the arsonist followed up with a hail of bullets. "Are you hurt, baby?"

What if he had hurt Willow? Max hadn't had a choice. If she had a concussion or a broken bone from him tackle, she'd recover. A bullet could be fatal. He wouldn't apologize for protecting her.

"I don't think so." She sounded breathless and shaky.

"Jesse, you good?"

"No injuries. Callie and Jason have minor cuts. Jason called for help. They'll be here soon. Are you injured?"

No choice except to admit the truth. Jesse and Willow would notice when he refused to sit to prevent driving the shrapnel deeper into his body. "Yeah."

Jesse's attention shifted to Max, his gaze assessing. "Shrapnel?"

"I feel like a pin cushion."

Willow gasped and pushed at his shoulder gently. "Turn around, and let me see."

"It's too dark, and I don't want to pinpoint our location with a light. I need to scout the area before first responders arrive." Max doubted the arsonist was still around but he didn't want first responders walking into an ambush if he was wrong. "Stay here."

"Max, no."

"I'll be fine." He brushed his mouth over hers and looked at Jesse. "I've got her. Go. Don't do any more damage to yourself."

He acknowledged the order with a chin lift and headed across the yard to the corner of the house, weapon in hand. With his back against the wall, he peered around the corner. No signs of a threat.

As first responders neared, Max eased to the side of the house, hugging the shadows, and walked toward the front of Callie's home. On the front lawn, the flames inside the house cast writhing shadows on the grass.

Neighbors gathered across the street to stare at the burning house. No one in an Orioles cap stood among the watchers. Would have been too easy, and nothing about this situation had been easy from the beginning.

Holstering his weapon, Max used his phone to take photos of the crowd. They might get lucky. Arsonists liked to admire their handiwork but this didn't feel like a typical arson case. Either Callie or Willow, possibly both, had been targeted.

He considered that as he snapped photo after photo of the milling people on the opposite side of the street. Arson was a sloppy way to kill. Too many ways for the plan to fail.

Why hadn't the arsonist shot them as they fled the flames? Max and the others would have been easy to pick off.

Maybe this was a crime of opportunity. If the arsonist was Orioles Cap, the man had proved himself comfortable with a knife. If he wanted a gun, Orioles Cap could easily score an illegal weapon on the street.

When a patrol car rounded the corner and raced toward Callie's house, Max shoved the phone in his pocket. Behind the police car, a fire truck and a rescue arrived.

Time for him to return to the others. He and Jesse would be grilled by the police, probably handcuffed and placed in the back of the squad car unless they were lucky.

In less than five minutes, Max and Jesse were in cuffs. Although he hated to be treated like a criminal, Max couldn't blame the cops for the precaution. When they first rolled up on the scene, the officers had taken one look at Max and Jesse's weapons and, despite their identification as employees of Fortress Security, confiscated their weapons and handcuffed them. At least the officers agreed to allow Max and Jesse to remain outside the patrol car after Max's explanation about the potential threat to Willow's life.

"This isn't fair, Max," Willow said. "You and Jesse didn't do anything wrong. You're not criminals. You saved us. I would have run out the front door like Jason wanted to do. You prevented us from taking a bullet."

"Everything will be sorted out soon." Max scanned the crowd across the street again. No one new had joined the watch party but he felt eyes on him.

"I still don't like it."

"I'm not a fan, either."

A tan sedan stopped a few houses away. Two men exited the vehicle and strode toward the patrol car.

He sighed. Fantastic. Let the fun begin. Cohen and Warner stared at Max and Jesse.

"You're like a bad penny, Norton," Warner said, a sneer on his face. "Always turning up at the wrong place and time. Still say you're innocent?"

"It's the truth."

"Got proof this time? Any convenient security-camera footage to keep you out of jail?"

"Two eye witnesses, one of whom owns the firebombed house." Max shifted, his muscles tightening. His pain level was edging higher by the minute. He'd have to let Jesse or one of the waiting paramedics evaluate his injuries.

Cohen narrowed his eyes. "You injured, Norton?"

"I was closest to the Molotov cocktail when it exploded."

"Max needs to go to the hospital," Jesse said. "He's bleeding from several cuts to his back and shoulders."

"Thought you were a paramedic. Why didn't you treat him yourself?"

"We were a little busy escaping the fire and making sure Willow, Callie, and Jason were safe. Plus, it's too dark out here to ensure all the glass has been removed."

Cohen grunted. "Stay here." The detective motioned for one of the patrol officers to watch Max, Jesse, and Willow, then he and his partner had a quick conversation with Callie and Jason. When they returned, Cohen ordered the cuffs removed.

"Yes, sir." A rookie released them. "What about their weapons, sir?"

"Return them." The detective looked at Max and Jesse. "Lock the weapons in your vehicle while you're in the hospital. We'll catch up with you there and take your statements. Officer Donnelly will follow in his patrol car to be sure you make it to the emergency room."

Max could live with a babysitter. The concession was more than he'd expected from the detectives. He inclined his head in silent agreement. Once the officers returned the weapons, Max stored them in the weapons safe in the floor of his vehicle, then tossed the key fob to Jesse. "You drive." His lips curved. "Not a good idea for me to do it." He opened the back door of his vehicle.

"You should allow the ambulance to transport you," Warner snapped. "Unless, of course, you're faking injuries to get out of another interview."

"Forget it." He could lay face down on his backseat as easily as he could on a gurney, and he'd be able to help if someone attacked them. "Jesse and Willow will take me." Max looked at Donnelly. "Coming?"

"I'll be on your six, sir."

He'd bet the rookie cop would tailgate them all the way to the hospital. The kid was so green he made Max feel ancient.

"Let's get you set up in the backseat," Jesse murmured. "Officer Donnelly."

"Sir?"

"Call the hospital. Tell them we're transporting a patient with shrapnel wounds from a Molotov cocktail. Should arrive in ten minutes."

"Copy that."

The trip to the emergency room was an exercise in pain. If Max didn't know better, he'd swear Jesse hit every pothole dead center to torture him. Instead of tearing a strip off his friend's hide, Max gritted his teeth. No need to upset Willow more.

Finally, the medic parked near the emergency room entrance and opened the door for Max. "End of the line, buddy."

He glared at his friend. "Did you have to say that?"

Jesse grinned. "Want some help?"

He wanted to say no but could use the assist. "Yeah."

"How much did that hurt to admit?"

More than he wanted to say. "Shut up."

Outright laughter from his friend. "Let's go. Your woman looks worried."

With Jesse's help, Max maneuvered from the vehicle. "I'll need clothes from my Go bag. The ones I'm wearing are toast."

A nod. "I'll bring them when the doc is ready to release you."

Didn't escape Max's notice that Jesse avoided saying how soon that might be. He wondered how long it would take to pluck shards of glass from his body. Max wasn't looking forward to the next few hours.

Willow met him on the sidewalk, threaded her fingers through his, and walked inside the emergency room with him. Jesse flanked his other side, keeping a close watch on him.

"I'm not going to face plant in the lobby," Max muttered. Probably. He'd hate to hit the deck with Willow watching. "I'm okay."

"You look like you should be in ICU."

He glared at Jesse. "Laugh it up, buddy. Your time is coming. By the way, Willow needs to be checked by a doctor, too."

"I'm standing right here," she protested, "and I'm not hurt. You made sure of that."

"I tackled you."

"And took the brunt of the impact with the floor."

Max stopped in the middle of the emergency room lobby. "If you want me to have medical treatment, then you'll see a doctor. If you refuse, I'll turn around and walk out."

"That's dirty pool, Norton."

"Deal with it, Knox."

She narrowed her eyes. "I won't forget this."

He smiled, feeling smug that his tactic had worked.

The medic went to the desk to register Max and Willow.

"Do you think they'll let me go into the room with you?" Willow asked.

Officer Donnelly walked into the ER entrance and stopped a short distance away, watching them.

"That might not be a good idea, baby."

"You don't want me with you?" Hurt filled her eyes.

"In order for the medical staff to clean and treat my wounds, I'll have to strip down. They can't remove the glass otherwise."

Her cheeks turned red. "I don't want to make you uncomfortable."

"This has nothing to do with my comfort level, Willow. If you want to go with me, I'll make it happen."

"You don't mind?"

"Nope." Max cupped her cheek. "I don't want you to be afraid of me or uncomfortable. I'll always have your back and protect you, even from me. I need you to trust me." With everything.

Willow raised her chin. "I want to know what's happening first hand. I can close my eyes but at least I'll hear the doctor's assessment of your injuries and be there for you."

"The injuries aren't bad," he insisted.

"You can't see them." Her hand tightened around his. "Max, your clothes are sliced everywhere. The material is soaked with blood."

"I've had worse injuries and survived." Much worse.

Willow's eyes widened. "When?"

"We'll talk later." He wouldn't discuss his past in the waiting room of the hospital.

"Mr. Norton? Ms. Knox?" A tall, heavily-muscled man stood in the doorway of an interior hall.

With his hand cradling Willow's, Max started forward. Jesse joined them. "I'm Norton. This is Willow Knox."

"Chance Ford, your nurse. Come with me. Officer Donnelly said there would be three of you in the same room. You okay with that?"

"It's perfect. Thanks for the accommodation."

"Ms. Knox, is that all right with you?"

She nodded.

Donnelly greeted Ford.

"Normally, we only allow one extra person in a room, but Garrick said we should make an exception." He cast a curious glance at Jesse, then turned his attention to Max. "What's the story, Mr. Norton?"

"My girlfriend is in danger. Jesse and I are her bodyguards. I won't leave her alone in the waiting room."

"Truth or ploy to take your girl into the exam room along with your friend?"

"Truth."

After a nod of confirmation from Officer Donnelly, Ford motioned Max and the others into the exam room ahead of him and closed the door. The rookie remained in the hallway. "What happened?"

Max summarized events at Callie's home.

The nurse whistled. "A Molotov cocktail, huh? Where are you hurt?"

"Back, shoulders, legs."

He glanced at Willow. "What about your injuries?"

"None that an ice pack or two can't fix. Max took the brunt of the explosion and protected me in the process."

"Guess that means your visit with the doctor will be faster than Mr. Norton's. Wait in the hall while I help him into a hospital gown." When Jesse escorted Willow out of the room, Ford closed the curtain to block the view through the window.

"Do you know who tossed the cocktail through the window?" Ford asked as he circled around behind Max.

"Never saw the guy." Max should have asked Jesse to keep an eye on the surroundings. Willow could have been seriously injured because of Max's lapse. Never again, he vowed.

A moment later, the nurse said, "Your shirt isn't salvageable. To make things easier, may I cut the material?"

"Go for it. I always have a change of clothes with me."

"Let's see what we're dealing with."

Soon, Max was sporting a blue-and-white hospital gown. He scowled. Nothing like having a cold breeze blowing on his back.

Ford patted the exam table. "Face down, Mr. Norton. Looks like you need stitches in several places. I'll let the doctor know you're ready. After you're taken care of, he'll check Ms. Knox."

"Thanks." Stitches. He stretched out on the exam table, wincing. Wouldn't be the first time for stitches. Given his career, these wouldn't be the last, either.

However, Willow would see the scars on his back from his captivity. Would they bother her? The scars would remind Willow of her time with Armando.

Once Ford covered the lower half of Max's body with a sheet, he shoved the curtain aside and opened the door. "You can come in now. I'll be back with the doctor."

Willow stood at the head of the exam table and wrapped her hand around Max's. "Officer Donnelly said Detectives Cohen and Warner would arrive within the hour."

Max grimaced. "Hope they wait until the doc removes the glass. I'd rather not answer questions in this condition."

"I don't know." Her gaze skimmed over him. "You look good to me."

He chuckled. "Glad you think so."

Jesse groaned. "Please, spare me. There's nowhere to hide from the sap in this room."

"Jealous?"

"Yeah, so give me a break."

"Not sorry, buddy."

The door opened and a man in a white coat with a stethoscope draped around his neck walked into the room followed by Ford. "Mr. Norton, I'm Dr. Reagan. Chance tells me you got up close and personal with a Molotov cocktail. Let me take a look, and we'll decide the best course of action. Would you prefer for your friends to step outside?"

Max shook his head.

"What do you want me to do, Max?" Willow whispered.

He kissed her palm. "Keep your eyes on my face. My body is beat up from previous injuries, Willow."

"You'll tell me about them?"

"If you want to know, I'll tell you. As much as possible, no secrets between us," he murmured.

After examining Max, Reagan said, "You need stitches, Mr. Norton. Four cuts are deep. Do you remember the date of your last tetanus shot?"

"Six months ago. I'm in black ops, Doc. We're vaccinated against everything under the sun."

"Good. That will make things easier. I'll leave you in Chance's capable hands."

The nurse left the room and returned soon with a suture tray. He washed his hands, tugged on rubber gloves, and smiled. "Now the fun begins."

Max rolled his eyes.

Chapter Sixteen

Although Willow kept her gaze locked on Max's face while Chance cleaned and stitched cuts, the stoic man on the exam table showed no sign of the pain he must feel.

How was he able to maintain a neutral expression? She'd be wise to remember his skill at hiding pain was excellent.

Willow thought about his scarred back. He had a story she wouldn't like. However, if Willow wanted a real relationship with him, painful truth was part of the package. He'd listened to her for hours. For six long months, Max had listened any time of the day or night and talked if she needed conversation. He'd shared light, fun stories of training with his team or entertaining incidents during missions without giving classified details.

He'd been careful with her. Willow hated that word, hated more that Max felt as though she needed protecting. Time for his habit of cocooning her in bubble wrap to stop.

The days and nights with that Mexican sadist had almost broken her. Almost. Willow's hand tightened around Max's. She was no longer on the verge of falling apart. Inch by inch, Willow had clawed her way back. She was stronger and would grow stronger still. She'd have to be as strong as steel to tango with Max Norton, the battle-scarred warrior of her dreams. And, oh boy, did she want to dance with him.

He frowned. "Do you need a soft drink or herbal tea? Jesse will go with you."

Willow shook her head. "I'm fine."

"The scars...."

"Don't bother me."

His body visibly relaxed despite Chance's continued work. "Tell me if you need a break. There's no shame in it."

"I can handle it," she insisted, and leaned close to his ear. "I can handle you."

A slow smile curved his mouth. Max kissed the back of her hand.

Her heart did a slow roll in her chest. This man was lethal in more ways than one.

After what seemed like forever, Chance straightened and tugged off his gloves. "Finished, Mr. Norton."

Max snorted. "After the time you spent stitching me back together, call me Max. We're friends now, right?"

The nurse chuckled. "I'd say we're besties." He turned to Willow. "Your turn, Ms. Knox."

The idea of any man she didn't know touching her still made Willow's skin crawl. Chance might be Max's new best friend but he wasn't hers. "I don't need anything."

Max raised an eyebrow. "You welshing on our deal?"

How could she back out gracefully? Great. She'd boxed herself in. Willow sighed. "Fine. Let's do this, Chance." At least Max was with her. Even injured, he was dangerous.

"I'll get the doctor."

She grimaced. She'd seen too many doctors over the past six months. This exam was unnecessary. A pain reliever or two, and she'd be golden.

However, Willow understood this was another way of Max showing his care. What woman in her right mind would reject him? Not her. Max said they were dating. She had the right to take care of him, too.

The door opened, and Dr. Reagan returned. "Your turn, Ms. Knox."

It took every ounce of courage she had to allow the doctor to poke and prod, and answer a million questions. Five minutes in, Willow's breathing accelerated and her skin grew clammy.

The doctor lifted his hand from her arm. "What's wrong?"

Max's hand tightened around hers. "Look at me, Willow."

Her gaze locked on his.

"Breathe with me." He counted to four. "Hold for four, exhale with me." Several times, he repeated the process, the breath count lasting longer for each round until she drew in a full breath. "Better?"

A nod. "Thanks."

"You have panic attacks?" the doctor asked.

A side effect of her time with Armando. "It's recent."

"Are you receiving treatment?"

"Counseling. No medication."

"What caused the onset of the attacks?"

"It's not relevant here." She refused to go through her story with a doctor and a nurse she'd never see again. Recounting those events always made Willow feel dirty. She knew what happened wasn't her fault. Didn't change her reactions.

Although he appeared dissatisfied, Dr. Reagan gave a curt nod and continued with his examination. This time, however, he paid close attention to how she reacted to his touch.

Fifteen minutes later, he scooted his rolling chair away from Willow and stood. "Clean bill of health. Use ice packs and over-the-counter pain reliever for aches. If you need help with the panic attacks while you're in town, come back to the hospital."

"I won't need help, but thanks."

"Offer is always open." He shook their hands. "Chance will take care of the final paperwork and prescriptions for antibiotics and pain for Mr. Norton, then you're free to go. Come back if either of you begin to feel worse."

"Thanks, Doc," Max said.

With a wave, Dr. Reagan left the room followed by Chance.

On the heels of their exit, a brisk knock sounded on the door. Detectives Cohen and Warner strode in.

Warner's lips curled. "Nice look for you, Norton. Trying out for the role of Frankenstein in a movie?"

"Ha ha. Don't quit your day job, Warner. After forty stitches, I'm not in the mood for your twisted sense of humor."

Cohen held up his hand to forestall a comeback by his partner. "Fair enough. Do you feel up to answering a few questions about what happened tonight?"

"Yeah, fine," Max said. "Let's get on with it, all right? My bed is calling me."

The detectives peppered Willow, Max, and Jesse with questions, taking them through the events at Callie's home over and over until they were satisfied.

Too little information. Events had seemed to unfold in slow motion at Callie's. In reality, less than two minutes passed from the time the firebomb was thrown through the window and when Max had carried Willow from the house.

How had he accomplished that? Max had been injured and losing blood. She knew firsthand how quickly blood loss could weaken and debilitate.

"So much for you two being hot-shot cops," Warner muttered. "You didn't see squat. Guess you've been out of the game for too long to be of help to real professionals."

"You want us to speculate?" Jesse folded his arms across his chest. "We've got theories. Didn't think you wanted us to muddy the water with speculations, seeing as how you're the ace detectives."

"You're right. We don't care about your theories. We just want facts. No bias. Nothing but pure, unadulterated facts." Cohen slid his notebook into his pocket. "Stop by the station tomorrow afternoon to sign your statements."

"We'll be there," Max said. "Callie and Jason all right?"

"You got the worst of the injuries. The Westovers have minor smoke inhalation and cuts from flying glass. We took their statements before they left the hospital. Ms. Westover is staying with her brother."

"How bad is the damage to her home?" Willow couldn't imagine the devastation the other woman must feel. First, she lost the man she loved, and now she faced the prospect of rebuilding. Callie's whole future had changed in a few short hours.

"Most of the house is intact. Smoke damage throughout. The living room and the first bedroom off the hall will have to be rebuilt."

"If the fire department hadn't arrived as fast as they did, the house would be a total loss," Warner said. "As it is, Ms. Westover is looking at months before she'll be able to return to her home. Trouble seems to follow in your wake, Norton. How did trouble follow you to the Westover house?"

"Good question," Jesse said. "We'll let you know when we have the answer."

Willow frowned. That was an excellent question. If someone followed them from the inn to the Royal Hotel and to Callie's, Jesse and Max would have noticed. She shivered. Maybe the arsonist had already been near Callie's and seen them go into the house.

Warner snorted. "Yeah, you do that. I'll wait by the phone for your call. Oh, wait. Don't bother." He sneered. "With your track record, I'm sure we'll see you soon anyway."

The detectives left the room.

"How much trouble will I be in if I punch Warner?" Jesse asked, tone mild.

"Forget it," Max said. "I'm not in the mood to post bail for you."

"Ouch, man. That hurts."

Chance appeared at the door. "Ready to get out of here?"

"More than." Max and Willow accepted discharge their paperwork. Max handed his prescriptions to Jesse.

"Fill the prescriptions, and take all the medicine," the nurse said. "You don't want to risk an infection."

Max held up a hand. "Save the speech, Chance. Jesse is a paramedic. He'll stay on my case."

"Excellent. Need scrubs, Max?"

"I'll be back in a minute with his clothes." Jesse left the room.

"Do you need anything else?" Chance asked.

"Nope." Max held out his hand. "Thanks, my friend. I appreciate the help."

"No problem. I'll return soon. Take it easy for a few days. I don't know what you do for a living. I'm guessing military or cop, so I know you're tough. However, you'll feel rough for a few days, and things will be worse before they improve. Give yourself a break."

Max chuckled. "You're a ray of sunshine."

"That's what all my patients say." And then he was gone.

After Jesse returned, Willow stood on the other side of the curtain while the medic helped Max into fresh clothes. When they finished, Max was on his feet, beads of sweat on his pale face. She longed to offer help or sympathy, and knew either wouldn't be welcome. Instead, she wrapped her hand around his without a word and started walking.

Must have been the right move because Max relaxed and Jesse gave her a nod of approval. "Do we need to stop by the pharmacy?"

"No." Jesse opened the door. Officer Donnelly was gone, probably back on patrol. "I have what Max needs in my mike bag."

"You do?"

"Fortress medics are well stocked. With our job, we're prone to injuries in the field. We can't show up at a hospital or doctor's office with knife or gunshot wounds and ask for treatment in a foreign country." He winked at her. "Tips off the enemy. I treat the team's injuries. If I need a consult with a physician, I call one of the Fortress doctors for advice."

Good to know Max and his teammates had immediate medical care when they were on missions.

In the SUV, Max stretched out face down on the backseat with a groan.

Jesse drove from the parking lot and headed toward the inn.

"What's the next step?" She twisted in her seat to look at Max.

"Sleep. We'll visit Enright's home tomorrow." He sighed. "I need to call Brody and the boss."

Jesse gave a bark of laughter. "Sounds like a boy band."

Max's lips curved. "Shut up and call Brody."

Willow shook her head, amused at their verbal sparring. A testament to their close relationship.

Less than a minute later, Max and Jesse's team leader answered their call. "Better be good," he growled. "Sage is sleeping. If your call wakes her, you'll pay."

"Sorry, Brody. You're on speaker with Max and Willow. Go to another room. Our update will take a few minutes."

"Hold." Over the car's speakers, they heard a soft murmur, a door closing, then, "Go."

Jesse gave a summary of the past few hours, ending with, "Once again, we're on the bad list of the Tucker's Gap police detectives."

"Great. That means they're unlikely to cooperate with us. No sugar coating, Jesse. How bad are Max's injuries?"

"Hey," Max said. "I'm right here, and I can speak for myself."

"Ha. You downplay everything. You could be bleeding to death and would still tell me it's just a scratch. Jesse?"

"Forty stitches in his back and shoulder. He took the brunt of the explosion while he protected Willow."

"No chance this is a random attack."

"None," the medic agreed.

"What about you, Willow? Are you injured?"

"Bumps and bruises. The doctor prescribed ice packs and over-the-counter pain medicine for me. I told Max I didn't need to see a doctor but he insisted."

"Don't give him grief. He's taking excellent care of you. Sage and Poppy will be glad to hear you're okay. Max?"

"Yeah?"

"The rest of the team will arrive at the inn around noon. We'd arrive earlier but Sage pulled an eighteen-hour day to finish her recording. The three of you have a chance to rest. Take advantage of it. Things will heat up when we start investigating in earnest. Enright's killer will fight back. He already fired a warning shot with the firebomb. Next time, he'll come at us harder. When we arrive, we'll decide on a plan of attack and get to work."

"Copy that."

Jesse ended the call to Brody and placed a second one to their boss who answered on the first ring, sounding more alert than Brody.

"Yeah, Maddox. Talk to me."

Between them, Jesse and Max updated Mr. Maddox. He asked several questions and made them go through events again. "What do you need from us?"

"Tracking jewelry for Willow along with a sat phone," Max said.

"Done. I'll have them delivered by noon. Anything else?"

"Check Willow's house."

She straightened. Check her house? Willow fisted her hands. Of course. She should have thought of that herself. Hartman was only a few hours from Tucker's gap. Wouldn't take someone with an ugly purpose long to drive there and search her house. But why bother? She was within easy reach here.

Cold chills surged up her spine. Unless an intruder had a different purpose. What if he left something behind? Assuming the phantom intruder was the same man who threw the bomb into Callie's house, how difficult would it be for him to create an explosive device set to explode when she returned home?

Anyone with computer skills would be able to find the information on the Internet. Still, wouldn't Fortress have known if someone slipped into her home? "I have a Fortress alarm system. Wouldn't one of your techs be notified if someone broke in?"

"No system is foolproof," Maddox said. "However, I doubt you've had a breach. We'll check anyway to eliminate the possibility someone searched the place or left behind something harmful or incriminating."

"Incriminating?" She hadn't considered that.

"If the bomber can't reach you because of the team protecting you, his next best alternative would be to implicate you in the murder. After an anonymous phone call or email to the Tucker's Gap detectives, you're no longer a threat."

Willow clenched the edge of her seat. This was crazy. She wasn't a threat to anyone. Apparently, Enright's killer might believe otherwise.

"Anything else we can do, Max?" Maddox asked.

"No, sir."

"If you think of something, ask. You'll get it."

"Thanks."

"Jesse?"

"Sir?"

"No injuries for you?"

"Nope. I was the furthest from the blast. Small bottle used for the Molotov cocktail."

"Good. All of you rest. I want an update in six hours." Then he was gone.

Willow blew out a breath. "Your boss is an intense, intimidating man."

"You don't know the half of it," Max muttered. "I've seen him make the toughest black ops soldiers I've ever met cry like a baby."

"Underneath that tough exterior, though, is a man who would die for any one of his people, especially his wife and daughter." Jesse reached over and squeezed her shoulder. "He's someone you want in your corner or at your back in a fight."

She had to give the man credit for organizing her rescue in Mexico. Her father said no one else could have made the arrangements and set up everything necessary to get her away from Armando as fast as Brent Maddox.

Also, when the team had transported her back to Texas for treatment by their doctor, Maddox and Max ran interference to give her a few days to recover before she talked to her father and brothers. Maddox also provided months of counseling free of charge.

Willow respected him for the way he cared about his employees. Every time Max and his teammates returned from missions with injuries, Maddox pulled out all the stops to ensure his people had the treatment they needed to fully recover.

The three of them fell silent as Jesse drove the SUV out of Tucker's Gap. By the way the medic frequently checked the mirrors, he was watching for a tail.

Willow twisted in her seat to stare out the back window. Although she noticed a few cars in the distance, none appeared to be aggressively pursuing them.

"Relax," Jesse murmured. "No one's on our six."

She glanced at Max. He was sound asleep. How was that possible? Perhaps he would teach her the enviable skill.

Willow turned to Jesse. "You're sure Max will recover without any ill effects?"

"Positive. Max will be as good as new in a couple of weeks. He was truthful when he said he'd had worse injuries. This is nothing compared to the recovery he went through two years ago."

Two years. Was that when Max's back had been scarred? "Can he tell me what happened?"

"Most of it." A quick glance. "He has to be ready to tell you, Willow."

"In other words, don't push?"

"He'll withdraw if you do. Sharing the information has to be his choice."

"I understand." In the months since she'd left Mexico, too many people to count had tried to pry into her experiences with Armando. Some were genuinely concerned about her health and wellbeing. Others were nosy and wanted titillating details to share with their friends or the news media. All the inquiries were unwelcome.

She'd made herself talk to Marcus Lang, her counselor. To her father and brothers, she gave enough details for them to get the gist of what happened without being explicit. Too much detail was uncomfortable for her and them. They loved her. Because they did, she felt a deep-seated need to protect them from the worst parts of her experience.

Funny, her wanting to protect her family from too much knowledge. The men were soldiers and used to seeing all manner of violence and the aftermath. However, they had worked as a unit to protect her as she grew up. Ironic that now she worked hard to protect them.

The one person she'd been brutally honest with other than the counselor was Max. He'd never pushed, always listened without comment, and accepted without judgment.

She and Jesse lapsed into silence for the rest of the drive to the inn. When the medic parked the SUV, Max stirred.

"Any problems?" he asked.

"Nope." Jesse exited the vehicle and opened Max's door. "Come on, old man."

Max waved him off. "I've got it. Help Willow."

After rolling his eyes, the medic left Max to get himself from the vehicle and circled to open Willow's door.

"Stubborn, much?" she murmured.

"You don't know the half of it."

"I heard that," Max snapped.

"Truth hurts." Jesse closed the door and nudged Willow toward the sidewalk.

She met Max at the front of the SUV and walked inside the lobby. Willow didn't mention him moving slower than normal.

The desk clerk glanced up from his book when they walked in and smiled. "Welcome back. Need anything?"

Max rested his hand against Willow's lower back. "Herbal tea for Willow. Thanks, Jerry."

She smiled. Brody was right. Max was taking excellent care of her.

"I'll bring it to your suite," Jerry promised. "What flavor is your favorite, Ms. Knox?"

"Blueberry. If you don't have that one, surprise me. I've yet to taste an herbal tea I don't like."

"I'll see what I can find. What would you gentlemen like?"

"Water for both," Jesse said.

"Yes, sir. I'll deliver your drinks soon."

After they climbed the stairs to their suite, Jesse entered the room first while Max and Willow stood in the hall. A moment later, the medic returned. "Clear," he murmured and stood back for them to enter.

Max nudged Willow toward her room. "Why don't you get ready for bed? Your tea should be here by the time you finish."

Excellent idea. She stood on her tiptoes and brushed her mouth over his before walking into her room and shutting the door.

While Willow washed her face, she considered what she should wear to sleep in. She didn't want to be far from Max in case he needed something overnight. That meant sleeping in the living room on the couch or one of the recliners.

Ten minutes later, she walked into the living room and stared at the tray sitting on the coffee table. The front desk clerk had brought up a tray with their drinks, and several different snacks. Fruit, muffins, chips, cookies, and protein bars.

Max gave Willow a to-go cup. "Jerry found blueberry tea for you. He said he'll be on duty the rest of the night and will be happy to bring up something else."

"Sweet kid, and amazing customer service. I wish I'd known about this place earlier. I would have stayed here instead of the Royal Hotel." She sipped the hot drink, eyeing Max over the rim of the cup. "How do you feel?"

"I'll be better in a few minutes. I just swallowed the meds Jesse shoved into my hand."

Guess that was as close he'd get to admitting he was in pain. "Don't want you to be cranky."

Jesse chuckled.

Max scowled. "I'm never cranky."

That brought outright laughter from the medic. "I'm not touching that one."

"No one asked your opinion." He slanted a look at Willow. "Do you need a snack before you sleep?"

She shook her head and lifted her cup. "This is all I want. You should lay down, Max. Where are you sleeping?"

He gestured to the couch.

Since she'd waste her breath arguing that he'd be more comfortable in a bed, Willow returned to her room and grabbed two blankets and a pillow to join him in the living room.

When she returned, Willow laid one blanket and the pillow at the foot of the couch, and chose the closest recliner for herself. She picked up her tea, sat down, and spread the blanket over her legs.

Max stared at her, his brow furrowed. "Aren't you going to bed?"

"I'm sleeping here."

He glanced at Jesse who held up his hand.

"Don't look at me, buddy. She's your girlfriend. I say if she wants to stay with you, let her."

Max sighed. "Are you sure, baby? You'd be more comfortable on a bed."

"I want to stay. Let me."

A small smile curved his mouth. "All right."

"Sleep, both of you." Jesse lowered the lights and took up a position near the balcony doors. "I've got the watch, Max."

"Wake me in three hours." Max stretched out on his stomach.

"Forget it. You need the rest to heal. I'll catch a nap later."

As Willow sipped her tea, she watched over Max. When she finished her drink, she reclined her chair and dropped into sleep.

Chapter Seventeen

The sun's rays caressed Max's face, warming his skin and bringing a sense of deep contentment. Until he moved. He shifted and grimaced. Stiff? Check. Sore? Double check. Pain from his healing cuts? Annoying but tolerable. Might be a different story when he stood.

A pain capsule washed down with a large cup of coffee was in his near future. Caffeine for the win today. No doubt Jesse would ply him with meds first thing to ensure Max could function, a priority with Willow's safety at stake.

He glanced at the recliner where Willow still slept. Tenderness filled him. The promise of what grew between them gave him hope for the future.

He admired Willow's courage and strength, and she had integrity in spades. Max loved her grit. To battle her way back took teeth-gritting determination and a never-give-up attitude.

None of the women he'd dated had been as concerned when Max was injured on the job. Willow sleeping in a recliner in case Max needed her was extraordinary. These injuries were minor compared to the ones from his undercover assignment with the cult. Memories of long weeks of infection and recovery were still fresh.

Jesse turned away from the balcony. "How do you feel, Max?" he murmured.

"Decent."

The medic snorted and retrieved his mike bag. "You're a master of understatement." He shoved two packets into Max's hand along with a bottle of water. "One capsule from each. No whining. You don't want to worry your woman."

"Yeah, yeah. It's not an understatement, just a comparison to earlier injuries." Max gave his friend attitude on principle. Couldn't make his job too easy, after all.

He swung his feet to the floor, gritting his teeth as the stitched wounds tugged and ached with movement. Yeah, this would be a fun day. He swallowed the meds without further argument and inclined his head toward Willow. "She do okay overnight?"

Max would have awakened if Willow was distressed but didn't know if she stayed awake watching over him. Blood loss and staying awake for more than 48 hours would do that to a man.

"Once you were asleep, she dropped off herself. Hasn't moved except to look over at you every half hour or so to make sure you're all right. She's been sleeping off and on for four hours. I didn't have the heart to tell her you're as tough as old shoe leather and hard to keep down even when you should rest."

He hoped Willow would be ready to hit the ground running when his team arrived. Having Sage and Poppy nearby would be good for her. The three women were a strong unit who supported each other through the tough and the easy.

"Want a shower?" Jesse asked him.

"Oh, yeah." Scraping off sweat, the scent of gasoline, and streaks of blood Chance missed? A definite priority when Max's goal was to win Willow's heart, not chase her off.

"Come on." Jesse grabbed his mike bag and headed for the second bedroom. "I have waterproof bandages."

Five minutes later, Max stepped into the shower, groaning as the hot water sluiced over him. Man, the spray felt good.

Mindful of his short time clock with the bandages, he soaped up and rinsed off. After toweling dry, Max tugged on his jeans, socks, and running shoes and returned to the living room. Willow was no longer in the chair.

His muscles loosened. Good. He'd rather hold off on an explanation about his back for the moment. He stepped out of the bedroom with a black t-shirt in hand. "Where's Willow?"

Jesse inclined his head toward her bedroom and sipped his coffee. "Hungry?"

"Starving."

A chuckle. "Good sign." He motioned toward the breakfast bar. "Jerry brought up breakfast before he went off shift."

The medic poured coffee into a to-go cup for Max and handed it to him. "Sip this while I check your stitches and replace the bandages."

"Thanks, Jesse."

"For putting up with attitude from you?"

He grinned. "For that, your medical expertise, and your tolerance of grumpy operatives."

"Of which, you are chief."

"Can't argue."

Max had to hand it to his friend. Jesse was fast and efficient. In less than two minutes, the waterproof bandages had been replaced with regular ones.

"Planning to tell Willow about your back?" Jesse asked as he tossed the medical detritus into the trash.

"Yeah. Not looking forward to it." He shrugged into his shirt.

"I bet. Soon, my friend. She's asking questions."

"Figured." How could she not be curious? Although she kept her gaze on his face throughout his treatment in the ER, Willow couldn't help but see some of the damage from the whip and knife. Maddox had offered more than once to set up an appointment with a plastic surgeon for Max. He'd never wanted to take time away from his team for the recovery.

Perhaps Max should consider the idea, especially if the scars upset Willow. "When we have some time alone, I'll talk to her."

A pointed look. "As soon as the team arrives with the Reynolds sisters, your time for a heart-to-heart talk will be over."

Max almost hoped his friends would arrive fast enough to forestall the discussion. He rubbed his jaw. Nothing like realizing you had a small pocket of cowardice hiding under all the first-responder instincts to confront trouble head on instead of running the other way.

Willow's door opened and she stepped into the living room. Her face lit up when she saw Max. "How are you?"

"Better."

"That's a relative term. You have to be better than last night."

Max chuckled. "Caught me."

"Jesse, what's your assessment of Max's condition?"

The medic winked. "Better."

"Both of you are hopeless." She set her crossbody bag on the coffee table and approached Max. Standing on her tiptoes, Willow brushed her mouth over his.

Pleasure flooded him because of the kiss and her initiating the contact. "What's this? No hug?"

"I don't want to hurt you."

"There's pain, and there's pain with a capital P. A little pinch from your hug is well worth it." He reeled her in gently for the hug he craved. A hug from Willow soothed his rough edges and made him temporarily forget the discomfort. "Are you hungry?"

"A little."

He took her hand and headed toward the breakfast bar. "If this doesn't appeal to you, we'll go out and get what you want."

Willow's eyes widened when she saw the spread of food laid out. "There's enough food here to feed an army."

Jesse handed Willow a to-go cup. "Hardly. Get what you want. Max and I will polish off the rest."

"Seriously?"

He shrugged. "We're growing boys."

She gave Max and Jesse a skeptical look but filled her plate and sat down to eat.

After they finished eating, Max glanced at his watch. An hour, maybe less before the rest of the team arrived. Sage and Poppy wouldn't wait as long as Brody and Logan thought before they wanted to head this way.

Jesse stacked the empty dishes and plates on the serving cart. "I'm taking a nap and a shower." He speared Max with a pointed look.

He gave a slight nod. Nothing like receiving a directive from the team medic. "I've got the watch."

Jesse walked into the second bedroom and closed the door.

Max held out his hand to Willow. "We need to talk."

Her eyebrows rose. "I won't like this conversation, am I?"

He led her to the couch and sat beside her. "The information will answer some questions. You asked me about the scars. Do you still want to know what happened?"

"Yes." No hesitation in her response. "If you're not ready, we'll table the discussion until you are. I can wait."

He was tempted to take her up on the offered delay. Coward's way out, he reminded himself. Not his character or style. She deserved the truth. Max shook his head. "It's time you knew some of what I went through." Max refused to subject her to the gory details.

Willow wrapped her arms around his waist and rest her head in the space between his shoulder and neck.

When she said nothing, Max glanced down at her. It struck him then that Willow knew he dreaded the conversation, and she'd positioned herself to hear him and offer comfort without staring him in the face.

He tightened his hold on the woman in his arms. Her kindness touched him as nothing else had and made him fall deeper in love with her.

Max nuzzled the top of her head. Yeah, he was falling in love with this extraordinary woman. If he didn't want his heart shattered into a million tiny pieces, he had to win her heart and put a ring on her finger. If she'd have him. That was the catch. She could do better than Max Norton.

He steeled himself and began the ugly story. "Two years ago, a frantic mother contacted Brent and asked for his help in finding her daughter. The girl had been missing for three months. The police detectives had placed the case on the back burner."

She tensed in his arms. "Why would they do that? She was someone's daughter."

"The case went cold. The detectives kept the case active but other cases had to take priority. It's reality in law enforcement. You work hard and fast to follow leads but the mother didn't do the detectives any favors."

"What do you mean?"

"She waited three weeks before reporting her daughter's disappearance. The girl was eighteen years old and free to leave home at any time."

"Oh, man. Did she suspect foul play?"

He shook his head. "According to the mother, her daughter had become interested in a man."

Willow kissed the side of his neck. "An all too familiar story."

"I can't tell you the girl's name, so let's call her Jane. Since Jane's boyfriend was involved in what the mother thought was a new-age group traveling around Texas, Maddox asked my team to find out if Jane joined the group or if she fell victim to a crime."

She frowned. "How hard is it to hide a body?"

"Bodies have a way of showing up."

Willow remained silent a moment. "Do you know how to make a body disappear?"

"Sure you want an answer to that question?"

"Yes."

"If Armando escapes custody and I find him first, the authorities will never locate his body."

She squeezed his middle briefly. "Can you tell me the name of the group this girl joined?"

"New Dawn. Took two weeks to find them. We tracked them to a very remote area in the Texas panhandle. Lots of nothing out there. The guy's name was Malcolm. No last name. He went around Texas and the surrounding states touting his brand of religion. Typical cult stuff. Everybody except the leader goes out and begs for money to deposit into the general fund which only Malcolm controlled. Share and share alike, he claimed but he kept sole control of the fund along with his two main henchmen."

"I heard news stories about New Dawn. Someone inside the group blew the whistle on the leader's practice of sleeping with all the women in his flock."

"The problem wasn't that he had his own harem. Malcolm slept with every female from age thirteen and up."

"You turned him in, didn't you?"

"Made me sick to watch the girls go into his home at night and not come out until the next morning, most of them beaten and bruised."

"How were you injured?"

"Took a day for the local cops to organize a raid with the state police. A few hours before the scheduled raid, Jane was to be Malcolm's latest guest. I tried to persuade her to leave the compound."

"She didn't listen?"

"Jane said sharing Malcolm's bed was a great honor, and the boyfriend who claimed to be desperately in love with her would beat her if she refused."

"She told Malcolm?"

"Yep. Four enforcers grabbed me and took me to the punishment room."

"What caused the scars?"

"A whip and knife."

"Max." Her voice broke. Warm liquid splashed on his neck.

"Don't, Willow. It's in the past."

"Why would he do that to you?"

"Malcolm was bloated with his own power. Most cult leaders believe they're untouchable and their followers should worship them. Malcolm believed he had the right to determine whether a follower lived or died."

"He planned to kill you?"

"If he had the chance. He didn't."

"Is he still alive?"

He looked down at her. "No."

"Good. I hope you or one of your teammates took him out." She wiped tears from her checks. "What happened to Jane?"

"My teammates got her out. She wasn't happy."

Her eyes narrowed. "Why didn't they help you?"

"They did, but whips and knives don't take long to do a lot of damage. My team infiltrated the compound but had to fight off enforcers to reach me."

"How long did they have you?"

"Thirty minutes." A lifetime when you're hanging by the wrists, unable to protect yourself effectively from four angry men determined to break or kill you. Two minutes into the punishment, Max knew the intent was for him to die, especially when he killed an enforcer who made the mistake of getting too close.

"I'm so sorry, Max." Willow tightened her hold around his waist.

Unable to stop himself, Max cupped her chin, tipped her face up to his, and kissed her. No light, butterfly kisses this time. He didn't have it in him. To distract her and himself from the brutal past, he took her mouth in a fierce, hot kiss designed to make them both forget the pain and focus on a possible future between them.

The taste of her sweet mouth was addicting, an addiction he had no intention of giving up. How he'd survived 37 years without Willow was a mystery.

Her soft moan and his slip in control yanked Max back to reality. If he pushed too far too fast, he'd lose her. Willow was too important to risk for a few moments of pleasure. He wanted more, so much more from this woman. He wanted a lifetime.

Max slowed their kiss from hot and fierce to gentle brushes of his lips against hers until he finally eased away. Her beautiful mouth was red and swollen, her breathing elevated, and her cheeks flushed. Willow was stunning. "I'm sorry," he murmured.

She blinked. "You better not be apologizing for kissing me."

"I didn't mean for the kiss to get out of hand."

"I liked it. Feel free to repeat the experience any time."

He chuckled. "Yes, ma'am."

A knock sounded on the door.

Max stood and pulled Willow to her feet. "Go into the bedroom. Don't come out until I tell you it's safe."

He palmed his weapon and headed for the door. Once Willow was inside her room, he checked the peephole. Max holstered his Sig. "It's safe, Willow." He unlocked the door to admit the rest of his team, Brody's wife, and her sister.

"Where is she?" Sage demanded as she pushed past Max into the suite. "Willow?" she called.

"Here." Willow hurried into the living room to join Max and the others who crowded into the space.

Sage looked into her face, and gasped. "Willow!"

Silence fell on the group. Varying degrees of anger appeared on their faces. Brody walked to Willow and tipped her chin up with his forefinger, then glared at Max. "You have five seconds to explain before I punch your lights out."

Chapter Eighteen

Willow glanced from one person to another, puzzled at the fury that almost sizzled in the atmosphere. All of the ire was aimed squarely at Max. What was wrong with the lot of them? They hadn't said more than a few words since they arrived.

Logan, one of Max's teammates, folded his arms across his chest. "Better be good, Max, or you'll be out of commission for several days."

A threat? Seriously? Willow felt as though she'd walked into an alternate universe. This was nuts.

Sawyer, the last member of the team, remained silent but glowered at Max as he inched closer with his hands fisted.

All right. Enough. This was ridiculous. Had they lost their minds? "Hey," Willow snapped. "Look at me. What's wrong with you? You drove up here to help Max but now you're turning on him? I don't understand what's happening."

"Simple." Sage's sister, Poppy, punched Max in the arm. Based on his flinch, Poppy hadn't pulled her punch. Worse, she'd punched the shoulder that sported new stitches. "Max made you cry. He has to pay for that."

She stared. "Are you insane?"

"He doesn't have the right to hurt you, Willow," Sage said. "No one does. We won't let him or anyone else hurt you again."

"First, I can take care of myself. I'm not totally helpless. Max and his teammates have been training with me to add to the skills I learned from Dad and my brothers. Second, Max didn't hurt me. He's never been anything but kind and protective of me since the moment I first saw him."

"Dial it back, Willow," Max murmured.

"I won't. This is outrageous. Their reaction makes me wonder how well your friends really know you."

"He made you cry," Poppy said. "No matter whether it was intentional or not, the fact that he brought you to tears isn't acceptable."

"I cried because he told me what caused the scars on his back and because I have some of the same marks on mine." Her voice thickened. "I know exactly how much pain he was in while he healed, and my back doesn't look anywhere near as bad as his. My heart broke knowing how much he suffered trying to save an ungrateful girl. If not for his teammates, Max would have died doing his job. He tried to spare that girl unnecessary pain and suffering. She blew him off and threw him to the wolves as thanks." Willow raised her chin. "He made up for my tears in spades."

"Yeah?" Brody's eyes narrowed. "How?"

She smiled. "He kissed the sadness right out of me." Willow sounded smug. She felt smug and maybe a little giddy, too.

More stunned silence followed that announcement, then Brody moved close enough to poke a finger in Max's chest. "You get a pass. For now."

"Yeah, yeah. I understand." He wrapped his arm around Willow's shoulders, drawing her close to his side. "If I hurt her, I'll pay."

"In spades." Sawyer shrugged. "She's ours now. We protect our own, even from one of our own if necessary. If you mess up, Jesse or I will step up to show Willow how a real man treats a woman."

A snort from Max. "Not happening. Get your own woman."

The door to the second bedroom opened. Jesse came to an abrupt halt seeing the group gathered near the door. "What happened?"

"A misunderstanding." Brody urged Sage toward the couch. "Got a plan of action, Max?"

"Started on it but Jesse and I didn't have time to nail down details."

Willow stared. That was news to her. When had Max and Jesse put the bare bones of a plan together?

"You can tell us what you have in a minute." Brody drew a brown envelope from his back pocket and gave it to Max. "Special delivery from Brent and Zane."

"Excellent." He led Willow to the couch to sit beside Sage. Max ripped open the envelope and pulled out a phone. After turning it on, he checked the contact list, then handed the phone to Willow. "Your satellite phone. The number is the same as your current cell number, and your account has been shifted to Fortress."

Poppy folded her arms. "What if you and Willow break up?"

The possibility sent a sharp stab of pain in Willow's heart. Every muscle in her body tightened.

"We won't," Max said.

"But if you do?"

"Willow will give back the phone, and Zane will reactivate the account with her current carrier." His gaze locked with Willow's. "She won't be giving back the phone."

She breathed easier. That sounded encouraging. At least he wasn't looking for a short-term relationship. She was falling in love with this man, a quandary if he didn't feel the same.

Willow's mouth curved. Perhaps she should fall back on the tactic her grandmother had used with her grandfather. A lined piece of paper with boxes for her grandfather to mark if he loved Grandma or not. Old school but it took the guesswork out of her problem.

For her to admit she was falling in love with Max only six months after being victimized by human traffickers was a miracle and a major indication of her recovery progress. Willow covered Max's hand with hers.

After pressing a kiss to her palm, Max poured the rest of the envelope's contents onto the coffee table.

Jewelry? Willow picked up one of the clear plastic bags and peered at the contents. Daisy earrings. Sweet. This had to be GPS jewelry like Sage and Poppy wore. "Thank you, Max."

"You'll wear the pieces?"

"Of course. They're beautiful, and I know about the GPS chips embedded in the pieces. Sage and Poppy told me about them."

"You don't mind that I'll be able to track you wherever you go?"

"Why would I? I don't have anything to hide, and my work isn't a national security issue. I'm sure Zane is able to track my phone, too. Besides, if I'm separated from my phone, hopefully I'll still be wearing at least one piece of this jewelry so you can track me." Her worst nightmare was being kidnapped again. No, she didn't mind the extra sense of protection.

Even if Max and his teammates were out of the country, someone at Fortress would find her and send a rescue team. A fair trade for what some people would see as an invasion of privacy. She called it a safety net and welcomed the security. Never again did she want to be spirited away with no hope of rescue. She had a lot to live for, starting with the man watching her.

How many other women could claim that their boyfriends or husbands paid such close attention to them? Rather than feeling hemmed in, Willow felt protected and maybe loved by one of the most important people in her life.

One by one, she donned every piece of jewelry until she was down to the watch. "This too?" she asked Max.

"Please." He lightly tapped one of the buttons on the side. "If you press this button, you'll alert Fortress that you're in trouble, and they'll activate the tracker and send a team. It's an emergency beacon." He tapped the second button. "Push this button when it's safe, and you'll be able to talk to Zane or someone else manning the comm station. Whoever answers the phone will be able to help you."

More safety and protection from afar. She removed the watch already on her wrist.

Max helped her fasten the Fortress watch and turned to Brody. "Thanks for being the delivery boy."

"Happy to oblige. What plan did you and Jesse devise for the investigation?"

Before Max could respond, Willow's new phone rang. She glanced at the readout. Recognition had her eyebrows rising. What did he want? Couldn't be good. Was this call to tell Willow he wanted a different researcher?

"Who is it?" Max asked.

"Oliver Enright."

"Answer on speaker. Let's find out what frame of mind Enright is in."

She hoped Graham's father didn't say anything to embarrass her or himself. Would Oliver blame her for Graham's death? Willow swiped the screen and tapped the speaker button. "This is Willow."

"Willow, this is Oliver Enright. I need to see you at my home right away." The older man's words were clipped. He sounded like what he was, a man in command of himself and everyone in his wide circle of influence.

"Before we get to that, I just want to say how sorry I am about Graham's death, Mr. Enright."

"So am I, my dear. How soon will you arrive?"

Her brows knitted. Oliver didn't sound broken up about Graham's death. In fact, he sounded as though he had taken it in stride and already moved on.

Max glanced at his watch and held up two fingers to indicate she could be at his home in two hours.

"The earliest I can be at your house is three o'clock."

"That's two hours from now. Are you sure you can't be here sooner?" He sounded dismayed.

"Yes, sir. I'm involved in a meeting at the moment. I won't be free until two at the earliest, and my hotel is an hour from your home." That gave them two hours to discuss options and come up with a plan.

"That's quite inconvenient." Enright sighed. "I suppose three o'clock will have to do. Bring your computer and all your research. Don't be late." He ended the call.

Willow slid the phone into her pocket. "That was a surprise. I didn't think he would want to see or talk to me again."

"It is curious," Max agreed. "Any idea what he wants?"

"I'm afraid he wants to terminate his contract with Ballinger. But I don't have my computer. If he wants to see my work to date, I can't show it to him."

"You said you can access your work from the cloud. We'll take my laptop, and you can email a copy of your work to Enright if he wants to terminate the contract with Ballinger or switch to another researcher."

Relief flooded her. "That would be perfect. Thanks, Max."

"Since that's settled, can we get back to the plan we haven't heard yet?" Brody walked to the small kitchenette and returned with a bottle of water he handed to Sage. "While you and Willow visit with Enright, we'll get started on the research here."

"We need help with background on the list of major players we've compiled to date. I'm sure we'll add more names as we move further into the investigation. Also, I haven't checked in with Zane yet but he's hunting for traffic cam footage that shows the killer's face."

Poppy grabbed a pad of paper from the coffee table and a pen. "We can help with all of that. Give us the list of people you've compiled so far, and we'll get started while you're gone."

Max reeled off a string of names, including Phillip, the restaurant host.

"Why are you investigating Phillip?" Willow asked. "He's just a college kid trying to earn enough money to pay for school. You know he's not a killer."

"I talked to him for two or three minutes, not long enough to know anything except what he wanted me to know. Phillip might not be the killer, but he could have hired one."

"A poor college kid?" Skeptical, she shook her head. "I don't believe that for a minute. You're going down the wrong path, Max. Use your research time on someone else."

"What do you really know about him? You met him a few days ago and passed the time in surface conversation for a few minutes at a time. Perhaps he had something against Graham Enright long before you arrived in Tucker's Gap, and his feelings boiled over. He might have money stashed away in an offshore account or in a trust fund that he used to hire Orioles Cap."

"Oh, come on. What about the drugged drink? Do you believe he drugged me, too?"

"It's easy enough to score Rohypnol on the street. All he had to do was meet the killer somewhere away from the hotel, hand the drug to him, and tell him when to strike. Phillip could have been the one to lure Enright to the hotel for the date with you."

"No." Willow frowned, sick at heart to think Max believed the worst of that sweet college kid. "He wouldn't do that. Besides, how would he have known Graham would come for a fake date? The man was married."

"If you're a player, word gets around, especially in high-income circles," Jesse said. "Tucker's Gap is small, Willow. No secrets in a small town. If Phillip is responsible for dumping Rohypnol in your drink, it explains why you're still alive."

She glared at him. "You believe the worst of him, too?"

He shrugged. "It's obvious he likes you. Not as much as the cute waitress, but enough to set things up to spare your life. Wouldn't have been difficult. Phillip knew when you usually needed a break from work. After watching your routine for a few days, he'd know you didn't leave the hotel once the sun went down."

"My original plan was to order room service. What if I had stuck to it?"

"Easy enough to set up the rendezvous with Graham Enright anyway and send up your favorite soft drink or herbal tea with Phillip's compliments. He might have asked someone to cover his station while he delivered the drink himself to ensure you consumed it."

"Say you're right. What if I remembered him showing up in my room? Wouldn't that implicate him?"

"Not necessarily. With the drug, your memory would be questionable at best and considered totally unreliable at worst."

Her heart sank. "I don't believe he's guilty." She didn't want to believe the worst of everyone. She refused to allow bitterness and suspicion to become the dominant forces in her life. Willow had worked too hard to put the past behind her to let it control her life in small, insidious ways.

She was still a work in progress. Going out after dark was the next big hurdle, one she was determined to scale. Now that she and Max were dating, Willow didn't want to be hobbled by fear. What if she wanted to surprise Max one night by meeting him at the airport when he returned from a mission? To do that, she had to walk out her front door after the sun set.

Jesse sat on a stool and leaned back against the breakfast bar. "For what it's worth, my gut says Phillip had nothing to do with the drug or Enright's murder. If he's innocent, we'll eliminate him from our suspect list. No harm, no foul. However, if he hired a killer, don't you want to know the truth before the killer takes another shot at you or Max?"

A hired killer. Her stomach lurched. "Why didn't I think of the killer-for-hire possibility myself?" It made sense. If you had money, why do the dirty work yourself? You wouldn't unless you were worried about the hired killer turning on you. Although she didn't know much about the killer-for-hire business, turning on your employer didn't seem like a good business practice. Word would surely get around the criminal circles that you couldn't be trusted.

"Why would you think of it? You don't want to kill someone." Max threaded his fingers through hers. "Look, to be honest I don't think Phillip is our guy, either. I'm not willing to risk your life making an assumption without eliminating the possibility first through every means at my disposal. You mean too much to me, Willow. Losing you would destroy me."

Willow teared up. For once, she wished her friends weren't close. That one comment made her long to throw her arms around Max's neck and share more of those scorching kisses that melted her from the inside out. With one comment, he slid even deeper into her heart. How was she so blessed to have Max Norton in her life?

"Brownie points for that one, Max," Poppy said. "Maybe I'll forgive you for upsetting Willow earlier."

"Thanks." He sent the other woman a wry glance before shifting his attention to Brody. "Got a feeling Enright's murder is more complicated that it seems."

He snorted. "Isn't it always? We'll get to the bottom of things, then turn the killer over to the local cops and go back to training for the next mission. You can court your lady while you heal."

Sawyer huffed. "Nice plan if the killer and his employer will cooperate. No guarantees. Murderers have their own agenda and timetable."

Poppy waggled the piece of paper on which she written the names of the people to research and laid it on the coffee table. "We'll split up the list while Max and Willow are gone."

"Many hands make light work," Sage said, quoting something her mother was famous for saying. Beverly Reynolds wasn't wrong.

"Want me to contact Zane while the others dig into the backgrounds of the major players?"

"Thanks, Sawyer." Max glanced at Willow. "When can you be ready to leave?"

"As soon as I grab my purse and your laptop."

He helped Willow to her feet. "I'll meet you at the door, and we'll go. We'll take a few detours to make sure we aren't followed."

Her stomach knotted. Great. Just when she was starting to relax, reality slapped her in the face. When she walked to her bedroom, Sage followed her and shut the door.

"Are you all right, Willow?" her friend asked.

"As well as I can be with a killer circling. Why?"

"Why?" Sage stared. "Are you kidding me? First, you were drugged, and an acquaintance was murdered feet from you. Second, for a while you were suspected of Graham's murder. Third, someone tried to kill you by throwing a Molotov cocktail through a glass window. If that wasn't enough, you're dating a black ops soldier whose face is in the dictionary beside the definition of stoic."

"You're worried."

"Do you blame me? It's a lot to process in a short span of time."

There were several things to address, so Willow picked the one most important. "I thought you liked Max."

Sage held up a hand. "Don't do that. You know I like and respect Max. That doesn't mean I like him for you. He's cold, tough, and grim. You don't need that. You need someone gentle and kind, someone with the ability to be sympathetic to your trauma. That's not Max."

Fury sent a zing of adrenaline into her bloodstream. "He's exactly what I want and need. He's been nothing but kind and gentle with me, and who better to understand what I went through than someone who survived a similar experience? I don't want to hear another word against him, Sage."

Her friend stared, eyes wide. "I'm too late."

"What are you talking about?"

"You're in love with Max. How does he feel?"

"I don't know. We've only had a few minutes alone since he arrived in town. I need to take things slow. I'm still working through baggage." If Max loved her, he'd be patient and wait for her to work through her issues.

"What if Max pushes for a commitment?"

"Then he's not the man I've come to know in the past few months. I know you love me, Sage, but you don't need to worry."

"Easier said than done," her friend said. "I almost lost you. You can't blame me for being concerned."

"Trust me. Trust Max. Neither of us are in the market for a heartache. We're not racing into this blind."

Sage sighed. "All right. I'll shut up for now. But if he hurts you, I'll rip him to shreds, then toss him to Poppy and his teammates. We'll wipe the floor with him before we're finished. Trust me. He will suffer if he hurts you."

Willow hugged her. "Max is a good, honorable man. If things fall apart between us, we'll handle it." They'd have to manage. She was friends with Brody, Sage, and Poppy, and Max was in their circle as well. She'd never hurt his relationship with his teammates. That meant an award-winning acting job so his work with Texas team could go on unimpeded.

"I don't want to see either of you hurt."

"Life has bumps and bruises."

Her friend scowled. "I've been saying the same thing to Brody. He wants to wrap me in cotton and stick me on a shelf when I have a flare up."

Willow's heart squeezed. Her friend's battle with rheumatoid arthritis was almost as difficult for Brody to handle as it was for Sage. "Then you understand how I feel when you and the others try to protect me. I want to live my life to the fullest, Sage. Bumps and bruises are part of the full-life package."

A knock sounded on the door. Brody opened the door and peered inside the room. "Everything okay?"

"We're fine, sweetheart." Sage smiled at him. "Just a little girl talk."

"Do I need to take Max out behind the barn and have a heart-to-heart talk with him?"

Willow and Sage exchanged glances and laughed. "Not necessary." Willow grabbed her purse and the computer, and headed for the door. "Save the talk behind the barn for Graham's killer. Max doesn't deserve it."

Brody rolled his eyes. "You take the fun out of everything, you know that?" He moved out of the doorway.

She laughed and walked to the suite's entrance where Max waited. The expression on his face was neutral but his gaze was locked on his team leader and Sage. His eyes were ice cold.

Oh, boy. Willow rested a hand on Max's chest. "I'm ready."

After exchanging a long, pointed glance with Brody, Max cupped Willow's elbow and ushered her from the suite. They walked to the stairs in silence and made their way down to the first floor and out the front door of the inn.

He escorted her to his SUV and lifted her to the front passenger seat. Instead of closing the door, Max leaned in and captured her mouth in a long, blistering kiss filled with passion and heat and more than a hint of desperation. When he broke the kiss a minute or ten later, his eyes glittered and his cheeks were flushed. "Don't," he whispered. "Please."

"Don't what?"

"Don't run from me."

"The only place I'm running is into your arms, Max."

"Promise?"

Willow brushed her mouth over his and whispered, "I promise."

He rested his forehead against hers and shuddered. "Thank you for trusting me." After another brief kiss, this one gentle, the black ops warrior eased back and shut the door. When he slid behind the steering wheel, he said, "Let's find out what Oliver Enright wants."

Ninety minutes later, Max drove up to the locked wrought-iron gates and lowered his window. He pressed the speaker button on the security panel.

"Enright estate. May I help you?"

"Willow Knox to see Mr. Enright. He's expecting her."

A beat of silence, then, "Mr. Enright wasn't expecting anyone else."

"I'm Max, Willow's boyfriend. She was attacked last night. I'm not letting her go anywhere alone. If Enright wants to talk to her, he'll do it with me by her side."

"Hold." Two minutes later, the guy manning the communication system said, "Drive to the front door. You'll be met." The gates parted.

When he parked, Max said, "No matter what Enright wants, I'm not leaving you alone with him or anyone else. Being here is like being in the enemy's camp, Willow."

"I understand. If Mr. Enright won't agree, we'll leave."

He came around the front of the SUV and opened her door. After helping her to the driveway, Max grabbed his laptop case and escorted Willow up the sweeping stairs.

The front door opened, and a man dressed in a black suit motioned them inside. "This way, please. Good to see you again, Ms. Knox. Mr. Enright is waiting for you in his office."

They followed one of Mr. Enright's security team through a maze of hallways to the office. The guard rapped twice on the closed door, then twisted the knob. "Ms. Knox and her companion, sir." He stepped to the side and motioned for Willow and Max to enter the office.

Oliver Enright came around the desk. He extended his hand to Max. "Oliver Enright."

"Max Norton. Thanks for allowing me to accompany Willow."

A wry smile curved the older man's mouth. "I was under the impression if I didn't agree to your stipulation, I wouldn't see Ms. Knox at all."

Max inclined his head. "I won't apologize for the precaution. I almost lost her twice in the past few days."

Oliver waved them to the two chairs in front of his desk. "Please, have a seat. Ms. Knox, did you bring your results so far?"

"I have access to the digital files. I'll send them to your email."

"You didn't bring your computer?"

"The police confiscated it."

Max brought out his laptop and booted it up.

"Do you need the Internet password?" Oliver asked Max.

"No, sir." After a few keystrokes, he handed the laptop to Willow.

She keyed in the necessary information to access her digital files, then sent a copy to Oliver's email. "Done."

"That fast?"

She studied his guarded expression. "Why did you want me to come, Mr. Enright? Did you want to tell me in person you want another researcher from Ballinger to take your case?"

"No, my dear. You misunderstand my intent." He rubbed his jaw, his hand trembling slightly. "I want you to keep tracing my genealogy with all haste."

"You don't blame me for Graham's death?"

"Why would I? The police detectives assured me you weren't responsible, that you had been drugged and were unconscious at the time of my son's death."

"What's the hurry on the family tree?" Max asked.

"Simple, Mr. Norton. I'm dying."

Chapter Nineteen

Max took the laptop from Willow's unresisting hands. She was pale again. He needed to get her out of here soon. "I'm sorry, Mr. Enright." Shocked to learn about his illness, too. The old man looked and acted healthy. Was he playing on Willow's sympathy or stating the truth? Another avenue for Zane to check. Medical information wouldn't be accessible except to a hacker of Z's caliber.

Good thing Max's team was already at work digging into the backgrounds of people involved in the investigation into Enright's death and the hunt for the killer.

"Nothing can be done to treat your illness?" Willow asked.

"The doctors have done all they can." He sat back in his chair. "Bone cancer."

"Now I understand why you're so interested in my progress."

"I don't think you do, Ms. Knox. I need to find an heir for my vast fortune. My estate is large and requires training to handle properly."

Max stared, puzzled. Nothing like bragging about the size of your bank account. But what did the size of the estate and Enright's illness have to do with pressing Willow to work faster?

She frowned. "Won't your wife inherit everything?"

His eyebrows soared. "Of course not. We signed a prenuptial agreement before we married. Besides, she has her own money. She'll be fine without mine."

Cold. Perhaps the current Mrs. Enright should go on the suspect list because she was angry at her husband for cutting her out of a billion-dollar estate. Perhaps Graham was dead because the current Mrs. Enright believed with the heir apparent out of the way, she'd have a better chance to inherit her husband's wealth despite the prenuptial agreement.

FALLOUT   195

When he'd been in Willow's hospital room, Max glanced at the
elder Enright's accounts. The bottom line had taken his breath away.
Good thing he wasn't the type to envy another man's riches nor was
he prone to jealousy.

His gaze went to Willow, and Max corrected himself. He wasn't
the jealous type when it came to money. Different story if Willow
was involved. If another man made a move on her, Max would have
something to say about it. He didn't want to lose her.

"I need you to find every potential heir in my family tree as
soon as possible," Enright continued. "I have to begin making legal
arrangements to transition my affairs and to train my successor in the
fine art of dealing with Enright investments and businesses."

"You could sell the businesses outright."

"Never. The Enright family became wealthy during the Great
Depression and added to the family coffers ever since. We pass on
family assets to children or grandchildren if possible, or another
family member, but never to an outsider. It's not done, and I don't
intend to break family tradition. So you see, my dear, time is of the
essence. The estate is complicated with stock portfolios, multiple
properties, and six corporations my heir will guide long into the
future. I need as much time as possible so I can leave the proper
legacy behind. I'm counting on you to help me accomplish that
goal."

No pressure or anything. Max watched Willow from the corner
of his eye and saw her eyes narrow.

"You're talking about finding current heirs, not ancestral family
members as you indicated in your contract with Ballinger. You lied."

"My priority changed the moment my son died. My medical
team informed me the morning after his death that my condition
was terminal. They tried everything, even an experimental drug trial
as a last resort. Nothing has stopped the progression of the cancer."

"Do you suspect you have children you don't know about?"

He shrugged as though an unknown son or daughter didn't matter. "It's possible."

"Graham had two sons. You're not planning to pass the Enright fortune to them?"

A bark of laughter. "Have you met my grandsons?"

She frowned. "No, sir."

"They're fools, both of them. I wouldn't trust my estate in the hands of either one. They would sell off everything and live the high life on my hard work and the hard work of my ancestors." His expression hardened. "I'm also not impressed with any other known Enright family members. Find me another heir. Now."

"I'll have to dig deep in your life. It's a serious invasion of privacy, and I still may come up empty. I can't create an heir out of thin air."

"Just do your job. It's what I'm paying you for."

"That's enough," Max said, voice low and hard. No one disrespected Willow and got away with it. No one.

She laid her hand over his in a silent warning.

"I'll expect an update on your progress tomorrow," Enright continued without missing a beat. "Don't disappoint me, Ms. Knox."

"You know more than you're saying, Mr. Enright. Why not save me some time and tell me what you suspect?"

"I'm not doing your job for you," he snapped.

Max's eyebrow rose, irritated at Enright's attitude. A clear dismissal from the lord of the manor. No more. Willow deserved respect. Max rose and held out his hand to Willow. "While you have my sympathy for the loss of your son and your health, your next conversation with Willow will be conducted with more respect or it will end without you receiving any information from her. Am I clear?"

"You wouldn't dare."

"I'd dare more than you can imagine to protect Willow."

Enright sneered. "Protect her? She's so weak that you have to stand in front of Ms. Knox to protect her from a dying man?"

"I protect her because she matters to me, not because she's weak." He guided Willow to the office door and escorted her from the mansion. After she was seated in the SUV, he set his laptop behind her seat and closed the door with a gentleness he didn't feel.

Fury zinged through his veins as he circled the hood and slid behind the wheel. If Enright had treated his wives with the same disrespect, Max wasn't surprised the man had married so many women.

Had Enright's disdain for others carried over to his son? Enright's priority was money and power, not people. Max drove from the estate and headed into downtown Tucker's Gap to fulfill a promise.

"Where are we going?" Willow asked.

"Police station to sign our statements." And if they were lucky, ferret out information from reluctant detectives.

"Why did you confront Mr. Enright?"

Max glanced her way before returning his attention to the road. He tightened his grip around the steering wheel. "He treated you like a hired servant instead of a skilled researcher. He should value your skills, not bully you into performing faster."

"He has a contract with Ballinger and I'm a contracted employee with the company. To Mr. Enright, it amounts to being a hired servant. Don't let it bother you. I don't. He wouldn't be the first Ballinger client to treat me that way."

Didn't mean he liked it. "Based on Enright's attitude, he expects you to produce an heir like a magician pulling a rabbit out of a hat. You can't create someone who doesn't exist."

"I don't know, Max. I have the impression he definitely knows something he's not telling me."

He snorted. "If Graham's anything like his old man, it wouldn't surprise me to find out he has a son or daughter he hasn't acknowledged from an affair."

"It's odd that Oliver is pushing me to investigate his background, not Graham's. I don't want to leave out a possible heir, so I'll shift my research focus to Graham and Oliver's wives and mistresses." She sighed. "He's bound to have a mistress or two in the background. Otherwise, he wouldn't have spoken so casually about the possibility of an illegitimate child."

Max would shift his focus to Graham and Oliver Enright as well. He didn't like the desperation in Oliver's eyes. What if Willow found an heir who was an impressionable kid? A word of advice to his or her guardian might be in order.

Then again, advice was usually not well received, and it was none of his business. His only concern was finding a killer before he made another attempt to murder Willow.

Ten minutes later, Max parked in front of the police station. Together, they walked inside the building and approached the desk sergeant. "Norton and Knox to see Cohen and Warner. If they're not in, find out who else can help us. We need to sign our statements."

The gray-haired cop indicated the plastic chairs set against the wall with a tilt of his chin. "I'll see if they're available."

Another power play. Nice. Max sat in one of the uncomfortable chairs beside Willow and threaded their fingers together. "Thank you," he murmured.

"For what?"

"Taking a chance on me, for giving us a chance to be together." He kissed her palm, then reached into his cargo pocket and pulled out the small gift he'd been holding onto for four weeks.

Willow gasped, her eyes lighting. "He's adorable." She cradled the small stuffed bear in her hands. "Thank you, Max."

"Like it?"

"I love it." Her brows knitted as she studied the vest the bear wore, focusing on the pocket. "He has something in his pocket."

"Unbutton it and reach inside." Praying he hadn't made a mistake, Max waited for her reaction.

She obeyed and pulled out the second part of his gift. Her gaze shot to his. "A key?"

"To my house. In case you need a change of scenery while I train with my team or I'm deployed." His stomach knotted. This was probably the dumbest idea he'd ever had but he wanted Willow to have a safe haven to run to when he was out of pocket. He had installed every security measure Fortress offered. His home had a large safe room and escape tunnels from each room. Just in case. He never knew when one of the cult members would come after him or one of the terrorists he and his team encountered on missions. Although Fortress did their best to protect operatives from exposure, no system was foolproof. "You can water my plants for me."

She smiled. "You don't have plants."

"I'll buy some."

Willow leaned in and kissed him. "I love your gift."

Cautious, he said, "I have it on good authority that stuffed bears are always a big hit."

"He's cute but I meant your gift of safety. If I need to take you up on it, I promise to water the plants and, if you're very lucky, prepare a meal for you. I won't intrude on your privacy, Max. You have my word on that."

Relief swept through him. "I don't care if you rifle through all the drawers and closets. I want you in my home."

"I won't abuse the gift."

He couldn't resist taking her mouth. Yeah, he was well and truly addicted. Mindful of the desk sergeant glaring daggers at them, Max eased back a fraction of an inch, his gaze locked on Willow's.

The door to the bullpen opened, drawing his attention, and Cohen motioned to Max.

"Come on. Let's get this over with." Max walked into the bullpen with Willow.

Cohen led them to an interrogation room and waved them to the table. He left the door open and stood in the doorway with his shoulder propped against the jamb. "How do you feel, Norton?"

"I'm fine." Or he would be soon enough.

"Ms. Knox?"

"Same." She sat at the table, keeping the stuffed bear out of sight.

Max liked that Willow kept the bear to herself. From the way she acted, she was protecting the toy from a surly cop who would sneer at a sentimental gift.

"Glad to hear it. Stay put. I'll return with your statements." The detective came back with a folder. He sat across from them and placed their statements on the table. "If you have changes, write them down, then sign the statement, and you'll be on your way."

Max scanned the statement, frustrated that he hadn't been much help to the detectives or himself. He was a trained investigator and still had next to nothing to offer about the firebomb. After scrawling his name at the bottom of the page, he sat back and studied the detective who watched Willow while she read her statement. What was that about? "Problem, Detective?"

Cohen's gaze shifted to Max. "Nope. Have any news to share about the case?"

"Do you? Share and share alike, right?" He considered pursuing the detective's concentrated attention on Willow but decided to bide his time. If the other man made a move on her, threatening or otherwise, Cohen would regret it.

A snort. "You know better than that. Game's not played that way."

Fair enough. He'd never been keen on sharing from his side of an investigation, either. With Zane's hacking skills, what the detectives knew Max and his team would find out. "Oliver Enright called Willow and asked her to come to his home this afternoon. We just came from there."

Cohen frowned. "I'm surprised. What did he want?"

"For Willow to work fast to find him another heir."

A stare. "You're kidding."

"Afraid not."

"Doesn't make sense. Graham has two sons and a wife. Wouldn't Mr. Enright pass the family fortune on to them or his own wife?"

"Not going to happen. Oliver said his grandchildren are fools, and he can't trust them with his wealth and businesses. He won't leave anything to his wife, either. Prenuptial agreement."

The detective rubbed his jaw. "Graham's wife didn't say anything about illegitimate children or a prenuptial agreement. Then again, she didn't appear to be broken up about her husband's death. Might be interesting to find out if she knows Oliver is looking for a different heir."

Interesting? Possibly. Could be a motive for murder, too, if the lady knew about the legacy plan before now.

Willow signed her statement and pushed it toward Cohen. "Are we free to leave?"

A wry smile curved his mouth. "In a hurry to ditch me, Ms. Knox?"

"I have work to do."

"Right." He stood. "I'll be in touch if I have further questions."

"Not going to share information, Detective?" Max's mouth curved.

Cohen gave a bark of laughter and strode from the room.

Max and Willow followed. As they neared the bullpen door, Warner stepped inside the room.

His gaze trailed down Willow and paused on the stuffed bear. He smirked. "Carrying toys around with you now, Ms. Knox?" He chuckled at his own joke and shifted his attention to Max. "Doesn't say much about her interest in you, does it, Norton?"

"Let's go, Max," Willow said quietly.

After a hard look at the sneering detective, Max took Willow's arm and escorted her from the station. At the SUV, he set Willow on the passenger seat. "Back to the inn so you can work?"

"We should talk to Graham's wife."

Chapter Twenty

Max gripped the SUV's overhead frame. Talk to Graham's wife with Willow by his side? This was such a bad idea on every level. What if Graham's wife was behind her husband's murder? He could be walking Willow into a trap.

The video footage showed the killer was a man. If Graham's wife hired the killer and made a move against Willow, Max would be there to stop the attack before it went too far. That would end the danger Willow was in and allow him to move their dating relationship to the top of his priority list instead of tracking down a killer.

Max frowned. He still didn't like Willow walking into a potential danger zone. What if he was wrong about Graham's wife? The thought of losing Willow was like taking a knife to the gut.

Willow cupped his cheek with her soft hand. "Before you say no, consider the time element involved. If Graham and his wife lived in Tucker's Gap, we're already here in town. If you take me back to the inn to work first and then return to town, you'll waste two hours before the interview."

"And if she's the reason her husband is dead?"

"Better to find out now while we have her cornered, right?"

"Cornered people come out fighting."

"I'll follow your lead and watch your back in case she has a partner in the house. We're a team, right?"

Max didn't like taking her into potential danger but she was right. Time was short to find the killer. "All right. We'll go see Graham's wife together." He brushed his mouth over Willow's before climbing behind the wheel. Activating his Bluetooth, Max called Zane.

His friend answered on the first ring. "Yeah, Murphy."

"Max Norton here. I need an address."

"Go."

"Celia and Graham Enright."

"Hold." A few keystrokes later, Zane said, "Two different addresses are listed."

Max frowned. "Explain."

"Trouble in paradise. They separated two months ago. Rumors in their social circle say they were heading for a quiet divorce."

"Do you know the reason?"

"Infidelity."

Cold chills surged over his body. Had Celia met Willow? If so, did she kill her husband and target Willow for revenge? "Give me Celia's address." After he keyed the address into the navigation system, Max said, "Is the boss available?"

"I'll check. By the way, I should have results from the security camera search for you in a couple of hours. I've been putting out fires all night and had to work on it between providing tech and communications support for two different teams in hot zones."

"No problem. I appreciate the help, Z."

"Yep. Hold."

Seconds later, Brent Maddox's voice filled the SUV. "Maddox."

"It's Max Norton, sir. You're on speaker with Willow."

"Understood. Sit rep."

As he drove to Celia's address, Max updated his employer.

"Do we have a picture of this guy yet?"

"Zane's working on it. He should have results soon."

"He's been up more than 36 hours. I'm sending him home to sleep. If he hasn't finished the search by the time he leaves, I'll assign another tech to finish the task. How do you feel, Max?"

"I've been worse."

His employer chuckled. "I hear you. Willow, need anything?"

"No, sir. Thank you for sending the phone and jewelry."

"You're one of us now. I'm glad to provide more safety for you and peace of mind for Max."

"I appreciate your thoughtfulness."

Maddox cleared his throat as though uncomfortable, and he probably was. "Watch your back, Max."

"Yes, sir."

"Later." Maddox ended the call.

In minutes, Max turned into a long, winding driveway and parked his SUV in front of Celia Enright's three-story home. He glanced at Willow. "You sure you want to do this? Might not be pleasant, especially if she thinks her husband was interested in you."

"The only person Graham was interested in was himself."

"Will Celia believe that?" He helped Willow from the SUV, and they walked to the double front door. Unsure of their reception, Max eased Willow behind him and pressed the doorbell.

A middle-aged woman opened the door. She was dressed in a black sweater and black trousers with matching flats. "May I help you?"

"Celia Enright?"

Her hand clenched into a fist. "If you're a reporter, I have no comment. If you don't leave my property, I'll call the police and have you arrested for trespassing."

"We're not reporters, ma'am. We're investigating your husband's death and would appreciate a few minutes of your time."

Celia's gaze shifted to Willow before returning to Max. "If you aren't reporters, then what do you want?"

He handed her his business card. "May we come in, Mrs. Enright?"

She glanced at the card before studying him a moment, then she stepped back to allow Max and Willow inside. Celia led them to a large living room to the right of the foyer and motioned to the sofa. "Please, have a seat."

"Thank you for seeing us, Mrs. Enright."

"We're sorry about the loss of your husband," Willow said.

"Thank you." She frowned. "I feel like I've seen you somewhere before. Do I know you?"

"No, ma'am. I don't live in Tucker's Gap. I'm here on business for a few days."

"I didn't catch your name."

Willow tensed. "Willow Knox."

Celia stiffened. "The detectives said my husband was in your hotel room when he died."

"Yes, ma'am. Someone dumped Rohypnol into my soft drink, and Graham was kind enough to help me to my room."

The other woman's face reddened. "My husband would never drug a woman."

"The security footage at the hotel showed the man who drugged me. It wasn't Graham."

Celia's eyes widened. "Who was it?"

"We haven't identified him yet, Mrs. Enright, but we're working on it," Max answered. "We've given the security footage to the detectives investigating your husband's murder."

"How do you know my husband, Mr. Norton?"

"I never met him. I came here because Willow and I are engaged, and I was worried about her safety."

Graham's wife sank into the recliner and sighed. "I see. I apologize, Ms. Knox. I assumed that you and my husband were having an affair. That was an unfair assumption on my part."

"Under the circumstances, it's understandable."

"Detectives Cohen and Warner assured me you weren't involved with Graham. However, I was afraid to believe them."

"Your husband was cheating?"

"I could never prove it."

"How long did you suspect he was cheating?"

Celia uttered a wry laugh. "Six months into our marriage. We've been married for 30 years, and I ignored what I suspected on my mother's advice. 'Men always stray,' she said. 'Good wives pretend their marriage is perfect.' I followed Mother's advice until I overheard my so-called friends at the country club laughing about my husband's ability to pull the wool over my eyes. I'd had enough. That night I confronted Graham about what I overheard. He denied it, of course. I told him to pack his bags and leave."

"Did he?" Max asked.

A sad smile formed on Celia's mouth. "Graham was gone within fifteen minutes, and he never returned." Her gaze dropped to her tightly clasped hands. "I must sound bitter and pathetic."

Her husband sounded like a jerk who was never satisfied. "No, ma'am. How was the relationship between Graham and his father?"

"Rocky. Oliver has very high standards, and Graham never felt he lived up to his father's expectations. He spent long hours at work and traveled extensively for his father. He was out of town for weeks at a time. Why are you asking about the relationship between Graham and his father?"

"Did you know Oliver is looking for an heir to inherit his estate?"

Celia stared. "He has heirs. My sons."

"What about you?"

She waved that aside. "I never expected to inherit anything. Oliver has always been clear that the estate would pass through the bloodline. My sons will inherit the estate when Oliver passes away, but that's a long way off. The man is the picture of health."

"He hasn't told you about his medical diagnosis?" Willow asked.

Celia's brows knitted. "Medical diagnosis? What about you talking about?"

"Oliver has terminal bone cancer."

Silence followed her announcement. "Are you all right, Mrs. Enright?"

"Why didn't he tell anyone? At the very least, he should have told Graham. This is unbelievable. Do you know how long he has left?"

"No, ma'am."

"You talked to him recently?"

A nod. "An hour ago."

Celia sighed. "No wonder he's talking about heirs to inherit his estate. He loves his grandsons. Perhaps he's looking for another heir because of his insistence on family bloodline. If he located another heir of his bloodline, he'd insist on including him or her in the will along with my sons."

"Does he suspect Graham fathered more children?"

Celia blanched. "You'll have to ask Oliver."

"Mr. Enright won't cooperate, only instructing Willow to find another heir."

"I don't understand." She turned her attention to Willow. "Why would Oliver tell you to find another heir to split the Enright estate with my sons? Are you good friends with my father-in-law?"

"He's a client of Barrington Research, my employer. I'm a genealogist. Part of my job is to locate heirs for clients. I've been in town for the past few days to create an Enright family tree."

"Sounds like you have an interesting job."

"I enjoy it."

"What do you do for Fortress, Mr. Norton?"

Couldn't tell Celia he was a black ops soldier tasked with hunting down and taking out terrorists. "Security and investigations. Do you know anyone who wears a Baltimore Orioles baseball cap, Mrs. Enright?"

She looked puzzled. "I don't think so. Why?"

"The man who forced his way into Willow's hotel room wore an Orioles cap."

A gasp. "You think I know who killed Graham?"

"Do you?"

"No! If I did, I would have told the police."

Not if she hired the killer. "Do you know anyone with a reason to kill your husband?"

"The women he slept with or their husbands, boyfriends, or family members."

"Did you hire a private investigator to follow Graham?" Willow asked.

Celia's cheeks turned red. "How did you know?"

"I would have wanted to know the truth."

"Did the investigator find proof?" Max asked.

She shook her head. "When my husband was in town, he was at home or the office. He'd have business dinners at local restaurants but the investigator said he came straight home afterward."

"Did he follow your husband on his business trips?"

"No. I should have asked him to follow Graham everywhere for a month."

"Do you have his report?"

"Of course. Would you like a copy?"

"I'd appreciate that."

"Don't expect much." She left and returned a moment later with a flash drive that she gave to Max. "Do you have other questions? If not, I have an appointment with the funeral home."

"Will you give us permission to search Graham's residence?"

"That's an invasion of his privacy," she snapped. "I've been willing to bare my soul and answer your questions, but that's too much."

Graham wouldn't care of Max and Willow poked around his place. He wasn't in a position to argue. "We might find evidence that points to the killer in Graham's personal space."

"My sons are already devastated by the loss of their father. I don't want them hurt more."

"No matter what we learn, we won't talk to the media."

"Information might get out anyway."

"We have to share any information with the detectives investigating your husband's murder. What they do with it is up to them." He helped Willow up. "Do you want to find your husband's killer?"

"Of course I do, but not at the expense of tarnishing the Enright name. Oliver wouldn't be pleased, and he could take it out on me and my sons. You don't know the kind of power Oliver wields in this town."

"Do we have your permission to search Graham's home?"

"When?"

"As soon as possible. The more time passes, the greater chance the killer will go to ground." Unlikely since Max believed the guy would come after Willow again. However, if he pushed to search the house now, he hoped the killer wouldn't have time to set a trap.

"I don't have time. I can't keep the funeral director waiting."

"You have two options. You can trust us with a key to search while you're at the funeral home."

She frowned. "I don't think so. What's the other option?"

"Call Cohen and Warner, and ask them to meet us at the house with a key." Not his favorite option but he'd take it if it meant he had access to the house now.

Celia stood. "I'll call the detectives on the way to my appointment and have them meet you. I'm not comfortable letting strangers wander through the house."

"We understand," Willow said. "Thank you for accommodating us. We'll be careful not to disturb anything."

"If you find anything, I want to know." The other woman's voice broke. "Even though my husband and I were separated, I still loved him and hoped for a reconciliation. Now, that dream is gone." Celia wiped tears from her face and scooped her purse from the floor. "You'll call me, Mr. Norton?"

"Yes, ma'am." He rested his hand against Willow's lower back as they walked to his SUV.

Once Willow was inside, Max slid behind the steering wheel and keyed in Graham's address. As he drove toward the other side of Tucker's Gap, Max called Detective Cohen.

"Yeah, Cohen," the detective snapped.

"Max Norton here."

A growl. "You're stirring up trouble and costing me precious time, Norton."

"How soon will you be at Graham Enright's home?"

"An hour. That better be good enough because some of us have a real job."

He let that dig pass. No point stoking the detective's animosity even higher. "We appreciate your time. Do you take your coffee black?"

A slight pause, then, "Yeah, why?"

"Willow and I will go to the coffee shop so she can work before we meet you at Enright's place. We'll pick up coffee for you and your partner."

A snort. "I don't know how you talked Celia Enright into letting you look through her husband's belongings."

"We want the same thing she does. Answers."

"I'm not sure we all want the same thing."

"I want to know who drugged Willow and why so he can't hurt her again."

"This is our case, Norton. You're not on the job any longer."

"I haven't forgotten. Everyone can use a hand now and again, Detective. Even cops."

"I don't need a vigilante poking around in my case."

"I'm an investigator looking for answers, same as you. You get the joy of locking this guy up and filling out all the paperwork."

A short laugh from the detective. "Don't rub it in."

"See you in an hour." He ended the call.

Willow squeezed his forearm. "Coffee for the enemy to sweeten their attitude?" she teased.

"Won't hurt."

He parked in the front of a coffee shop a short distance from Graham Enright's home, grabbed his laptop, and escorted Willow inside the shop. "Want anything in particular?"

She shook her head. "Surprise me."

"Choose a table away from the windows," he murmured.

Willow headed for the table in the corner farthest from the door and windows.

Perfect choice. Willow had paid attention to the tables he and his teammates chose when they ate in restaurants. Always the back corner, preferably with their backs to the wall, not easy to do when all five of them were together.

Max walked to the counter and ordered coffee for himself and blueberry tea for his girl as well as a large chocolate cookie shaped like a heart. Sappy, but Willow owned his heart and she deserved to be spoiled. This was part of his cunning plan to capture her heart and keep it.

When their order was ready, Max carried the small tray with their purchases to the table and set Willow's tea and cookie beside her.

She smiled. "A chocolate cookie. Thanks, Max. You didn't get a snack for yourself?"

"Nope." He needed caffeine rather than a pastry. Max inclined his head toward the laptop. "Any luck?"

Willow's smile slipped. "Not so far. I started with Mr. Enright and his possible offspring. I'm not getting anywhere through my normal search engines and databases. Only a list of his marriages and divorces. No offspring except Graham. Nothing about his affairs or possible children from affairs."

"Let me know when you run out of search options. I have a few resources we can tap to give us more information."

"Deal." For the next hour, she dug deeper while sipping her tea and eating the cookie.

Max enjoyed watching Willow consume the cookie. His woman loved chocolate. He made a mental note to send chocolate and perhaps flowers each time he was deployed. Maybe he could grow into a flowers-and-chocolate kind of guy after all.

While Willow worked, Max did his own research into the background of Oliver Enright. The further he dug, the more sympathy he felt for each of Oliver's wives. No question Oliver worked very hard to run the Enright empire and did so at the expense of his family life. Why didn't he guard his most precious treasure, his family?

Max's gaze shifted to Willow who studied her screen. If she trusted him with her heart, Max would never take Willow for granted.

She glanced up at him. "Something wrong?"

"Oliver Enright is a fool."

"No argument from me but why do you say that?"

"He's supposed to be all about family, yet he doesn't value his. His priority is the estate and the family name, not the people he should cherish. That's his real legacy." He tapped the top of his laptop. "Find anything?"

"Same as you, I imagine. A lot of nothing. Unless you find something in Oliver's past that makes him a target for revenge, I'll shift to digging into Graham's background when we return to the inn."

Max checked his watch. "I'll buy coffee for the detectives while you shut down the computer, and we'll leave for Enright's house."

Minutes later, he drove to the Winter Garden subdivision and parked on the street in front of Graham's house. When he opened Willow's door, a neutral-colored sedan swung into the winding drive and stopped. Cohen and Warner exited the vehicle and walked to the front door to wait for Max and Willow.

Max took the coffee carrier. "Thanks for meeting us," he said when they reached the grim-faced cops. He handed each a cup. "Peace offering."

Warner grunted but accepted the drink. "Let's get on with this. We have more important things to do."

He gestured toward the door. Might as well let the cops take the lead. More protection for Willow.

Warner slid a set of keys from his pocket and unlocked the door. He walked inside and turned on the lights. After a quick scan, he gestured the others inside. "Clear."

Max wasn't buying it. The back of his neck prickled, not a good sign. He eased Willow in front of him and nudged her inside the house.

Once he crossed the threshold, Max turned and scanned the neighborhood. Nothing stirred except a few birds, a cat, and a dog. A bicyclist rode by at a fast clip, not even glancing in the direction of Graham's home.

No curtains twitched, and no neighbors stood outside to watch the proceedings. Still, Max felt more prickles surge up his spine. His gut urged him to grab Willow and get out of the house but he knew she wouldn't leave yet.

After a slow survey of the neighborhood, Max wrapped his hand around Willow's upper arm and urged her toward the hall. "Office or bedroom?"

"Bedroom."

"Bedrooms are upstairs," Cohen offered. "Last door on the right is the master suite. I'll show you."

And stick around to keep an eye on them. Worked for Max. Celia Enright would know he and Willow hadn't taken anything with an eagle-eyed cop in the room.

Like the rest of the house, the master suite had been professionally decorated for its male occupant. "Take the bathroom, Willow. I'll search in here."

"What are you looking for?" Cohen asked.

"Something that doesn't fit." Max started with the dresser, searching each drawer for a hidden compartment.

When he came up empty, he shifted his attention to the nightstands on either side of the bed. In one drawer, he found a bottle of prescription pills. Max had a pretty good idea what the pills were for but he took a picture of it to show Jesse and returned the bottle to the drawer.

He headed to the closet as Willow returned to the bedroom. "Anything?"

"Expensive linens and personal care items. You?"

"Not really. I snapped a picture of a bottle of pills in the nightstand. Jesse will be able to tell us what the medicine is for."

"But you already suspect, don't you?"

"Uh huh." He opened the door to the large walk-in closet. "You take the right. I'll take the left. Focus on boxes. I'll do the same and look for hidden compartments."

"In a hurry, Norton?" Cohen drawled.

"Like you, I have better things to do than search through a dead man's belongings." Plus, that pesky nagging told him something was wrong.

Willow glanced at Max but she started to search without comment.

Max made fast work of searching the boxes on his side of the closet. Shoes, more shoes, and more shoes. Holy cow. How many pairs of shoes did one man need? His own closet held five pairs of shoes. Two running shoes, two pairs of tactical boots, and one pair of dress shoes gathering dust. Graham could have opened his own shoe store.

Shaking his head, he tugged the last of Enright's boxes off the shelf and found a smaller box inside. He removed the small box's lid. Max frowned. What was this? He recognized Enright but not the woman he was holding so close.

"Hey," Warner called up the stairs. "Come take a look at this, Cohen. I think someone's been in here since the crime scene team left."

Max pivoted, box still clutched in his hand. "Cohen, wait."

A deafening explosion rocked the house.

Chapter Twenty-One

Willow fell against Max, and both of them tumbled to the floor. Somehow he managed to flip them so he took the brunt of the impact on his back with her falling on top of him. Again. A heartbeat later, he had flipped their position and covered Willow's body with his as smoke drifted into the closet. Nearby, a man moaned.

She gasped and coughed because of the smoke. Cohen sounded like he was hurt. They must help him.

Max got to his knees. "You okay?"

She blinked rapidly, her eyes stinging. "I think so. What happened?"

"Bomb. We need to get out of the house in case more bombs are hidden inside."

"We have to help the detectives."

He stood and plucked her off the floor as if she weighed nothing. "No matter what happens, stay right behind me. I don't want to lose track of you with the fire and smoke."

Fire. She swallowed hard. Oh, yeah. They definitely needed to get out of the house.

Max scooped up the box he'd dropped and thrust it into Willow's hands. "Hold onto this." He wrapped his hand around her upper arm and led her from the closet.

When they stepped into the bedroom, a haze of smoke hung in the air. Fire crackled nearby, the sound sending shards of fear through Willow. Max was right. They needed to get out of here. Who knew how long Graham's house would hold together before the structure's integrity was compromised.

A strange creak sent her heart rate into the stratosphere. Oh, man. That wasn't good. Sounded as though they didn't have long before part of the house collapsed.

Max released her and hurried to Cohen who was sprawled in the doorway, slumped against the jamb. "Cohen, you hurt?"

No response.

He pressed his fingers to the detective's neck. "Got a pulse." Max hauled Cohen over his shoulder in a fireman's carry. "Can't wait for medical help. Let's go. We need to find Warner and get out of the house."

"I'm right behind you." Willow wrapped her arms around the box and hurried after Max and the detective. They descended the stairs quickly.

"Warner?" Max yelled. He coughed. "Warner."

No response.

"Detective, where are you? We need to get out of the house."

Still nothing.

"Come on." Max took Willow's arm and propelled her toward the back of the house. Coughing, he checked the back door before unlocking it and throwing the door open. He rushed her outside.

"We can't leave Detective Warner in here," Willow protested between bouts of coughing.

"I'll go back for him after you and Cohen are safe." He led her to the back of the yard to a dark corner behind a row of bushes. "It's not perfect but it has to work." Max eased Cohen from his shoulder to the ground. "Call for help. I'll be back in a minute."

"Be careful, Max."

After brushing his mouth over hers, Max raced to the back door and disappeared from sight.

Willow set the box she held on the ground and grabbed her phone. She called the emergency services operator and reported the fire. "Send an ambulance, too. At least two people are hurt." She feared Max would need medical assistance by the time he hauled Warner outside. The detective had been closer to the explosion than the rest of them.

After being assured first responders were on the way, Willow ended the call and checked Cohen. "Detective Cohen, can you hear me?"

He groaned, eyelids fluttering. "What happened?" he asked, voice hoarse.

"A bomb blew up in the house."

Cohen's eyes flew open. "Warner." He tried to sit up and gasped. Blood drained from his face, leaving him nearly colorless.

Willow pressed gently against his shoulder. "Stay down. Max went back into the house to get your partner. They'll be out in a minute."

Her gaze shifted toward the burning house. Where were they? Max and the detective should have been outside by now. Had something happened to Max? She envisioned a number of things, each one worse than the last.

Willow's stomach knotted. She couldn't leave Detective Cohen unprotected. What if Graham's killer was close, watching and waiting for an opportunity to finish all of them off? Although she wasn't anywhere near Max's level of proficiency, Willow could slow down an attacker long enough for Max to arrive and take over. Although Cohen would do his best to protect Willow, he was hurt. He likely had a concussion and possible internal injuries.

The detective attempted to roll onto his side and cursed. "Hurts," he said, groaning.

"I'll bet. Stay still. Help will arrive soon." Sirens sounded in the distance.

At that moment, Max staggered from the house with Warner over his shoulder. He crossed the yard in seconds, coughing and gasping for breath as he lowered the detective to the ground beside his partner.

"How is he?" Cohen asked him.

"Don't know. He has a head injury and was buried under a bookcase. I think his leg is broken, too. What about you? You okay?"

"Feels like I was run over by a bus. What happened?"

"Bomb in the office blew out the outside walls of the room and three other interior walls. Front of the house is already a total loss, and the fire is spreading fast. I hope the crime scene team was finished because there won't be much left by the time the afternoon is over."

Cohen coughed and hissed, clamping a hand over his right ribs. "Finished this morning. Lucky break."

Sirens came to an abrupt halt and brakes squealed.

Max stood. "I'll bring the EMTs back here. Stay put, Cohen."

"Yeah, yeah." The detective stretched out on the grass again with more harsh cursing. "Bet you're happy about this," he muttered, glaring at Willow.

"Why would I be?"

"Convenient that the house of the man you're suspected of murdering will be a pile of charred rubble, destroying any evidence we missed."

"You said the crime scene team was finished. Have you decided I'm guilty after all?"

"Jury's still out but makes me suspicious when you and Norton keep popping up in conjunction with a Tucker's Gap crime wave. We had a low crime rate before you and your boyfriend arrived."

"No matter what you think, we didn't bring trouble to town. It was already here." But she might have started a cascade of bad events when she began to poke into the Enright genealogy. Was someone worried about what she might find in her investigation or was the timing a coincidence?

Max returned with two EMTs. Before long, both detectives were on the way to the hospital and two Tucker's Gap police officers headed toward Max and Willow.

The older of the two officers narrowed his eyes. "You armed?" he asked Max. Both he and his partner reached for their weapons.

Max held his hands away from his body and shifted to put himself between the officers and Willow. "Yeah, and I'm licensed to carry. My identification is in my right cargo pocket along with my gun permit."

"Move slow, buddy. Ma'am, step out from behind your friend."

"Not happening," Max said. "Lower your weapons first. I don't want my girlfriend shot by accident."

"We're not trigger-happy vigilantes," the younger cop snapped.

"You're green and nervous. I'd say you've been on the job a year or less."

"I'm trained." The cop sounded defensive.

"So am I. I used to be on the job. No offense, my friend, but my priority is my girlfriend's safety not catering to your ego."

"Lower your weapon, Kirkwood," the first cop said. "Any funny moves on this guy's part, and I'll take care of him myself."

Willow scowled. Really? This was going downhill fast. She needed to do something or the situation would deteriorate further. "Max," she murmured. "It's all right."

He stepped to the side, arms still spread. "My girlfriend is not armed. If you have to confirm that with a pat down, call in a female officer. Willow is a trauma survivor."

Willow's cheeks burned as the officers looked at her with speculation in their eyes. "I was raped six months ago."

"I'm sorry to hear that, ma'am," Senior Cop said.

Max shifted slightly, again drawing the attention of the officers. "I'm reaching for my identification."

"Go slow," Kirkwood snapped.

Willow sighed. So much for a truce between the three men.

Max followed orders and handed his identification to the senior officer. He edged closer to Willow. "You sure you're okay, sweetheart?" he asked softly. "I can take you to the emergency room as soon as we're finished here."

"You're the one who took the brunt of the impact again." Jesse needed to check Max's back. "I'm fine except for a minor sore throat. You swallowed more smoke than I did."

He didn't look happy at the news about her throat. "I'll ask Jesse to check you when we return to the inn."

She nudged his arm. "I'll agree if you let him check you over, too. Fair's fair, buddy. Suck it up and deal."

Max chuckled. "Yes, ma'am."

"All right, Mr. Norton," Senior cop said as he handed back Max's identification. "What happened here?"

For the next few minutes, Willow and Max filled the officers in.

Another explosion came from the front of the house. Max wrapped his arm around Willow's waist and tucked her close to his side.

If they'd still been inside the house when this bomb went off, would they have found their way out? "You were right," she whispered. Good grief. Willow shivered despite the warmth of the afternoon. How many more bombs were in the house, and why hadn't the Tucker's Gap police found them when they searched the house?

Senior Cop glanced over his shoulder and whistled. "Good thing you got out of there when you did, Norton. Although you shouldn't have gone back in, I appreciate you risking your neck for Warner. He's a long-time friend."

Max gave a slight nod.

"I should have asked before now but were you injured in the blast? Do you need medical attention?"

His hesitation had Willow glancing up at him, heart skipping a beat. "Max?"

"It's nothing."

Definitely something. Max took stoic to a new level. "Where?"

"Left arm. Got too close to the fire when I lifted the bookcase off Warner."

"Do you need a ride to the emergency room?" Kincaid asked. "I'll be glad to call for an ambulance."

"No, thanks. My teammate is in town, and he's paramedic who always travels with a med kit. Are we finished? I'd like to take Willow to the hotel."

"Answer one more question before you go," Senior Cop said.

"What's that?"

"Why did you park on the street instead of in the driveway like the detectives?"

Max lifted one shoulder in a shrug. "We've already been targeted with an arson attempt. I didn't like the odds that a trap had been laid here for us. I hoped we would get ahead of any potential traps. I was wrong."

"Yet you brought Ms. Knox here despite the probable danger to her and yourself?" Skepticism rang in his voice. "Some boyfriend you turned out to be. I would never put my girlfriend at risk that way."

"I insisted he bring me," Willow said. She couldn't let these officers think the worst of Max. It wasn't fair when he'd done everything possible to protect her despite her insistence on coming along. "I thought he needed someone to watch his back in case of trouble."

Suspicion glimmered in Senior cop's eyes. "Mr. Norton, Ms. Knox, don't leave town. I'm sure detectives will follow up with you soon."

"We're not going anywhere until Graham Enright's killer is in custody." Max handed the officer his card. "The detectives can reach me here. Tell them to leave a message, and I'll return their call as soon as possible."

"Shy about giving your personal cell phone number?"

"Do you give out your personal cell number to anyone who asks? I don't give out my number. It's a security issue. Fortress always has someone manning the switchboard. When the detectives call, Fortress will notify me immediately."

A sharp look from both officers, then Kincaid said, "It seems trouble follows you, Norton. Might be wise not to poke your nose into official business for a while."

"I'll keep that in mind." Max didn't promise to follow Junior's advice.

Willow stooped and picked up the box, expecting the officers to question her about the contents. They didn't. Max led her to his SUV, giving the burning house and fire crews a wide berth. He kept her close, constantly scanning the area as they walked.

He stopped several feet from the SUV and eased in front of Willow before using his key fob to unlock the vehicle. "Stay here while I check things out."

Max slid a small, black device from his pocket and slowly circled his vehicle, watching the chaser lights on the device.

When he returned, Willow indicated the black gadget. "What is that?"

"An electronic signal detector. Fortress issues one to every operative."

Her blood ran cold. "You were searching for a bomb?"

"That or a tracking device. The detector didn't find either one." He escorted her to the vehicle, climbed behind the wheel, and drove from the subdivision.

Max activated his Bluetooth and called Brody.

"Sit rep," the Texas team leader said in lieu of a greeting.

"Trouble with a capital T."

"Hold." A moment later, Brody said, "Go. You're on speaker with the team plus Sage and Poppy."

"We met the detectives investigating Enright's murder at his home. While we were inside, a bomb exploded."

The sound of a feminine gasp came through the speaker. "Please tell me you and Willow are all right," Sage said.

"We're fine."

Willow frowned at Max. Fine? Not quite. "Max is a little singed around the edges, and we're both coughing from smoke inhalation. Max breathed in more smoke than I did when he went back into the house to get the second detective."

"How bad are your burns, Max?" Jesse asked.

"Sunburn."

"Blistering?"

"Nope."

"Stitches still intact?"

"I think a few popped loose when I hit the floor with Willow. We're on the way back now. You can check both of us."

"Willow, that okay with you?"

She relaxed. Now that he knew Max was hurt, the paramedic would be sure to examine the injuries. "It's fine, Jesse."

"Did you find anything we can use to point us in the right direction before the bomb blew up?" Logan asked.

"Bombs."

"Plural?"

"Yeah. At least three."

A soft whistle followed that announcement. "So, back to my question. Did you find something useful?"

"A box with interesting pictures," Max continued.

"Pictures?" Willow twisted to face him. Was this a much-needed break? "If the pictures are so interesting, why didn't the detectives confiscate them when they searched the house?"

"The box was hidden inside another, larger box, and both were on the highest shelf in the darkest corner. Would have been easy to miss the smaller box."

A huff, then Brody said, "I'd say Cohen or Warner was in too much of a hurry to be thorough."

"My money's on Warner being the culprit. I wouldn't have wanted him as a partner when I was on the job. The officers who questioned us at the house didn't confiscate the box. They must have assumed the detectives knew we had it. If it turns out the box is a key to the case, we'll give it to the detectives." He paused. "After we make copies of the box's contents."

Of course. She shook her head, amused. "Do you think Cohen and Warner will eventually give the box to Mrs. Enright?"

"She won't want them unless she plans to feed them to a bonfire."

Her eyebrows rose. What kind of pictures did Max find?

"Brody, what did you discover while Willow and I dodged bombs?" Max asked.

"We'll talk when you get here. I want your full attention on getting the two of you here safely. Logan will meet you halfway to watch your six."

"Not necessary. My ride was clean, and I'm watching for a tail. I haven't seen signs of trouble."

"You're getting the protection anyway, so don't argue. You've already had multiple attempts on your lives. We're not taking the chance that the killer comes after you again and this time succeeds in taking one or both of you out."

Max scowled. "I'm capable of protecting my girlfriend and myself, Brody."

"Suck it up, cupcake," Sawyer said. "You're not going to win this argument. We talked about it before you called, and you're outvoted. Deal with it."

"Yeah, fine. But I'll be sure to bring this up when it's your turn to give in gracefully to pressure like I did."

His teammates laughed.

Willow smiled. If that was a graceful capitulation, she'd hate to see Max give in with a bad attitude.

"See you soon, Max. Watch your six."

"Yep." He ended the call.

"You have loyal friends, Max."

He glanced at her. "They're your friends, too."

True. The Texas team had become as close to Willow as her own siblings and Sage and Poppy. Max had always occupied a different place in her life and heart. What she felt for him was nothing close to affection for a sibling. "Brody said Logan would meet us halfway. How will he know where to intercept us?"

"Phone tracker."

Of course. She should have guessed. Although the drive to the inn remained uneventful, Willow was glad to see the headlights of Logan's vehicle in the rearview mirror.

Max's teammate parked beside them at the inn and met them at the front of their vehicle. "The bomber didn't stick around to make sure he took you out. Sloppy work on his part."

"Didn't want to attract attention. If the cops are any good at their jobs, they took photos and videos of the bystanders watching the action."

"They'll upload the evidence to the police department's database where Zane will access it. Did you see anyone hanging around?"

"A bunch of folks. None of them stood out. Didn't see an Orioles cap." Max wrapped his arm around Willow's waist and walked into the inn with her. "Then again, I was a little busy after the bomb went off. I only got a quick video of the gawking neighbors when I met the ambulance and guided the EMTs around to the back of the house."

"Maybe we'll get lucky."

"Doubtful."

As soon as they were in the suite, Sage threw her arms around Willow. "I was so worried. Are you sure you're all right?"

"Just a nagging cough." Willow stepped back and turned to Jesse. "Please check Max."

The medic inclined his head toward Willow's bedroom door. "You heard the lady, my friend."

"Go, Max," Brody ordered. "You, too, Willow. After Jesse gives you both a once over, we'll talk."

Willow wrapped her hand around Max's and led him to her bedroom with Jesse on their heels with his medical bag.

"Take a seat," Jesse said. "Max, you first. Let's see your arm." The medic examined the injury. "A decent burn. Should heal up fairly quickly, though. I have cream to calm the pain. Show me your back."

Max's expression was neutral as he glanced at Willow. "Do you want to close your eyes or leave the room?"

Still protecting her. Her heart turned over in her chest. "Take off your shirt, Max."

"Are you sure?" he murmured. "It's not a pleasant sight."

"The scars are part of you, and I'll never reject any piece of you that you're willing to share with me."

Max reached back and tugged the t-shirt over his head, his gaze locking on hers as though gauging her reaction.

Willow managed to keep her distress buried deep. So much pain he had endured, and she was only seeing a small part of Max's back. Jesse's body hid most of it.

"You were right." Jesse opened his medical bag, tugged on a pair of rubber gloves, and pulled out a box. "You popped several stitches."

"Can you use butterfly tape?"

A head shake from the medic. "Sorry, Max. They won't hold." He left the bedroom and returned with a chair. "It will be easier to work on your back if you sit in the chair, facing backwards. Willow, sit on the bed and whisper sweet nothings in Max's ear while I clean him up and numb the cuts I need to stitch."

Perfect set up to preserve Max's privacy. She had to admire Jesse's careful maneuvering. Willow sat on the side of the bed. "So, Max, tell me something about you not everyone knows."

Amusement lit his eyes. "If I tell you in front of the nosy medic, my secret will get out."

"Hey, I'm not a motormouth," Jesse protested.

"If more than one person knows something, it's not a secret."

The other man scowled. "You're planning to tell Willow something juicy."

Willow grinned. "I'm special."

Max laughed.

Jesse rolled his eyes and ripped open a package of alcohol wipes. "Let's hear this awesome secret, Romeo."

Max glared at his friend. "You're sworn to secrecy."

"Maybe. Depends on how juicy this secret is." He tossed the bloody wipe into a plastic bag and reached for a clean one. "I might have to be bribed to remain silent."

"I happen to know a juicy secret of yours."

"Yeah, you do. What about it?"

"You keep mine, and I'll keep yours." Max looked pretty pleased with himself.

Jesse blew out a breath. "Yeah, fine. So, what's the big news?"

"I'm teaching myself a new skill."

Jesse paused mid swipe with the alcohol pad. "You teaching yourself to cook? If you are, I'm not volunteering to be your taste dummy."

Willow laughed as Max slid another glare toward the medic. "Don't get too crazy, Jesse."

"Hey, at least that's a useful skill. We could use a decent cook out in the field if we run out of rations."

"Does that happen often?"

"No, thankfully. We all suck at cooking. Well, Max?"

"It's not cooking," Willow's boyfriend muttered.

"What is it, then? And you can't tell Willow about your magician skills. That doesn't count because it's not a deeply held secret."

Willow stared. "Wait a minute. You're a magician, Max?"

He nodded.

"Why didn't I know this?"

"The subject never came up. I don't do magic shows often these days."

"Only for children, especially the children of Fortress employees," Jesse added. "He's very good, Willow. Puts on a great show. The kids love it."

"You'll have to tell me when you perform again. I'd love to see your act."

"Sure. I'll make sure you have a front-row seat. In fact, if you talk to me really sweet, I'll train you to be the magician's assistant."

"That sounds like fun. You've got a deal."

Jesse tapped him lightly on the shoulder. "Your secret? I'm dying here."

Max chuckled. "All right. You win." He drew in a deep breath and said in a rush, "I'm teaching myself how to knit socks." His cheeks turned red as he waited for their reaction to his announcement.

Silence followed for several seconds, then Jesse said, "So that's what you've been doing with the yarn. We thought you were practicing a new trick for the kids."

"Are you any good at knitting socks?" Willow asked.

Max snorted. "I'm terrible. I seem to be all thumbs. Instead of a solid sock, I'm only capable of making a sock with holes."

"How hard can it be to knit?" Jesse smirked. "You use two pointy sticks to make knots with string, then tug your creation onto your foot. Easy peasy."

"It's harder than it looks," Max said, his ears red now. "Try it sometime, and you'll see what I mean."

"Forget it, man. I don't intend to be the object of our teammates' ridicule."

"If you decide knitting isn't for you but you still want to try your hand at doing something with yarn, I could teach you to crochet," Willow offered. "I haven't done it in a few months, but I enjoy it." She hadn't picked up a crochet hook since she'd returned from Mexico. In retrospect, that had been a mistake. Crocheting always reduced her stress level.

His brows furrowed. "What's the difference between crocheting and knitting?"

"You use a hook to crochet. You can watch videos online to learn different stitches."

Jesse shook his head as he grabbed a syringe and a bottle of medicine from his bag. "Why are you torturing yourself with yarn and knitting needles, Max? Easier to buy socks than make them."

"Stress reliever," he said. "Counselor's orders."

"A little stick," Jesse murmured as he injected medicine into Max's skin, and continued their conversation. "Marcus Lang told you to learn to knit?"

"His wife, Paige, is teaching him to knit. He says it's a good way to reduce stress. He and Paige knit socks for themselves, family, and friends."

"Is it a stress reliever?"

"Not yet. I might have thrown a skein or two of yarn at the wall and broken a few needles."

"I'll teach you to crochet," Willow promised. "It's fun and faster than knitting. And the bonus? I'll get to spend time sitting very close to demonstrate various techniques."

"Deal. I'm definitely in." Max looked over his shoulder at Jesse. "No spilling my secret to the pack of wolves out there. Otherwise, I'll never hear the end of it."

"As long as you promise not to make me a pair of holey socks for Christmas and keep my secret from the wolves, my lips are zipped." Jesse finished injecting the medicine and stood after stowing the medical detritus. "I'll be back in a few minutes to stitch your cuts." He left the room without looking back.

Willow grabbed her phone. "While we wait for the medicine to take effect, let's find a video online to teach us to crochet socks." By the time Jesse returned, Willow and Max had decided on a pattern to try and ordered the supplies.

"Let's see if the lidocaine has taken effect." Jesse pinched a few places. "Any pain?"

"Nope. Just pressure. Let's do this. Clock's ticking." He looked at Willow. "What about teaching me to crochet a blanket? Something repetitive and easy enough for a child to do."

"I have just the blanket for you to try. Let me show you." She returned to the Internet and found the video she wanted and watched it with him.

When the video ended, Max looked thoughtful. "You know, the stitch doesn't look all that difficult. Want to help me choose the yarn?"

"You sure you want to order that much yarn? You might not like crocheting."

"I have to do something to satisfy Lang, and I think I can handle one hook better than two needles. Besides, if I don't like it, I can give you the yarn, right?"

But that wouldn't help Max's stress. "We'll make it work. I think you might be surprised how much you'll enjoy it."

"Finished, buddy." The medic tugged off his second pair of gloves and tossed them into a bag along with the other medical trash. The needle went into the hard container with the used hypodermic. "Try not to rip out my version of needlework, all right?"

"Yeah, yeah." He waited until Jesse checked Willow, declared her in good shape, and left the room before Max cupped her cheek with his hand. "Thanks."

"For what?"

"The distraction." He grimaced. "Want to know another secret? I hate needles."

"I'm not a fan myself so you're welcome."

Max studied her a moment. "You really don't mind teaching me to crochet?"

"Not a bit. My grandmother taught me. She'd be pleased to know I passed the gift to someone I care about." She leaned forward and kissed him softly. "She and my mother would have loved you, Max." Like she did. Willow was head-over-heels in love with Max Norton.

His lips curved. "Yeah? Good to know. I wish I could have met your mom. If she was anything like her daughter, she was a very special woman." He stood and held out his hand. "Come on. Let's see what Brody and the others discovered while we were out."

Max walked with Willow to the living room and led her to the couch. Instead of sitting on the cushion beside her, he sat on the arm of the couch.

"Tell us what happened," Brody said. "Don't leave anything out."

Max and Willow did as ordered, ending with, "The only thing that we were able to save was a box from Enright's closet."

Sawyer frowned at Max. "What was in the box?"

"Pictures of Graham Enright with different women."

Logan's eyebrows rose. "So? It just proves the guy was having affairs like his wife thought."

"There's a little more to it than that. Each one of the women wore a wedding dress, and he was wearing a tuxedo. The photos looked like the pictures taken on wedding days."

Poppy folded her arms. "I know you've been looking into Graham's background, Willow. Did you find evidence of multiple marriages?"

She shook her head. "The only marriage in the record is the one to Celia."

"What's your next step, Max?" Brody asked.

"Run Graham Enright's face through our databases and facial recognition system."

Chapter Twenty-Two

"What do you expect to find?" Willow asked. "Wouldn't running Graham's name through background searches turn up any criminal activity?"

"Not necessarily," Max said. "Enright's name won't pop for criminal activity if he used a different name and wasn't caught."

"I'm on it," Sawyer said. He grabbed his laptop and typed rapidly. "Search is ongoing. I'll let you know when it's finished."

"Any news about the arsonist?" Poppy asked Max.

"Nothing yet. We may not have anything for a while. Zane was awake all night as tech support for two teams, and Maddox planned to send him home to sleep for a few hours."

"I have news about that," Brody said.

Max straightened, wincing as the new stitches tugged his skin at the abrupt movement.

"Before Zane went home, he sent me recordings from various cameras in and around the hotel as well as all security and traffic cameras. I ran the footage through his computer program to clean up the images."

Now they were talking. "Get anything?"

"A reflection from a store window and a mirror. I'm still tinkering with the program to clean up the images," he admitted. "I think I can get a decent image by the time I'm finished with the process."

"I can help," Poppy said. "Logan showed me how that program works a few weeks ago."

He sent a narrow-eyed glance toward Logan. "Is that right?"

A careless shrug. "Poppy needed to clean up a digital image from a cold case she's researching. I taught her how to use Z's program."

"Does the boss know?"

Silence.

Brody scowled. "At least tell me Poppy was supervised when she used the program. You know how she is."

"Back off." Logan's voice was soft. Not a good sign.

"Hey," Poppy snapped. "Right here, Brody. Do you want my help cleaning up these images or not?"

"Go for it." Brody pointed a finger at her. "Don't poke your nose into our databases, Poppy. The boss will go ballistic if you do."

"Yeah, I hear you." She tossed a pointed look at Logan. "He said the same thing when I learned to work the program, and swore me to secrecy."

"Go for it, Poppy. Logan, we'll talk about this breach of protocol soon."

A snort. "Bite me."

"Who looked into Oliver Enright's background?" Max asked.

"That would be me," Sawyer said. "Oliver is something else."

"What do you mean?" Sage asked.

"He has the morals of an alley cat. Oliver keeps a string of women on the side along with his current wife."

"How many times has he been married?" Jesse asked.

"The current Mrs. Enright is wife number four. He trades them in every ten years."

"Wonder how many more times he'll get married."

Max exchanged glances with Willow. The news about Enright's health would spread soon. "I doubt he'll look for wife number five or add another mistress to his list."

Brody frowned. "Why not?"

"Terminal bone cancer."

Jesse whistled. "Guess that why he's pushing Willow so hard to find another heir."

Poppy glanced up from her computer. "Wait a minute. His wife as well as Graham's wife and sons should inherit. Why is he looking for someone else?"

"Oliver doesn't respect his grandsons," Willow said. "Celia isn't a blood relative and won't receive a penny of the Enright money. Oliver and his wife signed a prenup. She doesn't expect to inherit and has money of her own."

Logan shook his head. "Cold."

Sage frowned. "Why doesn't he respect his grandsons?"

"Oliver believes they'd sell the businesses and live off the Enright money instead of continuing the family legacy," Max said. "He thinks they're lazy bums who don't understand the value of a dollar and can't be trusted with the Enright legacy."

"He should have trained and groomed them to take over his holdings." This from Brody.

"It's sad." Sage leaned her head against her husband's shoulder. "Oliver is so focused on preserving the family coffers that he doesn't value the most important thing he has. Family."

Brody looked at Willow. "Max said you researched at the coffee shop. Come up with anything?"

"A lot of nothing on Oliver. Multiple affairs and four marriages. Pillar of the community. Generous charity donations. Strong work ethic. He spent a lot of time with his grandsons when they were young. When they hit their teen years, that stopped and he never reconnected with them."

Jesse scowled. "That's the time his grandsons needed him most."

"Agreed," Brody said. "Max, what do you know about the box of pictures you found?"

"Not much. I didn't have time to do more than glance at the photos before the first bomb detonated. However, I noticed a definite age progression in Graham. Some of the photos appeared to be family portraits with Graham, the women, and children."

"No, he wouldn't," Willow whispered, horror growing in her eyes. "Would he?"

"Graham wouldn't be the first man to do it." Max squeezed her hand. "I might have misread what I saw, Willow."

"You didn't," Sawyer said, his gaze glued to his laptop screen.

"Have something?" Brody asked.

The other man blew out a breath and sat back in his chair, hands clasped behind his neck. "I ran Graham Enright's name through the system and came up with zip, so I ran his image through facial recognition. Enright has been reported missing by four women other than Celia. Each of the women filed a report on a missing husband and submitted a photo of Enright. He's married to five women under different names and social security numbers. Celia is his legal wife. His second marriage came ten years after his first. From then on, the marriages came at five-year intervals."

"Wonder what his will looks like," Jesse said. "That's a nightmare in the making."

"No kidding. Just think about all those wives and kids in one room, and Graham's lawyer tasked with explaining that the man they loved was a bigamist."

Logan scowled. "Enright had to know he would be caught."

"I don't know," Sawyer said. "He's been getting by with it for more than twenty years."

"How?" Poppy demanded. "Tucker's Gap isn't a huge city. If these women moved in the same circles, they'd know each other."

"I don't know if they're in the same social class, but every wife lives in a different city and in a different county from Celia. Graham set things up to protect himself and prevent the women from meeting."

"What about social media?" Sage asked. "Everybody has social media accounts these days. What's to prevent his families from posting his picture?"

"Good question." Brody kissed the top of her head. "We'll look into it."

"What do we do with this information?" Willow asked. "Those women need to know their husband isn't coming home."

"Glad I'm not tasked with breaking the news to the widows," Logan muttered.

"Same." Sawyer went to the kitchen and poured coffee into a mug. "It's your case, Max. This is your call. What do you want to do with the information?"

"Bury it in a deep hole and run as fast as possible. Since that's not an option, I say we turn the information over to the Tucker's Gap police and let them handle the notifications. That's not our job any more. Since we have the names of the women who filed the missing persons reports on Enright, we should look at their social media and see what they posted. We might be able to piece a few things together that way. If not, we ask Zane or one of the other hackers to look into it."

Max grabbed his phone and sent Cohen a message. The detective could inform his partner when Warner was stable. "Done."

"Anything else?" Brody asked Max and Willow.

"Nope." Max stood. "I'll get the box of pictures. Might be good to split up the families and start on the social media pages. If we can't find anything useful, we'll pass the task to the Fortress techs or Zane." He retrieved the box from Willow's bedroom and set it on the coffee table.

Willow removed the photos. "Graham Enright was a sleazy man," she murmured. "No wonder he was so eager to meet me for a date. Maybe he wanted to add me to his harem."

Sage stared at her friend. "He asked you for a date?"

"He came to the hotel restaurant because someone claiming to be me left him a message and asked him to meet me."

Max fisted his hands. "Makes more sense now that we know about his other wives. He was prowling for another wife and believed you were a good candidate to continue his game."

If the man wasn't already dead, Max would be tempted to punch Graham Enright in the face. More than once. Jerk.

"Oh, come on. I didn't pay attention to him, and he was too old for me."

"I don't know," Poppy said with a slow drawl. "I can see where women would find Graham more attractive than Max. He was in good shape and had distinguished gray hair at his temples. And the money? Oh, man." She fanned herself, amusement in her eyes.

"Very funny," Logan said, scowling.

"Graham didn't appeal to me." Willow returned to the couch. "Since I barely interacted with him, why would he think I was interested?"

"Every other woman he met was. Why wouldn't you be into him? Besides, he didn't know about Max," Sage pointed out. "Too bad they didn't meet. It would have been entertaining."

Entertaining? Max glared at his friend who burst into peals of laughter at his expense.

Brody divided the names of Graham's four other wives between the team, and said, "Let's get to work."

Although his order ended the teasing for the moment, it wouldn't last. The situation would provide endless entertainment for Max's teammates for a long while.

When the rest scattered to different parts of the suite to work on their laptops, Willow turned to Max. "Who should we focus on?"

"Celia Enright and her sons. If one of them knew what Graham was doing, he or she would have the best motive for orchestrating his murder. It's possible one of his sons was the man in the Orioles Cap."

"I hope they aren't responsible. Bad enough to discover what kind of man he was without letting him destroy the rest of their lives when they're caught."

"People can be irrational in the grip of fury."

Willow frowned. "You may be right."

She didn't look convinced. "But?"

"I keep remembering the murders in the Enright family. They were committed with a knife. Did the same person commit all the murders?"

He wasn't a fan of coincidence, either. "The coincidence is too much, isn't it? If the deaths are connected, the culprit can't be the children from his fake marriages. They're too young."

"The wives aren't."

"We follow the leads to the end of the trail. If the trail doesn't lead to a killer, we'll keep turning over rocks until he crawls out. He won't be able to help himself." The likelihood concerned Max.

He took Willow's hand in his and walked to her bedroom. "Do you want to work in here or in the other room with the others?" He wanted her to be comfortable alone with him, but her trust couldn't be rushed. He had to be patient a little longer, and he'd have everything he wanted and needed. Willow.

She scooped the laptop from the bed and carried it to the table. "Here's fine." Willow turned one of the chairs around so he could sit backwards. "I trust you completely."

His heart leaped. "You do?"

A shy glance came his way. "You're the only one I trust to that level. Let's start the search with my databases."

Max joined her at the table as she booted up the laptop. "You can't drop a bombshell on me and in the next breath say let's get to work."

Amusement danced in her eyes. "I can't?"

He turned her to face him. "No, ma'am, you can't. Are you sure?"

"I ought to know how I feel, Max."

His hands trembled as he cupped her cheeks. "You don't know what that means to me. I've waited six months to hear those words from you."

Max brushed her mouth with his, intending for the kiss to be light and gentle. In less than a minute, the heat shot up one thousand degrees. He lost himself in the heat and silken texture of her mouth and the honeyed sweetness of her taste until his teammate's laughter broke the spell. He lifted his mouth from Willow's and stared at her for a moment. "I'm crazy about you, Willow Knox."

She smiled. "Good thing because I'm crazy about you, Max Norton. Ready to work now?"

Not really. He longed to continue kissing her. "Let's do it. Start with Graham's sons." He sat on the chair she'd pulled out for him.

Willow sat at the table and keyed in the oldest son's name. "Killian Enright is married, no children although his wife is expecting their first child." She glanced over at Max. "If I can't find another heir, do you think Oliver will leave everything to the child?"

"If he has no other option and ties everything in a trust with an executor to manage the holdings. I can't see him handing the estate and holdings to Killian to manage when he doesn't trust his grandson."

"Max." Logan stood in the doorway with a grim expression on his face.

He knew that look. Trouble. He stood, reluctant to take bad news sitting down. "What is it?"

"Poppy cleaned up the image of the man who drugged Willow and murdered Enright."

"And?"

"She ran the image through our database. We have a name."

Chapter Twenty-Three

Max tugged Willow to her feet. Together, they followed Logan to the living room where the rest of the team waited with Sage and Poppy. "What do you have, Poppy?"

She shoved back from the table and stood. "Trouble. You need to keep Willow under lock and key. Better yet, take her on a vacation someplace warm and sandy far from here. Keep her hidden away for a few weeks until your team resolves her problem."

Willow stiffened and glared at her friend. "I have a job to finish, Poppy, and I refuse to hide."

"Shut up and listen," the other woman snapped. "I'm trying to keep you alive. I don't care if you like my methods. You living is a lot more important than protecting your delicate feelings."

"That's enough," Max warned. No one was going to abuse Willow again, not even a friend who yelled at her out of love because she was afraid for Willow's safety. "Tell us what you found. We'll go from there."

Poppy glowered at Max. Instead of sniping at him like he expected, she turned the laptop around and pointed at the face on the screen. "This is the guy who drugged Willow and likely killed Graham Enright."

Since that was excellent news, why was Poppy so afraid for Willow? "Name?"

"Meet Dwight Mendez, killer for hire."

Adrenaline poured into his bloodstream. A mercenary who profited from the deaths of others. Great. Just great. "How good is he, Logan?"

"Very. The guy never gives up, and he's ruthless. Doesn't mind collateral damage, either. Worse, he enjoys his work. As you've seen, his specialty is knife work although he doesn't mind using other methods to get the job done."

"How long has he been hiring out?"

"Since the day he turned sixteen years old. He murdered his old man with a knife. Claimed self-defense."

"Was it?"

A shrug. "Maybe. Cliff Mendez beat his wife and kids. It's possible he turned on Dwight one time too many, and the kid pushed back with a knife in his hand. From that point on, Dwight was brought in for questioning about several murders similar to Cliff's. Nothing stuck. He left the states for a few years, went to Europe, and became best friends with Tommaso Ricci."

Max groaned. "That's not good." Understatement of the year.

"Nope. The kid honed his skills with a master assassin and returned to the US to ply his trade. He's been in business for himself for over twenty years, Max. He's highly sought after by people who need problems solved permanently. Cops at all levels of government have brought him in for questioning but he's never been charged with anything. No evidence."

Sawyer shook his head. "Great. Ricci did his usual stellar job of training a wannabe assassin. That guy is scary smart and slippery as an eel."

"So are his students," Logan said. "Dwight was seen on camera near the areas of a few knife murders which is why he was brought in for questioning. No charges stick."

"The feds want to nail Mendez's hide to the wall," Brody said. "With the footage Zane put together and Poppy's work cleaning up the images, the FBI would owe Fortress a boatload of favors if we handed them what we have, plus gift-wrapped Mendez, and provided free delivery of the trussed-up assassin to the nearest FBI field office."

"I get the picture." Max glanced at Willow. Her face was pale. "I'll keep you safe, Willow. Mendez won't get near you." Not while he was still breathing.

"You can't promise that. No one can."

"He's good. We're better. He prefers using a knife. Knife work is close quarters, and I'll be beside you every minute."

"Mendez might prefer knives but I don't think he's not afraid to branch out. Otherwise, we wouldn't have dealt with a Molotov cocktail and bombs. I'm tired of dodging danger everywhere we go."

"We don't know Mendez was to blame for the arson and bombs."

"Thought you didn't believe in coincidences," Poppy said. "The five of you harp about it often enough. Was I right to take your admonition as truth?"

Max wished he didn't believe the maxim himself. "Yeah, you should. Most of the time the statement is accurate. Now that we know who we're looking for, we have a better chance of catching him before he gets too close to Willow. Someone has to know where he is. We have to find him and extract the information." By using any method necessary. He'd cross any line to protect Willow.

"If it was that easy, Mendez would already be rotting in prison," Willow said. "Excuse me. I need a minute." She rose and walked outside to the balcony railing.

Max looked at Brody. "Call Maddox and Zane. We need to find Mendez before he takes another swipe at Willow."

After a nod from his team leader, Max followed Willow outside. He scanned the area around the inn, wishing the building had more floors so they were higher off the ground.

Max eased between Willow and the balcony railing and nudged her backward until she was against the wall of the inn with his body in front of hers, blocking a sniper shot. The skin at his nape crawled. He hated having his back exposed.

He took comfort in the knowledge that no one, not even the police, knew where they were staying. So far, Max had seen no signs of anyone watching the inn and no new guests had checked in since Max and Willow arrived.

He wrapped his arms around Willow and tucked her against his chest, careful not to make her feel trapped. Max held Willow until her body stopped trembling and melted against his. Oh, yeah. That's what he wanted and needed. "Better now?"

A slight nod. "Magic touch."

He snorted. "That's your touch, not mine. I might perform magic tricks, but you are magic. Everything about you is sheer perfection."

Her laughter was soft. "You're biased."

"Nope. I spoke the absolute truth. You saw Mendez's picture on the computer screen. Think back from the time you arrived in Tucker's Gap until now. Do you remember seeing him at the hotel, on the street, the coffee shop, or a restaurant?" He knew Willow's habits well. His girl would have found the closest coffee shop to feed her tea habit, and she would have remained in the hotel except for completing interviews and researching family files.

Willow shook her head. "I remember seeing a pair of expensive running shoes but not Mendez's face. I thought I had imagined the shoes."

"Since your memory has gaps, you don't trust what you remember is true. The running shoes might not mean anything. You're sure the person wearing the running shoes is a man?"

"If the running shoes were on the feet of a woman, she has a large foot. Max, when you and your teammates catch Mendez, will the danger to us be over?"

Max wanted to lie to her. Couldn't. He shook his head. "We need to find the person who hired Mendez. He doesn't work for free. When we stop Mendez, his employer will hire someone else if he feels threatened by you."

She shuddered. "I was afraid you'd say that. If I knew anything to help, I would have told the police."

"The killer doesn't know what you remember from the night of Graham's death."

"Wouldn't the police announce to the media they were looking for a person of interest?"

"Not with a man like Mendez. If he knows the authorities are looking for him, he'll disappear and come back when the heat's off. Better for us if the cops act as though they don't know who's responsible for Graham's death."

"Fair point. How is Mendez contacted for work? He can't have a website. What would he use for a domain name? Killers Are Us?"

Max chuckled. "Dark web. If you're careful, you can find anything you want, including an assassin to do your dirty work. Word gets around when you're available for wet work, especially if you work by referral. There's a trail. We just have to find it."

"Zane again?"

"This is his area of expertise." Among many others. The SEAL was handy to have around and deadly in a firefight. "If anyone can find the electronic trail, it's Z."

She sighed. "I'll owe him a million favors before this is finished. Think he'll trade for a free family tree?"

"You don't owe him. I do, and I'm happy to repay any favor as long as you're safe." He brushed a soft kiss over her mouth. "Ready to go inside and get to work?"

Willow nodded. "I needed a minute to pull myself together. It's hard knowing someone wants to kill you, harder still to see his face and know he's real and ruthless."

Max took her hand. "Come on. Time to turn the tables on Mendez and hunt him down."

"I like that idea. Let's see how he likes being the hunted instead of the hunter for a change. Where do we start?"

What would she think of him when he admitted the truth? "I have a few contacts on the dark web. We start there." Max knew someone else who had more contacts in that arena than he did.

Her eyebrows rose. "You're a man of many surprises."

Was that good or bad? Afraid to ask, Max guided her into the suite. "Logan, have a minute?"

His friend pushed away from the breakfast bar where he'd been working with Poppy and followed Max and Willow into her bedroom. He closed the door. "What do you need?"

That question was the perfect example of why he loved working with this team. Max knew Logan and the others on his team would do anything to protect him and Willow, legal or not. But if anyone took the risk and paid the price of failure, it would be Max. "Still have contacts on the dark web?"

Logan's mouth curved. "What do you think?"

Some things never changed. "The best way to lure Mendez into the open is bait a trap he can't resist."

Willow's hand gripped his forearm. "How do you plan to trap Mendez?"

"By using the perfect bait. You in, Logan?"

A slow, feral smile curved his mouth. "How do you want to do this?"

"Give him a prize he can't resist. Another contract on Willow."

#

Chapter Twenty-Four

Willow stared at Max. She couldn't have heard him right. "What did you say?"

"You said earlier you were the perfect bait. You're right."

Max's hand coasted up and down Willow's back and sent goosebumps zinging across her skin. Same thing happened every time he touched her. He just did it for her. Man, what chemistry they had together.

"We have to make the prize irresistible," he continued.

"I'm the farthest thing from irresistible. If you don't believe me, wait until I'm on a deadline and under a ton of pressure. I'm crazy cranky."

Logan chuckled. "I'm happy to say your crankiness is Max's problem to handle. But Mendez is a mercenary, Willow." He leaned one shoulder against the wall. "He's all about money. He doesn't have integrity or honor. Otherwise, he wouldn't make a profit from killing people. Mendez won't be able to resist cashing in twice for killing the same target." He gave a polite bow. "You're looking at a second man who wants you dead."

She rolled her eyes. "Nice to know I've ticked off so many people. What did I do to you to make you want to kill me, too?"

He looked at her a moment, his gaze assessing. "I think you broke up my marriage."

"What does that say about you?"

"Nothing good but Mendez won't care as long as my money is good."

"Whatever. Won't Mendez check out your story before he accepts the contract? You could be an undercover police officer hoping to lure him into the open."

"We'll have Fortress create a solid backstory," Max said. "Mendez doesn't know Logan. As soon as the killer is in police custody,

Fortress will remove the backstory and erase all images of Logan from the Internet."

But his face would still be on the Net for a time. What if Fortress wasn't fast enough? The wrong people might recognize Logan and track him down. Willow shook her head. "It's too risky. What if a terrorist happens to be looking for Logan and sees the pictures?"

"Zane will ensure that doesn't happen."

She still didn't like it. Poppy would be at risk, too. Her friend was very fond of the taciturn black ops soldier. Although she wouldn't say so, Willow suspected Poppy was falling for Logan. "You've worked under an assumed name before?" Willow asked Logan.

He shrugged. "It's a sting. I've done my share of undercover work. I'll be fine."

"I want to do it myself, but Mendez knows my face as well as Jesse's," Max said. "That leaves, Sawyer, Brody, and Logan. While Brody and Sawyer could pull this off, Logan is the best at sliding deep into a role, so deep the mark has no clue he's being set up."

She eyed the operative in question. "Max better be right about your acting skill. I'll never forgive myself if you're hurt during this operation, and Poppy won't forgive me, either. So, don't get hurt." Willow gave a mock shudder. "Mendez has nothing on Poppy. She's ruthless."

He saluted. "Yes, ma'am." Logan straightened. "Anything else, Max?"

"That's it for now. I'll put out some feelers myself on the dark web, see if my contacts have heard of Mendez and know how to contact him."

"Only trusted sources. I'll call the boss and tell him what I need from the tech geeks before I start cast out the lure for Mendez."

A slight nod. "Thanks, man. I owe you."

Logan waved that off. "No debt." He left the room.

Max placed a light kiss on Willow's mouth. "You're a homewrecker, huh?"

"Who knew?"

"I foresee punching the lights out of men who believe you're more interesting and beautiful than their own spouses and girlfriends, and think you're fair game."

"How long do you see yourself having to do this?"

"The rest of my life."

Her gaze shot to Max's face. He wasn't kidding. "What does that mean, Max?" She was afraid to believe what she was seeing.

"You know what it means, Willow."

"Spell it out for me. Please." She prayed she hadn't misread him.

"I've been courting you for months, baby. Is it any surprise I want everything? I'm in love with you, all the way to my soul. You own my heart."

And there it was, the one thing she longed to hear and terrified Willow to her bones. Was it too soon after Mexico to trust her own heart, to trust his? "Max." Her throat tightened to the point where she struggled to draw in a breath.

"Follow my breaths, Willow." He pressed her hand onto his chest and breathed to the count of four, held it for four beats, then breathed out to the same count. "Good. Again. This time to six."

She matched her breathing to his. When they reached an eight count, Willow's breathing was easier, almost natural. Thank God.

She dove into his open arms and nuzzled against him. "I'm sorry," she whispered. "I didn't expect that to happen." And was aggravated it had. She'd worked hard to overcome those panic attacks, and this was the second one in as many days.

"It's my fault. This was too soon. I should have waited. I'm sorry for upsetting you."

Willow shook her head. "It's a gift. I won't let you take it back."

"Gifts shouldn't cause panic attacks."

She wrapped her arms tighter around his waist. "Are you sure, Max?"

"Sure that gifts should bring joy instead of panic, absolutely."

"Are you sure you want to tie yourself to me?"

He stilled. "Why wouldn't I?"

This was so hard. She hated Armando and what he'd done to her even more at that moment. "You know what happened to me in Mexico. You know everything." Max knew more than her own family. The thought of sharing personal details with her father and brother made her cringe inside. But Max knew it all. She'd turned to him on dark nights when memories plagued her and spilled her guts to the quiet man. He'd listened without judgment and helped Willow restore her equilibrium every time. "Are you sure you want to be involved with me on a personal level?"

"Not want, Willow. Need. I need you more than I need my next breath. So, yeah, baby, I'm sure. How I feel will never change. You're the one for me. The only one."

Relief swept over her. Thank God. "In that case, I have a gift for you, Max."

He started to pull away. "You don't have to...."

"I love you, Max." She had to tell him the truth. He'd exposed his heart for her. Willow wanted him to know he had her heart as well. "I think I've been half in love with you since the moment you walked into that horrible cell where I was held captive. You brought me hope and a gun."

He chuckled at that last bit, but it was true. Max walked into the cell to rescue her and enabled her to help herself by giving her a gun. "I fell the rest of the way in love when you walked into my hospital room in Tucker's Gap and declared you weren't leaving my side."

Max cupped her face between his palms. "It's my turn to ask if you're sure. I don't want you to feel obligated or, God forbid, sorry for me. Are you sure?"

"I don't say things I don't mean. My heart is yours." Her eyes burned. "A once-in-a-lifetime gift, slightly damaged, but all yours if you want it."

"Oh, I definitely do." He kissed her tenderly. "Your heart isn't damaged, Willow. It's perfect, and I'll treasure it until my last breath."

"I'll do the same with yours."

"I meant what I said a few days ago. This is a commitment, one I'm giving you for our lifetime. There's no hurry and no time line here. We'll take as much time as we need, all right? I want to marry you when you're ready, whether it's tomorrow or ten years from now. As long as I know you're mine and you love me, I'll be content to wait until the time is right. I need a promise from you, though."

"What promise?"

"You'll tell me when you're ready to be my wife. I won't push or pressure you because it's not fair to you, so the ball is in your court."

Oh, goodness. She fought a losing battle against her tears. They trickled down her cheeks. Max was such a good man. How had she been so blessed to have him walk into her life and, more important, to stay there? "I'll tell you when I'm ready."

A slow smile curved his mouth. "Do you realize you just agreed to marry me?"

"I don't remember you asking a question."

"No take backs," he warned. "You agreed, and I'm not letting you back out." Max wiped her tears away and rested his forehead against hers. "Will you allow me to buy you an engagement ring?"

Willow smiled. Sneaky. "What sane woman would turn down an engagement ring from the man she loves with her whole heart?"

He blew out a breath. "Thank God. As soon as we get home, I'm sliding my ring on your finger so everyone knows we belong to each other."

"I'll be proud to wear your ring." And show off the symbol of his love for her.

He held her close for several minutes, exchanging kiss after kiss with Willow, each one more passionate than the last. By the time Max eased away from her Willow's knees were weak and her lips felt swollen.

"We need to get to work." Max lifted her hand to his mouth and kissed her palm. "I'm hanging onto my control by a thread."

Willow smiled. "We can't let Logan accuse us of slacking off." She sat at the table and booted up his laptop. "You want to work on the computer?"

"You go ahead. I have some calls to make first, then I'll help."

Willow logged onto her work database as Max talked to someone named Javier. She stared at the screen a moment, considering where to go first. Oliver Enright was pushing her to find an heir. He had two grandsons and a great-grandchild soon to arrive. Yet he wasn't satisfied with any of them. She wasn't a miracle worker. Unlike Max, she couldn't make someone appear out of nowhere. What if there wasn't anyone else to find?

She considered what she knew of Oliver and his history with women. What were the odds of Oliver having a child born to one of his mistresses?

Willow frowned. If she discovered one of his women had given birth to his child, would Oliver accept the child as his next heir, especially if the child was born to a mistress rather than a wife?

All she could do was follow the trail and give him the results. Whether or not he accepted the heir was on him.

She slid her phone from her pocket and pulled up the list of Oliver's mistresses. Willow flinched at the sheer number. The list contained at least twenty names, and she wondered if the list was complete. Max's teammates were good. Zane was better. How good were Oliver's skills in discretion?

With a sigh, she typed in the current mistress's name. By the time Max finished his calls, Willow had marked three women from her list. They didn't have children.

"What are you doing?"

"A search on Oliver's mistresses. I'll do the same with Graham's other wives. Perhaps one of them gave birth to an Enright child Oliver will accept."

"How's it going?"

Willow grimaced. "Between Oliver's mistresses and Graham's wives, I'm looking at 25 women and their children for Oliver and four women plus Celia for Graham."

He whistled. "Wow. It's good we have several people in the suite to help."

She glanced over her shoulder toward the living room as their friends laughed at something Poppy said. "They're already looking into Oliver's wife and ex-wives."

"They can't have made much progress. Might be best to give the list of women to Fortress and ask them to weed out the possibilities. If you don't want to do that, we'll split the work between the eight of us."

Willow hated to hand over the research to Fortress and owe more favors to the company CEO but she didn't have unlimited time to plow through the work herself. "Ask Fortress to look into Oliver's mistresses and wives. We'll keep working through the list of Graham's wives and children."

"I'll send the request for tech support to Maddox. He'll either assign it to Zane or one of the tech geeks. We'll have results soon."

Willow didn't see how with 25 women to look into. However, she sent the list to Max's Fortress email address. "You should have the list now."

He pulled out his phone and tapped a few keys, then made another call. "It's Max Norton. I need a favor." Max explained the request, listened for a moment, then said, "Thanks, boss." He ended the call. "Done. The techs will give this top priority. No one is better at background research. We should have results in two hours."

"Thanks, Max. This will help cut hours of work for us. How did you make out with your calls?"

"Javier had never heard of Mendez. Crash was a different story."

She blinked. "Crash?"

"Long story involving lousy driving skills and a boat load of bad luck. Anyway, Crash said Mendez goes by Troubleshooter in the chat rooms mercenaries haunt."

Troubleshooter? Really? "Does he work by referral only or research each person who contacts him?"

"Both. Once Fortress creates a background for Logan, Crash will tap one of his sources to generate an introduction to Mendez if necessary."

"Why won't Crash recommend Logan to him?"

Max remained silent.

Uh oh. She stiffened. That wasn't a good sign. "He's too afraid Mendez will slip through the trap and come after him and his family?"

"Yeah."

"What will we do if Logan's friends are too scared to contact Mendez?"

"His friends are deeper in the underground market than mine. One of them will step up, especially when they find out Logan is after Mendez to protect a friend."

"He's that close to these people?"

"Let's just say they owe him huge favors. To protect you, he'll call in all the markers." Max held out his hand. "Come on. Let's update the others." They walked back to the living room. "Logan, any progress?"

"Talked to a friend who promised to contact Mendez once we have the background set up and a name for her to contact."

Poppy's head whipped his direction. "Her? Your contact is a woman?"

His lips curved. "Problem?"

She glared at him. "Maybe. How good of a friend is the woman?"

He laughed.

Poppy lightly punched his arm.

"Lay into him later, Poppy. What do you have, Max?" Brody asked.

"The name Mendez uses in the mercenary chat rooms."

"Now we're talking. Let's have it."

"Troubleshooter."

"Lame," Sawyer muttered.

"We also asked Fortress for assistance with the research. Turns out between them, Oliver and Graham were involved with 30 women."

Jesse shook his head. "The Enright men are nuts."

"No kidding. Fortress is looking into the women Oliver was involved with, 25 in total. We opted to look into Graham's wives and children ourselves."

"Give us one wife a piece," Brody said. "We'll help."

"Good grief," Poppy said. "We have a ton of work to do in a short period of time."

"Would anything else help with your research?" Brody asked Willow.

"We have so many people to research, having white boards to write everything out would be a great help. Large pieces of paper we can stick on the wall will work, too. I need to map the families and see if anyone overlaps more than one family group besides Graham and Oliver." With that many people in the mix, she'd bet the farm at least one person, perhaps more, crossed family or friend groups.

Sawyer stood. "I'll take care of that. I noticed an office supply store down the street."

"Need a hand?" Jesse asked.

"Sure. Willow, do you have a preference between white boards or paper?"

She considered the advantages and disadvantages of each. "Paper. We won't be able to hide the white boards when housekeeping comes to clean."

"Paper and markers. Anything else?"

Willow shook her head. "Make sure the paper is thick enough to prevent the names from bleeding through to the wall, is self-adhesive, and won't damage the paint when we peel it off."

"You got it. Paper, markers, and no home remodels. If you think of anything else, call me. Should Jesse and I pick up dinner while we're out?"

"Excellent idea," Poppy said. "I'm starving. Mexican all right?" When everyone agreed, she looked at Jesse and Sawyer. "Buy a variety in volume."

"Yes, ma'am." Sawyer and Jesse left.

Max's phone rang. He glanced at the screen and grimaced. Swiping a thumb across the screen, he said, "What can I do for you, Detective?"

Chapter Twenty-Five

Max held the phone away from his ear as Cohen cursed a blue streak, glad he hadn't placed the call on speaker. When the storm of heated words slowed, Max said, "I guess you're as surprised by the news as we were."

"How did you find out Graham Enright was a bigamist?"

"Sure you want to know?"

"Is it illegal?"

"No." He had access to facial recognition software through Fortress. Accessing law enforcement databases was another matter and one he didn't plan on discussing with the Tucker's Gap detective.

"Tell me."

"The only thing I carried out of the house besides you and your partner was a box containing pictures of Graham with four other women. Some of those pictures were wedding photos with the women. Others were of Graham, his wives, and their families."

"Why didn't you tell me?" Cohen snapped.

"When? You and Warner went to the hospital not long after I carried you outside. We didn't know if the pictures meant anything. It was possible Graham followed in his father's footsteps and married a succession of women. We never expected to learn he'd married each woman without divorcing any of them.

"Celia Enright told us she hired a private investigator to prove Graham was having an affair but the investigator struck out. The photos gave me the idea to run Enright's image through our facial recognition software, and we hit pay dirt. Four other women filed missing persons reports on their husbands. Each woman submitted a photo of the man she had married."

"Enright."

"He used a different name and social security number for each relationship. When you ran a standard background check on him, the system wouldn't have caught it. We checked the marriage dates. His only legal marriage was to Celia. Graham married the second wife about ten years after his first marriage, then added another wife every five years."

"Another man with an average salary wouldn't have been able to afford five wives at once," Cohen muttered.

"No kidding. Celia said he traveled extensively for his father. The five women live in different cities and counties around Tennessee. They wouldn't have traveled in the same circles. What we don't know yet is why the women didn't post pictures of him on social media."

"Unheard of these days. Everybody spills way too much information online."

"Could be something as simple as Enright wanting to protect his children in case someone who knew Celia happened upon his photo while scrolling through social media. No picture of him meant no way to connect the fake name to his face and his fake families."

More vicious cursing. "He had kids with these women?"

"Yeah, he did."

"How old are they?"

"I'm not an expert but it looks like the youngest is only a few months old."

"Send me everything you have."

"Right now, we only have names and addresses, plus the names he used and the social security numbers. You'll need to notify these women about Enright's death and about their illegitimate marriages. I don't envy you the task, Cohen."

"I don't want to tell Celia she was right about her husband, either." He sighed. "Enright was a fool. If he was unhappy in his marriage, why didn't he divorce Celia and marry the next wife? Had to be cheaper than maintaining five separate households. Want to trade jobs for a few hours, Norton?"

He chuckled. "Sorry, man. I resigned from the job for several reasons. Death notifications and irate relatives are two of them."

"I'm stuck in here until tomorrow, and this isn't something I can do over the phone."

"One more night won't make Graham less of a fool or his wives any worse off."

A grunt. "You have a point."

"How's Warner?"

"In surgery for internal injuries but his prognosis is good. Keep me updated. If you learn anything, I want to know yesterday. Got me?"

"Yeah, I got it." Max wouldn't be thrilled if he was in charge of an official investigation with private detectives holding back information. As a former cop, he wouldn't make the police detective's investigation harder. They all wanted the killer behind bars.

Max ended the call. "Detective Cohen is livid about Graham Enright's multiple marriages."

"More likely he's ticked off because he and his partner missed some important facts," Brody said. "They would have found the information themselves if they dug deep enough."

Logan's phone vibrated. He checked the screen. "Maddox must have put all the techs on my request. Fortress has my fake social media profile up and running."

"How dangerous is that for you?" Poppy demanded. "You can't have your face on the Internet, Logan. It's not safe."

"How safe is it for me to be friends with the daughters of the Vice President of the United States?" he countered.

Sage nudged her sister. "He has a point."

"We keep a low profile," Poppy protested. "In the past six months, we've been to D.C. twice and only once in the public eye. Brody and Logan weren't in the country at the time so there was no danger to them. This is different. What if terrorists see his photo and track him down in Hartman? There must be a better way to handle this."

"Fortress understands the risk and negated it," Logan said. "When Mendez searches for my fake name, he'll be directed to my social media pages in a private room that mirrors the public social media sites. No one except Mendez will see these pages."

"No loopholes?"

"None. Fortress only hires the best."

"We'll see. If they screw up, I'll be in your boss's face." She froze. "Wait a minute. You said Willow is the other woman who broke up your marriage."

"You hussy," Sage teased Willow.

"Who is the woman to whom you're supposedly married?"

"One of the other operatives. The techs took pictures of her and her husband, who is also an operative, and photoshopped my face over his."

"No kids?"

"Nope. My fake wife didn't want to ruin her girlish figure and I'm selfish enough not to want her to be anything other than runway perfect."

Willow stared. "Fortress has operatives who are also runway models?"

"Two. My fake wife isn't one of them. Both of the runway models are too high profile to pull this off. The woman I'm fake married to is named Lily."

Poppy scowled. "You sure you don't have a thing for Lily?"

Logan snorted. "I'm not stupid. Her husband, Remy, would kill me and feed me to the gators in his beloved bayou. He's easy going except when it comes to his wife."

Brody laughed. "You forgot to mention Lily is more dangerous than her husband. She might look like a grown-up Barbie doll, but Lily is creative in her vengeance and lethal."

Poppy relaxed. "Sounds like a woman I should meet."

"You'd like her," Max said. "And you'd love Remy. All the women do."

Logan stared at Max with an expression that would have made his insides turn to ice if they weren't close friends. He held up his hand in a silent apology. Funny that the quiet, intense operative was possessive of a woman he wasn't officially dating.

"Back to business." Brody retrieved a bottle of water for Sage and broke the seal for her. "We need to research Graham's wives and see if anyone in their backgrounds stands out. We'll work on that while Sawyer and Jesse are out."

Poppy returned to the breakfast bar where her laptop was set up. "Names, Max."

"Misty Wolcott, Jana Dean, Lucy Walters, and Nina Grace." He gave the address and name Graham had used for each of the marriages.

"We'll take Misty Wolcott," Brody said. "Max, you and Willow continue to looked into Celia Enright and her sons. Poppy, you and Logan investigate Lucy Walters. We'll leave Nina Grace and Jana Dean for Sawyer and Jesse. They should be back before soon with office supplies and dinner."

"The Fortress tech geeks should have something soon on Oliver's mistresses, wife, and ex-wives." Holy smoke, Max thought. What a mess in the making that was.

"Does Oliver's wife know about his mistresses?" Sage asked.

Willow nodded. "The current Mrs. Enright ignores his affairs as long as he's discreet."

"People already know," Poppy said. "They may not say so in her hearing to spare her feelings, but her friends and acquaintances know."

"As long as Mrs. Enright doesn't have to listen to people talk about it, she can pretend it's not happening." Max took Willow's hand. "Let's call Celia before we dig into her background."

She walked with him to her bedroom. "Why do you want to talk to her?"

"I want the name of Graham's lawyer and Celia's promise to contact him or her on our behalf. I'd like to know if he's aware of the other wives and children, and if Graham made provisions for them."

"Motive for murder?"

"Can you think of a better one?" Max sat at the table. "People have killed for less than millions of dollars."

Willow logged onto the computer. "People can be a disappointment."

People could be downright evil but he didn't point that out. She had experienced it firsthand.

Max's phone rang in a pattern indicating the call was forwarded from Fortress. He checked the screen, surprised to see Celia's name. He swiped his thumb across the glass and said, "Norton."

"Why did I have to find out from Detective Cohen about my husband's house?" Celia Enright snapped. "You should have called to inform me about the fire."

Max relaxed when he realized she wanted to talk about the fire and not the other wives. "When did he contact you?"

"A few minutes ago. Why didn't you tell me that you started a fire at Graham's?"

"Willow and I didn't start a fire. We were inside the house with the detectives when an explosion occurred."

A gasp. "An explosion? A gas line ruptured? I didn't know Graham had gas logs or appliances. He was paranoid about fires."

Celia paused. "Wait. Are you implying the arsonist who almost killed you and Willow struck again while you were at Graham's?"

"The cause of the fire is still under investigation. Detective Cohen will tell you when he knows what caused the blaze."

"You know more than you're telling me."

"I suspect things still unconfirmed. I don't want to tell you something that may turn out to be false."

"How soon will I find out more?"

"Tomorrow, possibly the day after at the latest."

Celia uttered a loud huff. "This is ridiculous. Are our detectives so lazy or untrained that they can't work faster to provide information to waiting families?"

"They're waiting for the arson investigator to determine the source of the fire."

"I see." She still sounded suspicious. "Can you pressure the detectives to contact me sooner?"

"No, ma'am. I have no influence here."

"I doubt that. You convinced me to let you search through my husband's things without much difficulty. Speaking of your search, did you find anything?"

He flinched. Not the question he wanted to hear. "We didn't have time to do a thorough search before the fire started."

"This is frustrating, Mr. Norton. I need answers. My sons need answers."

"Yes, ma'am. The detectives are working on it but they were both injured in the fire."

"What? I didn't know that. How bad are their injuries."

"Cohen doesn't appear to be too bad. I don't know about Warner." He could find out through Zane but figured Cohen would share the information when Max talked to him the next time. "Cohen should be back on the job tomorrow."

"I suppose that will have to be good enough. Please call me if you hear anything."

"Yes, ma'am. Get some rest. Nothing will change in the next few hours. Do you have family in town?"

"My sons live here."

Excellent. She shouldn't have to deal with the shocking news about Graham's other wives by herself. "Spend time with your sons. They're hurting as much as you are."

"Yes, of course. You're right. I've been selfish, thinking only of my own loss. My sons lost their father."

"I have a request."

"What's that?"

"I'd like the name of Graham's lawyer and for you to call him."

"Why?"

"I'd like to ask him a few questions about Graham. He'll need your permission to talk to me."

"What do you want to know? Perhaps I can answer them for you."

"This is something only the lawyer will know."

Another pause, then, "His name is Sam Parker." She rattled off his office phone number. "I'll call him now. He's a good friend and answers calls from me day or night."

Now that was interesting. "Must be a close friend." Or he was very conscious of the size of the estate connected to Graham Enright.

"He is. May I give your phone number to Sam?"

"Of course. Thanks for contacting him."

"I'm warning you now. I'll ask him what this mysterious conversation is about."

"I wouldn't expect otherwise, Mrs. Enright." When she ended the call, Max slid his phone back into his pocket. He indicated the computer. "We have one more name to investigate."

"Who?"

"Sam Parker."

Willow's eyes widened. "He's Graham's lawyer?"

"Yeah. Why?"

"He's also Oliver's lawyer."

Chapter Twenty-Six

"Have you met Parker?" Max asked Willow. May not be anything to the intersection. After all, how unusual would it be for father and son to use the same lawyer?

She nodded. "The first day I met with Oliver, Sam was in the office for a meeting with him."

"What was your impression of him?"

"He came from old money and went to an Ivy League law school. No confirmation on that. Just a feeling based on his speech, manner, and tendency to look down his nose at me."

Max chuckled. "Can't say I'm surprised. I doubt either Enright would hire a lawyer without a degree from one of the top schools in the country. They would also be inclined to hire someone the people in their social circle trusted."

Willow turned back to the computer. "Do you want to research Sam first or focus on Celia and her sons?"

"Celia first."

"What do you expect to find?"

"I'm not looking for anything in particular, just something that doesn't ring true or points in another direction to investigate."

Willow tapped a few keys and turned the computer so he could read what was on the screen as she scrolled down the page. When she reached the end of the document, she glanced at Max. "Want me to input her name into the Fortress system?"

He nodded. "We should be able to find a photo of her for our facial recognition system."

"Personally, I hope we don't find anything. One louse in the family is enough." Willow paused. "Okay, two less-than-honorable men in one family is enough." She accessed the database and typed in Celia's name.

A minute later, information on Graham's wife filled the screen. A few more pieces of information, more layers, more depth. Nothing new.

When he finished reading, Max rubbed the back of his neck, wincing as the new stitches tugged again. His initial assessment was correct. "Nothing we didn't already know. What about her sons?"

"Killian and Noah, both work for Enright Enterprises." She entered Killian's name first.

The son's information filled the screen a moment later. Impressive. Killian had a bachelor's degree and an MBA from Harvard. He was currently working on his doctorate in Economics. This degree was online so he didn't have to move away from Tucker's Gap. His wife, Cheyenne, was expecting their first child in a few months.

Max frowned. Why didn't Oliver want Killian as his heir? On the surface, the guy looked perfect to run the Enright empire. Who wouldn't want a man at the helm with three degrees in business and economics?

"This doesn't make sense," Willow said. "Killian seems like an excellent choice for Oliver's heir. Why did he reject his grandson?"

"Maybe his opinion has more to do with Killian's future plans."

"How do we find that out without asking him? Never mind. Social media, right?"

"People do tend to spill everything online."

"Let's find out if Killian Enright is one of those who spills his guts to the world." She searched the social media sites and came up empty. "Struck out."

Since Killian was working full time and working on an advanced degree, Max doubted he had time to waste on social media. "Check Cheyenne's name."

She entered the name and sat back. "Wow. Cheyenne's whole life is on social media."

"Focus on the posts where she mentions Killian."

A short while later, she pointed at the screen. "There it is. That's why Oliver won't name Killian as his heir."

Max scanned the entry and shook his head. "Oliver is short-sighted. Who says you can't teach on the college level and hire a stellar board and management team to oversee an empire?"

"Most of Killian's time would be spent on his university responsibilities instead of Enright. Oliver wants his heir to be as driven and consumed with the family legacy as he is."

"I don't see how Oliver or Graham had much time for their wives and mistresses."

Willow laughed. "Remember that if you ever consider straying, Mr. Norton."

"Never going to happen, soon-to-be Mrs. Norton. You're the only woman for me. It's you or no one."

Her smiled faded. "How do you know for sure? You might change your mind."

Max shook his head. "The only woman I notice in a room is you. The rest are assessed for threats, then dismissed. I love you, Willow. Why would I look at another woman let alone have an affair when the only woman I'll ever want is you?"

A soft gasp at the doorway had Max and Willow turning in their seats.

Sage stood at the entrance, hand over her mouth, tears glittering in her eyes. "Sorry to interrupt that sweet moment, but Jesse and Sawyer are back with supplies and dinner." She moved further into the room. "Did I hear right? You're getting married?"

Max kissed Willow's palm. "We are. No date yet, and we're not in a hurry. She'll have a real engagement ring on her finger as soon as we return home."

Their friend wiped tears from her cheeks and smiled. "I'm happy for both of you. Anyway, come eat while the food is hot." Sage returned to the living room.

As Max approached the doorway with Willow, Brody's voice reached them.

"Sage? What's wrong, baby?"

"I'm fine." She laughed. "These are happy tears."

Brody glared at Max. "You sure I don't need to punch someone in the face for making you cry?"

"It's our fault," Max said. "Sage overheard a good conversation."

"Spill, Sage," Poppy demanded. "I can use some happy news." She slid a narrow-eyed glance Logan's way. "Especially now."

Her sister shook her head. "Nope. It's not my news to share. This information must come from Willow or Max."

Poppy turned her gaze and unspoken demand on Max.

Oh, man. Logan would have his hands full with Poppy Reynolds if he ever wised up and convinced her to give him a chance.

Max looked at Willow. "Do you want to share the news or wait? Your choice."

She smiled. "Tell them. They'll guess anyway."

"You heard her, Norton." Poppy folded her arms. "Spill already."

He tucked Willow against his side. "Willow and I are in love. I'll buy her a real ring when we're home to make our engagement official. When we get married is totally up to her. I'm content knowing she's mine."

The two accepted hugs and hearty congratulations from his team and the women.

Sawyer squeezed his shoulder lightly. "When do you plan to ask her father for permission to marry her?"

Oh, man. "Soon," he muttered. "Don't rush me." His teammates laughed, the jerks. "I have time," Max insisted.

"Not much," Logan said, amusement in his eyes. "Word gets around fast."

Just wait until Logan had to talk to Poppy's father. Colonel Knox had nothing on Vice President Reynolds. Then they'd see who was laughing the most. "I just asked Knox for permission to date her. Can you imagine what he'll say when I ask permission to marry her this fast?"

"You should worry about her brothers' reactions," Jesse said. "They're both Special Forces."

He scowled. "Trust me, I'm aware of that. However, her father has teams of Special Forces soldiers at his disposal."

More laughter from his teammates. "Face it, Max," Sawyer said. "You're toast."

"Thanks for the support, buddy. I'll return the favor one day."

"All right. That's enough," Willow said. "He'll be fine. Max can handle my father. We need to eat while the food is hot. Who knows what we'll face before the night is over."

Brody gestured toward the breakfast bar where several covered containers were set out along with plates and utensils. "Ladies, fill your plates."

After they finished eating their meal, Max brushed his mouth over Willow's. "I have a call to make." He sent a glare toward his grinning teammates. "Start researching Noah Enright. I'll join you shortly." He hoped. Depended on what kind of mood her father was in. Man, he hated to admit it but his teammates were right. This wouldn't be a cakewalk.

He stepped onto the balcony and closed the door behind him, praying Colonel Knox was open to the idea of a marriage between him and Willow, and placed the call.

"Knox," Willow's father said, his voice a hair above a growl.

Max flinched. Maybe this wasn't the best time to talk to Willow's father. "Max Norton here, sir."

"How's Willow?"

"She's fine."

"What's happened?"

He took a deep breath and updated Willow's father. "She's fine," he repeated. "I would have called you immediately if she'd been injured."

"This is becoming too dangerous, Norton."

"I agree. My team and I have a plan to draw out the killer and squeeze him to learn the name of his employer."

"You know who he is?"

"We have an identification. When we capture him and obtain the name we need, he'll be handed over to law enforcement."

"Too bad," the military man grumbled under his breath. "I'd like a few minutes alone with him before you turn him in."

Max smiled. "I feel the same way, sir." He sucked in a deep breath. "I need to talk to you about something else, Colonel."

"Let's have it, son."

No point delaying the inevitable. Wouldn't help and might hurt his case. "I want your permission to marry Willow, sir."

An extended silence followed his statement. Was that good or bad? Sweat broke out over his body. Probably bad. Why would any father want Max Norton, former magician, former cop, and former troublemaker to marry his daughter? Finally, he couldn't stand the silence any longer. "I love Willow, Colonel. She owns every piece of my heart."

"You know what she's been through."

"Yes, sir. She told me everything."

"Everything?"

"All of it. When Willow can't sleep because memories haunt her, she calls me. We've spent hours on the phone in the middle of the night."

"Why didn't she call us? We would have been glad to listen."

"Some things are too personal to share with your father and brothers. The abuse she suffered is one of those things."

"Why did she tell you details she hasn't shared with her own family?"

Max sighed, knowing his next words would trigger an investigation by her father and might well torpedo his relationship with Willow if the colonel voiced his objections to their future marriage. "I told you I've been through a similar experience. While she didn't know the details at the time I met her, Willow cobbled together enough information from my teammates to have an idea why I understood the trauma she suffered."

"I'm sorry, Norton."

He froze. What did that mean? Sorry that he'd been injured or sorry that Max couldn't marry Willow? "Sir?"

"I hate that you suffered as well. A lot of misguided and evil people fill our world."

"Someone has to fight back. That's what I did as a cop and what I do now."

"You fight terrorists for a living, Norton. Willow is too fragile to be with a black ops soldier. This isn't a good idea. She needs someone kind and gentle, someone who will handle her with the utmost care and pampering."

Stunned, Max rubbed his jaw. How could Gray Knox view his daughter as weak? She was as much a warrior as his Special Forces sons were. "I'm sorry, sir. I disagree. She's one of the strongest people I've ever met. I'm proud of her and honored to belong to her. I want Willow to be happy. Wrapping her in cotton isn't the way to give her what she needs." She wouldn't thank them for treating her as though she was weak. She wasn't and never would be.

"Son, I don't want her to be hurt again."

"Neither do I, and I'll do everything possible to protect her from further harm. But she's not delicate. Willow is a warrior and fighter to the bone."

"Come on, Norton. You say you'll protect her but you hunt terrorists for a living."

"With all due respect, sir, so do you and your sons."

"Fair point. I still think this engagement is too soon."

"I want my ring on her finger, Colonel. The ring is another form of protection. It tells people, especially men, that she's loved and protected. The ring tells Willow the same thing. How fast Willow and I move our engagement forward to a wedding day is up to her. I won't push her to set a date. Whether it's a day or ten years, I'll be content as long as I know she loves me and is working her way to me."

Knox chuckled. "You sound like I did when I spoke to my father-in-law about marrying Willow's mother. You're sure you won't change your mind about her down the road? The kind of trauma she suffered raises its head when you least expect it."

"There is no one else for me, sir. She's the love of my life. If Willow turns me down, I'll remain single the rest of my days. I won't settle for anyone else."

"I still don't believe the timing is right but I won't stand in your way. However, if Willow says it's too soon, you will back off. You hear me?"

"Yes, sir. You have my word I won't pressure her in any way." No matter how much it cost him.

"I'm a good shot, Max. Willow's brothers are better. You might want to remember that."

"I won't forget." He shuddered as relief swept over him. "Thank you, Colonel. You won't regret this. You have my word."

"See that you keep it, Norton. Otherwise, we'll talk again, and the next time won't be so pleasant." Knox ended the call.

Max shoved his phone into his pocket and took a moment to calm his racing heart. That had been intense. He wondered how soon he could expect similar phone conversations, including the warnings, with Willow's brothers. At least he had some time there due to deployment with their teams.

After a slow survey of the area, he returned to the living room. His teammates glanced up from their work with varying degrees of curiosity on their faces. "Well?" Brody asked.

"Well, what?"

"How soon will the hit squad be here to take you out?"

Max's teammates laughed. Even Sage and Poppy smiled at that one. "Very funny. You're a real riot."

More laughter from his so-called friends as Max stalked into Willow's bedroom.

"What's going on?" she asked. "What did I miss?"

"I just finished talking to your father, and the guys were giving me grief, as usual." As close as brothers, he and his teammates took every opportunity to tease each other. They might have given Brody the same treatment when he was dating Sage.

Willow turned in her chair to look at him. "How did it go?"

"About like you'd expect." He dragged a hand down his face. "If you look close, you'll see that I now have several more gray hairs on my head. Your father isn't someone I'd want to meet in a dark alley, baby."

She laughed. "I bet it wasn't that bad."

"Ha. You'd lose that bet. He's a father determined to protect his only daughter. Trust me, it wasn't pretty." He bent and kissed her. "However, he gave me his blessing as long as you agreed to accept my proposal without pressure from me. You're going to agree, right? Tell me I didn't put myself through that torture for nothing."

Willow tapped her chin with her forefinger. "Hmm. I don't remember you asking me a question."

Well, if that was the hold up, Max could fix that problem. He dropped to one knee, took Willow's hand in his, kissed the back of it, and said, "I love you with everything I am, Willow Knox. When the time is right and you tell me you're ready, will you marry me?"

She smiled. "I would be honored to be your wife, Max Norton. Yes, I'll marry you."

He blew out a breath. "Thank God. I think it would kill me to call your father back and tell him you turned me down."

Willow wrapped her arms around his neck and hugged him. "I love you too much to let you go."

"Excellent. Just remember that when I make you angry in the future."

"Deal."

Max's phone signaled an incoming forwarded call. He pulled out his phone and glanced at the screen. His eyebrow rose. That was fast. "It's Sam Parker." He swiped his thumb across the screen and said, "Norton."

A slight pause, then a man said, "This is Attorney Sam Parker. Mrs. Graham Enright told me to answer your questions about her husband." The disapproval in his voice made it clear what he thought about the request.

"Thanks for calling, Mr. Parker. When do you have a ten-minute window for a meeting?"

"I'm a very busy man, Mr. Norton. I don't have time in my schedule."

Max wanted to see Parker's face when he asked the questions. "Ten minutes, sir." If he didn't agree, Max would wheedle his way past the man's administrative assistant. "I'll bring you coffee or meet you at your favorite coffee shop on your way home. The coffee is on me, of course. Isn't ten minutes worth a cup of coffee?"

Parker sighed. "All right. I'll meet you at World of Coffee on Fifth and Main. Do you know where that is?"

"I'll find it. What time?"

"In two hours. Don't be late, Norton. If you're not there by the time I arrive, I won't wait. I have a pressing engagement this evening and mustn't be late."

"I'll be there."

"How will I recognize you?"

"I know who you are." He ended the call on that subtle threat and turned to Willow. "I see what you mean about the Ivy League thing. Parker wasn't happy about meeting me."

She narrowed her eyes. "Us."

"Right. Us."

"When are we meeting him and where?"

"In two hours. A place called World of Coffee. Know it?"

"I should have known he'd choose that shop. It's not a run-of-the-mill coffee place. The shop is out to make a statement by selling coffee for a minimum of ten dollars a cup."

Max winced. "Ouch." No coffee was worth that much in his opinion. Then again, he was used to cups of coffee that tasted like burnt sludge. In his line of work, you got caffeine however you could get it.

"Tea is just as expensive there."

"Max." Logan walked in. "Lena is ready to throw out the lure for Mendez."

"Good. Willow and I are meeting Sam Parker, Graham's lawyer, in two hours. If Mendez schedules a meet while we're gone, take Sawyer or Brody for backup."

A snort. "I don't need backup to handle one assassin."

"We need this guy alive. Take backup."

"Yeah, yeah, Mom. I hear you." Logan rolled his eyes and returned to the other room.

"He won't go alone, will he?" Willow asked, worry in her eyes.

"No." He reconsidered. "Probably."

She glanced at him. "Make sure he doesn't."

Max saluted. Logan always did what he wanted. The only one who could rein him in was Brody, and that wasn't a sure bet. "I'll take care of it before we leave. Parker made a big production out of me being there when he arrived and said he wouldn't wait. We should go now and wait for him to show. Have a feeling he'll show up early enough to miss us at the designated time."

"What if he doesn't show up at all?"

"We track him down and persuade him talk to us." Before he called the cops.

Willow shut down the laptop and scooped up her crossbody purse. "Ready."

Max told Brody where they were going and pulled his team leader aside. "Make sure Logan has backup if he meets Mendez," he murmured. "I don't trust him."

Amusement lit Brody's eyes. "Logan or Mendez?"

"Mendez won't play fair, and Logan will be inclined to rid the world of a terrorist."

"Can't blame Logan. I agree with him."

"Same, but we need Mendez alive to answer questions."

"Logan won't go alone," Brody said. "No promises on what condition Mendez will be in when we finish with him."

"Don't care. Just make sure we have answers." After all, who would Mendez whine to? The cops would plead ignorance, pointing out he'd arrived on their doorstep with bruises. Better yet, Max and his teammates could make an anonymous call to the feds and leave Mendez trussed up for them to collect. They would appreciate the gift of an international assassin.

Logan and Brody were the best at extracting information without leaving a mark behind to tell the tale.

A slight nod from Brody. "Go. Watch your back."

"Copy that, sir." Max ushered Willow from the suite. Soon, they were driving toward Tucker's Gap. Halfway to their destination, his phone rang.

He glanced at the dashboard display and tapped the screen. "You're on speaker with Willow, Z. What do you have for me?"

"I sent the information you asked for on Oliver Enright's wife, ex-wives, and mistresses. The man's been busy," Zane said dryly.

"That is the understatement of the century. I'm surprised someone hasn't called his hand on his behavior in the past 50 years."

"When you have money, people turn a blind eye to behavior others wouldn't get by with."

"Anything stand out in the backgrounds?"

"Besides the sheer volume?"

Max smiled. "Besides that."

"Your woman is right."

Willow jerked. "Good to know," she said sounding cautious. "What am I right about?"

"Someone is targeting Oliver Enright's family. What's interesting is the killer is probably the same one who killed Graham. Do you know who this guy or gal is?"

"Dwight Mendez. We isolated his picture from security and traffic cam footage, and cleaned it up for an identification."

The sound of keys clicking filled the cabin of the SUV. A moment later, a soft whistle sounded. "Nasty character. This is the man after Willow?"

"Yeah. He'll fail. No one is going to hurt her." They'd have to go through him first.

"You still set on the plan?"

"Can't think of a better way to reel this guy in, Z. He's slippery but he's also a mercenary. He won't be able to resist getting paid twice for the same mark."

"Will someone warn Remy before he learns the information on his own?"

Max flinched. "I'm not telling him, that's for sure."

Laughter from the Navy SEAL. "You're not immune from retribution, my friend. It's your plan."

"Don't remind me. In my defense, I wasn't the one who came up with the idea to use Lily as the fake wife."

More laughter from the other man. "Yeah, that was the boss's contribution to the plan. I'll enjoy the fireworks when Lily's husband confronts Brent about the scheme."

"Maybe Remy will cut me a break when he learns the plan was created to protect Willow. Anyway, Logan's friend Lena is initiating contact. We'll see if Mendez bites."

"He will. Be careful, Max. Mendez is an ugly piece of work. He'll enjoy pitting himself against you."

"I have to find out who hired him. It's the only way to protect Willow."

"Agreed. Don't let down your guard. If you need anything, say the word."

"Thanks. I hope I don't have to take you up on the offer but I'm not holding my breath."

"Whatever I can do, I will. Willow, do everything Max tells you to do, all right? He'll keep you safe."

"I promise. Are you working tonight, too?"

"I am. I'm covering for another tech who came down with the flu. Max, want me to keep digging into Oliver's women?"

"That would be great. Let me know if you find anything."

"Copy that. Later."

He parked in front of the World of Coffee minutes later and circled the SUV to open Willow's door. Max held out his hand. "Ready to enjoy some liquid gold?"

Willow laughed. "For the price their charging, I'm expecting spectacular tea."

"We'll see about the coffee." He escorted her inside the coffee shop and paused in the doorway, surprised by the posh atmosphere, elegant tables, and plush chairs in a dimly lit shop with a glass-enclosed fireplace in the center of the large room. Looked more like a five-star restaurant than a coffee shop.

"Nice, isn't it?" Willow murmured.

"Have you been in here before?"

She shook her head. "While I was in Oliver's office, his assistant brought him coffee from here. She said the drinks are amazing."

"Guess we'll find out."

They were seated at a table near the door to Max's displeasure. It was there or nowhere. For a place selling overpriced hot drinks, World of Coffee was packed. After a wink at him, Willow took the seat with her back to the door, allowing Max to relax slightly and keep an eye on the door.

He scanned the menu and resisted the urge to roll his eyes at the pretentious-sounding names of the various coffees and teas. "Looks like you can have every tea ever known to mankind, Willow. What do you want to try?"

"Pomegranate orange tea." She smiled. "A large pot since we'll be here over an hour."

He stared. "Pot?"

"Look around, sweetheart. They serve tea in china tea pots here."

Max glanced at the tables around the room. Several of them had tea pots in various shapes and sizes sitting in the centers. "Right." Perhaps that explained the pricey tea.

One of the wait staff stopped at their table. "Are you ready to order?" she asked with a bright smile.

"A large pot of pomegranate orange tea for the lady and a large coffee for me."

"What kind of coffee?"

"Just a plain cup of joe."

She stared a moment. "Um, all right. I highly recommend cinnamon sugar twists with your order. They're absolutely divine, guaranteed to melt in your mouth."

"Sold." He slid a look toward Willow. "A chocolate muffin, too, please."

"Yes, sir. I'll return soon with your order."

Max waited until she disappeared in the kitchen before he said in a low voice, "She looks twelve."

Willow grinned. "She makes me feel old, too."

"You're perfect. I feel like a dinosaur compared to her." He rubbed a hand over his face. "I don't think I've ever been that young and innocent."

A full 30 minutes before Sam Parker had scheduled their meeting, he strolled through the door and headed for the hostess station.

Max stood. "Be right back with our quarry." He walked up to the hostess station as she was apologetically explaining that Parker would have a fifteen-minute wait to be seated. "That won't be necessary," Max said. "We've been expecting Mr. Parker."

Parker pivoted to stare at Max, mouth agape.

"Max Norton. Thanks for meeting us, sir." He gestured toward the table where Willow was seated.

"What are you...?"

"Doing here this early?" Max finished softly. "Figured you'd pull something like this, and I have to wonder why you're reluctant to speak to us when Mrs. Enright asked you to do so. Have a seat, Mr. Parker. You're drawing attention to yourself. Ten minutes and a cup of coffee won't hurt you, right?"

The attorney glared at Max, then walked to the table, his posture projecting extreme displeasure.

He motioned for the attorney to take the seat nearest the window and made it more difficult for him to leave. Max signaled the waitress.

"Yes, sir?" the perky twelve-year-old asked.

"Coffee for my friend. Mr. Parker, what would you like?"

"The Himalayan Mocha Latte, please."

Max manfully maintained a pleasant expression on his face when the attorney ordered the most expensive cup of coffee on the menu.

"Yes, sir." Perky girl hurried away and began to prepare the fancy coffee.

"Thank you for agreeing to meet with us, Mr. Parker," Willow said.

He gave a slight nod. "I wasn't aware you were joining us, Ms. Knox."

"How are you acquainted with Mr. Norton?" Parker stiffened. "Is he harassing you? If you want to press charges, I'll be glad to take your case as a favor to Mr. Enright."

Willow laughed. "That won't be necessary. Max and I are engaged."

He sat back, his lips pressed into a thin line. "I see." Parker switched his attention to Max. "What exactly do you want, Mr. Norton?" He made a point of glancing at his watch. "The clock is ticking on your ten minutes."

Max eyed the attorney with his flat, cop stare. "I'll remind you that Mrs. Enright asked you to cooperate. Does she know about Graham's other wives?"

"Excuse me?" Parker's voice rose.

"Save the dramatics, and answer the question. Does she know?"

The attorney glanced around. Satisfied no one appeared to be paying attention to them, he leaned closer to Max. "Of course she doesn't know about the affairs," he whispered. "What kind of foolish question is that?"

"Is Mrs. Enright the type of woman to take him to the cleaners over it?" He smiled as the other man sputtered. "Never mind. I have a pretty good idea of the answer. If I was in her shoes, I'd take him for every penny he had. Did Graham mention the four other wives and families in his will?"

"Mistresses, and he included a bequest for each of them. I was instructed to bring the mistresses to the office separately to inform them of the bequests. It's a generous amount of money."

How much did he feel marrying each woman under false pretenses was worth? "Wives. At least, they believe they are. They have no idea he married them under a false identity while he was legally married to Celia."

The attorney lost all color in his face. "Wives? That's absurd. Graham was having affairs with them. He couldn't marry them since he was already married."

"Want proof?"

"Do you have any?"

"I wouldn't have said anything if I didn't."

Parker swallowed hard. "Poor Celia. She'll be devastated." His expression hardened. "You won't tell her. I forbid it. She's been through enough without you dragging her through a scandal."

Good friend indeed. Was he more than a friend or longing to be more? Excellent motive for murder. "The detectives investigating her husband's murder will notify her."

"Why? What would they gain by doing so? She'll be devastated when she learns he was having affairs. Is it necessary to twist the knife by informing her that he was tied to those women in fake marriages and established families with them?"

Parker knew about the children. Interesting turn of phrase, twisting the knife. "Are you fascinated by knives, Parker?"

He looked puzzled. "What are you talking about?"

"How much do you know about Graham's death?"

"Only what Celia told me and what I heard in the news. He was stabbed to death." The man scowled. "Wait a minute. You can't suspect me of murdering my own client because I mentioned twisting the knife. That's insane. I had no reason to want Graham dead."

"Not even to have his legitimate wife for yourself?"

"How dare you? I'm a happily married man, and Celia is a good friend."

"Know what I think? I think Graham wasn't the only unhappy spouse in that marriage. Perhaps Celia found proof her husband was cheating and decided to find some happiness for herself."

"That's an irresponsible thing to say. You have no proof. You're fishing for information. Well, you won't get it here."

"Here you go." Perky waitress set her tray on the table and handed out the drinks. "Would you like anything else? I'll be happy to bring it to the table."

The attorney frowned. "I need my coffee to go."

"Oh, of course." Perky picked up the large coffee and hurried off. "I'll return in a minute."

Parker waited just long enough for the waitress to scurry out of earshot, then said, "I don't want you harassing Celia or spreading malicious gossip around town about me." His voice lowered to just above a whisper. "I've never killed anyone in my life. I warn you, I will sue you for every penny you have if you come after me. Better think long and hard before you do." He rose as Perky approached with his to-go cup.

Max stood and moved aside.

"Thanks for the coffee." Without looking back, Parker strode from the shop.

Chapter Twenty-Seven

Willow turned to Max after Sam stormed from the coffee shop. "That was fun." If you were a glutton for punishment. "What should we do now?" They hadn't gained much information from the interview except to confirm he knew about the other women but not the marriages and false identities.

"Enjoy our snacks and drinks before we return to the inn. We'll find out if Logan's friend made contact with our target." He covered her hand with his. "If nothing else is breaking, we'll start organizing your genealogy research with the information we have."

"The key is somewhere in the research." Willow didn't know where yet but she would find it. When she did, they'd have the answer to put the puzzle pieces together. "Do you think Graham's death is tied to money?"

"The top motives for murder are love, lust, loathing, or loot. Millions of dollars are at stake in the Enright holdings. The sheer volume of women involved in this situation adds another layer of trouble."

What an understatement. Not only might one of the women in Graham's life have discovered his lies, no one would be surprised if she or a male relative chose a path of vengeance. "So many facets involved in Graham's death," she murmured and sipped her tea. Willow sighed, pleased with her choice. This tea was a true luxury.

"Good?"

"Heavenly. It's a shame Sam showed up so early. I would have enjoyed drinking the whole pot."

Max winked. "We'll ask Perky Girl to figure something out so we can take it with us."

"Deal. How's your coffee?"

"Excellent but not worth twelve bucks. The cinnamon twist thing makes up for it, though. It's great." He gestured toward her muffin. "How's the muffin?"

"Melts in my mouth."

His eyes darkened and his gaze dropped to her lips. "Shouldn't say things like that, baby," he murmured. "Makes me want to find out for myself how good the muffin tastes. I don't think the patrons in this place approve of public displays of affection."

"Probably not. Sorry, love. You'll have to wait until we're back in the SUV."

"Promise?"

She shivered and smiled. Yes, explosive chemistry between them. "Promise."

When Perky waitress zipped by the next time, Max asked for a way to take the tea with them. "Want a refill on your coffee, sir?"

He smiled. "No, thanks."

Within minutes, they walked outside the shop and headed for the vehicle. Max kept his arm around her waist while she carried the drink carrier with her two large to-go cups of tea. His right hand remained close to his weapon.

He ushered her to the SUV and opened the door for Willow. "I need to be sure the vehicle is clean of tracking devices, then we'll go."

She set the tea in the cup holders between the seats and watched while Max circled the vehicle with his electronic signal detector.

After a complete circuit, he slid the device into his pocket and climbed behind the wheel. "We're clear." Max cranked the engine and scanned the area carefully instead of putting the SUV into motion.

"What is it?" What had he seen? Willow looked around. She saw vehicles driving along the street, pedestrians walking along the sidewalk, and shadows shifting as the wind caused tree limbs and bushes to sway in the breeze. No threats.

"I don't know. Something but I can't put my finger on it." He waited and watched another full minute before heading toward the street. "Do me a favor."

"What?"

"Keep the drinks in the cup holder."

Her heart skipped a beat. "You think we'll have trouble?"

"Maybe. Something is off."

As Max drove through Tucker's Gap, Willow's gaze shifted constantly, searching for threats. Her hands gripped the seat.

"Relax," he murmured, reaching over to cradle her hand in his. "If we run into trouble, we'll handle it."

"You don't have backup."

Max glanced at her. "I have you."

"That's a nice to hear but I don't have a weapon."

"I can fix that." He pointed to the keypad in the floor. "Seven-fourteen-forty."

Willow keyed in the code and opened the floor gun safe to find a Sig with two magazines. "Perfect. That's the weapon Dad bought me when I graduated from college."

He chuckled. "He gave you a weapon instead of a car?"

"Dad wanted to give me a way to protect myself when he and my brothers weren't close to handle the job for me." She checked the Sig, then loaded the magazine, and immediately felt more in control. At least she had a way to protect Max if they came under attack.

At the halfway point, headlights flashed in the rearview mirror. Willow twisted in her seat to look out the back window. A vehicle trailed behind them, lights on bright, and closing fast. "Max." Could be nothing. Could be something. Her bet was on trouble.

"I see him." He activated his Bluetooth and made a call.

"Sit rep," Brody said.

"We're 20 minutes out and coming in hot. We picked up a tail."

Despite the tense situation, Willow's mouth curved. Max sounded disgusted by that fact.

"I assume you checked for trackers."

"Yeah. Found zip."

"Sawyer is on his way. You know the drill."

"I got it. Evasion. If that's not possible, capture and question. That would be a fine plan if I was alone."

"Then your evasion tactics better work until Sawyer arrives," Brody said in a mild voice. "The rest of us will be on standby. Otherwise, expect Sawyer to contact you soon." He ended the call.

Two minutes later, Max's phone signaled an incoming call. Max tapped the screen on the dashboard to answer. "Where are you, Sawyer?"

"Eastbound on Highway 32. I have you on the GPS tracking program. I'm fifteen minutes out. What's your situation?"

"We picked up a tail a few minutes ago. No tracker so he must have been waiting off the highway."

"Wouldn't be hard. The highway doesn't have much traffic. Still, he'd have to know you were coming this direction."

"Not hard to figure it out when there's only one main highway through Tucker's Gap."

"Mendez?"

"Probably. Nothing indicates he's a team player but I'm not ruling out a partner."

"Is the driver aggressive?"

"He's inching up on us. Willow, face forward in case the driver makes a run at us."

She twisted in her seat and watched the vehicle creep closer with the side mirror.

"How did the interview go with Parker?" Sawyer asked.

"He's not our biggest fan," Max said.

"Count me as shocked. He didn't appreciate your sparkling wit, huh?"

"Surprising, isn't it? Parker knew about Graham's other women but not the marriages and families." He summarized the information they'd learned. "He's interested in Celia as more than a client."

"Sam denied it," Willow said. "He claimed he was happily married but I think Max is right. Sam was protective and possessive."

"A great motive for murder. Kill off the cheating husband and sweep the wealthy widow off her feet."

"After you divorce your current wife," Max said. "Wouldn't do to make the same mistakes as your good friend, Graham, made."

A snort from Sawyer. "No kidding. Nothing like turning off the new widow because you played the same game as her husband."

"Parker's the right body type, too."

"Willow, do you remember seeing Parker the night you were drugged?"

Flashes of blurred images, including the expensive running shoes. No faces. "I'm sorry. My memories are still fuzzy and chaotic."

"What about in the hotel, the restaurant, or around town?"

"Only at Oliver's office."

"What was your impression of him?"

"He was snooty and unhappy to see me. He acted as though I interrupted an important meeting."

"We should dig deeper into his background."

Max glanced in the rearview mirror, and pressed the accelerator pedal closer to the floor. "Location, Sawyer?"

"Ten miles out."

"The driver is maneuvering into position. Hold on, Willow." He whipped the wheel to the right and sped down the exit ramp. He turned left into a large subdivision and floored the accelerator. "Took the Raintree exit and hung a left."

"Copy that." Sawyer lapsed into silence except to keep them apprised of his location.

Max tightened his grip on the steering wheel. "Get ready, Willow. There's a cubby in the door. Slide the Sig inside and hold on."

Willow did as he instructed. "You don't want me to use the gun?"

He shook his head. "Too many homes around. You'll have to wait to show off your sharpshooter skills."

"Ha ha. Very funny." Why was he so relaxed? Willow felt as though she'd shake apart any minute.

"Sawyer, the driver is speeding up. I'll try to shake him."

"Copy. One mile out."

As Max's speed increased, he growled. "I need to get out of this neighborhood. I didn't realize how crowded the area is."

A slight pause, then, "Water Tower Road is your best option."

"Copy that." Max guided the vehicle through a series of quick turns, taking a winding route out of the subdivision. He skidded around a final corner and stomped the pedal to the floor. The SUV surged forward and slowly widened the gap between their vehicle and the driver pursuing them.

"Half a mile," Sawyer said.

Max continued to create distance between them and their tail.

Willow breathed easier. Maybe they'd make a clean getaway.

"Quarter of a mile," Sawyer said. "I see your headlights coming and the vehicle trailing you. What am I looking for?"

"Tan car, early model, 2008 or 2009 Toyota, four doors."

Willow stared at Max. He'd gotten all that from glances in the mirror?

"Got it. I'll take care of the tail. Get Willow to the inn."

"You're not dealing with this guy alone. I couldn't see how many people were in the car."

A sigh. "Why do all of you assume I can't handle a two-bit thug?" The big black ops soldier sounded aggrieved.

"If this is Mendez, he's a dangerous two-bit thug, and he might have recruited help despite his track record."

"Yeah, yeah. Willow, you doing all right?"

"Peachy."

He laughed. "That's what I like to hear. Good to know Max has a flair for exciting dates."

"Hey, that's right." Max grinned. "Can't say I don't know how to keep my dates entertained."

"I'd rather see a magic show next time," Willow said. "We can check off a car chase from the date list."

"Good girl," Sawyer said. "Make him work for it."

"No help from the peanut gallery." Max glanced in the mirror again. "Taking the next right in two hundred feet."

"Copy that."

"Hold on, Willow." Max slowed just enough to slide into the turn and race from the highway.

Willow twisted in her seat to see what was happening behind them. The pursuer tried to take the same exit but Sawyer cut him off.

The tan car veered back onto the highway with Sawyer in pursuit. Max hit his brakes, executed a three-point turn, and raced after Sawyer and the tan car.

"Will we catch him?" Willow asked as they gained ground on the caravan.

"We have the speed," Max said. "Let's hope no one pulls onto the highway in front of us. At this speed, we could have a major problem."

Ice water poured into her veins. "How fast are we driving?"

"You don't want to know."

"He's taking the Canton exit," Sawyer said. "Then left." The sound of tires squealing came through the speakers.

"Sit rep," Max snapped.

"Hold." Seconds later, his teammate said, "A truck pulled out in front of me. I'm resuming pursuit, east on Canton." Long seconds ticked by, then Sawyer growled. "Lost him. I'm starting a grid search on Tulip and going east to west for six blocks."

"We'll take north to south. Willow, look for a tan Toyota. Let's see if we can flush this guy out."

"You think he's hiding?" Wouldn't the driver of the tan car want to get away as fast as possible? Anyone in his right mind would want to avoid a one-on-one confrontation with Max. Now that Sawyer had joined the party and turned the predator into prey, the unknown driver would be smart to disappear.

"Depends on how bad he wants us."

Willow shuddered. Her. How bad the driver wanted her. Max wasn't the primary target. She was. "Why doesn't Mendez move on to another contract? He must know you won't step aside and let him kill me."

"His reputation is on the line. Mendez's claim to fame is he never fails to fulfill a contract. If he fails to take out one lone woman, his reputation takes a hit and so does the price he can charge for his services."

Ten minutes into the grid search, a vehicle raced toward them from the left, headlights on bright.

"Hang on," Max shouted. He floored the accelerator and spun the wheel to the right.

Seconds later, a vehicle slammed into the left side of their SUV.

#

Chapter Twenty-Eight

Max grabbed his Sig. "Sawyer, the Toyota broadsided us at the intersection of Magnolia and Canton."

"Copy. I'm two blocks away."

"You all right, Willow?" Max swiped his forehead with his forearm. The material came away wet with blood. He sighed. More work for Jesse.

"I'm fine."

A black SUV raced into sight as the driver of the car sprinted away from the accident and plunged into a stand of trees near the road.

Scowling, Max forced his driver's door open with an ear-splitting screech of metal and hurried around to open Willow's door.

Sawyer's SUV skidded to a halt. A second later, he was out of the vehicle and running toward them. "You okay, Max?"

"Stay with Willow." He sprinted toward the trees where his quarry had disappeared and plunged through the dark, noisy undergrowth. So much for sneaking up on him. No chance of that with this stuff dragging at Max's clothes.

Once he cleared the underbrush, Max headed toward the right where his target had left a trail of broken branches and bent grass blades. A road lay on the other side of the woods and was the driver's best chance to escape Max and Sawyer. Cross the road, and he'd disappear like a ghost into another part of the subdivision.

Max slowed as he approached the tree line to avoid making himself a target in case the driver hid nearby, lying in wait. He scanned up and down the road. No movement.

Sirens sounded in the distance. He didn't have long before he had to return to the scene of the accident to talk to the police.

Max also wanted to check on Willow. Despite her assurance she was okay, he'd seen fellow cops and operatives swear they were fine because adrenaline in their blood stream masked serious injuries.

Another slow visual sweep of the neighborhood netted him nothing. He sighed. Sawyer would have searched the Toyota by now. If they were lucky, something inside the vehicle pointed to the identity of the driver. Faint hope. Mendez didn't gain his reputation by being careless. Chances were excellent the tan car was stolen.

After another swipe at his forehead, Max secured his weapon in his holster and retraced his steps. He broke through the underbrush at the accident site as law enforcement rolled up, blue-and-white lights swirling in the darkness.

Willow saw Max and hurried across the distance separating them. She wrapped her arms around him. "You're all right?"

"Fine, just frustrated. He's gone. Didn't get a glimpse to confirm his identity." He eased back and looked Willow over from head to foot. "You sure you're not hurt?"

"Nothing over-the-counter medicine and ice won't cure. Looks like you didn't fare so well." She trailed her fingertips over his forehead. "You'll know all the emergency room doctors by name at this rate."

"Jesse will take care of it. Like you, I've had enough of emergency rooms."

"Come on. We have questions to answer. How should we play this? We can't tell them Dwight Mendez rammed your vehicle. I didn't see anything except headlights."

"We play it straight. Hit-and-run by an aggressive driver."

By the time they reached the scene, one of the policemen was interviewing Sawyer. The other was searching the tan car as an ambulance and fire truck rolled up.

The cop interviewing Sawyer glanced at Max and whistled. "Ouch, buddy. Good thing the EMTs are here. You're Max Norton?"

"Yeah."

"Let the medics check your head while I get information from Ms. Knox."

Max glanced at Sawyer who gave a slight nod. He'd raise too many questions if he refused all medical assessment. For the moment, Willow was safe and the car's driver was in the wind. They'd regroup and resume the hunt as soon as the cops turned them loose.

He bent and leaned close to Willow's ear. "Sawyer will stay with you while the EMTs look at me," he murmured. "Don't volunteer information."

"Go. I'll be fine."

Max squeezed her hand and walked to the back of the ambulance. While the medics checked him, Max watched Willow and the patrol officer. As the minutes progressed, Willow remained composed. That was good.

The EMT cleaning Max's cut assessed his work. "You should go to the hospital, Mr. Norton. You took a good hit to the head and might have a concussion. You need stitches."

"I have a friend who's a paramedic. He'll take care of the stitches. Can you use butterfly tape for now?"

"I can do that. Make sure to have the cut treated. Otherwise, you could end up with an infection and scar."

Not like he didn't have scars all over his body. However, he didn't want to do anything to distress Willow. "Thanks for your help." Max returned to Willow and Sawyer as she was finished her statement to the police.

"Your turn, Mr. Norton," the officer said.

An hour later, the first responders were gone, and Max stared in dismay at his SUV. "Bear will kill me," he muttered.

"Who's Bear?" Willow asked.

"The mechanical genius who retrofits our SUVs. The Fortress fleet vehicles are his babies, and he takes it personally when we wreck them."

"This wasn't your fault."

Sawyer pulled out his key fob. "Bear won't see it that way. As far as I can see, your SUV is drivable, Max. I'll follow you back to the inn in case you have a problem."

"Appreciate it. I'll call Bear on the way in."

"Good luck." His friend grinned. "You'll need it."

"Thanks a lot." He glared at Sawyer who laughed as he jogged to his own vehicle. Soon, Max merged onto the highway and resumed their journey toward the inn. Since the SUV wouldn't fix itself, Max made the dreaded call to Bear.

"Talk to me," a deep voice said in lieu of a greeting.

"Max Norton here."

"What do you need, Norton?"

"First, you're on speaker with Willow Knox. Willow, this is Bear, our genius mechanic."

"Nice to meet you, Bear," she said. "Max speaks highly of you and your skills."

After a short pause, the Delta operative said, "Pleased to meet you, Ms. Knox. Norton, your woman is buttering me up. What did you do?"

"It wasn't my fault."

"Likely story." A sigh. "All right. Let's hear it."

He swallowed hard and explained what happened, ending with, "I need a loaner. This is the fourth attempt on Willow's life in the past week."

"Address?"

Max rattled off the address of the inn.

"Drivable?"

"Yes, sir."

"Hold." Bear's voice came through the cabin's speakers a minute later. "You'll have a loaner by midnight. Meet me in the parking lot. Don't be late."

"Thanks, Bear."

"Didn't do it for you." He ended the call.

Max breathed out slowly. The notification was over, and he'd survived. A win-win, in his book.

"What did he mean by that?" Willow asked. "Isn't he replacing the vehicle for your benefit?"

"Despite what he said, that's partly true but Bear is giving me a loaner to make sure you're protected. He has a soft spot for the women in our lives."

"What did your mechanic do before he came on board with Fortress?"

"Delta Force."

"I should have known. Your mechanic has intimidating down to a science."

Max chuckled. "That's the truth. Relax while you can. Barring further trouble, we'll arrive at the inn soon. Once we're there, we'll start on the Enright family tree."

"Not a job for the faint of heart." Willow covered his hand with hers. "We'll start the family tree after Jesse repairs the damage to your head."

Right. More stitches. Woohoo. Max enjoyed the drive through the quiet countryside, holding Willow's hand. Being with her brought him more joy and peace than he'd ever felt with anyone else. Didn't matter what they were doing. He simply enjoyed her company. She was everything, and he was grateful Willow agreed to marry him.

As the miles passed, he thought of the future with hope and anticipation. Having a family with Willow one day? A dream of his. When they had some time, Max would broach the subject of children and a dog or three. If she wasn't on board with kids and pets, he'd deal. All he really needed to be happy was Willow.

When they entered the suite with Sawyer, the women hurried to Willow. "What happened?" Poppy demanded. "Brody just said someone was tailing you." She glared at her unrepentant brother-in-law before pointing at Max's head. "That looks like the guy did more than follow Max."

"Hey," Brody protested. "Blame Max for withholding information, not me."

"The driver broadsided us." Max held up his hand to stop the barrage of questions from his teammates. "I didn't see the driver. He was already out of the car and running by the time my vision cleared."

"Get the license plate of the car?" Brody asked.

Max sent the picture he'd taken to his team leader. "I'm betting the car was stolen."

"Probably. We'll run the plates anyway."

"Sit down, Max," Jesse said, pointing to a chair close by. "Let me check your head. Everything else will wait."

He sat. You didn't argue when your paramedic issued orders. Max submitted to Jesse's poking and prodding without many complaints.

His friend reached into his mike bag. "You need stitches."

"Let's get it done. We have work to do."

"Willow, while Jesse is working on Max, we can start the Enright family tree," Sage said.

"Good idea." Poppy broke away from the other two women, picked up the oversize pads of paper, and handed them to Logan. "Peel and stick."

While he created a large writing surface across two walls with the paper, Willow retrieved Max's laptop and booted up the system. "Who has the best handwriting?"

"You know how to set up the tree best for your use," Sage said. "Poppy will work the computer, and I'll read the names for you to write down."

"That works." Willow took the markers from Poppy. "Let's get started. Max, if you and your teammates think of something to add, sing out."

"Copy that." He hissed as antiseptic hit the cut. "Ouch. Watch it, Jesse."

"Suck it up, cupcake."

"Where's the love?" Max groused.

"In reserve for serious injuries. A little scratch like this doesn't qualify."

"Little scratch?" He eyed the syringe filled with lidocaine and the stitch kit. "If it's so little, why do you need those?"

"Practice. Got to upgrade my skills. You're an excellent test dummy."

He glared at his friend. "Jerk."

A wink. "Back at you, buddy."

Max held still while Jesse injected the medicine, then watched Willow do her thing with paper and markers while waiting for the meds to kick in. By the time his forehead was numb, several pages were filled with names.

He studied the lists, frowning. "The only connection seems to be the Enrights."

Sawyer leaned back in his chair. "I thought we'd find overlapping."

"I don't know." Brody rubbed his jaw. "Graham's women all lived in different areas of Tennessee."

"What about Oliver's harem?" Logan asked. "With more than twenty women, there should be overlap. Discretion didn't mean separation by geography."

"We'll look into that." Willow glanced over her shoulder. "That's a good point, Logan. I didn't think to compare the locations of Oliver's ladies and Graham's. If two of them are in the same location, the women might know each other."

"Women talk," Sage said. "If a mistress and wife talked, the fake wife might discover Graham's lies and plot revenge."

"Wouldn't that be a disaster," Jesse said as he completed the first stitch. "Can you imagine comparing notes and realizing your lover is the father of the other woman's fake husband?"

Max grunted as the needle slid deep into his skin. "Those men were begging for trouble."

"Oh, yeah," Brody said. "Let's find out who gave them the basket of trouble that led to Graham's murder."

Once Willow wrote the names of the women, Poppy started tracking their locations. When they finished, Willow returned to Max's side and motioned toward the walls. "What do you think?"

He studied the papers. "Jana Dean, one of Graham's wives, and Nora Torville, one of Oliver's mistresses, live in Blue Ridge."

"Lucy Walters lives in Killene along with Taylor Ainsley," Logan pointed out. "Focus on those four women and their families, Willow. If there's a connection, that's where we'll find it."

"Any overlap between Oliver and Graham aside from bloodline?" Jesse asked as he finished the last stitch.

"The lawyer," Max and Willow said at the same time.

"Could be a coincidence," Sage pointed out. "Makes perfect sense if Graham used his father's lawyer to handle his own legal affairs."

"Still, we should rip into Parker's life and find out if that's the only connection," Poppy said. She walked to the breakfast bar where Logan's laptop sat. "Logan and I will check for more connections between Lucy Walters and Taylor Ainsley."

"Sawyer and I will do the same with Jana Dean and Nora Torville," Jesse said. He tossed the medical detritus into his hazards bag and used needles into his sharps container. "No more stitches, Max. Otherwise, I'll have to request a special delivery of medical supplies. Got me?"

"Yeah, yeah. I got it." He rose, glanced down at his shirt, and grimaced. At the rate he was ruining his wardrobe, he'd need to hit a big box store soon to buy more shirts.

Max kissed Willow's temple. "I'll be back in a few minutes." He went to the second bedroom, stripped off the stained shirt, and tossed it into the trash bin. No point in trying to salvage this shirt, either.

After a quick shower to rinse off the blood from his injury and sweat from his run through the woods, Max grabbed clean clothes from his Go bag and dragged them on. He pulled a comb through his hair, tied on his tactical boots, and called it good.

When he returned to the living room, Willow was studying the family tree, a puzzled expression on her face. He walked up behind her and rested his hands on her shoulders. "What do you see, Willow?"

"I'm wondering about Sam Parker and his connection. We know he's the lawyer for Oliver and Graham." She turned to look at Max. "How do we find out if he's the attorney for the other women?"

"The Fortress tech geeks. They can find anything. Want me to ask Zane to look into it?"

"If he has time, the information might be helpful."

"Consider it done." He kissed her forehead and stepped back, reaching for his phone. Max called Z as he walked to the balcony door and stared out into the night.

"Yeah, Murphy," his friend said.

"Max Norton here. I need another favor."

"Name it."

"Information on an attorney named Samuel Parker. He was Graham Enright's attorney and is the attorney of record for Oliver, Graham's father. I'd like to know if Parker is the attorney for any of Oliver's women or Graham's wives aside from Celia. We already know he's taking care of Celia's affairs." And wanted to be more involved with the widow than he admitted.

"I'll get on that as soon as I can. Might be a while, Max," his friend warned.

"Assign the task to one of the geeks."

"Might be best. I'm tech support for Shadow unit tonight, and they're in a hot zone."

"Shadow unit stays in hot zones."

"They have a soft spot for women and children caught in human trafficking. It's difficult, gut-wrenching work with a fast time line."

"I know," he murmured. He'd seen it as a cop and saw more now as an operative. "I have a soft spot myself for human trafficking vics." Especially after meeting Willow, although Max had never thought of Willow as a victim. She was a survivor.

"I'll bet. As soon as Nico and his team are out of danger, I'll take over the research if the geeks haven't finished. Give us a few hours."

"Thanks, Z." He ended the call and made another to his boss. Maddox would not be happy about the vehicle. Of course, knowing Bear, he might have already informed the boss that another body shop order was in the works.

"Maddox. Where are you and what do you need, Max?"

"I'm at the inn with my team, checking in." Among other things.

"Sit rep."

Max updated the Fortress CEO. "Zane or the Fortress tech geeks will run a search on the attorney. We're digging into the backgrounds of the four women who live in the same towns."

"You and Willow are all right?"

"Yes, sir. I have a few more stitches to add to the collection. Otherwise, we're good."

"All right. I'll authorize any overtime Bear needs to repair your ride. You owe me, Norton."

"Yes, sir. Any time, any where. I appreciate it, boss."

"Yep. Watch your back." Maddox ended the call.

Max slid the phone into his pocket and turned to Willow. "All set. Zane and his crew will look into the lawyers for the women."

"Good. Let's look into Sam Parker's background."

"Excellent idea."

She laughed. "You're looking for any excuse to dislike him."

"I already do. Just avoided the rush." He led her to the couch and retrieved his laptop.

Logging into the Fortress system, Max entered Parker's name. Data filled the screen. "Father is Wayne. Mother is Nora. Sam grew up in Leeville, Tennessee. Four siblings, all younger." He smiled, amused. "All girls."

Willow nudged him with her elbow. "You're enjoying that, aren't you?"

"Oh, yeah. He deserves all that aggravation and more." Max scanned the details of Parker's life. No question the attorney was intelligent. He'd earned many academic accolades as he sailed through school. Top grades in every course.

His lips curled. Sure left Max's associate's degree in the dust. He'd had opportunities to further his education but hadn't worked on another degree. His interest centered on fighting terrorism at home and abroad instead of spending more time in a classroom.

As he read further into Parker's background, Max stopped mid-sentence to go back up a few lines. "Huh."

"What?"

"Parker did a short stint in the public defender's office. I thought he'd go directly into private practice as soon as he graduated with his law degree from Yale."

Willow scanned the information on the screen. "He clerked for a judge in Leeville. Hold on a second. May I?" She gestured toward the computer.

Max shifted the computer to her lap. "What are you thinking?"

"Family connections." She opened another window, and her fingers flew over the keyboard. A moment later, she pointed at the bottom of the screen. "There."

He moved closer. "His father and the judge are good friends, and the judge and the district attorney Sam worked for are brothers. My guess is the judge recommended Sam work as public defender to gain experience, perhaps to set up his career as a criminal defense attorney."

"Sam's not doing that now. He shifted to corporate law."

"Criminal defense is a hard field."

Willow looked at Max. "You should know."

Yeah, he did. Working on either side of the aisle in law enforcement was tough. Still didn't make him feel sorry for the jerk, though. "We're still looking for connections and overlaps. What do you think about doing family trees for Nora Torville, Jana Dean, Lucy Walters, Taylor Ainsley, and Sam Parker?"

"Good idea." She stood. "Let's set up another row of paper and start forming the trees."

Max climbed to his feet and snatched up the tablets of paper. He peeled off five sheets and pressed them to another wall. If Willow's gut feeling was correct, somewhere in the family trees of the people surrounding Graham and Oliver Enright lurked a killer.

Chapter Twenty-Nine

Max stepped to the side to give Willow access to the papers on the wall. "How can I help? Would you rather I write names or read off information from the database?"

"Do you have a preference?" she asked.

He rubbed his hands together, grinning. "Who doesn't want permission to write on a wall?"

"Then take over the role of scribe." She handed him the marker. "Let's start with Taylor and Lucy, then move on to Nora, Jana, and Sam."

Max shrugged. "Works for me." Didn't matter as long as they mapped out the information on the five people for easy comparison.

"Taylor first. She lives in Killene and owns a...." Willow's voice petered off.

He glanced over his shoulder and noted her flushed face. "What's wrong?"

"She, um, owns an escort agency. Taylor Escorts."

His lips twitched. "How long has she operated the agency?"

"Fifteen years, and listen to this. Taylor Escorts is franchised. She has businesses set up all over the country." She keyed a few things into the search engine and said, "According to your database, Taylor Escorts is a clean business. No arrests for her or any of her escorts."

Surprising and impressive. "When was she involved with Oliver?"

More typing, then, "Sixteen years ago." She glanced up. "Do you think Oliver gave her seed money to get her business going?"

"The timing is interesting. We can look into that possibility." He turned back to the paper with Taylor Ainsley's name scrawled in the center. "Taylor's family members?"

"She married Alan the year she opened Taylor Escorts. They have two daughters, Paisley and Lauren, ages ten and twelve. Parents of both Taylor and Alan are deceased as are the grandparents."

"Anyone else to add to Taylor's tree?"

"Aunts and uncles on both sides are deceased, too. Alan and Taylor have two cousins each." She gave the names of the cousins which Max wrote down. "That's all for the families."

He moved to the next sheet of paper. "Lucy Walters is next. What do you have on her?"

A moment later, Willow said, "Like the other four women, she believes she's married to Graham. They have four children. Good grief. That's a lot of kids."

He chuckled. "I've heard of larger families. I knew a cop in Texas who was the fifth of twenty children."

Silence, then Willow choked out, "All from the same mother?"

"Yes, ma'am. Tom said Christmas was a wild and chaotic affair with his brothers and sisters, their spouses, and all their children. Also a ton of fun, too."

"Christmas was crazy with just me and my brothers. I can't imagine so many children, spouses, and whoever else joins the party."

He wanted to ask if she wanted children one day but wouldn't broach the subject with an avid audience listening to every word. Turned out, he didn't have to bare his soul. Poppy charged in where Max hesitated to tread.

"Hey, Willow, have you thought about having children in the future?"

She glanced at her friend. "Of course. I'd love to have kids. Not twenty. Perhaps two or three." Willow smiled at Max. "Depends on Max's preference."

Excellent news. He would have been satisfied without children as long as he had Willow but longed for sons or daughters of his own, perhaps one of each. Once Max's mother learned he was engaged to

Willow, she'd start subtle inquiries to find out how soon they were getting married. Then she'd give hints about more grandchildren to love and spoil.

Poppy shifted her question to him. "Well, Max? How many kids?"

"Leave him alone, sis," Sage said. "That discussion is for Willow and Max."

"He can tell me to butt out if he wants." She gave him a smug smile. "But you won't, will you? So, what's the word, Max?"

"I'm voting for three as long as Willow doesn't have complications. If she has difficulty, we'll talk about other options, including adoption. I can handle being childless. I can't handle losing Willow."

"Thanks for sharing that information with the class," Logan said dryly. "Get back on task, Norton."

"Yes, Dad," he shot back. "The taskmaster is cracking the whip. What does Lucy Walters do for a living?"

"Oh, you're going to like this one," Jesse said. "She's the administrative assistant for the principal of Blue Ridge High School. Graham and Lucy have been together for ten years."

"There's a note in the Fortress research on Lucy that says Graham put her through college." Sawyer flinched. "I looked at her social media posts. She might have become involved with Graham soon after she graduated from high school. No pictures of him, of course. Just gushing over her mature, handsome boyfriend, then a short while later, she brags about marrying her rich boyfriend and how he's going to be the perfect father."

"Yuck," Poppy muttered. "Talk about robbing the cradle. He had worlds of experience, and she likely had none."

"Sugar Daddy," Logan said.

"Double Yuck." Sage rested her head against Brody's shoulder. "I can't think about that too long or my stomach turns upside down."

"Same. Moving on," Max said. He turned back to Jesse. "Do Lucy and Graham have children?"

A nod. "Adam, Kelsey, Grace, and Evan. Lucy's parents and both sets of her grandparents are still alive. Orville and Laura are Lucy's parents, and Peter and Wynonna are Orville's parents and Charles and Nancy are Wynonna's parents."

He filled in the names on the chart and stood back. "Anything else?"

"Private school, of course," Sawyer added. "Lucy and Graham's four kids attend an expensive, exclusive private school. I'm not seeing how Lucy's family could afford it, so Graham had to be footing the bill."

"Anything else to add to the tree, Willow?"

"Not at the moment. Let's move on to Nora Torville."

He printed her name in the center of the paper. "What information do we have on her family?" When she remained silent, he turned. She had an odd expression on her face. "What's wrong?"

"Maybe nothing."

And perhaps something. "Let's hear it."

"Nora has four children. The oldest is named Samuel. It's a common enough name. Must be a coincidence."

Max turned back to the paper and entered the information. "What are the names of the other children?"

"Thomas, Randall, and Elise. Nora is married to Harris. No grandparents on either side. Do you have anything to add since you researched her, Poppy?"

"Nora owns Blue Ridge Public Relations."

"Wait." Brody frowned. "That's a big company with a reputation for handling the elite in Washington, D.C. and New York. They tried to get Fortress to sign a contract with them but the boss refused."

"If the company is so good, why didn't Mr. Maddox want to sign their contract?" Willow asked.

"Fortress doesn't need a public relations firm because they don't advertise. They only take business on referral."

She stared. "How can they possibly have enough business to survive?"

"Oh, trust me. They don't have any problems. In fact, the boss is constantly turning away business because we don't have enough operatives to handle the missions. Word of mouth in the military community was enough to get them off the ground, and they haven't looked back."

"Anything else interesting in your research, Poppy?" Max asked.

"All four kids went to Yale."

Yale. Max paused, marker hovering over the paper, and looked over his shoulder at the true-crime writer. "Is it possible the oldest of the kids, Samuel, is a child of Oliver's?" If so, didn't that raise an interesting problem for Oliver. By his own admission, he didn't recognize children outside of wedlock. Was Samuel his son? If he was, would he change his policy now that Graham was dead?

Jesse rose. "I'll check into it."

"Let's move on to Jana Dean while Jesse looks into that. What do you have on Jana, Willow?"

"She lives in Blue Ridge along with Nora. Jana has three children with Graham. Abigail, Gabrielle, and Serenity. No grandparents listed."

Max frowned. "Any evidence that Nora and Jana know each other?"

"Give me a minute and I'll tell you," Poppy said. She typed rapidly for a minute, then studied the screen. Finally, she sat back with an expression of satisfaction on her face. "They're members of the same country club."

Yet another ping went off inside Max. "Wonder if these two women compared notes and realized their men were father and son."

"Even more important," Willow said. "Did Nora know Graham was married to Celia? She might have kept in touch with Oliver over the years, especially if Sam was Oliver's son."

"A realistic assumption," Poppy said. "Nora's company takes care of the public relations for Enright Enterprises."

"Look at this." Jesse set his laptop on the coffee table.

Max walked to the medic's side while everyone gathered around to see for themselves what Jesse found. "What do you have?"

"A family picture of Nora's children. Samuel doesn't look like the other three. He looks like this mother, but not like his father, Harris."

Willow gasped. "Max."

He stared at the screen and whistled. Sam Torville, also known as Sam Parker, stood with three other members of his family. "Why does he have a different last name? Did he change it?"

"I've got that," Poppy said. "Nora's maiden name is Parker. Sam uses his mother's maiden name since Harris never officially adopted him. By the way, Nora started her PR firm a few months after Sam was born. Sudden infusion of cash with an instant high-powered client list from the moment the business opened its doors."

"Oliver's work," Max said. "Had to be."

"Sam must know the truth about his father," Sawyer said.

"I guess the real question is how long he's known."

Max sifted the pieces of the puzzle in his mind and came to a horrific conclusion. If he was right, the answer made a kind of terrible sense. "Poppy, when did Sam appear on the scene in Tucker's Gap?"

More fast typing, then, "Ten years."

Max and Willow exchanged glances. "Can't be a coincidence," he said softly.

"What isn't?" Brody demanded.

"The serial killer who's been stalking the Enright family has been at work for the past ten years."

"Hold on," Jesse said. "Are you saying Sam Parker is a serial killer and the same guy who attacked Willow?"

"That can't be true," Sage said. "You identified Dwight Mendez from the hotel security cameras and the traffic cameras. Mendez definitely killed Graham."

"No," Brody said slowly. "Parker didn't kill his brother. But he could and probably did hire Mendez to do the job for him."

"Why? He would have had easy access to Graham." Willow shoved a hand through her hair. "Graham would have let him into the hotel room since Sam was his lawyer. Sam could have claimed to see Graham helping me and offered to help."

"It's one thing to hire an assassin to do your dirty work," Max said. "It's something else entirely to do the job yourself. Killing someone is a messy business." He and his teammates knew that first hand.

"And we saw Mendez slip into the hotel room on camera," Sage reminded them. "Sam didn't kill Graham."

"Sam pretended to be a friend to Graham but was a snake in the grass, waiting to strike," Willow said.

Max nodded. "If he's paying Mendez's bill, then, yeah. He pretended to be a friend and betrayed Graham in the end."

"Makes me wonder if Oliver knows about Graham's wives and about Sam." Willow swallowed hard. "Would Oliver have become so angry that he hired Mendez himself to kill his son?"

"Interesting question," Logan said. "And one I hadn't considered."

"Surely not," Sage said, her eyes filled with distress. "A father wouldn't kill his own child, would he?"

"Your father wouldn't, sweetheart," Brody said. "Not every father is a good one."

"That's just evil."

"If it's true," Max pointed out. "We're speculating. We need cold, hard facts."

"How do we find out if it's true?" Willow asked.

"Follow the money," Sawyer said.

"Finding it would take too long with Oliver's vast holdings," Brody pointed out. "Be easier to see if there's a trail between Mendez and Parker."

"Let's make that happen," Max said. "The faster, the better."

"Legal?"

"Don't care. If we find what we need, we'll have Zane drop an anonymous tip into Cohen's email. He and his partner can work the legal angles to get what they need to make a case." Thank God that wasn't his problem any more. He could follow the trail wherever it led as long as he didn't cross the line into illegal territory. Most of the time. Truthfully, he'd do whatever it took to protect Willow, legal or not.

"Won't the police trace the email back to Zane?" Willow asked.

"Zane's too good to make a mistake like that. Don't worry. None of this will blow back on him."

"I'll call Fortress and get them started," Brody said as he stood. "I don't know how fast we'll have answers."

Max returned to the sheets of paper. "Let's finish filling out the information we have and do a comparison for more overlaps."

When they finished, Max stepped back to stand beside Willow. He studied the notes scrawled across the sheets. "I don't see more overlaps," he said after a few minutes. "Guess we'll see if Fortress finds the money trail to confirm our suspicions."

"And if they do?" Willow asked. "What then?"

"The guys have a nice, long chat with Parker," Poppy said.

Logan grunted. "More likely we'll catch Mendez and squeeze him for information on his client."

"Have to catch him first."

"That's what the bait is all about."

A moment later, Logan's cell phone signaled an incoming message. He glanced at the screen. A slow smile curved his mouth. "Mendez took the bait. He wants to discuss terms."

"Set up a meeting," Brody said.

The other operative responded to the message and waited. Two minutes later, his phone pinged again. "Got him."

"When and where?" Max said. Logan wasn't meeting this guy alone.

"Three hours." Logan frowned as he entered information into his phone. "He wants to meet at a warehouse on Pinhook Road."

"Set up," Poppy said. "You can't meet this guy in a deserted area. He'll try to kill you."

He sent her a cool look. "You have a better idea? We need to shut him down fast. We all agreed this is the best way to bag the assassin and get answers."

She glared at him. "It's a dumb idea."

"Have a better alternative?"

"No," Poppy snapped.

"Then we go with the plan we have."

"You're taking backup."

"Don't need it."

She got in his face. "You're taking it anyway. Not negotiable, Logan." Poppy looked at Brody. "Go with him."

Her brother-in-law chuckled. "Planned on it since Mendez saw the other members of the team."

"Good. Don't come back with so much as a scratch or I'll never hear the end of it from Sage."

"Yes, ma'am. You heard the lady, Logan. Gear up."

"Yeah, yeah." He left the suite with Brody on his heels.

Poppy shoved her hands through her hair and began pacing. "This is a terrible idea."

"Chill, sis." Sage caught Poppy's hand on the next pass and tugged. Her sister dropped onto the couch beside Sage. "This is what they do. We have to let them handle it."

"I want to go."

"No," Max and his teammates said simultaneously. "The last thing you want to do is endanger them," Max continued. "And you will if you go with them. They've got this. Trust them to do their job."

Two minutes later, he admitted them to the suite. "All set?"

"Yeah." Brody went to his wife and kissed her. "Try to sleep, baby. I'll be back before you miss me."

"Not a chance," she murmured. "Be careful."

"Always." He headed for the door. "Ready, Logan?"

"Almost." Logan cupped Poppy's chin and planted a hard kiss on her mouth. After an intense stare, he straightened and started for the door. "Ready."

Chapter Thirty

Willow's stomach tightened into a knot as the door closed behind Brody and Logan. This was one of the worst things she could imagine. She felt terrible for endangering two good friends and didn't blame Poppy for being upset. Max would have gone himself if he could have found a way to do it and not alert Mendez.

Her breath caught as another thought occurred to her, a nightmare of epic proportions. What if Mendez didn't meet them? What if he set off another bomb instead? Now she felt like running after the men and begging them to avoid the meeting altogether. Surely if all of them put their minds to the task they could find a better alternative.

"Brody is right, Sage," Max said. "You should try to sleep. He'll worry about you if you don't."

Brody's wife frowned at him. "That's playing dirty, buddy."

"Maybe. Did it work?"

"Yes, it did." She sighed and allowed Max to help her stand. "Come on, Poppy. Let's go to our suite to wait."

Sawyer followed them.

"Where is he going?" Willow asked.

"He's on guard duty until Brody and Logan return," Jesse said. "Did you see the glance exchanged between Brody, Logan, and Sawyer?"

"Oh." She was slow on the uptake tonight, perhaps because she worried her friends would leave that meeting in body bags instead of on their feet.

Max sat beside Willow. He raised her hand to his mouth and kissed her palm. "You thought of something that upset you a minute ago. What was it?"

She sighed. "Did anyone ever tell you that you might be too observant?" She'd never able to hide a surprise from him. He'd know she was hiding something the minute he saw her face. Clearly, she shouldn't play poker. She'd lose every game.

"Not lately. Tell me."

"What if Mendez doesn't show but leaves a bomb? He could set off an explosive device as soon as they're inside the building." Willow hoped he would discount her idea. He didn't.

"It's possible. That's why they're going early to check things out."

She shuddered. "I hate this, Max. I don't want anyone hurt on my account."

He wrapped his arm around her shoulders. "I know. The best thing to do is end this as fast as possible. Since Mendez is the key and the more dangerous of the two or three men involved, we start with him."

When Jesse's phone signaled an incoming call, he glanced at the screen, smiled a little, walked to the balcony door and went outside. He leaned against the railing, phone pressed to his ear.

"That looks interesting." Willow snuggled against Max's side. "Do you think Jesse has a female friend he's not telling anyone about?"

"Maybe."

Some off note in his voice had Willow turning to stare up at him. "You know something."

"Maybe," he repeated.

"Is that the secret he didn't want you to tell?"

"No. That secret is a different one. This is a recent development."

She shifted her attention to Jesse again. "Two secrets, huh? A challenge for me, Poppy, and Sage. You should know Jesse's secrets are as good as revealed to the masses."

Max flinched. "Man, remind me not to brag about having a secret around you three." He stood and held out his hand. "Come on. Time for you to go to bed, too."

"You have to be kidding." Willow narrowed her eyes. "Do you really think I'll go to bed while Brody and Logan are in harm's way on my account?"

"Sage is."

"Ha. That's what you think. Yes, I know she has rheumatoid arthritis and must be careful with her health. I'm not that delicate, and a wise man wouldn't treat me as though I am." Her voice held a warning. Before he could reply or defend himself, Willow's phone rang.

Nothing good ever came of a phone call at this time of night. Had something happened to her father or her brothers? She yanked her phone from her pocket and checked the screen.

The name made Willow's eyebrows soar. She turned the phone toward Max so he could see the caller's name.

He frowned. "Answer it on speaker."

She swiped her thumb across the glass and tapped the speaker button. "Is everything all right, Mr. Enright? It's late to be calling."

"I need to see you immediately." He sounded tense and upset.

Max shook his head.

"It's after midnight." The idea of going out now made her break out into a cold sweat. She could do it if Max was with her, but she didn't understand why Oliver needed to see her now.

"You work for me. You come when I say."

"I work for Ballinger Research, and my boss wouldn't expect me to go out in the middle of the night to meet a client."

"Check your email. I think you'll find orders to meet with me any time I request."

She frowned. Her boss knew how she felt about going out after dark although he didn't know the reason behind her reticence. "Hold on while I check."

Willow scanned her emails. Dread curled in her gut when she saw an email from her boss sent fifteen minutes earlier. The gist of the missive was that she was to do whatever Oliver requested along with a not-so-gentle reminder that the client was always right and to accommodate him no matter how odd the request.

"Well?" Oliver demanded. "Did you read the note from Ballinger?"

"Yes, sir."

"Then you must accommodate my request. Correct?"

"Yes, sir."

"Good. I'll expect you on my doorstep within the hour." A slight pause. "Alone. This is a private matter." He ended the call.

Willow turned her gaze to Max. "I don't understand what the rush is."

"I don't know but I don't like this. It's out of the ordinary." Max scowled. "I say he can wait a few hours for the sun to come up."

"I can't, Max. My job is on the line if I don't accommodate Oliver's odd request. I have to go."

"You aren't going alone. I don't care what Enright said, Willow. I'm going with you."

She smiled. "I wouldn't expect otherwise. Thanks."

"You might want to hold off on your thanks, baby. Oliver will soon find out I'm not happy about him dragging you out for work in the middle of the night. Nothing is that important."

"He can be a little quirky," she admitted.

"More like demanding," Max muttered.

And Max wasn't? Amused, Willow went to get her purse as Max alerted Jesse and the rest of his teammates.

Max was right to alert them. The timing for this meeting was odd and, combined with the sudden meeting with Mendez, suspicious.

By the time she returned to the living room, Jesse and Max were ready. The men were geared up and ready for trouble. She prayed the preparations were unnecessary.

#

Chapter Thirty-One

Max peered through the windshield at the multi-level mansion, the knot in his gut pulling tighter by the second. Why wasn't this place lit up light a Christmas tree? He didn't like anything about this meeting. Oliver should have been able to wait a few hours to see Willow. If Willow wasn't afraid she'd lose her job, Max would have called Oliver and told him they'd arrive when the sun rose. After one last sweep of the darkened grounds and home, Max opened the driver's door and got out.

Jesse met him at the front of the vehicle. "What do you think?"

"Something's wrong."

"Yep."

"Let's do this and leave. The sooner Willow is behind locked doors at the inn, the better. Keep your eyes open for trouble out here."

"Sure you don't want me to come in? Enright will never know I'm outside the office."

He considered the offer a moment, then shook his head. "If we're not out in ten minutes, storm the gates of the castle."

"You got it. Watch your six."

"Count on it." Max opened Willow's door. "Ready?"

"Not really. I appreciate you coming with me."

Max planted a hard kiss on her mouth. "I'm glad I was here rather than out of the country on a mission."

"Me, too." She accepted his hand and stepped onto the asphalt of the driveway. "Any instructions, Max?"

"Stay close. The faster we take care of business, the better."

"In other words, don't waste time. Copy that," Willow said with a snappy salute.

He chuckled as he escorted Willow toward the mansion. "Smart aleck." When they arrived at the door, Max rang the bell.

The door swung open, and Oliver's butler motioned them inside. "Mr. Enright is waiting in his office." He frowned. "I understood Ms. Knox would be alone."

"Would you allow your wife or daughter to travel by herself at this time of morning?"

"He won't be pleased."

"He'll have to get over it." Max turned Willow toward the hallway.

"I'll show you the way."

"No need. I remember." He waited until the butler left before walking with Willow to the office. He rapped sharply on the door.

"Come in, Willow. What took you so long?"

At Max's nod, Willow twisted the knob and stepped into the office. "I'm staying an hour outside of Tucker's Gap."

Max walked inside the room, conscious the clock was already ticking down to the ten-minute mark.

Enright rose from behind his desk with one hand in his pocket and a thunderous expression on his face. "Why are you here, Norton? I told Willow to come alone."

"Did you really think I'd let her drive by herself at this time of night?"

The old man sighed. "You made a grave mistake." He pulled his hand from his pocket and pointed a weapon at Willow. "Come here, Willow, or I'll shoot your boyfriend."

"Don't move, baby," Max murmured.

A cold smile curved Oliver's mouth. "Wrong choice, Norton." He gave a small nod.

A brush of fabric caused the nape of Max's neck to prickle. He started to turn. A snap sounded behind him and a split second later, pain ripped through his body as his muscles locked up. Max fell to the floor with a loud thud.

Stun gun. He'd be out of commission until the effect of the weapon worked its way through his system. His main concern was Willow. Without him, she was vulnerable. Not that he'd done a stellar job protecting her.

A familiar face appeared in Max's line of vision. "Hello there, Norton. I hear you've been looking for me." Mendez smiled, stun gun in hand. "You and I will be spending some quality time together after I get better acquainted with your girlfriend. I'd invite you to watch but this is a private party. I don't like to share."

"Get away from him." Willow started toward Max and was brought up short by Enright. "Let me go, Mr. Enright."

"Quiet," he snapped. "Take care of him," he ordered Mendez.

"No, please," Willow said. "Don't."

Max glared at the grinning serial killer who then kicked him in the ribs with a booted foot. Pain stole his breath. The crack he'd heard was probably a rib or two.

Mendez rolled Max onto his stomach and tied his hands with zip ties. "Stick around, Norton. I'll get back to you."

The creep got to his feet, slid the stun gun into his pocket, and pulled out his knife. He stalked toward Willow. "Come with me, or Enright will fire one bullet into your boyfriend every minute until the magazine is empty. Norton will bleed out while you watch." A smile curved his mouth. "I don't want my fun to end that soon, though. If it does, I'll take it out on you. So, what's it going to be? Come play with me or Norton dies while you watch. Choose."

Max forced his mouth to work. "No," he choked out. The word came out thick but understandable. If Mendez got Willow alone, she would die. Max would do anything to keep her alive, including sacrifice himself.

Mendez glared at him. "That's going to cost you more time with my knife before I cut your throat." He turned back to Willow. "Well?"

She shifted her right hand over her watch. Although the movement was subtle, Max could tell by the placement of her fingers that she pressed the panic button on her watch.

He breathed easier. Jesse would be alerted in less than a minute as would the rest of his team. Help would come. He and Willow had to stay alive long enough for rescuers to arrive.

When her gaze met his, Max mouthed, "Run, hide." She couldn't fight Mendez in a hand-to-hand confrontation for long. Yeah, she'd been training, but Mendez was stronger and wouldn't stop until he wore her down. Willow's best chance of survival was to run and hide from the killer.

"Time's up." Mendez waggled the knife near Willow's face. "Decide. Die now after I kill your boyfriend or play first, then die?"

Jerk. Max strained against the ties but his muscles still spasmed. A few more minutes and he'd have enough control to defend Willow. Unfortunately, Mendez wouldn't delay that long.

"All right. I'll come with you." Willow raised her chin, defiance in her eyes. "Don't hurt Max. I'm begging you."

Satisfaction filled his eyes. "That's better," he crooned. "I love it when women beg." Mendez crooked his finger. "Come to me, Willow. I've been looking forward to getting my hands and knife on you."

She shook off Enright's hold and stepped sideways. Instead of walking to Mendez, Willow executed a perfect roundhouse kick, and the knife flew out of his hand. She ran. With a roar of fury, Mendez scrambled to retrieve the knife and raced after her.

Enright sat on the corner of his desk with his Glock pointed at Max. "I would finish you off myself but Mendez enjoys his work. He'll be unhappy if I take away part of his entertainment for the night."

"Why?" Max croaked.

"I've been assured Willow Knox is Ballinger's best researcher." He shook his head. "Does she know the truth?"

"What truth?" He'd begun to regain controlled movement in his fingers, a positive sign. He needed to reboot the rest of his muscle control fast. Oh, and while he was asking for miracles, Max wanted his ribs to heal in the next five minutes, too.

"Oh, come now, Norton. If she hasn't found out already, she soon would have discovered Graham's unfortunate tendencies." He picked up a familiar notebook from the desk and waggled it. "Her notebook indicates she was on the right track. The truth is quite embarrassing. I can't let her divulge the information to anyone."

"Why hire her?" Ha. He'd spoken more than two words. Progress.

"I had good intentions. I didn't lie to Willow, you see. I needed an heir besides Graham." Enright shook his head. "I refuse to let my legacy fall into the hands of my grandsons. Can you imagine? A failed economist more interested in teaching than making money and running an empire, and another failure of a son who wants to go into the military as soon as he graduates from college instead of protecting the family name and legacy. A disappointment, both of them."

"Should be proud. Good men." A great deal better than their father and grandfather.

Enright gave a bark of laughter. "Now I understand why you're nothing but a washed-up cop. Too bad. You have an excellent reputation but it's exaggerated. I didn't intend to kill Willow until I discovered Graham had married all those women. Outrageous and embarrassing."

"You hired Mendez to kill Graham."

"When I asked my lawyer for the name of a person with creative, permanent solutions to problems, he recommended Mendez."

Convenient. "What about the others?"

The other man frowned. "What others?"

"The other murdered heirs in your family." Max flexed one hand, then the other. Yes. Better. He concentrated on moving his legs and feet.

"Victims of their own bad habits."

"Death by stabbing, all of them? Coincidence?"

Enright shrugged. "It happens. Keeping bad company leads to consequences."

The guy was an idiot or trying to sell a bill of goods to Max as well as himself. Why he'd want to convince Max didn't make sense.

The butler rushed into the room. He didn't bat an eyelash at Max lying trussed up on the floor and his employer holding a weapon. "Sir, Ms. Knox ran from the house."

Enright stood, glowering at his butler. "How did she escape? You were supposed to lock down the house."

Fury rolled through Max. They'd planned all along to kill Willow tonight. Even the butler was in on the plan and seemed a willing participant.

"Security breach at the back of the house. A guard and I went to check, and I saw her running across the yard with Mr. Mendez in pursuit."

"This is unacceptable. Have security sweep the grounds. If they find her before Mendez, take her to the basement."

"Yes, sir." He pivoted and left.

Where was Jesse? Impatient, Max jerked against the bonds. Not quite yet. Another minute or two. He chafed at the delay. Willow was out there with a crazed killer. Max needed to get on his feet and find Willow before Mendez captured or killed her.

"I should shoot you and be done with this business," Enright said.

"What about Mendez?"

"I'll kill him after he finishes with Willow. He's becoming too hard to control."

Idiot. Enright had never been in control of that junkyard dog. Time to distract Enright until Jesse arrived or Max's motor control returned enough for him to take down the old man. "How well do you know your lawyer?"

A frown. "I've worked with him for ten years. I know him very well. Why?"

"Ask him how well he knows Mendez."

"Obviously, you know something you're dying to tell me. Spit it out, Norton."

He wanted the news straight out? Fine with Max. "Sam Parker hired Mendez to kill the other four heirs in your family."

The older man stared. "That's ludicrous. He had no reason to have them killed."

"Much as it pains me to admit this, Norton is right." Sam Parker walked into the office with a Ruger in his hand. He aimed the barrel at Enright.

Chapter Thirty-Two

Willow sprinted from the back of the house, across the yard, and into the trees to the accompaniment of shouted orders to stop and Mendez's screaming curses and threats of retribution. She ignored them all.

Although she felt guilty for leaving Max behind despite his order to run and hide from Mendez, Willow believed Oliver wouldn't kill the man she loved. She couldn't see Graham's father doing his own dirty work unless absolutely necessary. If she had to guess, Enright would kill Mendez to tidy up the loose ends and protect himself. He wouldn't succeed. Mendez was too good at his work to fall prey to an amateur like Oliver.

Willow shoved through the foliage and dodged trees as she ran. Soon, she'd have to switch to stealth mode. If she survived, Max would have a new student in his next evasion class. Her.

While she ran, Willow searched for something to use as a weapon. A good branch with heft would be perfect. Barring that, a nice-sized rock.

She also needed a place to hide once there was enough distance between her and crazy Mendez. The only problem? No handy mountain or hill to hide behind.

Not only that, it was dark out here. Really dark. More than once as she ran, Willow stumbled. The shadows on the ground sometimes masked a depression in the soil or a small dip in the ground. Sometimes, the shadow was just that, a shadow hiding nothing.

Willow's watch vibrated. What on earth was that? She looked behind her. No sign of Mendez or one of Enright's cronies.

Praying she wasn't making a huge mistake, Willow slowed to a walk and glanced at her watch. Across the screen was a message. *To talk, push top button.*

Her eyebrows soared. She'd forgotten that feature of the watch. Grateful the tech on duty hadn't initiated contact without checking if it was safe, Willow pressed the button and started to jog. "I'm here," she said softly.

"It's Zane. Talk to me."

Oh, thank God. "Max is down. Stun gun. He told me to run, so I did." Her voice broke. "I should have stayed to help him."

"You did the right thing. He trusts you to protect yourself until we get you some help."

"Can you find me?"

"I'm tracking you. Mendez?"

Vicious curses and shouts from the man in question sounded closer. "On my heels."

"Can he see you?"

"Not yet."

"Can he track you?"

She blinked. Oh, no. Willow stopped running and looked behind her. In a patch of moonlight, her footprints stood out like a beacon. "Yes." Her voice shook. "Zane, what should I do?"

"Look for leaves, rocks, or hard-packed dirt to step on to hide your footprints. Find a weapon and a place to hide. Are you armed?"

"No, and don't remind me how stupid that was."

"Find a weapon of some kind and get ready. How close is he?"

The shouts of rage and vile threats sounded nearer. "Too close." Willow moved over to hard-packed dirt and leaves, and sped up. She needed more space between her and Mendez. Otherwise, he'd catch her before she found a weapon and hiding place.

No convenient guns or knives anywhere, so she grabbed a rock that looked good. She wrapped her hand around it and squeezed. Yes, this would work in a pinch although she'd rather have Max's Sig.

She picked up her pace. "Zane?"

"Still here."

"Max?"

"Don't know. Jesse went after him, and I haven't heard from either operative."

Mendez went silent.

Goosebumps surged over Willow's body. "Zane," she whispered into the watch.

"Quiet," he murmured. "I'll stay with you."

A good promise. What she wouldn't give to have one of the operatives with her. Max said Zane was dangerous. She could use his skill right now.

Footsteps pounded behind her. "You're going to pay," Mendez yelled. "You'll wish you had never run from me. Your boyfriend will suffer because of your actions."

"Stay focused," Zane murmured.

Right. Ignore threats of torture and death at the hands of a serial killer. She kept going.

Four hundred yards later, something hard hit Willow from behind and took her to the ground. "Got you." Mendez laughed.

"Get off me, you oaf. I can't breathe."

"Can't have that. Ends my fun too soon." He raised up enough to flip her over and leer at her. "Wasted all that energy running. Too bad." Mendez brandished his knife. "I planned to take my time with you in the comfort of a bedroom. Now, I think I'll string you up in Enright's basement and get to work." He stood, grabbed her wrist, and yanked Willow to her feet. "Let's go."

"All right, all right." She gave a half-hearted attempt to yank her arm from his hold. At the same time, she tightened her grip on the rock in her hand.

"Knock it off," Mendez snapped. "The more you fight, the more pain I'll inflict before I finish with you." He jerked her into him.

Willow was ready for the move. She allowed her body to fly toward him and used her momentum to help shove him off balance.

When Mendez fell to the ground, he took her with him, his face twisted in an angry mask. Willow twisted her upper body and slammed her elbow into his temple. His head snapped to the side and he lay still.

Keeping her grip on the rock, Willow leaped up and ran, terrified Mendez would be right on her heels. She figured the trick with the elbow strike would only work once. Hence, retaining the rock. "I got away for now," she said to Zane.

"How?"

"Elbow strike to his temple. Angle was wrong, though. Glancing blow."

"Nice job, Willow. Help is coming."

"Max?"

"Nothing yet. Stay focused."

"Tell him I love him."

"Tell him yourself when you see him."

Invisible spiders crawled on her skin. Oh, boy. Not a good sign. She ran faster and prayed. Before she'd taken more than two dozen steps, Mendez grabbed the back of her hair and yanked.

Willow screamed at the agonizing pain.

"Stupid woman," the man hissed as he shoved her to the ground and dove on top of her. He sat on her stomach and pressed the tip of his knife to her throat. "You're not worth the trouble. I get paid twice to kill you anyway. Doesn't matter if it's fast or slow, as long as you're dead."

"Can't handle one lone woman?" she taunted. "Some serial killer you are."

"I'm a professional."

"A professional lunatic." She poured as much scorn in her voice as she could manage.

Mendez cursed and raised his knife to stab her.

Willow slammed the rock against his temple, bucked her hip to throw him off balance, followed him over, and punched toward the center of his throat.

The killer turned his body at the last second so, once again, the angle was wrong. Mendez gagged, dropped his knife, and clutched his throat, eyes wide.

"Run," Zane snapped.

His order galvanized her. Once again, Willow jumped up and sprinted away from her attacker.

"Veer to the left. Hurry."

Despite the desperate circumstances, she smiled. "Yes, sir."

A soft chuckle. "Brat."

"My brothers call me that."

"Four hundred feet ahead is a ravine. Find somewhere to hide in there. Be careful climbing down."

Willow followed his directions. She found the ravine where Zane indicated. After a quick glance over her shoulder, she sat on the edge and felt for a toehold.

When she found one, she turned and eased herself over the edge. As she climbed down, Willow scanned for darker sections of the ravine. Although she longed to rush, that could lead to a fall with injuries or death. Willow wanted a long, healthy life as Mrs. Max Norton, and she would do everything possible to obtain it. She loved that man with every cell in her body.

Carefully, Willow edged further to the right to an area in almost complete darkness. Her throat tightened at the prospect of going into it. No, not now. She didn't have time for a panic attack. Later, Willow promised herself. She could fall apart when she was safe. Willow inched her way across the slippery terrain, praying she didn't slip and fall.

Small rocks and clumps of dirt rolled into the ravine. Rather than look up, Willow forced herself to move faster toward the safety

of Mead

of darkness. What an irony. One of the things that terrified her might save her life.

"I see you, Willow. You won't get away from me now," Mendez said. "You have nowhere to run."

She glanced up as the killer eased over the edge of the ravine and started to climb down.

Chapter Thirty-Three

Max slowly rolled to his side as Sam Parker stalked into the room, weapon aimed at his father.

"What are you doing?" Oliver Enright snapped, fury darkening his eyes.

"Haven't figured it out yet, have you?"

"I don't understand."

"Yes, I know you don't. Drop the gun."

His father hesitated.

"Drop it."

While the two Enright men faced off, Max made fists and began pulling at the restraints on his wrists. He could handle the two men without a problem if he was one hundred percent and unrestrained. Neither was true, which made the situation more challenging.

He hoped Jesse had gone after Mendez and Willow. Was she all right? Max needed to take care of these two men and go after the woman he loved.

Enright's weapon dropped to the floor with a thud. "You better have a good explanation for this, Parker."

"I have one." He paused for effect. "Dad."

"I'm not your father."

Huh. Max studied the old man as he increased the tug on his wrists. Enright was lying. He had known about Parker.

The attorney gave a bitter laugh. "Yes, you are. You had an affair with my mother."

Enright stared at Parker.

"Does the name Nora Parker Torville ring a bell?"

"She told you."

That stopped Parker cold. "You knew," he said faintly. "She said you didn't know."

"Some attorney you are," Enright said, contempt in his voice. "Your own mother lied to you, and you didn't catch it. Did Nora tell you the truth?"

Parker shook his head. "I found out by accident ten years ago. I ran across the legal document where you signed over your paternal rights in exchange for financial and educational support for me and my siblings until we finished college."

"I should have cut ties with her and forced Nora to sign a non-disclosure agreement."

"Too late now, isn't it? I know the truth." Parker waggled the weapon at his father. "You refused to acknowledge me. You planned to give Graham everything, a man who was married to five women at the same time, instead of splitting the estate between me and Graham."

A snort from Enright. "Never going to happen, Parker. You got every penny from me that you'll ever get."

With a shriek of rage, Parker aimed the weapon at Enright.

Already knowing what would happen, Max yanked his wrists hard and broke the zip ties. He hoped to rush Parker before the attorney pulled the trigger.

The Ruger bucked. Blood stained Enright's white shirt right over his heart as Max leaped to his feet and tackled the attorney. The weapon flew from Parker's hand and skidded across the hardwood floor.

He cursed and threw a roundhouse punch.

Max blocked and countered with two hard punches of his own. Both of his connected. Parker groaned and went limp.

"You okay?" Jesse rushed into the room, weapon in hand.

"Yeah." Max rose and flipped Parker onto his back. He zip tied the attorney's hands behind his back and stood. "Where's Willow?"

"Don't know. Zane contacted me, said you'd been hit by a stun gun. He's been helping Willow while I took out the guards and the butler. Z said she's one tough lady who's holding her own."

He glared at his friend. "You better hope she's okay." Max pressed the button on his watch to connect to Fortress as Jesse checked on Enright. He glanced at Max and shook his head.

"She's in trouble," Zane said, voice tense. He gave the coordinates. "I told her to hide in a ravine. Mendez is closing in on her."

Max pressed a hand to his ribs and took off running.

"What's wrong?" Jesse asked, keeping pace with him.

"Mendez nailed me with the toe of his boot."

"Want me to tape it?"

"Like I want my next breath but we don't have time." The second he cleared the threshold of the back door, Max sprinted toward the coordinates Zane had given him with Jesse close on his heels.

When they drew close to the coordinates, Zane said, "Hurry. Mendez is climbing down the ravine."

No. Max prayed as he ran. If Mendez reached Willow, he would kill her. A simple swipe of the blade across her throat or a shove off the side of the ravine, and Mendez would have completed the contract and salvaged his ruthless reputation. And Max? He'd lose the love of his life.

A scream ripped through the night's silence.

Max poured on another burst of speed and skidded to a stop inches from the edge of the ravine. He dropped to his stomach with a grunt from pain and peered over the edge. To his left, he spotted the serial killer with his hand wrapped around Willow's wrist, slowly tugging her to him despite her efforts to free herself.

He grabbed his weapon and aimed at Mendez. "Baby, drop."

She obeyed instantly, lifting her feet and dropping to the ground.

Max pulled the trigger.

Mendez jerked, froze, and listed to the side.

Using her feet, Willow shoved him away from her.

His body rolled to the bottom of the ravine. Mendez lay still.

Max scooted over the edge of the ravine, ignoring the sharp pain in his ribs, and hurried toward Willow.

She scrambled to her feet and started toward him. "Max!" Willow launched herself at him.

He planted himself and gathered the woman he loved into his arms. "Are you all right, Willow? Did he hurt you?" Max wanted to look for himself but didn't want to let her go.

"A few new bruises. What about you?"

"Cracked or broken ribs."

She gasped and started to back away.

He tightened his hold. "I'm fine, better because I have you in my arms."

"I should have stayed in the office and helped you."

"You did exactly what I needed you to do."

She refused to meet his gaze. "Ran like a coward? Yeah, I have that down pat."

Max tipped her face up to his. "You offered yourself as bait to draw the most dangerous man in the room away from me. You protected me when I should have been the one protecting you. If Mendez had murdered you, I would never have forgiven myself for my own failure. I'm sorry, Willow."

"You've been protecting me since the moment we met. Tonight was no different. You shot Mendez to keep him from throwing me into the ravine. Because of me, you have more blood on your hands. Thank you for saving me, Max."

He kissed her, long and deep. When he pulled back, Max rested his forehead against hers. "I love you."

"I love you, too."

"Hey, do you plan to stand there the rest of the night or climb back up to solid ground?" Jesse called down.

Max laughed and glanced at his friend. "We're coming up now, Dad."

"The local cops are on the way, including Cohen."

"We better go meet them."

"Should we check on Mendez first?"

"No need." Max had taken a kill shot, the only way to ensure Willow's safety.

"He's dead?"

He glanced at her. "Yeah, he is."

"I'm glad. He was evil."

Max squeezed her hand. No need to confirm what they both knew to be true. The world was a better place without Dwight Mendez roaming the planet, looking for his next target.

When they reached the top of the ravine, Max boosted Willow over the edge to solid ground, then hauled himself up and over.

"I'll bring the cops back here to retrieve Mendez's body," Jesse said.

"Will they arrest you, Max?" Willow asked. She pressed close to his side.

"We'll have to go to the station to answer questions but no one will question why I killed Mendez," Max said. "Everything will be fine."

"What happened to Mr. Enright?"

"Parker shot him. He didn't make it."

She gasped. "Oh, no."

He wrapped his hand around hers and started the return journey to the mansion. Max summarized the information he'd learned from Parker and Enright as they walked.

By the time he finished, tears trickled down Willow's cheeks. "Enright's behavior was the catalyst for five deaths plus his own."

"Fallout," Max agreed. "Every action has ripple effects. His actions cost people their lives."

"I don't understand why Mr. Enright hired me. He had to know there was a good chance I'd discover Graham's marriages."

"He didn't know until recently. By then, you had already begun to research, and he couldn't take the chance you would keep digging, discover Graham's five marriages, and disclose the information."

"Anything I learn is considered confidential. I'm not allowed to disclose anything I discover while researching unless I receive permission. I can't imagine Mr. Enright giving me permission to tell."

"He didn't trust you to keep silent."

Willow sighed. "Five people dead, and the only one left to pay the penalty is Sam Parker. I suppose that's some justice, but Graham's families will be devastated."

"In a way, Enright is responsible for Graham's actions."

"Why?"

"He followed his father's example."

They arrived at the house to find the police processing the various crime scenes. Brody and Sawyer met them at the edge of the tree line.

"Sit rep," Brody said. "Fast."

Max gave his team leader a rapid-fire report, ending with, "Mendez is at the bottom of the ravine."

"Alive?"

"No."

"Good. You know the drill."

"Yeah, yeah. Say as little as possible and call Fortress if things even smell like they're going south."

"You got it."

"What happened at the warehouse?"

"Mendez left three bombs. We had to dismantle them or we would have arrived sooner. Let's go."

The rest of the night passed in a haze of pain and fatigue. Max answered questions on the scene, then went through events of the night multiple times at the station. Finally, he said, "Look, we've been through everything over and over. My answers haven't changed. We're done here. I'm taking Willow back to the inn so she can rest." And so Jesse could tape his ribs. This time, Max would gladly swallow a couple of pain capsules without complaint.

He hurt all over and suspected Willow felt just as terrible. As the hours passed, he'd noticed more and more bruises forming on her arms and hands. Badges of honor, he reminded himself. His woman was as tough as nails. She'd basically defeated a serial killer on her own. While Max was frustrated with his own performance, he was proud of Willow's. Strong was an understatement.

Max pushed the wooden chair from the scarred table and stood. "Well, Cohen?"

The detective rolled his eyes. "Go. Stick around for a couple of days in case we have more questions. Get some sleep, Norton. You look like roadkill."

He snorted. "Thanks a lot. Looked in the mirror lately?"

"Avoiding it these days."

Max left the interrogation room and walked into the lobby. Willow surged to her feet and came into his open arms. "Ready to leave?"

"You're free to go?"

"For now."

She looked up, worry in her eyes. "What does that mean?"

He urged her toward the door of the station and stepped into the sunshine. Man, the sunlight felt good on his face. "Cohen wants us to stick around for a couple of days in case they have more questions."

"What about Jesse? Will he be in trouble?"

Max inclined his head toward his SUV where Jesse waited. "Doubtful but you can ask him yourself."

Jesse eyed them critically when they drew near and shook his head. "Get in the backseat, both of you. I'm driving."

Max tossed him the key fob and obeyed the medic's order. "How did the interrogation go?"

"Piece of cake. The security guards and the butler will be fine so the interview was to obtain a complete picture of the night's events."

Willow relaxed. "Good. I was worried."

"Sleep, guys. I've got the wheel."

#

Chapter Thirty-Four

Four days later, Max rang Willow's doorbell and waited on the porch, flowers in hand and a small velvet box in his pocket. He shouldn't be nervous. He loved Willow, and she loved him. So, why was his heart racing? His hands trembled, too. Didn't make sense. He was usually rock steady. Not today.

The door opened, and there she was. The woman he loved with every fiber of his being. Willow smiled and stepped back, opening the door wider. "Come in, Max. Look at those beautiful flowers. Thank you."

When he handed her the flowers and walked inside, Willow closed the door behind him. "Why are you all dressed up? I thought we were eating dinner here."

"We are." Couldn't ask for a woman's hand in marriage in fatigue pants and a black t-shirt, could he? "Seemed like the thing to do," he muttered.

She looked puzzled but took his hand and led him to the breakfast bar. "What do you think?" she asked as she filled a vase with water and arranged the flowers.

He stared at the loaded plates, the lit candles, and the gleaming silverware and glasses filled with iced tea. "Wow. This looks and smells amazing." Holy smoke. Pot roast, mashed potatoes, and some kind of vegetable casserole making his mouth water.

Max already knew he wouldn't taste a thing if he didn't take care of business first, so he said, "Sit down for a minute. I need to ask you something before we eat."

She sat. "Is something wrong?"

"No. In fact, everything is perfect." Well, provided she said yes, of course.

Max took Willow's hand in his. "I'm sorry about your job, baby." Her boss had terminated her employment in the wake of the publicity following Oliver Enright's murder and the sordid details of the case.

"So am I. I enjoyed working for Ballinger."

"You deserve a better job, and I've been tasked with offering you one."

She stared.

Good or bad? "Brent Maddox is always looking for new researchers, and he wants to hire you."

"What kind of research?"

"The same kind you did for Ballinger. Many of our cases hinge on family connections, whether blood kin or not. You'd be an asset for Fortress. The boss assured me that you'd be able to pursue your own research using company resources." Willow took research contracts with private clients to complete family trees. If she went on research trips, though, Max would go with her. He never wanted to receive another phone call informing him that Willow was in the hospital following an attack.

Max pulled from his pocket the contract Maddox had shoved into his hand earlier in the day. He gave it to Willow and waited while she read the terms of her employment.

Her eyes widened, and her gaze shot to his face. "Is Mr. Maddox serious?"

"Yes, ma'am."

"But the salary is three times what I made at Ballinger."

"Fortress believes in paying their employees what they're worth, and Maddox only hires the best."

"What do you think I should do?"

"It's your choice. You have plenty of private contracts already lined up. You don't have to work for Maddox although I believe you would enjoy the job. The only thing I'd rather you didn't do at Fortress is become an operative, but that's for my peace of mind, not because of your abilities. You would do well as a field operative. My heart couldn't handle the worry over your safety."

She smiled. "Good answer, Mr. Norton."

"Thank you, Ms. Knox. I'm learning."

Willow looked over the contract again, then reached for a pen, signed the paper with a flourish, and handed it to Max. "When do I start?"

"Monday morning at eight." He brushed his lips over hers. "We can ride together."

"I'd like that. Ready to eat now?"

"One more thing." Max sucked in a breath, grabbed the small box from his pocket, and dropped to one knee.

"Max?" Willow whispered.

"I love you, Willow Knox. I love you more than I can put into words. You turned my world upside down the minute I saw you. From now until the end of time, my heart will be yours."

Tears poured down her cheeks but happiness shone in her eyes. He could live with making her cry because she was happy. "Will you do me the honor of becoming my wife?"

She nodded. Once the pink diamond mounted on the platinum band was on her finger, Willow threw her arms around his neck and captured his mouth with hers.

Long minutes later, Max broke the kiss. "The deal we made still applies, Willow. We'll get married when you tell me you're ready. No pressure, all right?"

"I'll have to coordinate schedules with my brothers and Dad, but I've always wanted to be an April bride. Sound good to you?"

Stunned, he rested his forehead against hers. "Sounds perfect. I'll tell the boss we're taking a two-week honeymoon in April as soon as you give me a definite date."

April wedding to the woman of his dreams? Nothing could be better. Life was good now. In April, his dreams would come true, and his life would truly begin.

* * *

About the Author

Rebecca Deel is a preacher's kid with a black belt in karate. She teaches business classes at a private four-year college in Nashville, Tennessee. She plays the piano for her church, writes freelance articles, and runs interference for the family dogs. She's married to an amazing husband and is the proud mom of two grown sons. She delivers occasional devotions to the women's group at her church and conducts seminars in personal safety, money management, and writing. Her articles have been published in *ONE Magazine*, *Contact*, and *Co-Laborer*, and she was profiled in the June 2010 Williamson edition of *Nashville Christian Family* magazine. Rebecca completed her Doctor of Arts degree in Economics and wears her favorite Dallas Cowboys sweatshirt when life turns ugly.

Read more at rebeccadeelbooks.com.